THE QUEEN RISES

KRISTEN CIPRIANO

Cover design by Kerry Ireland
Editing by Laura Silverman
Proofreading by Claire Rushbrook
Author Photography by Heather Nan

ISBN: 979-8-9922601-0-6 (eBook format)
ISBN: 979-8-9922601-1-3 (Paperback format)

Produced by Iconic Publishing LLC
An independent publishing house in Keller, TX

www.kristencipriano.com

For my husband. I'd make it rain for you, too.

You are about to enter into an era known as the Dark Ages of the Light Realms. Within these realms, the Elven Kingdom is plagued by a brutal patriarchy led by their tyrant ruler, King Vilero. On this journey, you will witness instances of intense violence, hand-to-hand combat, drowning, death, suicide, elements of war and battle, attempted rape, graphic language, alcohol use, and sexual activities shown on the page. Readers who may be sensitive to these topics, please use discretion. Prepare yourself, and welcome to the Dark Ages of the Light Realms...

"When the masculine steals from or seeks to control the feminine, it is not merely a violation of the natural laws of the Light Realms. It is an abomination, a sickness of the mind that causes the masculine to descend into his most violent and reprehensible nature. He controls the feminine by force, by any means necessary, and grows insatiable for more and more power. He is stronger, he is in control, and she appears (at least for a time) rather weak. He does not immediately feel the cost of these crimes, and he is able to delay his debts for as long as the feminine remains a victim.

But the moment the feminine awakens to her true power— one not defined by physical strength nor logical action—but a power so raw and fierce and infinite that it can rival the destruction dealt by the fiery breath of a Havordian, the masculine learns very quickly that he was never in control.

He was a fool to think he had any power over her.

For she is the truest essence of power that exists."

— Zyrran, 1500 B.V. (before Vilero)

Present day
599 a.v. (After Vilero)
Ador, Syra

1

Magic would be infinitely helpful right about now.

I grit my teeth, feeling the familiar wave of anger burning my insides as I stare at the entrance to the Light Realm's only prison.

The Cave, aptly named, is carved beneath the eternally snowy Ador, which is the biggest mountain in Syra in the northernmost territory of the Elven Kingdom. A small village of the same name lies a little more than halfway up the mountain, and at the peak is the castle that houses our tyrant ruler for the past six centuries.

King Vilero.

I pull my cloak tighter around me, unsuccessfully fighting to keep out the frigid air. Frigidity that—if I had magic—I could protect myself against. Males often enchant their cloaks in Ador to keep the cold at bay.

Because they can.

Because it's easy for them.

Because *they* still have magic.

But I don't. Because *I* was born female.

I repress a groan, unwilling to make a sound despite the rising fury that always seems to be lingering just under the surface of my skin. It never fully goes away; it's like a mouse trap always on the verge of going off whenever I am confronted with situations like this.

Ones where I desperately need magic.

I let out a hot breath, and the air fogs up the space in front of me. I watch it dissipate, fading to nothingness, revealing the peaceful white landscape before me.

All smooth lines of fluffy snow, interrupted by jagged points of rock and tree at the base of the mountain. The sky is dark, and yet somehow still grey, the moon hidden behind a blanket of clouds.

I'm hidden at the thickest part of the powder-dusted aspens, just before the slope abruptly flattens. In front of me and to the left, the arched entrance of The Cave beckons like a promise of safe shelter and warmth for a hibernating bear.

It's anything but.

Shelter? Yes.

Warm? Perhaps.

Safe? Not even for a fucking grizzly.

Magic keeps the prisoners in, in addition to the King's lethal Guards. No one's ever escaped.

No one who's been formally *incarcerated*, that is.

I've snuck in *and* escaped eighteen times.

It's a fool's errand, these little midnight quests of mine. Grandmother must be turning in her grave as she watches me risk my life again and again. Not that she's surprised—I can't imagine she would be.

I was always sneaking into places I shouldn't be once she became my guardian seven years ago—after my father was arrested for a murder he did not commit. Especially when the High Guard seized our home and froze my father's assets. We were left destitute.

And though she was the adult, I took it upon myself to keep us well fed.

Wealthy homes. Markets. Even the occasional bank vault.

These became my stomping grounds in the darkest hours of the night. I was too young to get a job, but you're never too young to steal.

And I'm good at it.

Really good at it.

So good that I've deluded myself into believing that I'll succeed in stealing *my father* out of prison.

A fool's errand.

As if in response, Raven (the black mare I stole from the stables up in Ador) lets out a frustrated snort. I eye her apologetically. She's probably freezing, too.

Or just bored out of her mind.

We've been here for over an hour. I make it a point to come every time a new prisoner is expected, but despite what I overheard some Main Guards discussing on my way home from work, tonight's new inmate is still nowhere to be found.

I shiver. September is a brutal trick here in Ador. It's as cold and barren as January.

Fuck, I miss the warmth. And the *sea*.

I miss where I came from. Abyssia.

Though *not* for the people.

With my father's arrest, it took less than a week for my friends to decide I was also guilty in their eyes. Tarletan, the young male who had been courting me, was forbidden from seeing me.

For the next five and a half years, Grandmother became my only anchor. In Abyssia, and for my sanity. At least until she passed.

Once she was gone, I decided pretty quickly to move to Ador.

Because living amongst people who hate you is a cruel kind of torture; one that leaves no visible scars, but in many ways cuts deeper.

That was a year and a half ago.

I thought I would be here for six months at most.

The wind dies down a bit, and I watch the snow fall languorously to the ground, as if gravity itself has been suspended.

Each flake falls onto a pile of more snow, accumulating slowly and purposelessly.

Each one is meaningless.

They do nothing to change the picture.

They just stack on top of more of the same substance, which never even melts anyway.

Nothing ever *changes* here. Not in a year and a half, nor in five hundred and ninety-nine years. It's the same cold, unforgiving place it's always been. Especially for females.

Perhaps it will always be this way.

I shake my head, attempting to clear the darker thoughts lingering at the edge of my consciousness.

Despite the endless winter, the poor job prospects, the village overrun with High Guards and Main Guards, and the distressing proximity to the King's palace... I've chosen to stay in Ador. Though it's becoming a challenge to remember why.

Because my father is innocent.

Is he, though?

At first after he'd been taken, I certainly believed that. But then the evidence started to stack against him.

The body was found, for one, with *his* magical signature all over him. That still didn't prove he was the one to kill him, because he'd been killed by a knife wound, not magic.

But it *did* prove he was in fact dead, which was something I hadn't come to terms with until then.

The snow picks up and I shiver again, deciding that if the prisoner doesn't arrive in the next few minutes I'll leave. Raven gives me a satisfied snort, as if she can sense my train of thought.

The body was one thing, but when the High Guards eventually found the knife buried in our backyard, it took much more creativity to imagine a scenario where he could be innocent.

Eventually I decided that my traitorous mother and her demon captor likely had something to do with it. When you sell your soul to the Shadow Realms like she did, it often infects your whole family, too.

She made that fateful choice when I was four. She even had the gall to tell my father he would 'understand one day' before she walked out on us.

Twenty years later, I still have yet to figure that shit out.

So when your good parent gets arrested for a murder you could never imagine him committing (my beloved private tutor who had been with us for over a decade no less), the logical next step is to blame your bad parent.

Especially when she sells her soul to a demon.

Demons can possess the mind and force elves to do their bidding —so maybe my father *did* kill him in the sense that he was holding the knife, but the demon pulled the strings and was ultimately to blame.

That explanation satisfied me enough. I've clung to it like a life raft in a raging sea, through the years with Grandmother and since.

I take a painful breath—the air is so icy that it *hurts* going in— and stand up, dusting the snow off the back of my cloak.

I hesitate another brief moment, warming my hands against Raven's body heat before climbing on top of her. A subtle *crack* forces my eyes back toward The Cave entrance, where out of thin air, two High Guards flanking a struggling prisoner have appeared.

"No—NO! Not The Cave. *Please!*" the prisoner begs.

"Can we knock him out yet?" one Guard says to the other.

The other simply hits him hard on the back of his skull. The prisoner lets out a strangled sound and then sinks like a sack of potatoes between his captors.

I quickly dismount. I shoot a warning look to Raven then creep forward in the trees, readying myself to sprint the thirty-odd feet between my hiding spot and the entrance at the perfect moment, once the three males are just out of view.

I hear the front gates creaking open. Just a few more seconds. Their footsteps become louder as they shift from packed snow to hard rock. I take a breath, and then I launch myself toward the gates.

My heart rate picks up as I dance the fine line between making it through the gates and being discovered by the Guards.

They can turn at any point—this part is always the most dangerous—but there's a hiding spot just inside the gates. One where I won't be seen and can wait until night fades to early morning. A time when the prison is fairly empty of Guards.

I slow my steps as I watch the Guards turn the corner at the end of the hall, exhaling with relief when their magically conjured lights finally fade out of view.

The gates are less forgiving. I brace myself and launch across the remaining distance, turning sideways to wedge through the shrinking gap.

My heart skips—I'm through, but my cloak is caught. I yank on the fabric, silently cursing myself for not gathering it up tight. Footsteps sound somewhere down the hall, so I frantically search the darkness to determine if I've already been seen.

I can't see a thing—there's no torches lit in this section—and the one approaching doesn't appear to have a conjured light like the previous Guards.

Maybe that's working in my favor too.

Even so, I need to get out of the open *now*.

I yank harder on the cloak, which begins to tear. I sigh and pull the dagger out of my boot to cut through the remaining threads that are keeping me attached to the gate.

The footsteps are growing louder, but I finally free myself, inching quietly and much too slowly toward my hiding spot. I slide into the gap in the rocks and back all the way up against the cave wall until my entire form is hidden by the shadows.

I cover my mouth with my hand to stifle a gasp as the gates already begin reopening and a chunk of my cloak falls to the ground.

Please don't let him find that, I beg the Maker.

Please.

The Guard is dressed in grey—the Main Guard uniform. Less dangerous than the High Guard, but still. He hesitates for a fraction of a second after the gates part. My heart stops.

Keep moving forward, I urge uselessly.

Finally, he does.

Seconds later, there's a *crack* as he dissolves somewhere else from just outside The Cave's entrance.

My heartbeat gradually slows its alarming pace. I stare at the spot where my torn piece of my cloak likely fell, considering the merits of retrieving it.

And the risk of being seen again.

I could leave it, but if someone skilled with magic comes upon it —a High Guard, perhaps—they will be able to determine *who* the piece of fabric belongs to.

And if they happen to figure out that it belongs to a Fiana Willowbark, the lone employee of the dusty old bookshop up in the village, who mysteriously arrived here a little over a year ago...

The same Fiana Willowbark whose father is incarcerated in The Cave...

They will realize very quickly that there's no reason why I should be here.

No *legal* reason, that is.

And at that point, they may very well decide to throw me in my own damned cell.

Not ideal.

The hall is silent and has been for over a minute. I take a soundless breath then sneak out of my hiding spot, dropping to a crawl once I'm through the narrow opening.

My hands sweep across the floor as I inch toward the gates, mercifully catching on the soft fabric before I have a chance to panic. I snatch it up and shove it into my boot then shimmy back into the tight enclave to wait.

More silence stretches on. I fight my sleepy eyelids as I wait for the nighttime shift to end and the vast majority of the Guards to leave.

Several minutes pass and then finally, the footsteps start—dozens of Guards leaving their posts for the night. I hold my breath as the lot of them pass through the gates, counting the seconds it takes for them to dissolve away.

Forty-five seconds later, they're gone.

I wait another three hundred seconds, just in case there are any stragglers leaving shortly after expected.

There aren't any.

Time to move.

The last time I snuck in—at least a month ago—I successfully located the file room but didn't have enough time to rifle through and find my father's file before the sunrise shift was expected.

Tonight, I know exactly where to go.

I move as quickly as I can without making a ton of noise, keeping one hand glued to the wall on my left as I advance. I have matches in my pocket if I really need the light, but it's better to feel my way through versus risk being seen.

The Cave stretches deep underneath the mountain. Thousands of prisoners are housed here. Some are elves, but many are creatures from other realms—vampires, demons, and other unthinkable beings. It is said that the prisoners eventually go mad due to the darkness, isolation, and magic keeping them in.

It's ironic, in a way. These prisoners are caged *by* magic, while females in the Elven Kingdom are imprisoned by the *lack* of it.

I round my first corner after a quick glance in either direction.

I make a right turn next, into a section with torches at the far end. I wait thirty seconds, ensuring there are no sounds of Guards approaching, before half jogging to the edge of the light and pausing to listen again. Still good—so I sprint through the light, around the corner and down a darker passage. I pause in the darkness to catch my breath.

The air grows damper and thicker here. I creep down the

passage towards another lit section, waiting for thirty tense seconds to ensure I am alone. I sprint through the light to the fork at the end of the passageway, hanging a sharp left and then a quick right into another enclave.

I found *this* hiding spot on my tenth break in—six months ago. I shudder as I remember that night. If I hadn't found this spot, I would have certainly gotten caught. That night, I swore I would give up this stupidity.

Of course that only lasted a few days; I can only avoid my guilt for so long.

My father's been here for *seven years*. If he hasn't descended into insanity yet, he doesn't have much time left.

So I set a limit, backed by nothing other than my gut feeling: I'm getting him out by the time I turn twenty-five, which is six months from today.

And I still have no clue which cell he's in.

I slither out of the enclave, then hesitate again. This is the passage that leads to the dining hall, where the remaining Guards camp out at this time of night. I tiptoe toward the hall, holding my breath as I get close enough to see the light.

They're chattering. My stomach knots as I inch forward to catch a glimpse. I stay away from the edge of light, pressed against the wall as I count them.

Ten in grey, three in black. Clustered around one of the tables, playing cards. I shiver as one of them erupts into laughter that echoes off the cavern walls. Others join in, and I recognize my moment. I tiptoe the final few feet toward the Guards, hanging left immediately to get out of view.

I pick up the pace slightly as their laughter grows louder, passing six different archways that lead to various rooms. There's the kitchen, the bathrooms, a meeting room and a few storage rooms. The file room is the seventh archway, and as I slide inside, I exhale in relief.

It's unfortunate that High Guards are still in the dining hall.

They might be able to hear me, even in here, if they're immortal. I resist the impulse to light a match, and instead run my fingers over the drawers. They're etched with letters. It takes me a minute or so to find the *W*.

I listen intently, though the dining hall is behind a thick wall of stone, and the chatter and laughter are muffled here. I take a breath then opened the drawer, cringing at the sound it makes.

I wait.

Tense.

Listening.

Forty-five seconds later, I pull out my matches. I pause, holding the tip of the match against the striking surface. I wait for another loud wave of laughter then strike the match, holding it over the files as I scan the names.

Willowbark...

Willowbark...

Willowbark... *There!*

I pull out the file just as my match burns to my fingertips. I drop it hastily and put it out with my boot, picking it up seconds later and stuffing it into my pocket. I wait another thirty-five seconds until the chatter in the dining hall swells again, then strike my second match at the same time I open my father's file.

My eyes skim over words like *murder* and *unprovoked* and *violent stabbing* before I find his cell number: 2534.

My match is at its end again, so I snub it out and jam the file back into place. I pick up the match and wait another fifteen seconds before laughter erupts full force and I gently slide the drawer shut.

I've never seen cell 2534, but I do know what wing the 2000s are in.

I tiptoe out of the file room and back toward the passage, pausing at the edge to sneak a peek at the dining hall. I wait for another golden opportunity to escape without being seen.

It takes a hundred and seventeen seconds before that moment

comes. One of the Guards in grey *finally* kicks back his chair in frustration—he's lost the game—and launches himself across the table at one of his opponents.

I roll my eyes but thank the Maker as I slide around the corner and down the hall. I sneak a glance back, only to see one of the Guards in black is missing.

Shit. Now I have to worry about running into *him* on my way out.

I push that thought aside as I retrace my steps, pausing before each corner to listen in both directions. I bolt across the first lit section, creeping into the shadows as fast as I can. I sneak a quick glance over my shoulder. My heart stops—a Guard in grey has rounded the corner, a mere fifty feet behind me.

I hang a quick right into a passageway that takes longer, but is completely unlit. I start slow and then pick up my pace as fear takes over. I take a left and a right, then press myself tight against the wall as the Guard passes through the passageway ahead of me.

An agonizing two hundred seconds later, I decide to make a run for it.

I sprint toward the entrance, cringing at the echoes my footsteps make, but I can't afford to slow down now.

I have exactly two hopes for escape.

If, by some miracle, a Guard just left, I can sprint out of the gates before they close. The timing has to be *absolutely* perfect and the Guard has to have dissolved away immediately for me to not get caught.

My other hope—which really isn't a very good option since I am making *a ton* of noise now, is to hide back in the enclave until someone else leaves and hope no one knows the concealment exists.

I've never seen anyone even *look* toward my hiding spot, so it's not out of the realm of possibility that I can safely wait things out there.

But I would much, much rather get the fuck out *now*.

I round the last corner and nearly cry tears of joy—the gates are audibly moving.

I bolt, as light as I can on the tips of my toes, slowing just slightly as I near the gates to make sure whoever opened them is out of view. The light is minimal, but I can't see a figure; I risk sprinting full out the rest of the way, making it through the gate seconds before it seals shut, clutching my cloak tight to my body as I slide through.

I want to stop and catch my breath, but I don't dare wait to be discovered. I pause at The Cave's entrance only to ensure no one is waiting outside, then dash across the snow towards Raven, my pulse pounding so hard I can feel it in my ears.

The mare gives me a look that tells me I'm in *deep shit,* but I ignore her. Instead, I round to her side and start to climb into the saddle.

One foot's in and I'm about to push off with the other when someone's firm hands grab me by the hips, yanking me away from the horse and stealing the breath from my lungs.

"What do you think you're doing?" the male asks in a low voice, his breath tickling the back of my neck.

I choke. "I—"

"Why do you have Raven so far from her stables?" he says before I can respond. His grip tightens on my hips.

"The Guard let me take her," I breathe, carefully choosing my words.

It's a version of the truth; the Guard certainly didn't *stop* me, though he also didn't notice she was taken. Still, it's better than an outright lie. Some males—like those of the Premonic bloodline— can detect them with magic.

"Have you done this before?"

I want to turn and see his face, yet I'm also very aware that any movement I make might be interpreted as a threat.

"No," I lie—a test. I want to know if he *is* Premonic.

"Try again," he growls.

Fuck. "Yes."

"How often?" He pulls my body closer to his, though not quite touching.

I swallow, my throat feeling tight. I need a truth—but one that won't reveal too much. "More than I should," I admit.

"Even *once* is more than you should and you know it." His voice is low and dangerous. "What the hell am I going to do with you?" It's a question that feels more like a taunt.

"You could let me go," I suggest. "Raven is fine, and I can get her back before sunrise. Before anyone else has to know."

"Clever, but no." There's a hint of amusement in his tone, though his hands are tightening around my hips again.

Like he owns them.

And with what he knows—in a way, he does.

"I could—owe you one?" I offer. My stomach twists at the thought of being indebted to a male, but I have no options left.

"You'd make a deal with a High Guard warrior?" he says skeptically.

I cringe. *Of course it's the one in black that catches me.*

"If there's another option available to me, by all means, share it," I snap.

"Stop stealing horses. Can you promise me that?" His voice is edged with anger.

No. I can't promise him that.

He hears as much in my silence. A hand snakes around my front to press low on my belly. I tense under his sudden movement. My dagger is too far away, but I swear to the Maker, if that hand starts to drift—

"You're reckless too, I see." His voice drops lower. "Why do you steal them?"

"I—" *Shit.* Another question I can't answer without revealing too much. "I like riding," I hedge.

There's a long pause.

The hand on my stomach feels heavy and far too *fucking* warm.

I fight the urge to look over my shoulder, and I clench my jaw to stop the curse words that are threatening to spew out.

"If I let you ride mine, will you stop stealing Raven?" His tone is playful again.

My breath catches. I glance down at his hand, which is still squarely pressed against my lower stomach.

"We're—still talking about *horses*, yes?"

He snorts, but his fingers flutter against my belly. "Yes."

Not. Fucking. Likely.

"I guess I can agree to that." It's not like I have another choice. *And his hands are still on me.*

"Good. Then I *guess* I won't have to arrest you," he quips. His arms tighten around my stomach, pulling me tight against his warm body.

I jerk, wanting to fight his sudden closeness, but before I can react, matter swirls around us and through us. There's nothingness, blackness, a void. No obvious way in or out of this in-between place.

The Ether.

A chill runs down my spine as I feel the wind-tunnel effect of traveling through space and time.

I hold still, even as my heart races, even as his grip around me becomes less sturdy and my own body feels like melted butter in his not-fully-solid arms.

Not even a full second passes before our feet land on the cobblestone sidewalk of Ador. My legs give out underneath me, but his arms hold me up.

"I'll take care of Raven, you go home and stay out of trouble," he orders. His hands slide to the sides of my waist. Finally—they release me.

I whirl around to look at him.

But he's already gone.

2

Morning comes much too quickly; I manage to get four hours of sleep in before I'm due for my shift at the bookshop.

I've grown rather fond of this simple job, though it's far from glamorous.

The shop reeks of dust and mothballs and is dimly lit by nothing more than a few narrow windows. There's a small table and chairs amidst the various shelves, but the table is shrouded by shadows and the chairs are extremely uncomfortable.

It's as if the owner designed the whole shop to discourage patrons from wanting to stay and read, which works quite well for me, considering my true motives for being in Ador. It lets me fade into the background and become rather forgettable, while still having the opportunity to make a livable wage.

Barely livable, but beggars can't be choosers.

Plus to his credit the owner, Wort, has never once laid a hand on me. A rarity in this town.

The patrons are usually males brushing up on various branches of magic. Females have no use reading such tomes; they usually opt to read for an escape. Fiction dominates their choices, though occasionally they'll purchase a cookbook or history book. But only on those rare occasions when they have enough money to even shop here.

It's not a pricy shop, but females don't often have extra to spend given our second class status in this kingdom.

My first hour goes agonizingly slowly. I'm deep within the dusty shelves restocking some books, letting out a spectacular yawn, when the bell on the front door finally sounds with the first patron of the day. I stifle another yawn as I go to the front to greet the newcomer.

Please be female.

I weave through the towering maze of leather bound books from centuries past and present, mentally preparing for inappropriate remarks should my wish not be granted.

I round the corner, and my stomach drops. The male is tall, muscular, and uniformed in all black.

The one from last night?

I'm not sure.

His dirty blonde hair is cropped short to his skull, his pointed ears sticking out to either side of his head. A long scar runs from his eyebrow toward his hairline. There's a curious expression on his face as he appraises me—like he *does* recognize me.

I hold my breath as I wait for him to speak.

His eyes take their time as they rake over me. They linger on my lips, the points of my ears, my breasts. I'm wearing an unshapely sweater that hangs low to my hips—surely he can't see much of my figure.

But maybe he felt it *last night...*

"Give me turn. I want to see the rest of you," he demands.

I narrow my eyes at him. His voice is different—too brash and not at all rich like the male's in the forest. A different High Guard, then.

I straighten up to my full height, bringing me eye level with his chin.

"What are you looking for today, sir?" I croon in my sweetest voice, a polite smile plastered to my face like a mask.

"Oh come on—just one turn," he sneers.

I ignore that. "Fiction or nonfiction, sir?" My face melts into an even lovelier display of politeness. Meanwhile, my insides are like a cat sharpening her claws.

"Mmm... got something lacy on underneath that sweater? Can I see it if I ask nicely?" His eyes fixate on my breasts again.

"*What book, sir?*" I fight unsuccessfully to keep the fury out of my tone.

The male sighs, rolling his eyes. "Just point me in the direction of the Shadow Realms histories."

My answering smile is a touch vicious. I lead the way to the appropriate section, mentally cringing that I have to *turn for him* after all. I hope the heavy sweater obscures most of his view.

"Nice," he grunts. I can practically feel his eyes on my ass.

So much for obscuring anything.

I bite the inside of my cheek, trying to hold back the retort on the tip of my tongue that's aching to be spoken.

Or more accurately... shouted.

I *really* don't need another High Guard prick having leverage over me right now. I push down the urge to insult or maim and turn with another curt smile.

"This section, sir. I'll be in the front."

"Not so fast, you," he says, grabbing my arm. "How about a kiss?"

I wrinkle my nose at him. "I have diseases."

He cackles with laughter. "You know I like my females dirty. Come on, just a quick one."

"No." The word is sharp and final. My fingers twitch toward the dagger hidden in my boot.

His nostrils flare. "What's gotten into you? It's just one kiss."

"Let go of me, please," I seethe.

He grips my arm tighter. "I don't think so."

I'm seconds from doing something stupid—but before I do, the bell rings again as another uniformed fellow pokes his head in from outside.

"Are you done yet, Nasgardo? What's taking so long?" The male sounds annoyed.

"He's trying to assault the attendant, that's what," I say loudly.

"Ah Nas, we don't have time for this. Leave the poor bitch alone."

The original male—Nasgardo—rolls his neck. His anger seems to diffuse slightly and he finally unhands me.

I stalk swiftly to the front, giving a grateful smile to his companion. He returns to his post outside the shop.

Nasgardo makes it to the front a moment later with *Rituals and Spells of the Shadow Realms* by Vladimir Dragovich.

"Fifteen notes, sir," I say as I mark down the title in the ledger.

"No." He gives me a hard look over his shoulder, then leaves with the book in hand. The door swings shut behind him with another *ding* of the bell.

My heart rate spikes. I sprint around the counter, racing after him.

"Sir, you haven't paid for that!" I shout loud enough for nearby pedestrians to hear.

Nasgardo's companion glares at him then shakes his head in annoyance. He doubles back, pushing his messy red hair out of his eyes. "How much?" He whips out a fat stack of notes.

"Fifteen," I say. "Guess Nasgardo's too poor to afford that," I add louder, for the blonde's benefit.

"Careful, you," the redhead warns, handing over the payment. My throat feels tight.

"Thanks," I say quickly, rushing back inside the shop.

When the door slams shut and they start walking again, relief washes through me.

"Worth it," I say to myself.

At least now I won't get fired for that asshole.

I shake off the nerves and return to my private stack—including the ancient volume I found last year that has a thousand-year-old map of The Cave.

I found it by pure accident.

Shortly after I arrived here, I decided to attempt breaking into the prison, and I even did once completely blind. But I nearly had a panic attack looking down that long dark hall the first time, not knowing what lay beyond it. I left quickly after that, without so much as rounding a corner.

The next day, I felt like a failure. I was overcome with guilt and anxiety, so much so that I knocked this book off the restock carriage by accident. It landed face down, open to this page.

Like the Maker himself wanted me to break my father out.

I could never have succeeded without it. The map details hundreds of tunnels interweaving in complicated curving patterns. The hiding spots aren't marked, and some tunnels have collapsed or been rebuilt over the years, but it gives me a huge leg up. One that I desperately need.

I study the wing where cell 2534 is located, tracing my finger over the winding path that leads to the only exit. It's a long way out.

I jump as the front bell rings again.

Please be female.

The smell of jadowin greets me the moment I look toward the door. The male is short with a curved spine, ratty clothes, and a cloak too thin for the harsh winters of Ador. An alcoholic.

I groan. He's not here for books—he's here for warmth. He probably got kicked out of the tavern already, though it's hardly afternoon.

He gives me a wave then hobbles toward the stacks. A hand falls to his stomach and he coughs, curving over himself. His face is thin and sunken, and his collarbones are poking out sharply underneath his sweater. I keep hawk eyes on him as he ventures toward the back.

He coughs again, the sound gargling from deep within his chest. Then he bends forward and retches all over the floor. I cover my nose and mouth as bile threatens in my own throat.

"Uhh!" I gasp behind my hand. "Get out!"

The drunkard is still clutching his belly as he staggers back to the front, a stream of sickness dribbling down his chin. I shake my head, looking away as my own disgust threatens to add to his mess. He stumbles out of the bookshop with another *ding* of the bell.

It fucking *reeks*.

I hurry to the storage closet before the odor overwhelms me, quickly grabbing a few rags, the mop and the soap bucket. I go to the offending spot in the stacks and sop up as much as I can with the rags then pour the mop water over the stickiness and mop it up. I throw the rags in the laundry bag by the back door and seal it shut to keep the smell contained.

I wash my hands in the back, and my thoughts are little more than a string of curse words as that barely buried rage dares to *snap* at any moment.

With magic, this would have been *far* less disgusting.

I don't remember the process of having it stolen, but my father did it as all fathers do under King Vilero's rule.

I groan, feeling resentful.

How *weak* and *pathetic* the males of this kingdom are. No one stands up for females or tries to challenge the King.

Not now, not in the past six centuries, likely not ever.

Like the snow that never melts, the injustice stays, forever frozen in place.

And no matter how hot my rage gets underneath my skin, it's never enough to burn this stupid kingdom to the ground.

I dry my hands and return to the books with a bitter taste in my mouth. I start shelving the restocks with force.

A bit violently, even. As if they might somehow travel through The Ether and smack King Vilero in the face.

I picture the rectangular red marks staining his ivory skin. The image brings a vindictive smile to my face.

Apparently there was a time when magic *wasn't* stolen from females, and some days I have the fleeting thought that I was born in the wrong place at the wrongest of times.

Ding, rings the front door bell.

It's a couple of poor villagers, dressed in thin cloaks and worn leather boots. Their faces are lined—due to poverty and stress, not age. Both are male and look no older than thirty.

"*The Origins of the Light Realms*, please," one croaks with a frown.

"Of course. This first section, third shelf from the top on the left."

They disappear into the stacks. I wait at the counter, my stomach muscles tense.

Moments later, the one who spoke returns to the front, handing me the necessary twelve notes.

"Thank you," I say with my signature forced smile.

The second male emerges from the stacks with the book and they leave with a *ding*.

My shoulders relax.

What a day.

The rest of it passes much like the first half. Customers (all male) *dinging* in and out of the front door. Unnecessary power struggles over my body and books. Restocking volumes in the stacks, taking payment, and marking down new orders. Bitter thoughts about the King and the entire opposite sex.

Another typical day at work.

Ding. I race to the front from deep in the stacks. It's—Wort. *Strange.* He never comes to the shop this late.

Wort is bald, overweight and sweaty, despite the constant

winter. He never wears a cloak and always has an air of fear about him whenever he's around me, though I can't imagine why.

He gives me a wave and goes to the back room briefly before meeting me in the front again.

I arch a brow, waiting for him to explain why he's staring at me like he just accidentally killed my cat.

He lets out a colossal sigh. "I hate to do this to you, Fiana."

I swallow hard. "Do what?"

His eyes crinkle in pity. "I have to fire you."

What the—?

"Why?" I demand. I've worked here a full year, and *tirelessly* without complaint.

"Do you remember a High Guard fellow from this morning? Nasgardo?"

Shit.

"I remember him," I say, my jaw tight. Something like dread creates a sinkhole in my stomach.

Wort lets out another sigh, rubbing his bald head nervously. "He has an order from the King to seize my home if I don't fire you." He takes an involuntary step back, nearly bumping into the stacks behind him.

I stiffen. Wetness pricks at the corners of my eyes, but I ignore it. Instead, I lift my chin.

"I understand. I'll just take this week's pay and I'll leave." My voice is somehow still steady.

Wort's face crumples in—what is that? Shame?

"I'm not allowed to pay you, either. It's all in—in the order."

*Not allowed to—*I clench my fists at my sides. "You won't *pay* me?" My fingernails dig into my palms.

He grimaces, stepping back further into the depths of the stacks. I follow him.

His eyes dart frantically across my face. "I can't. They magically bound the order so even if I pay you under the table, they'll know."

We stare at each other in silence. A long moment passes.

"I can't believe this," I finally say.

"I'm sorry. I wish I could help you in some way, but my hands are bound." He clasps his hands as if in emphasis.

I glare at him. Willing the situation to be different. Willing away the unbreakable magical binding. With all the stores of elven magic I *don't* have, that cannot break such a binding anyway.

There's nothing left to say. Nothing left to do.

I exhale with force, pushing past him and grabbing my cloak off the hook near the back alley door. I pull the cloak around me, buttoning it up to the top, and wipe away a lone tear.

I take a final look back at Wort, guilt and pity still evident on his face. I open the back door and step outside, hesitating, the door still ajar, letting cold air into the shop behind me.

Briefly, I consider forgiving him. It's not his fault, as much as I want to blame him.

But then again, he's another weak male full of stolen magic.

I snort at that.

I turn to leave without saying a word, slamming the door shut behind me. Snow comes tumbling off the roof onto the hood of my cloak. I shake it out violently, cursing under my breath as I leave the shop behind.

My steps are more like stomps as I punish the snow underneath my boots. Forgiving him would have been mistake, I can sense that now.

Let his stupid guilt eat him alive.

3

The streets of Ador are freezing. Light is dimming rapidly behind the near constant cloud cover, and street lamps are already lit in preparation for dark.

I hardly make it two blocks before a large snowy owl swoops down from the clouds, nose diving toward me. I groan as it settles into a graceful stop, perching on a bench a few feet to my left.

"Not tonight, Haldric. I can't tonight," I mutter, avoiding his piercing yellow eyes.

The owl squawks in protest.

"I need to take care of myself." I quicken my pace as my cloak billows behind me. "I'm sorry. I just can't."

He lands fluidly on one of my shoulders, his claws gripping my cloak and the flesh underneath.

A wing nudges the side of my face. Once. Twice. A third time. Urgency emanates like heat waves from his plumage.

"Alright, *alright*, I'll help. Show me where."

Haldric squeals in delight and flies ahead of me, landing on a lamppost several paces ahead. We continue like that in slow succession, past my decrepit apartment building toward the nicer section of town. My heart sinks when Haldric lands on a roof set back behind the main strip.

It's the stables.

The horses aren't in trouble—I can sense that much already. Haldric is leading me somewhere outside of town. Somewhere I'll need to *ride* to get to.

I curse under my breath.

"I can't, Haldric. I got caught last night," I murmur. I know from experience that he can hear me even over the roar of the wind.

His eyes are full of reproach.

I groan. "North or south?" I ask, my jaw tight.

I'm not agreeing yet.

Or at least that's what I'm telling myself.

Haldric turns his hyper-mobile head northward. My stomach lurches. Toward the King's castle. As if stealing a horse again isn't risky enough.

You've already been fired. What more can you lose? A voice sounds in my head, as if Haldric is speaking to me directly.

But of course, he is not.

It's just my own misguided need to tend to an injured animal no matter the consequences.

Turn around and go home, begs a more practical side of me, especially as the Guard at the front glances back toward the stalls. Especially as I remember the promise I made to the male last night.

I creep around to the back of the building.

It's not guarded tonight. *Of course.*

Haldric perches on the snow-covered branch of an aspen, eyes darting to either side of the barn.

The perfect silent watchman.

I inch my way toward the opening. I take a breath, steeling myself, then sneak a quick look around the corner.

The stables are empty, as are most of the stalls. Only a lone black mare remains. Raven again.

Of course.

The streets are fairly quiet, too. Only an elf or two is still milling about, heads ducked against the light snowfall that has just begun. Their pace is an eager one. Eager to return to the warmth of home, or perhaps the local tavern.

By some stroke of luck, the Guard at the front pulls tobacco out of his cloak pocket and starts packing his pipe, seemingly fixated on the task.

I roll my eyes.

This is how I get into trouble. They make it too damn easy up front, and then I lull myself into a false sense of security and end up making mistakes that later result in me getting caught.

Like last night.

I throw a quick glance at Haldric, who is radiating calm and is unnaturally still. His tell that we're still in the clear.

I slither around the corner, keeping my body pressed against the stall doors. Raven is on my side and just a few stalls down.

A treat basket hangs from the stall next to hers, so I fish for a carrot before sliding her door open and creeping inside. Her bored eyes light up with excitement at the sight of me—or perhaps the carrot. I feed it to her, stroking her mane.

"Be good again, Raven, and I promise there's more where that came from," I whisper near her ear. She snorts once in response. It feels affirmative enough to me.

I grab a saddle and loop it over her as silently as I can, then swap her halter for a set of reins. I sneak a glance down the length of the stables again—the front now seemingly a ghost town—and the back, guarded by Haldric whose eyes are alight with encouragement. The Guard still has his back to us, fiddling with his matches. *Of course.*

I shoot a warning look to Raven then lead her out the back just as the wind picks up, muffling the sounds of her horseshoes against the frozen dirt.

I stick three more carrots in my cloak pocket on the way out, and quickly guide Raven out of the stables and deep into the trees behind. Haldric looks positively gleeful as I climb into the saddle.

A quick look back up the stables shows the Guard happily smoking his pipe, still none the wiser.

I soften in relief, letting out a long held breath. I nudge Raven into a gentle trot up the mountain, Haldric leading our trek in the air.

The pounding of my heart rivals the roaring of the wind by the time we reach the fallen animal. I can feel its agony—like phantom wounds carved into my own flesh—as we approach.

King Vilero's palace is only a hundred feet up the mountain from where we stop. I shoot Haldric a glare, though he can't see from his perch high in the aspens.

It's a doe.

The poor creature's legs are utterly mangled—broken in such a way that only the highly destructive Havoc magic or pure brute force could have caused her injuries.

Some High Guard prick probably did this out of sheer amusement. I clench my teeth. *They're all the same.*

There's also a huge gash running up her abdomen, spilling blood into the white snow beneath her shivering form.

"When did this happen?" I gasp as I kneel by the animal, the full force of her suffering causing a lump to form in my throat. By the amount of blood, it's hard to believe she's still alive.

I pull a rag out of my cloak pocket to dab at the wound, which soaks bright red far too quickly.

"I don't know if I can help her," I admit in a strangled whisper.

Even if I can get the bleeding to stop, it's not like I can keep a fully grown doe safely immobilized in my one room apartment while her legs heal. Even if I splint her, she won't be able to walk in this condition.

What she really needs is a Curic—the kind of elven magic that heals elves and animals alike.

I throw my middle finger up and jab it northward toward the King's castle. It's *his* fault she has to suffer.

The snowy owl lands on the ground next to me, eyes wide and insistent.

"I can't, Haldric," I groan. "The best I can do is—put her out of her misery." I bite my lip as tears fill my eyes for the second time tonight.

Haldric glares at me. I can practically hear his tone.

Try harder.

I ignore that, reaching in my boot for my dagger, feeling an ache in my heart as I prepare to slice her carotid artery.

It will be a quick death, though not entirely painless. I raise the knife—

"I can heal her," says a familiar male's voice near the edge of the trees. "But first you need to tell me why you broke your promise."

I stand with a start, the dagger lowering to my side. My heart races as I realize he's the High Guard from last night.

His skin is pale from the winter, but warmer than my own pallor, as raw power emanates from every pore, giving his skin an aura of other-worldly glow. Like his magic is too intense to remain wholly invisible.

Though the lightness ends there.

He's uniformed in black and uncloaked, his arms crossed over his chest, with lethal bands of muscle bulging underneath his armor.

His hair is a dark brown mess of snow-dusted waves that hang low enough to graze his cheeks. Though a thick beard obscures the bottom half of his face, I can tell his jaw is tense, his lips curved downward into a disapproving frown.

His eyes—even at a small distance—are piercing, and set beneath a prominent brow.

They're the kind of eyes that miss no detail, however small.

They see you right to your core on first glance, beneath all your masks and walls.

I shiver, and not from the cold.

He's still waiting for me to answer, but my response is caught somewhere in my throat.

"Is this why you steal horses? To save dying animals from their eventual fate?" He takes a step toward me, uncrossing his arms. "Is this what you were doing last night?" he adds, his voice quieter.

The beard suits him, as does the messy hair. They give him a rough edge that counteracts the aristocratic beauty of his face. Without them, his straight nose and prominent cheekbones would look far too noble for any enemy to consider him a real threat.

But he *is* a real threat. A big one, by the looks of his biceps.

I need to tread carefully.

"Borrow," I rasp, my voice weakened by fear. My heart rate climbs as he inches closer. "I only borrow them, and I always bring them back."

"You broke your promise," he says again, his eyes accusing.

"I know," I admit. The doe's pain is still throbbing throughout my body, and my eyes drift to the pool of red at my feet. "Please, you have to heal her."

"Hmm," he says, prowling closer, studying me with intensity. His eyes are unlike any I've seen before, hinting at a rare mix of magic. A rich cobalt blue fades to icy blue toward the center.

Two-toned eyes. I find myself struggling to look away from them.

And worse, struggling to want to.

I can feel Haldric watching me. If he senses danger, he'll attack.

I force myself to breathe. To remain calm.

The owl won't win that fight.

I sigh. "Will you heal her then or not?" My heart stutters as he comes closer.

He looks amused.

"Are you not afraid of me? I should arrest you for this," he says, jerking his head toward Raven. "Especially since you've already received a warning." His tone is deceptively light. Like a prince holding court with a fascinating guest.

I say nothing.

"Hmm." He kneels in the snow at my feet, looking down at the doe. For a split second I consider using my dagger, though I squash that urge as he lowers his hands gently onto her legs.

An earsplitting series of *cracks* fills the otherwise silent air, and Haldric squawks from his perch up above.

The deer yelps once, then pushes herself to standing, the wound at her belly now fully sealed. Her eyes meet his in silent thanks, then she bolts through the trees and down the mountain.

I inch back away from the male, eager to bolt as quick as the doe.

"Not so fast." He turns and grips my wrist in an inescapable hold. My breath snags as his eyes meet mine. "You lied to me."

"I didn't mean—"

"Give me one good reason why I shouldn't throw you in The Cave tonight," he seethes, his tone harsh. I pull against his grip, which only tightens further.

Haldric is squawking again. I shoot him a warning look.

"One good reason," he presses, with more urgency this time.

"I—I can't stand their suffering," I admit rashly. "I can *feel* it when it's close by. I know that sounds crazy, but it's true. It's worse than my own suffering. Worse than any pain you could imagine. I cannot bear it."

He grows silent. Thoughtful.

His jaw softens subtly. "I believe you."

"It's the truth," I sigh.

"I know." He studies me. "Let me show you where I keep my horse."

"No—it's okay. I won't do it again, I swear," I say quickly.

He cocks a brow. "Even your owl friend knows that's a lie. Come. It won't take a moment."

I can't fathom why he isn't hauling me off to prison, but I keep my mouth shut as he lifts me onto Raven and then climbs on behind me.

His arms reach around me for the reins and he nudges Raven into a trot southward. Haldric follows us in the skies.

I try not to notice his proximity as we descend the mountain, but it's impossible not to fixate on the feel of his hard body pressed against my back, his arms circled loosely around me.

There's an unsettling heat building in my body, and I'm not sure if he's using magic or if I'm feeling something... *else*.

"What animal was it last night? And how did you heal it?" he asks casually as we ride, his voice low by my ear.

"Um—" My thoughts scramble as I try to come up with something truthful I can say. "Last night didn't work out as planned." *There. That's accurate enough.*

"Shame."

I can feel the heat of his breath against the side of my neck. I risk a sidelong glance. He's leaning into me.

"Why would you let me use your horse?" I fix my eyes forward again.

He snorts. "I don't like arresting pretty little things like you. Not if I can help it."

Odd. Most males in the High Guard relish *any* opportunity to oppress a female. Like Nasgardo.

"I'm not a *thing*," I mutter under my breath.

He ignores that, continuing his earlier thought. "And seeing as you can't control yourself, I may as well offer you mine. I usually keep Sterling at the stables near my home, but I'll move him down to town tomorrow."

"You don't live in town?" I question.

"No."

"Where do you live?" I can't help but ask.

"Elsewhere."

I repress a snort.

We ride in silence the remainder of the way back to the village. He pulls on the reins at one of the first buildings, a smaller set of stables used by the few wealthy villagers of Ador.

Raven skids to a stop, and the male climbs easily off before gripping my waist and pulling me off as well.

I land lightly in front of him, face to face and much too close. He's *tall*. Enough to where I have to look up to meet his eyes, and I'm not exactly petite.

His hands are still attached to me.

"From now on you will only ride Sterling. You will not steal—or *borrow*—anyone else's horse. Are we clear?" The words are probably meant to threaten, but his eyes are strangely full of humor.

"Fine," I agree, fidgeting in his grasp.

He leans in closer, abruptly serious now, his voice barely above a whisper.

"And don't think I don't know you *weren't* saving animals last night. Your scent went all the way to The Cave. Inside it, too. I don't know what the hell you were doing in there or *how* you managed to sneak in, but you need to *stop*."

I gulp.

"If I catch even the faintest hint of your scent in there again," he adds, tightening his hold on me as he leans in closer still, "You'll *wish* for the feel of suffering animals when I'm through with you."

My heart practically leaps out of my chest. "Understood."

He frees me from his grasp and climbs on top of the horse so quickly that I stagger backward, nearly falling on my ass.

Immortal—he must be immortal.

I steady myself and start sprinting to my apartment building, eager to get out of the open as fast as possible. The familiar *clump-clump-clump* of horseshoes on the cobblestone alerts me that he's staying close as I race home.

I refuse to look, quickening my pace even as my heart beats loudly in my ears.

As I open the front door, Haldric catches up with me and follows me inside, landing on my shoulder as I seal the door shut.

"I'm fucked, Haldric," I admit as I press my whole body weight against the door. I catch my breath for a beat before I walk us both up the stairs to my unit.

I have no job.

Rent is due in a week, and I'm ten percent short.

I have no savings to speak of; I barely survive on my earnings from the bookshop.

I've been here for over a year, and I'm no closer to getting my father out of The Cave than when I'd first arrived.

And now I have captured the attention of not one, but *two* High Guards in the same week.

Even the owl seems defeated by the time we make it to my door.

4

I sleep hard, waking the next morning shortly after dawn. I bathe, dressing myself in my nicest dress, a long-sleeved ankle-length silvery-white thing that clings to my body in all the right places.

I reserve this dress for when I need male elves to like me, and in the icy climate of Ador, it's the closest I can come to showing off my body.

I pull on my black leather boots and apply what little makeup I have to my face—just enough rouge on my cheeks to break up my paleness and a hint of color on my lips.

I don't wear anything on my skin, which is clear and luminous, glowing with some leftover elven genetic anomaly that somehow didn't fade when my magic was taken.

I twist my hair with a hot iron into thick, loose, mahogany curls that hang down to my mid back. My pointed ears subtly peak through the curls, a style elven males often find erotic.

Because *this* is where I've landed.

Jobless and so hopelessly unqualified for most of the jobs in this town that I have to use my curves and a teasing display of my ear points just to get an interview.

I move across my one-room apartment to the kitchen area, pulling a book down from on top of the icebox. I ruffle through the pages until I find what I'm looking for. A tattered old map of the village.

I sit at my tiny kitchen table, no bigger across than my skinny forearm, made of a bright cerulean blue-coated iron. The table is extremely heavy and a rather odd piece of furniture to have indoors. I stole it from outside of a coffee shop a few blocks away late one night, after closing up the bookshop, shortly after I secured this apartment.

The proprietor probably thought *no one in their right mind* would carry such a heavy table away in the blistering cold, and therefore left them out all night unchained.

Ripe for the picking.

Survival mode makes you do illogical things, I'll admit.

And sneaking away in the night with things I shouldn't have comes so naturally you'd think I have magic fueling it.

I used to feel guilty about it. I wasn't *raised* to steal.

But then again I had something far more sacred stolen from *me*.

Perhaps this is how I get some semblance of revenge.

In any case, my talent for thievery did come in handy when I needed to fill this apartment.

The only thing I bought for myself was my mattress, which is barely big enough for two. For me, it feels huge and I live for the moment when I get to stretch out in bed after a long day's work.

Alone, of course. *Always alone.*

My mind unwillingly drifts to the male from last night. The one with the prince's face and curious two-toned eyes.

He's had his hands on my hips two nights in a row, and I have yet to learn his name.

"I miss sex," I admit with a sigh.

Haldric squawks at me from his perch by the window, his expression disapproving.

I snort.

"Relax. It was just an errant thought." A highly illogical, incredibly stupid errant thought.

Haldric was the first animal I ever saved. His wing was caught in a shingle on the bookshop's roof, and I shimmied myself up there to help ease it out.

A few feathers dislodged, and he yelped at that, but the moment he was free, I could feel his pain receding rapidly. He flew away at once, and at first I thought I'd never see him again, but then he somehow found me at home later that night. He brought me a hunk of stolen cheese from Maker knows where.

A creature after my own thieving heart.

He's been my faithful (and *only*) companion ever since Grandmother died.

I purposely keep the Adorian elves at arm's length. I'm here for my father, not friends.

Nor lovers, I remind myself. *Especially terrifyingly lethal, unfairly sexy kinds of lovers.*

Haldric is my one exception.

Though he is so abnormally *aware* for an owl that I often wonder if he's not a shapeshifting elf born of the Chamelic bloodline.

My face twists at that thought. That would be *way* creepier than an unnaturally intelligent owl.

As if in agreement, the bird clicks his beak. I shoot him an amused look before returning to the map.

I spread it out on the table. With a dull pencil I study it, following the winding streets snaking up the mountains.

Syra as a territory is huge and yet small... The mountain range stretches so wide that it makes it the biggest of the Elven Kingdom, but the actual villages carved into the cliffs are quite minuscule—

including Ador—especially compared to the cities I grew up with back in Abyssia.

Ador is a difficult village to live in with air so thin that it took me weeks to stop getting altitude sickness; as if I needed another struggle to contend with. When the daily puking *finally* stopped, it then took me even longer to regain physical strength and stamina at this punishing height.

Back then, I stretched my money as long as I could, picking up jobs and quitting them just as quickly as I realized my bosses wanted to use me for my body.

That's why the bookshop position had felt like a gift from the Maker. I actually felt reasonably safe there.

Until last night.

It had been twelve glorious months of being well fed and (mostly) untouched, now positively ruined because of *one* stupid male in the High Guard.

My stomach roils underneath my calm exterior, but I force myself to focus. I need a job. Fast.

Ideally one where I won't be touched and prodded like a common whore.

I lightly mark the map with X's on all of my former employers.

The tailor, where one night he pinned me against the wall and forced his tongue down my throat. His breath tasted of garlic—I can still taste it now. I kneed him in the crotch and escaped before it went further.

Still, the memory makes me shudder.

I mark a big X over the shop.

And then there was the butcher shop, where only a week into my job one of the butchers held a knife to my throat when I refused to suck his... *sausage*. The boss walked in just in time, forcing him to quickly hide his knife so as not to get caught. I shoved past him as fast as I could, shouting "I QUIT" at the boss as I did.

Another X.

Fuck that place.

Haldric hisses in agreement.

There was the hotel, where guests frequently tried to strong arm me into their rooms. *Nope. X.*

And the dressmaker's, which I actually enjoyed working at and was the source of my current attire. But after about two months of employment, the shop was sold to a new owner, and the next week when I asked for my paycheck he unzipped his pants and asked how *badly* I wanted it.

I just turned around and left.

The next X I carve nearly rips the paper.

Luckily... I have never been raped. But I'm not about to put myself into a position where that might be the case again. I run my fingers over the X's I've drawn, including one over the bookshop, and assess what remains.

There's the market. The apothecary. The bakery. The coffee shop. The three restaurants. The male outfitter's. The salon. The blacksmith. The portal station. And the tavern.

Except I'm not *technically* old enough to work at the tavern. At twenty-four and a half years, I'm six months short of being able to legally work there.

I need to be twenty-five, the same age when our magic is said to be fully developed within us. It's a stupid law, considering I don't even *have* magic. But a law nonetheless.

So *not* the tavern.

I have twelve other options to work with.

Better make them count.

The market manager won't stop staring at my breasts. It's like he's having an entire conversation with them. I fight the urge to demand his eyes upward and maintain my polite smile, though it doesn't touch my eyes.

"So as you can see I am very reliable and have worked in retail for over a year," I say calmly, keeping my expression agreeable for his benefit.

"And why did you leave the bookshop?" he wonders idly. There's a slight glance back up at my face before he fixates on my nipples, which are showing through my dress in the cold, magically refrigerated back room where he's interviewing me.

Just openly staring at them.

His lips even part obscenely, as if he desires to suck them.

I bite back my anger. After all, this dress is *supposed* to get this type of attention for me, giving me a higher likelihood of getting hired.

Get through this so you can eat next week.

I let out a silent sigh and share my practiced response.

"I'm ready to grow into a more sophisticated role, and the bookshop only had the one opportunity. Here, you have a much larger facility and since I've made my own meals since I was a child, I will jump right into the work easily."

My next smile is pretty.

The manager's eyes drift to my crossed legs, back up to my breasts, fixate on that tiny sliver of my pointed ear showing beneath my hair, and then *finally* drag back to my face. I suppress a scowl.

"I'm sorry. I can't hire you."

Excuse me? "Why not?" I clasp my hands together tightly.

"You're Fiana Willowbark right?"

What does that have to do with— "I am."

He frowns. "This Guard—Nasgardo—came through yesterday and magically bound me not to hire a Fiana Willowbark. If I had known *you* were this Fiana," he sneaks a glance down the length of my dress again, "I wouldn't have agreed. Well, I probably would have, but I would have fought for better terms."

At least he's fucking honest.

I grit my teeth. "What were the terms?"

"He agreed to waive my taxes for the next month. I should have fought for the year..." he says regretfully, eyes lingering on my legs again.

No doubt imagining what lies beneath the dress.

"Thank you for your time," I say curtly, standing to leave.

"Wait! Would you like to get dinner with me? I'll buy..."

I turn and leave without a response.

Unbelievable. After twelve failed interviews, this cruel, repulsive High Guard has succeeded in binding the entire town from hiring me. I even went to the tailor—who was *way* too thrilled to see me again—and he too, had agreed to the binding.

I'm too disgusted to go to the butcher or the dressmaker's, but I'm also running out of options. I can feel tears fighting to spill over. *Damnit.* I can't afford to have my makeup ruined.

I blink back the tears, sitting on an ice-cold bench and closing my eyes, taking the deepest, slowest breath I can manage. Finding that place inside of me where I feel calm, even in utter chaos.

I open my eyes. The Ador Tavern stares back at me.

Six months isn't that long...

I'll be of age likely by the time anyone will be able to check. Ador isn't exactly good at record keeping and since I came here from another territory entirely, I doubt a record even exists of my true age.

I just have to play it cool enough that no one will feel the need to use magic to confirm if I'm telling the truth.

It's a risk... but I don't have very many options left. I take another deep breath and set an intention internally. I don't have magic, but I know this is how male elves do it, and something in me just needs the placebo effect of the action.

Please let me get this job. No matter what, let me get this job. Please. Clear every obstacle out of the way for me to get this job. Please let me get this job. Thank you.

I feel nothing, which really isn't a surprise since I was merely thinking to myself and not *actually* conjuring anything. But it does give me the *slightest* boost of confidence, enough to keep my head held high as I cross the street to enter the tavern.

The space is dimly lit and warm, with a large fireplace roaring on the wall opposite the front door. The fire is magically conjured, the flames changing colors on a slow, continuous loop. To my left are a handful of tables, some tucked so far back into the shadows that I can't see who sits at them, but most are full.

In front of the fireplace is a large U-shaped couch with a low table covered in beer steins and short glasses filled with brown liquor. Jadowin, most likely—the high octane spirit brewed from fermented witch's barley. A large group of males are clustered there, drinking. They laugh and clap each other on the back every now and then.

To my right is the bar. It's long and made of a thick dark wood, a magical seal evident to prevent drips and blemishes.

There's about eight barstools pulled up close, all of them filled with males of all different kinds, the width of the stools adjusted magically to the size of the male.

Some of them wear the dark grey uniform of the Main Guard, with their black belts and shoes, and holts filled with magical weapons of all sorts.

Others are village dwellers, wearing the typical Adorian garb of thick black pants, boots, and flannel shirts or heavy sweaters.

There's one male wearing the High Guard uniform, jet black from head to toe, weapons hidden from view with spells but most certainly there.

The Main Guards are the obvious ones—they *look* like soldiers. The High Guards just look dangerous, but you can't quite tell why.

Behind the bar is a pretty female, her golden hair piled high atop her head, pointed ears fully exposed with an array of golden earrings dangling from her lobes. Her cheeks are flushed and shiny with sweat, a flirtatious smile upon her lips as she keeps the bar entertained and quenches their seemingly endless thirst.

I smile to myself. *This* is a good sign. A bar that already has a pretty bartender could always use another one.

I approach the bar, sidling up on the end farthest from where the one in black sits.

"Hello, I'm hoping I can speak to your proprietor? I would like to be considered for a job." I puff my chest out subtly.

The female notices that, looking me over, and smiles. "Yeah he likes females like you. I'll let him know you're here."

Wonderful. I keep a polite smile on my face and step back from the bar a bit to give the drinkers some space.

One male follows my movements and turns slowly toward me. He glances briefly at my body sheathed in the tight bodice, and then fixates on my eyes, a warm smile spreading across his olive-toned face.

I don't shrink from the gaze, and instead take it in and smile back. I have to practice flirting working in a place like this.

May as well start now.

"Well aren't *you* delicious..." he says, a playful smirk playing at the corners of his lips. He's not unattractive. I don't have to work *too* hard to pretend to like his compliment.

"You're too kind," I say, letting my eyelids droop slightly while parting my lips, a look I know drives males mad.

He takes the bait. "You mean to tell me I get to see *you* tending this bar soon?"

The comment causes everyone at the bar to turn and stare, too. I scan their faces quickly, noticing the most attractive among them sits at the far end, in the jet black uniform.

Shit—the bearded one from the last two nights. *Of course.*

I ignore the panic already surging inside of me and rein in the urge to glare at him. I turn back to the villager in front of me, hoping against all odds I still have a chance at this job.

"Only if you help me convince the owner I'm worth his trouble..." I tease, a playful pout hiding my barely leashed anxiety.

His eyes catch on my lips. "Oh don't worry darling. I will..."

"So will I, gorgeous," the villager to his left adds.

"Me too!" the one to his left.

"Same!" the one after that.

"We'll make him hire you," says a Main Guard further down the bar.

"He won't have a choice," agrees his uniformed neighbor.

"Agreed," says the third in dark grey.

The one in black remains silent, just staring at me.

"Well I guess you're hired!" bellows a booming voice from behind the bar. I turn toward it.

The proprietor is huge, towering at least two heads length above my own height. I have to crane my neck a bit just to look into his eyes, which are a shimmering gold flecked with jet black.

His hair, pulled into a ponytail at the nape of his neck, is grey and wiry, as is his chest-length beard. His skin is pale as porcelain which gives him an eerie, somewhat mystical look, especially with those bright gold eyes.

I curtsy. "Hello, sir, I am Fiana Willowbark. I am pleased to make your acquaintance." My tone oozes charm.

"Hmm...yes I've heard of you. What did you do to piss off Nasgardo?" he wonders, eyes narrowing with curiosity.

"I- I wouldn't let him kiss me. Or leave without paying. And he didn't like that," I confess, attempting to ignore the sinking feeling in my chest. *Please let this male be exempt from the binding.*

The giant bursts out laughing, so loudly that a few of the fellows at the bar flinch. "And if anyone in here tries to steal a kiss, or skip on their bill, even if it's a High Guard warrior, what will you do to stop them?" he asks, his brow rising. It's a challenge.

I smooth my dress, smiling in a way that would have made my father squirm. "I have my ways. I could show you if you'd like... are there any volunteers?" My voice is light as I scan the bar for a victim.

Nearly all of them raise a hand, all except the one in black. I pick one of the villagers toward the middle, right next to the Main Guards. "What's your name, sir?"

"Elyon. Pleased to meet you," he says with a little bow of his head.

"You too, Elyon," I enthuse.

I pause, scanning his form, as if to size him up. All a part of the show. I look to the Guard on his left.

"Do I have your permission to incapacitate Elyon? I promise he won't be *permanently* damaged."

The three guards in grey look at each other and then chuckle. "Yeah, I'd like to see this..." one of them says while the other two nod in encouragement. I notice the one from last night still staring in my direction, but ignore him.

"Good. You wanted a kiss did you?" I demand, mostly for theatrics. My audience is now completely rapt.

"Give it to me, baby..." He purses his lips as his eyes slide shut.

"Tongue or no tongue?" I tease playfully.

"Uh—no tongue?" he says with a nervous chuckle. Unsure of what to expect.

Poor bastard.

I grab his forearm with one hand and yank him out of his bar stool. I pull him closer to me, close enough for that kiss, and his eyes widen in shock as I wrap one hand firmly around his shoulder and the other around his ribcage.

I give him a wicked grin as I tuck my hip behind him, pulling him backwards over the fulcrum made by my hip. I let him fall to the ground, landing with a thunk on his side.

I finish by sitting on top of him, my boots pinning his arms down, the smile on my face utterly victorious.

Elyon lets out a little groan. "Should have asked for tongue."

The bar erupts into laughter, the giant's the loudest.

"Me next!" says the villager to his right, giving me his hand to help me up. I take it.

The proprietor dissolves and reappears instantly to the other side of the bar. Now closer to me, he sizes me up one more time. "All that in a dress too. And you're of age?"

"Naturally," I fib, standing taller, that devilish smile back on my face.

"Alright. You can start tomorrow. Come at sunset. Wear something black in case of spills. I don't want you dirtying your good clothes."

My heart races. "Thank you, sir!"

"It's Credo. And we do use magic for cleaning here, so your main job is serving the drinks and keeping the customers happy."

"I don't doubt she'll succeed..." says the female from behind the bar. She gives me a wink. I smile back.

A genuine one, this time.

Credo leans down low to whisper in my ear, "I don't take bindings with the likes of Nasgardo, no matter what he tries to offer me."

I nod, my eyes meeting his with gratitude as he straightens up. "Thank you, Credo, sir." I curtsy again.

He gives me a wave (on a smaller male you might call it little, but there's *nothing* little about this giant) and dissolves back behind the bar, lumbering through a door that must lead to his office.

Relief washes through me as the customers continue to gawk at my performance. I give a sheepish grin to Elyon. "I didn't hurt you too badly, did I?"

He blushes. "Of course not, Miss Fiana."

"Where did you learn how to do that?" says a velvety voice from behind me. My heart stops.

I spin around knowing all too well exactly who it is.

His two-tone eyes are like magnets for my own, and his lips are curved into an amused smirk.

He's a cruel trick. Like a noxious flower that lures you in with its beauty, only to kill you the second you get close enough to take a good whiff.

"I—" I hesitate, wondering if he *will* turn me in for breaking into The Cave, despite what he said last night. I can't afford to be in trouble with the Guard again.

I take a shaky breath. *Just tell the truth*, I decide, though my heart is pounding erratically.

"I met a traveler once at the bookshop. He saw how badly other customers treated me and thought I should have a way to defend myself." I keep my chin up, refusing to break eye contact. *Go ahead and arrest me, I fucking dare you.*

"He taught you well." His expression is still amused.

It unnerves me. Last night he ended things so harshly.

Why so friendly now?

"I'm Evander, by the way. I don't think we've been introduced properly," he adds, extending his hand.

I shake it without thinking; he's already touched me a few times. I cringe as I realize this time it's voluntary.

I force myself to respond. "Fiana. But I think I'll be going now. Big day tomorrow..." I slowly edge past him.

"Wait," he insists, grabbing my elbow before I can pass.

I turn, keeping my smile polite. "Yes?"

His eyes penetrate mine. Intensely.

As if he's stripping me down to my bones, seeing through every careful wall I've constructed and getting to the truth of who I am and why I'm really here.

My mouth runs dry as I wonder if he actually *can* do that. Blue eyes are rare in elven bloodlines. And I can't remember what magic they align with.

If he's a Hypnotic, I'm totally screwed.

After a moment, his face falls slightly.

I hold my breath.

Finally... he speaks.

"Can I escort you home?" His tone is remarkably casual.

Seriously?

'You'll wish for the feeling of suffering animals' to *this*?

I scoff. "No, thank you." It's an effort to keep the rudeness out of my tone.

"Okay." He holds my arm a split second longer before letting go, his hand falling to his side.

The second he releases me, I'm gone.

5

The next day, I arrive at the tavern exactly ten minutes before sunset. As instructed, I'm wearing a pair of black pants and a tight black sweater, similar to what the female behind the bar was wearing. My hair is in a high ponytail with thick mahogany curls cascading down the center line of my back, pointed ears adorned with a pair of small golden hoops.

I enter the tavern, head held high, and make my way toward the bar. The tavern isn't nearly as full as it was yesterday. Perhaps the crowds come a little later in the evening.

I catch the bartender's eye.

"Fiana, right?" says the blonde from behind the bar. Same one as yesterday.

"Right." I give her a polite smile.

"You'll come around to this end." She points to a portion of the bar that can lift up with a little walkway underneath. "It doesn't lift anymore, so you'll have to duck," she adds.

I duck low and awkwardly walk underneath to the other side of the bar.

"I'm Mila," she says as she fills a large stein with an amber colored beer.

"Nice to meet you."

She sets the beer down in front of a portly villager and then comes close, leaning in to whisper in my ear, "It actually does lift, but the owner doesn't like it open in case the customers get out of control."

I give her a curt nod, thinking of my time in the bookshop. "That's wise of him."

"He likes to keep us safe, believe it or not. That's another reason why he didn't agree to the binding with Nasgardo. Honestly—he probably would have hired you just from learning of his prejudice," she adds in a low voice.

"Oh really?" My tone is skeptical.

"He's from before the King's time, so he knows how it was. Back when *we* had magic." She gives me a knowing look as if that says it all.

In a way... it does.

"I'm really happy he hired me," I admit. "I was out of options."

Mila frowns. "I can't believe Nasgardo would turn the whole town against you."

"I can," says a deep voice from the other side of the bar. "Nasgardo's in the High Guard. What did you think would happen? He's drunk off his power and status. He'll condemn anyone who forgets their place in his eyes."

It's that olive-skinned male, the first one who noticed me at the bar yesterday. He's got hair that's nearly black and a pair of eyes to match. Everything about his complexion and features are warm, yet something about his coal black eyes sends a chill down my spine.

And not the good kind.

I frown at him. "I've gathered that."

"Don't misunderstand me—*I* don't feel that way. But you can't expect one of the King's elite to just take it if a female tries to chal-

lenge his authority. They're an easily wounded bunch, you know..."
He shrugs.

"Mmhmm," I agree flatly. *Careful now.* I let out a breath. "Can I
get you anything?" I ask, shifting my tone to sound more polite.
Assuming my role as bartender. His short glass has only a sip of
liquor left in it.

"Another jadowin," he says with a little nod toward his glass.
And then he smiles.

Yeesh. His smile evokes a fox happening upon a rabbit. He's
handsome, but in the con artist kind of way.

"Your name's Fiana, right?" he asks as Mila shows me where the
jadowin is beneath the bar.

"Yes, that's right." Calm. Detached. All business.

"I'm Calimo." He offers his hand to me as I finish filling his glass
with the boozy brown liquor.

I hesitate, bending down to set the bottle back in its resting
place. When I straighten up, his hand still hangs there, waiting for
me. I look away for a beat. Others at the bar start to notice his still
outstretched arm.

And me, ignoring it.

With his other hand, he pulls out a bill that is probably too big
for a single shot of jad, and slides it across the bar toward me.

"No change," he grins. His stupid hand still waiting for me.

I sigh and finally take it. "Nice to meet you." It's a lie.

I feel something like fear in my gut... and then a wave of
something else overtakes me as his hand clasps mine, his grip
firm.

My mind goes back to another era. I'm back in Abyssia, sixteen
and in love. Craving the touch of a young male instead of shrinking
away from it. Sneaking out of my father's house for that first night
we shared together, all clumsy and awkward at first.

And then... *not.*

And the agony I felt when he left me so soon after, when my
father was arrested. His family forbade him from seeing me.

For years, I tried to write to him. I eventually gave up when I exiled myself to this wintery hell...

One where the touch of a male doesn't mean love.

Or even respect.

I pull my hand away and study Calimo, seeing him differently now, yet not quite believing my own eyes.

I see a male whose black eyes look gentle, and kind. A male who looks nothing like the young male in Abyssia, yet reminds me of him as he looks at me. Not with ownership or entitlement, like most in Ador do. But with appreciation. With respect, even.

I swallow, my throat now dry as I struggle to understand what I'm experiencing. Calimo just smiles at me warmly, seemingly unaware of the cataclysmic shift his touch has caused within me.

Mila shows me the ropes that night, and luckily the tavern isn't overwhelmingly busy.

Most of the work is remembering where everything is and the prices. The rest of the work is making conversation with our eager clientele.

As is probably true in most bars in Syra, the tavern is mostly frequented by males. The few females who do bravely venture inside are typically here *with* a male... or desiring to pick up one.

Avoiding drunk males full of stolen magic has become a learned response for females over the centuries, I imagine.

While most males still want females that *actually* want them back... there are a fair few who use their stolen advantages to sway things in their favor, at the expense of the female's own wishes of course.

Especially when drunk.

So as a gender and as a general rule, we tend to avoid taverns. Which makes Mila and me the targets of pent up male desire more often than not. At least from what I observe on this first night.

I watch Mila toy with the males from behind the bar, our little safe haven in an otherwise rowdy crowd. I watch how she flirts without ever touching anyone. How she leans in close, letting her breasts tease them. How she laughs at their jokes and gives them little winks.

I watch as she politely declines no less than ten invitations to dinner in an hour and take note of her responses, filing them away for future use.

And I watch as she refuses to bring drinks to the tables and couches, her face melting into an irresistible pout whenever a male complains about having to stand up.

"We *never* bring them their drinks," she whispers to me the first time it happens. "Behind the bar, it's safe. I think Credo even put magic back here for us, but he's never admitted it to me. Out there —they get handsy. They want you to sit in their lap or pull you toward the bathroom. One of the daytime workers—Lark—she didn't listen to Credo's warning and went out there on her second day. A Guard started dancing on her in a *very* untoward way if you can imagine, and she elbowed him in the ribs to get away. He slit her throat right then and there. If Credo hadn't been nearby to heal her right away, she probably wouldn't have made it..."

I shudder. "Stay behind the bar, no matter what. Got it."

The rest of the night is a blur of pouring drinks and receiving dirty compliments. I'm the shiny new thing, and they don't stop coming for me.

But it's also a blur of money. *So* much money. More money than I used to make in a week at the bookshop. I keep pocketing the tips, getting increasingly satisfied as the first pocket begins to bulge... and then the second.

Most of the notes are small, but I get a few twenties and even a fifty. I can hardly believe it as I do the math—my rent can be paid with the tips from a single week of work alone. Back at the bookshop it used to take me all month to save up.

So I tolerate the mild abuse from the customers. I even make it a game with the more attractive ones. See how much I can tease them... taunt them... see how much a bat of the eyelashes will get me. Or an absentminded stroke of my ears. Or a nonchalant stretch that shows off my breasts...

The hardest part is remembering that it's all a game. That they only play nice because they want me on my back, in their beds. That they can't really be trusted.

Especially the ones in uniform. Especially the ones in *black* uniforms.

As if to confirm my suspicions, Evander is the only male in the whole bar fraternizing with females. He has two of them sitting at his shadowy table near the back. They keep leaning into him. Touching his arm. Stroking his ears. Grazing his leg.

Mila catches me staring and tells me in a loud whisper, "He's at the top—and I mean *the top* of the High Guard. I think he's one of the last descendants of the Havoc bloodline, if you can believe that."

"Really..."

That explains the unique eye color. Havocs are nearly extinct. They're known for—well, causing havoc. Destroying things. Indiscriminately. They're absolutely lethal in battle. I can't help it, but my mind drifts to the doe. Was *Evander* the one who broke her legs?

"He's immortal, right?" I wonder, remembering his impossible speed.

She raises a brow and jerks her head toward the two females. "What do you think?"

My stomach lurches. "Ugh. That's *disgusting.*"

"I know. I see him here with all kinds of them. It's sad, really. They're like puppies to their master..." She fake-gags dramatically.

I shudder.

Immortal males are probably the *worst* part of this miserable existence. While there aren't many of them—about ten percent of the population—they have so much strength, power, and enhanced magical abilities that even one of them is a death threat to the average male, let alone female.

Females, in yet another cruel twist of fate, cannot be born immortal unless *both* their parents are immortal. Males can be born immortal from just one immortal parent or even from two mortal parents.

And nature has blessed the all-powerful immortal males even further...

If they happen to find a female they want to keep forever, they have the ability to *share* immortality during sex.

And the females—the Maker must *truly* hate us—because the females become eternally devoted to the immortal male during that... *process.*

Whether she wants to be or not.

My tutor, the one my father allegedly murdered, once told me that in centuries past when females still had their magic, the sharing of immortality was considered a sacred bond and was shared only in the case of a divine union, or when an immortal male met his ideal female counterpart and she accepted his love.

Divine unions were said to be more powerful than ordinary love for the immortals; completely altering the course of the rest of their lives, and even enhancing their magical abilities.

In the good times, this meant the immortal male became utterly devoted to the female who held the pull for him. When and if she accepted and they sealed the divine union, they would *both* be strengthened by the unbreakable magical bond. It was said that they would become of one mind, one body, and one energy.

One mind, meaning they could share thoughts with each other that no one else could discern, even with the most advanced mind reading magic, across great distances.

One body, meaning the female would become immortal as well, allowing them both to live in love and bliss forever.

And *one energy*, meaning their magic would cross pollinate. Each would grow stronger as they gained the abilities of the other...

and together they would become more powerful than they ever could have been apart.

It was a beautiful story, now merely elven lore, because the reality is that since King Vilero started the process of stealing magic from females nearly six hundred years ago, the divine union magic has been utterly tainted and destroyed.

Because immortal males don't *need* to be devoted to any female to gain her magic. They can just steal it.

And on the off chance they *do* feel the pull with a female, all they have to do is *immortalize* her and she becomes devoted to him forever... whether she wants to be or not.

In the King's times, this means that most immortal males simply rape their divine feminines instead of bothering with the lengthy process of courtship.

Worse yet—most of them don't even bother stopping with just the one. Although nature intends for immortalization to be used with *one* female—an immortal male's divine feminine—nothing technically stops them from sticking it to *any* female who opens her legs to them.

Willingly, or otherwise.

Thus the immortal males of King Vilero's time often have *dozens* of immortal females devoted to them. Like elven concubines, magically bound to an eternity of unconscious loyalty.

Like puppies to their master.

Like those females and Evander.

The one saving grace that nature provides for females in this twisted mess is that *if* a female has been forced into devotion—if she does not actively *choose* to be immortalized and agree to the divine union—the magic of *one mind* and *one energy* do not take.

She keeps her thoughts, safe and sound, all to herself. And her immortal male does not gain access to her magic.

Of course, none of us *have* magic to access anymore... but perhaps keeping her mind sacred is enough of a consolation prize to keep her sane.

Although eternity is a *very* long time.

And so this beautiful, wonderful, magical love was mutilated—like so many other things—under the rule of King Vilero.

When Evander comes up to the bar to order another round of drinks for him and his females, it takes everything I have not to spit in his face.

And he has the gall to leave a hundred note tip.

Despite myself, I pocket it hungrily.

Like a puppy given a treat by its master.

6

I t's been two weeks of successful shifts at the tavern, October rent is paid and I already have enough for next month ready to go. My fridge is stocked full of food from the market, and the top of my bookcase is littered with various potions I was able to acquire through the apothecary's back room, which illegally sells magic-infused potions to females. At a premium, of course.

It's another risk, but I've purchased from them once before and didn't have an issue. This time I got three vials of yarrow tincture infused with Curic magic, for healing difficult-to-treat wounds; forgetful serum, which is made with Hypnotic magic and causes the drinker to forget recent events; and essence of repulsion, which utilizes Chamelic magic to repel attention and essentially makes you invisible.

Even after all of that, I still have an extra hundred notes to spare.

So on my first night off, I reserve a table at the mid-priced restaurant at the top of the village.

The Alcove.

Though I received no less than *twenty-six* requests for dates in the past two weeks... I'm going by myself.

My hair is curled and my lips are painted dark red. I've dressed in a long, cobalt blue gown and my nicest pair of boots, topped with a heavy black cloak. While the materials are modest, it is an outfit I would wear if a male I truly liked were courting me.

Tonight, it's just for me. And maybe for the waitress, who compliments me as she leads me to my table.

The Alcove is dimly lit and carries a heady aroma of lush meats and savory sauces. It's the kind of food that truly chases away the cold, if only for an hour. There's a fireplace toward the back and a few booths with benches wrapped in plush velvet.

That section is moderately busy, filled mostly with couples or small groups of males—but the table she takes me to is flanked by two empty ones.

I sit in the chair that faces toward the rest of the room, while the one opposite me remains empty and still.

The waitress approaches and I order a glass of wine as she tells me the specials for the evening. I sigh in contentment at the act of being served—instead of being the one who is doing the serving.

I'm the only female here alone, but I'm not embarrassed by that. In fact, the thought makes me sit up straighter. Prouder.

The waitress brings me my wine and I place my dinner order, silently marveling at the fact that I can afford what I really want to eat. I sip my wine and lean back in my chair, all tension melting from my shoulders. It's nice.

It's short lived, though.

As I wait for dinner to be served, that familiar ache of guilt fills my stomach.

Here I am, sitting in a nice restaurant being served and acting like I have no cares in the world; meanwhile, my father is deep in the bowels of this mountain, approaching his eighth year of torture in The Cave.

And I haven't done a single thing since starting my tavern job that would help his escape.

Almost unconsciously, I pull out the two tattered newspaper clippings that have become a permanent fixture in my cloak pocket. I run my fingers over the print remembering each of those nights...

PROMINENT HERON NATIVE DISAPPEARS IN THE NIGHT

Lyla Araminta Willowbark, née Woodsen, was declared missing by her husband, Tarian Perceval Willowbark to the Heron Guard at 3 o'clock in the morning on Tuesday, April 15th. The Heron Observer interviewed neighbors close to the Willowbark residence about that night. Some report they startled awake around that time, citing a feeling of inescapable terror and dread. Others report remaining asleep, but becoming trapped in an endless loop of their worst nightmares. A few admitted they had sleep paralysis and one said they had trouble breathing. All of these signs suggest possible demonic activity. Local officials were unable to confirm or deny this assessment, citing this is still an ongoing investigation. Mr. Willowbark was also unable to confirm or deny demonic activity, but did confirm for the Observer that neither he nor his four-year-old daughter were harmed.

I repress a snort. No, we weren't 'harmed'.

Just traumatized. Abandoned. Betrayed. Confused. What mother sells her soul to a demon?

I shake my head, slamming that article down and picking up the other.

ECCENTRIC WIDOWER KILLS BELOVED TEACHER IN A SENSELESS FIT OF RAGE

Tarian Perceval Willowbark has been accused of the murder of Ellery

Roger Mason. Mr. Willowbark was taken into custody shortly after midnight on Saturday, August 28th. Mr. Mason was Mr. Willowbark's daughter's private tutor for the past eleven years. It is still unclear what the motive was, sources close to the investigation say. Mr. Mason was engaged to be married to Morgana Inessa Blackthorn. "Ellery was nothing but dedicated to the Willowbark family and was like a beloved uncle to Fiana. It's an absolute disgrace," a source close to Ms. Blackthorn told the Observer. Of note, Mr. Willowbark's late wife, Lyla Araminta (née Woodsen), was mysteriously reported missing in 579 A.V. and was never found. Neighbors at the time suspected demonic activity, but this was never proven by local officials. Is it possible Tarian Willowbark killed his wife thirteen years ago? Officials denied comment. Mr. Willowbark's mother, Chrysalia Lee Willowbark (née Rockwell) has taken custody of her son's only daughter, Fiana Marie. This is a pending investigation and the Observer will continue to release details as they are reported.

Tears prick my eyes as the memories of losing them both rush through me. My chest tightens, and I let out a ragged breath. Willing the past to be different. And yet knowing it never will be.

I don't notice that the waitress has seated someone at the table next to me.

"Who stood you up? I'll kill 'em..." purrs a voice I recognize. I look up, my pulse quickening.

Evander is sitting alone at the table adjacent to mine, in the chair across from mine. He's still in uniform and his dark brown hair is disheveled, as if he's had a long day. A hint of anger shines in his eyes, and the subtle glow of his skin seems to be tinged in red.

Fuck. I hate how my body instantly reacts, seeing his face up close. How my eyes drift to the muscles of his chest underneath his uniform, then drag up and linger on the rugged lines of his beard before catching on the sight of his mouth. This male exudes sex just by breathing. And not the kind I used to have with Tarletan.

The kind that's so intense and all-consuming that you lose hours—if not *days*—wrapped up in each other.

It's easy to see why so many females fall at his feet.

I will not be one of them.

I quickly wipe the wetness still lingering in the corners of my eyes, carefully so as not to smudge my makeup.

"No one stood me up. I'm here on a date with myself."

His lips twitch underneath his beard. "It must not be going very well then, by the looks of it. Guess I'll have to kill *you*..." he teases, his strange blue eyes full of cockiness.

I just glare at him. And take a sip of my wine.

"Is that a love poem you wrote yourself? Can I read it?" His immortal speed snatches the clippings out of my fingertips before I can react.

"Don't—" But his eyes scan the papers in an instant. He frowns.

"I'm sorry, I shouldn't have taken this," he says, passing it gingerly back to me, his face apologetic.

I narrow my eyes. "Where's *your* date?" I so rarely see him at the tavern free of his... puppies.

He shrugs. "Just me tonight." His eyes twinkle with some unshared thought. "But I'm curious. Why bring something like *that* on a night when you're clearly out celebrating?" He gestures toward the newspaper clippings.

"Who says I'm celebrating?" My tone is sharp with denial, but damn does he know how to read me.

"Aren't you? If memory serves, you've done well at the tavern so far..." Eyes still twinkling.

I want to punch him as I think of *his* role in that. He comes back every night, always with a new female or three—and always leaves a hundred note tip.

Does he think that gives him some sort of *ownership* over me? Am I the next female he wants to lock into immortal servitude? My stomach tightens into knots.

I choose to answer his former question. "I don't want to forget where I came from. Or what it took to get here."

The answer is truthful, and perhaps too revealing. I shut my mouth before I say something else I might regret.

The waitress stealthily gives him his drink—a tall glass of jad—and he takes a swill now.

"How old were you? When he was arrested?" he wonders, his face unreadable.

"Seventeen," I say icily. My tone implies he should ask no further questions. The waitress returns with my food. "Now if you don't mind, I'd like to eat in peace."

He makes a show of pretending I stabbed him in the chest, reacting to the invisible wound. I roll my eyes. He chuckles, but says nothing more.

His food arrives shortly after mine, and we spend the rest of the meal ignoring each other.

The food is delicious. Though I'm annoyed that Evander is still sitting next to me, I can't help but enjoy the complex warming flavors of the roasted duck and root vegetables. After years of little protein, this food brings me back to *life*, bite by bite. I sigh when I'm finished, feeling thoroughly nourished.

I can feel Evander's eyes on me, but I keep mine focused forward until the waitress comes by to clear my plate.

When it's time for me to pay the bill, the waitress just shrugs and says it's already been paid.

My eyes dart over to Evander as embarrassment heats my cheeks. "What did you do?" I accuse.

He furrows his brow dramatically, eyes taunting. "I have no idea what you're talking about."

"You had *no right* to do that," I insist, pulling the notes out of my cloak pocket to pay him back.

An invisible wall appears as I try to hand it to him, my knuckles knocking into it hard, like glass. "Ow!" I yank my hand back. I try again, more gingerly this time, and hit glass. "Stop that!"

Evander just cracks up as if it's the funniest thing he's ever seen.

"Fine. If you won't take it, I guess the waitress gets paid double tonight." I go to set the note down, but now it's stuck to my hand. I lift my hand away from the table and try peeling it off with the other hand, which works. And then I try dropping it on the table again—and I can't. It's glued to me like flypaper. Evander is laughing so hard the entire restaurant is staring.

"You are the most disgusting, annoying, insufferable male I have ever met!" I leave my table and stalk toward the door, my face turning beet red as everyone follows my movements with their eyes. The note is still stuck to my hand, so I shove it back into my pocket, where it finally magically releases me.

"Don't forget sexy, hilarious, and utterly irresistible..." he coos from behind me, quickly keeping pace with my hurried steps. "With the best, and the most *massive*..."

"Stop following me!" I hiss, turning around to glare at him. He's still shaking with laughter.

I take a deep breath, working to make my voice sound firm. My eyes blaze with the fury of six hundred years of mistreated females.

"I don't want to *know* you. I *don't* think you're attractive. And if you don't leave me alone, I'm going to *physically assault* you. And seeing as you're High Guard, I really don't want to do that and risk going to The Cave tonight. So will you *please*—for the love of the Maker—leave me *alone*."

The look of shock on his face tells me I win this round. I turn to walk home, head held high, with absolutely no regrets.

In fact, it's the best night of my life.

My speech works... for the next several days Evander isn't in the tavern. The satisfaction of telling off a High Guard immortal scumbag is so good that I almost don't miss his sizable tips...

Almost.

Luckily, there are plenty of others to pay me at the tavern, and though my haul would have been bigger had Evander shown up, I'm still pocketing more money than I made in a week at the bookshop every single night.

Calimo, the villager who insisted I shake his hand, keeps sitting at the bar and dominating my attention. Every night, he showers me with compliments and asks me about myself. And every night I play the game of being just interested enough to flirt with him... but not so interested to go home with him. He asks me out to dinner frequently. I always say no.

He's not the only one. Something's odd about this bar. The males are actually *nice*. Ador—a village overrun with the Guard, not to mention *the capital* of the King's anti-female agenda—isn't exactly the place where you'd expect to be treated well as a female. Mila's guess that perhaps there's magic in the bar driving this behavior is the only explanation that makes sense to me.

Because it can't be that males in Ador are actually... decent. *No. Can't be that.*

So I ignore the dinner requests each night and keep my guard up with the males in the tavern—especially with Calimo, who certainly seems to have his eye on me.

Tonight has me feeling confident with the repetitive tasks of the job. Glasses are clinking. Males are talking passionately. The fire blazes red, filling the tavern with a warm glow. The whole bar is jovial.

I've found a familiar rhythm, I know where everything is, and I've even started to trust myself in the games I play with the opposite sex. So much so that I'm actually having *fun*.

At work. With the males of Ador... who knew?

I smile to myself as I fill a few steins of beer for some villagers.

"So you *do* smile," says a voice from down the bar. "I was beginning to think your face is broken..."

It's Evander, returning at last.

I turn to glare at him. He's standing at the edge of the bar between two stools, a couple of attractive redheads giggling a few feet behind him. I ignore him at first, sliding the beers to Elyon and his friends, smiling at him sweetly as he passes me a ten note tip.

It's a stark contrast to the next look I give Evander. "What can I get you?"

"Oh there it is! The frown again. Must have been a fluke." He smirks, as waves of his power glitter in the air around him. "We'll take two glasses of the house white and a double shot of jad, neat."

I send another glare in his direction as I get to work. He just grins. Completely unbothered.

Like always.

Fucking prick.

I notice Calimo watching us in my periphery, his eyes flitting between me and Evander.

No one orders the wine in this tavern. Anyone for a taste of it would find it worse than lighter fluid. I tried a glass after one of my first nights—and nearly spat it out.

So I have to open a fresh bottle. It's like I'm on display as both Calimo and Evander study my every move. I cut the foil and screw the corkscrew into the bottle, and with each twist, I can feel them watching. I try quickening my pace, if only to get their eyes off me, but the corks are so cheap I can only go so fast without risking breaking them.

Eventually I turn to Calimo, just for someone to talk to.

Someone other than Evander.

"What are you doing this weekend?" I ask Calimo sweetly, letting my lips settle into an attractive pout. I slowly pull the cork out of the bottle.

He nearly chokes on his jad. "I uh... don't really have plans I guess. I might try to have lunch with my father..."

I see Evander scowl out of the corner of my eye, but I keep my gaze focused on Calimo's. "That sounds nice... what does your father do?" It's the first question I've ever asked him about himself.

Evander snorts, and my eyes dart unwillingly in his direction for a beat before centering back on Calimo.

"He's uh..." Calimo starts to say as I pour the first glass of wine. "He's the King..." My hand slips and I nearly drop the bottle, spraying white wine all over the back bar.

And all over my shirt.

"I didn't realize..." I say awkwardly as I pull out a rag to clean the bar. And my shirt.

The only son *I* have ever heard of has red hair just like the King's.

"Yeah. I know I don't give off the vibe of royalty and all. I don't live at the palace—I live here in town."

Evander is still staring at me, waiting for his drinks, so I give up on my shirt and start pouring the second glass of wine.

"So you and—" I glance at Evander, somehow unable to say his name out loud. "You two must know each other... right?"

"For centuries, yes," says Evander coolly. He looks annoyed.

"Centuries?" I repeat, my eyes widening slightly. "Are you *both* immortal?" I direct the question to Calimo.

Calimo shrugs, running a hand through his dark hair. "I've never tried to find out. But my father's bloodline is very... strong. Even if I'm mortal, I don't age as quickly as others with all of that extra... power..."

I shudder, thinking of the source of all of that *extra* power. Thinking of all the females who had been forced to sacrifice their own magic for the good of the King's bloodline.

"Although I would guess I'm likely *not* immortal. Otherwise there would be more females... staying close to me..." he adds with a sidelong glance at Evander.

I wrinkle my nose. Another confirmation of what Mila suspected... from someone who's known Evander for *centuries*.

"Can I just get my drinks, Fiana?" Evander asks lazily.

I exhale with force and hand him the wine glasses, then quickly pour his double shot of jad and slide that across the bar to him, too.

"Thanks... I fixed your shirt by the way," he says with a wink, handing the drinks to the females. My hands drop to my abdomen where my shirt was soaked with wine, and now it's indeed dry.

"I didn't ask you to do that!" I complain.

His eyes run greedily down my body. "As much as I'd love to see you in a wet shirt... I didn't want you to get cold." He pauses, piling several large bills on top of the bar. "For the nights I was away." He winks, and then takes his drink and finds a table back in the shadows with the two redheads.

I glare at the money on the bar for a moment, my stomach twisting as I imagine pocketing it.

Go away.

I don't want you.

I don't need you.

You mean nothing to me.

The money just stares back at me.

I get over myself and grab it. Five hundred notes, plus the cost of the drinks in exact change. I stick the five hundred in my pocket. *Like one of his whores.*

"He's revolting," I say to no one in particular, but Calimo catches my eye and gives me a nod.

"I've always hated him," he agrees.

Interesting.

And he's the King's son...

I run my hands along the tops of the bottles beneath the bar as a new idea starts to take shape.

Calimo likely has access to information about The Cave not found in the bookshop. And if he *hates* his father—he might be more than willing to divulge a royal secret.

It's wrong. I know it is. And it's dangerous.

And yet I find myself leaning in toward Calimo, widening my eyes in interest. "Why do you live down in the village?"

"Well... my mother wasn't my father's preferred... lady," he says carefully.

I get the deeper meaning.

"Does she live in the village too?" I keep my tone polite.

"No... she died. A long time ago. My father eventually—tired of her. She was a hundred and fifty when he decided he was done with her. I miss her sometimes, but then again I've been alive longer without her than with her."

My heart sinks. I've heard stories of the King's habit of *disposing* of his mistresses after a time. Everyone has.

No wonder Calimo hates him.

"I am so sorry he did that to her." My tone is kind. But—*a hundred and fifty years*—"How old *are* you?" the question escapes me before I can stop it. Calimo's features look like he's in his early thirties at most.

"I'm the same age as Evander, three hundred and eighty years old," he shrugs. "But my father much prefers Evander, even though I'm his son. He's at the top of the High Guard partially because of his power and immortality... but also because my father loves him so much. Evander's the son he never had, but always wished for. And I'm the son he *did* have, and always wished away."

"That's terrible," I sympathize, resting a hand on the bar. There's an opportunity here, I can feel it. But I need to play my part well.

I meet Calimo's eyes. "I had a parent like yours, too." I hesitate, editing the details a bit to prevent too many questions. "It was my mother. She just left us one day. For no reason. No explanation."

"I'm sorry," Calimo says, placing one of his hands on mine.

I don't flinch at his touch.

7

The guilt has gotten worse, judging by my nightmares.

The past several nights, I keep seeing memories of my father holding me in his arms after my mother left us.

"I will protect you," he whispers as I sob in his arms. "I won't ever let anything happen to you."

Then the dream morphs, and I see myself as a teenager screaming at my father for keeping me so excessively protected that I can't go to a public school or go out with my friends.

"I will not apologize for keeping you safe," he argues, locking me in my room.

"And just *what is it* you are keeping me safe from, Father?" I shout, banging on the door. It was raining that night, and the thunder booms so loudly that I jump at the sound.

"When you're old enough, you will understand," he says softly. "Until then, you will follow my rules. I cannot have you taken from me like your mother was."

Those words cut so deep that they take the fight right out of me. I stay there, my forehead pressed against the door, tears streaming down my face.

"I love you, Fiana," he murmurs. "I know it seems like I'm being unfair. And I hate putting you in this position where you can't be with your friends. But since your mother left us, we can't play by the same rules as everyone else. It's dangerous for reasons you do not understand. And that's okay. I'm willing to be the villain if it means you'll be safe."

"Demons aren't coming for me, Father. At most there's a sixteen-year-old boy who wants to take me to the theater," I complain.

"Even so, the answer is no," he says gently, and I hear him walk down the hall to his own bedroom. Then the dream morphs, and I'm trapped in the cloak room as two High Guards come to take him.

"Tarian Willowbark?" says the taller one, a brown-haired fellow I notice through the crack of the door.

"Yes," my father says far too calmly. Horror grips me as I realize his demeanor—one of resignation—is much like my mother's was the night she was taken.

"You're under arrest for the murder of Ellery Mason," says the second one, a blonde fellow.

"Murder?" I whisper. *He murdered my tutor—?*

This has to be a mistake. My father would sooner kill himself then *murder* an innocent person for no reason.

I'm seconds away from bursting out of the closet to try to defend his honor when I feel his magic block the door from opening. I clear my throat, preparing to scream, when my voice seems to evaporate right from my throat.

Tears start sliding down my cheeks as I realize *he isn't letting me help him.*

Magical cuffs are placed on my father's wrists. The kind that block *his* magic from flowing. My stomach churns. I could be stuck like this if they take him away!

Each warrior in black grips an arm and they all dissolve into thin air until nothing remains. I scream—soundlessly—into an empty house where no one will hear as the tears cascade faster down my cheeks. I shove and push and *fight* with all my might against the enchanted door, willing magic I don't have to force it open.

A split second passes, and then I'm tumbling out of the closet as an ear splitting sound fills my ears. A scream—my scream. My voice is back.

I land *hard* on my knees as agony rips through my chest.

He's gone—he's really gone.

I jolt awake, sweating profusely. Haldric eyes me sympathetically from his perch by the window. I sit up, catching my breath as guilt and dread fill me to my core.

For all his focus on protecting me, he forgot to protect himself from the demons. And I never once made it easy for him.

And it shouldn't, but it sure as hell feels like it's my fault.

For a brief moment after he was arrested, I wondered if my mother would come for me. I wouldn't have gone with her, of course.

But it would have been nice to properly greet her, I think to myself as I slide my dagger into my boot while I dress for my tavern shift. It's the same one I've kept on me at all times since my father was taken.

The same one I vowed I would one day ram through her heart should she ever show her face here again.

Every shift this week, Calimo comes back and sits right in the center of the bar, commanding most of my attention.

And now, I give it willingly.

Just... not for the reason he thinks.

I haven't dug into his potential knowledge of The Cave yet; it feels too risky doing it while the tavern's busy, and he always seems to come in during those times.

I have to get him alone soon.

It feels like progress, though. Even if I'm just winning Calimo's favor for now.

It's not enough to chase away the nightmares, though.

Meanwhile, Evander never ceases to shamelessly flirt with me, despite having a new gaggle of females following him around each night.

It's beyond irritating. I never see repeats either. Nor do I see him really *engage* with his females. It seems like he just... tolerates them.

And in a way, that makes it worse.

Each female is a living example of his absolute contempt for our gender. He isn't in love. Isn't in lust. Is hardly even interested in any of them. But he keeps bringing them around. Just because he can.

I've developed a bad habit of clenching my jaw every time I see him with a new female. I have to remind myself to relax otherwise I end my shift with a massive headache. He doesn't seem to notice or care... because he keeps on dropping those hundred note tips with that aggravating grin of his.

I even try to give the tips to Mila sometimes, who would take them gratefully, but the same annoying magic he did on the cash in the restaurant is on every single bill he's given me.

If I try to give it to her, it stays glued to my hand. If she tries to take it from my pocket—an invisible wall blocks her from even getting close. And if she tries to collect the money off the bar directly, before I even touch it—it's too slippery and slides right out of her grasp.

I even try giving her some of his tips from a previous shift that I'd already taken home and brought back. But the same magic occurs. I can only get rid of his money, it seems, by spending it on myself.

"I just don't get why he hasn't given the game up yet," I complain to Mila one evening after Evander tips me two hundred notes, one for tonight and one for last night when he didn't come in at all.

Mila rolls her eyes at me. "You haven't so much as gone on a single date with anyone else. Not even Calimo. He probably still thinks he has a fighting chance..."

I stare at her blankly. "You really think so?"

"A male like *that* doesn't give up on something he wants until it's clear he can *never* have it," she says wisely.

I purse my lips. "Then I guess I'll have to make things clearer..."

I consider my options. There's Elyon, but he's a foot shorter than me. There's a few Guards that are nice, but they're *Guards*.

Part of me wants to fight it, but Calimo does stand out as the obvious choice. Even Mila suggested him. It's a good plan for another reason too—it'll give me a chance to speak to him outside of the tavern chaos.

Later that night, Calimo comes in and asks for the hundredth time if I want to have dinner with him.

I finally say yes.

"Leaving so soon?" Evander asks from his shadowy table in the corner as I make my way toward the tavern door, my cloak draped over my arm.

"I worked the day shift today." I pull my cloak around my shoulders. "I have a date tonight," I add, buttoning the top.

He appears instantly at my side, his immortal speed practically giving me whiplash.

"And who's the lucky male you finally said yes to?" He sounds annoyed. *Good.*

"Calimo." I keep my chin up.

"Please be joking..." His tone is condescending.

"I'm not," I say, feeling my jaw tighten. I fight to keep my face neutral.

He groans, but I keep my eyes forward. Just a few feet to the door now, and—*how does he* do *that?* He's instantly in front of me, blocking my path now. Forcing me to stare into his cobalt-and-ice-blue eyes.

"Please be careful with Calimo. He's not as... *nice* as he seems." His nostrils flare.

I snort. "Not that it's *any* of your business, but he's been nothing but kind to me. Unlike *some* people." I push past him but he catches my arm.

"When have I not been kind to you?" he demands, his voice quiet.

"The suggestive jokes? The magical money that you won't let me share with Mila? The *threat* you gave me one of the first nights we'd met?" *The parade of females. The fact that you work for the King.* I glare at him.

Evander raises a brow. "That was a *warning*, not a threat." His eyes trace a heated line down to my lips. "And I can't help it that I find you irresistible..." His fingers tighten slightly on my arm. "And fuck me for being so generous," he says with a cocky grin.

Generous? Generous?

"So there's no *other* reason why you over tip me and only me? It's just pure, good-hearted generosity?" It comes out like a retort.

"It is with you." His eyes dance with unbridled amusement.

I bite the inner edge of my cheek. He holds my gaze, challenging me. *Your move, Fiana,* he seems to say.

Insult him. Take him down a peg. Wipe that stupid smile off his face.

A bitter sigh escapes me.

"Well... I'm going to be late," I say. He releases my arm and steps aside. He opens the door for me, too.

Fucking. Prick.

I make it back to my apartment to change.

Stupid, stupid, immortal scum.

I glance at the clock. Calimo will be here any minute, and I'm still wearing my all black unofficial tavern uniform. I force myself to breathe—blowing out all the hot air that has accumulated inside me since leaving the tavern.

I race into my bathroom to quickly check my makeup, and then root through my closet until I find the white dress I wore the first day in the tavern. I undress and slide it on, fluffing my curly brown hair, finding myself idly wishing that immortals could *somehow* get venereal diseases, though I know they're immune to most illnesses.

Haldric clicks his beak a few times disapprovingly. I can practically hear him saying *get it together*.

There's a knock at the door. I glance toward the sound.

I try to force Evander out of my mind, and it's a bit like shoving him into an overstuffed drawer.

The damn thing just won't shut.

I groan, jamming my feet into my nicest boots, the ones with a heel, then cross my apartment to open the door.

Calimo's eyes take me in, admiring the curves of my body underneath the white dress, lingering in some spots that cause me to blush.

Good—this is good. I can focus on Calimo. I'm here with Calimo. Tonight it's all about Calimo.

Though deep down, I know this isn't just a date with Calimo. I have an agenda. A purpose. My heart rate picks up.

This is for my father.

"You look beautiful," he says finally, giving me a light kiss on the cheek. His scent envelopes me for the first real time—a musky mix of toffee and pure male essence.

"Thank you," I breathe, still mentally forcing that stupid immortal drawer shut. I plaster a smile on my face as he pulls back.

Calimo wears what looks like his nicest villager uniform... a crisp tartan shirt in dark reds and browns tucked into a pair of straight black pants. His cloak is black and woolen tonight, giving him the look of an attractive vampire who lives somewhere cold. Though those only actually exist in the Shadow Realms.

He extends his arm. "Shall we go?"

I hesitate for the briefest of moments. It's my first date with a male in over seven years, and my first date with a male in Ador. I shouldn't be nervous—or better yet *afraid*.

And yet... I take a steadying breath.

Just then a wave of calm comes over me, so palpable I wonder if I imagined the nerves a moment before.

Maybe I had.

I reach for Calimo's outstretched arm.

The world dissolves around us and I feel my form and Calimo's arm become less solid, even as I clutch him tighter. My heart races as we pass through space and time.

I haven't dissolved since first meeting Evander, but I quickly push that memory back into the mental drawer. For good measure, I picture ramming my whole body weight against it. Finally, it feels like it's shut.

I exhale in relief.

Not even a full second has passed and we reappear in front of The Alcove—the same restaurant I took myself to a few weeks prior. *The same restaurant where*—no. I will *not* open that drawer again for the rest of the night.

"Have you been here?" Calimo asks casually, guiding me to the front with our arms still linked.

"Just once..." I say, still catching my breath from the dissolution. "Never with a date, though." I shiver.

"I love this place. You'll like the duck..." he adds.

As we make our way inside, the waitress guides us to our table. The same one as before. I curse under my breath.

Calimo gestures to the chair nearest the wall, pulling it out for me with magic from where he stands on the other side. I edge in between the tables to the chair and sit down. I fight tooth and nail not to look at the empty chair at the neighboring table where *he* sat.

Instead, I notice this is the first time I've ever seen Calimo use magic. That strikes me as odd considering his powerful bloodline. I don't know what to make of it, but I file it away for later.

We listen patiently as the waitress details the specials for us. Calimo orders a bottle of wine to share, and the waitress leaves to procure it.

"You look beautiful tonight. Did I already tell you that?" he wonders, a sheepish smile spreading across his warm-toned face.

I smile back. "You did. But thank you..."

"I'm surprised you finally agreed to go out with me. Don't get me wrong, I'm delighted you did... but it just seemed like you weren't interested in dating much of anyone," he confesses. I feel myself blush.

Still not... but I have a part to play.

"I haven't found the males of Ador to be very..." I hesitate, searching for the right words, "*Old world*. I like a male who still treats a female like a lady, even if we no longer have equal status in these realms."

Calimo nods, understanding in his coal-black eyes. Such strange eyes.

"It must be hard for you, living here. So close to the Guard. So close to... the King," he says delicately, and I hear the unsaid words in his pause. *My father, the King.*

"Do you see your father often?" I keep my tone warm. Reserving judgment.

I'm fishing, too.

He shakes his head. "I'm the bastard son, the failure in his eyes. The one he'd rather forget. Every once in a while I try to reconnect... but he isn't impressed by much from me. The only way I can see him turning around is if I offered him something... *valuable*." A shiver unexpectedly snakes down my spine at that, but I ignore it.

"That sounds really hard. To have him so close, and yet for him to feel so far away." I know *that* feeling more than he realizes. More than I'm willing to admit to him.

Calimo nods, a curt smile on his lips. The waitress returns with the wine then, and we place our dinner orders. I choose the duck again.

I watch the waitress walk away as something in my stomach flutters. I unroll the napkin at my place setting and pull it into my lap, twisting it in my hands under the table.

I originally agreed to this dinner to get Evander off my back and to get Calimo alone—to see what he knows about The Cave, if anything. Yet a part of me is suddenly struggling with the idea of using him. Doesn't *want* to use him. I even find myself relating to him.

I twist the napkin tighter.

What the hell is happening to me?

I clear my throat and meet Calimo's eyes again.

"I've been alone for a long time. Both my parents are—gone. So I know how you feel," I reveal.

Calimo's eyes soften. A bit like Tarletan's might have, I notice.

"You told me about your mother. I didn't realize your father was gone too," he says softly, leaning in.

I strangle the napkin with my fists. "Yes. He is." I can tell he has questions, but I speak again before he can ask. "When did your father kick you out of the palace?"

His forehead creases. "Your age—twenty-five."

Damn. Over three hundred and fifty years ago...

"Did you work with your father at all before you left?"

Calimo snorts. "I tried. He wanted me to join the Guard, but I barely have any Havoc in me. I trained anyway, learned how to fight. Learned to master what little Havoc magic I have access to. I was still quite the disappointment. My mother's genetic line was incredibly weak; just Relic magic mostly. Which is kind of useless. Unless you're looking for something." His eyes turn abruptly serious.

The way he's staring at me, I almost feel like *I'm* the thing he's looking for.

"And what do you do now?" I smooth the napkin out in my lap, giving my hands a break from their strangulation efforts.

His smile is wide. "Sin, mostly."

I smile, but inside I feel stuck. He isn't giving me much to go on. My questions have to get bolder.

I feign a look of rapt interest, clasping my hands on the table and leaning in toward him. I speak in a low voice, a smile dancing at the edge of my lips.

"Did you ever visit The Cave during your training? You hear such scary things about the place growing up. Is it as bad as they say?"

Calimo studies me for a long moment. I struggle to keep the guilt off my face.

He sighs. "It's worse..." But then he leans in, mimicking my posture. "You wouldn't believe the filth that's in there. Gorgons, maras, *loads* of demons. Vampires, chimeras, even manticores."

I shiver for his benefit, and to hide my ire at his use of the word *filth*. I fix my lips into an artful frown. "It honestly keeps me up at night sometimes, living so close to them. I need to know—there's no way they could escape and get us, right?"

Calimo chuckles. "Of course not! No prisoner has ever escaped The Cave."

I drop my hands back to my napkin again, gripping it tight to hide my frustration. I need him to give me *more*. "But it can't just be locked cells, right? There's got to be something more guarding them? Preventing their escape?"

He eyes me curiously. I widen my eyes in faux fear.

"There's magic keeping them in, too. Each cell has a different set of wards based on its occupant. You're safe here. None of them will get you in your sleep. And if they do," he leans toward me, "I'd be happy to protect you from them."

I sigh in relief. "That's good. What kinds of spells do they use, anyway?" I wince dramatically. "I can't imagine anything strong enough to keep a mara in line..."

Maras are the demons of demons. Also known as a demon's worst nightmare embodied, which is quite the accomplishment considering demons *are* the essence of worst nightmares embodied.

It's impossible to grasp what could possibly be horrifying *to* a demon—who's very existence *is* a thing of unimaginable horror.

But maras are exactly that.

"Fiana—what's with the questions? No one's escaped The Cave in fifteen centuries, since it was established. You have nothing to fear." He smiles, though his eyes are tight.

Shit. Time for damage control.

"Maker save me—you're right." I sigh dramatically for his benefit. "I haven't been courted by anyone in a long time. I'm still kind of new at this." I peek up at him from under my lashes.

Calimo laughs. I join him.

His eyes drift to my lips. And linger there. "I'm sure you'll pick up the nuances soon enough."

My next statement isn't an act.

"I haven't—I *don't* say yes to just anyone. I hope you know that." It comes out like a warning.

His eyes meet mine. "I won't let you down, Fiana," he says calmly.

Something in my stomach churns. Guilt? No. Nerves maybe. I take a sip from my glass. *What a mess.*

"Forgive me for saying so, but I am glad that you didn't say yes to Evander," he confesses.

I nearly choke on my wine. That mental drawer springs wide open all over again.

"Why do you say that?" I wonder.

Not that he asked me. Not that I want him to. Not that I would say yes. Ever. In a million years.

"Well, I know you understand what it's like to have a parent who doesn't want you. Now imagine if the same week your mother left you, she suddenly invited your arch nemesis to live with her like a daughter *instead of* you. Or like a son, in my and Evander's case."

"He did that?" I ask in disbelief.

Calimo nods. "He kicked me out of the palace on Monday. By

Thursday, Evander had moved in. I think my father even gave him my room, the old bastard."

I shake my head. "That's just evil. And—you don't have to worry about Evander. I have no desire to end up as one of his immortal concubines. I plan to stay *far* away from him."

"Good," Calimo says with a smile that touches his eyes. My heart skips. He really is attractive; all smooth skin and silky black hair. My eyes catch on his mouth, stained slightly from the wine.

Our meals arrive shortly after that, and for a time we eat in silence. I break it first.

"Do you date a lot? Am I one of... many?" I ask, feeling blush creep into my cheeks.

I guess I'm abandoning my agenda now.

Calimo's lips twitch. "I have had lovers over the centuries of course, but as of now I'm only focused on one female."

I take a sip of wine, admiring the way his dark hair subtly glows in the dim candlelight of the restaurant. His eyes, never leaving my face, feel like a fireplace warming my bare skin.

How easy it would be to fall in love with such eyes.

The King's bastard son... my new love?

My next sip of wine is bigger than I intend.

I don't recognize this version of myself. I haven't seen her since —well, since Tarletan.

At the end of the meal, he pays the bill even though I offer to split it, and we leave the restaurant arm in arm, making our way slowly back to my apartment.

We decide to walk this time. The snow is soft and fluffy, like fat balls of cotton gently descending from the sky.

"The last male I was with was back in Abyssia. His name was Tarletan. I thought I was going to marry him. Back then, at least," I mention, though I'm not sure why I do. Something about the softness of the snow and the warmth of the male next to me is bringing my guard down.

"Do you miss Abyssia?" he asks, giving me a sidelong glance.

"All the time," I nod. "It's so much warmer there, and the sea is beautiful. It never snows. There's all these flowers and beautiful insects. Butterflies and dragonflies and lightflies..."

"What are lightflies?"

I stop walking and turn to look at him. "You don't know what lightflies are?"

He shakes his head. "I know it's hard to believe with how long I've been alive, but I've never left the mountains of Syra..."

"You haven't? Oh—they're *magnificent!* Lightflies are like butterflies except they're a bit smaller and their wings glow all these different colors. They stay in swarms, too—they all fly together. If it's not too windy, sometimes the way they fly and the way their wings change colors it looks like a light show. There's really nothing like it!" I gush, remembering the last time I had seen it. My last night with Tarletan before my father got arrested—after we'd made love under the stars in his parents' garden.

It was my happiest memory.

We link arms again and keep walking.

"Maybe we'll have to go to Abyssia together sometime. So you can show me," he suggests casually.

My stomach twists. "I don't want to go back."

"Why not?" He sounds surprised.

"I—" How can I explain it? The fact that all of my friends believe my father is a ruthless murderer? The fact that no one—not even Tarletan—had cared enough to check up on me since he was arrested? Never wrote to me or tried to visit me, or even wished me a happy fucking birthday?

I clear my throat. "There's nothing left for me there. I wish there was, but that part of my life is over. It would hurt too much to go back now."

Calimo wraps his arm around my shoulders, hugging me in tight to his side as we walk. "I can understand that. I'm sorry I suggested it." His tone is gentle. I look up at him. He's staring at me.

"No, it's okay. You didn't know. And—it's nice that you would take me there. If I wanted to go. If I *could* go. I appreciate that."

"If you ever change your mind, I'll take you. Whatever you want, Fiana."

We reach the stoop of my apartment, and I find myself lingering outside. Not wanting to go in alone. Not wanting the night to end. The rapid change in my intentions with Calimo is making my head spin.

I turn toward him, looking into his warm black eyes.

To hell with my agenda, a timid voice offers in the far recesses of my mind. *You deserve a little fun in your life.*

Is that what this is? Fun?

The snow is so light tonight—uncharacteristically light. The snowflakes dance on my eyelashes and sink into my hair, dusting his hair, too. I itch to run my fingers through it.

I take a step closer and lean into him, giving in to the desire. I stare into those dark eyes as my fingers twine through the silkiness of his hair, feeling his arms wrap around my waist. The scent of toffee and wine envelope me, the flavors beckoning me to have a taste.

Yes, this could be fun.

I lean in closer, and his eyes slide closed. My lips part, and I taste his wine-scented breath on my tongue. I pause, letting the flutters in my heart build to a crescendo as he inches closer to me, our lips now only a hair's breadth apart. I close the minuscule distance as my eyes slide shut and his softness and warmth seep into my lips, my breath, my mouth.

My first kiss in over seven years.

I wasn't prepared for what happens next.

My body reacts wildly, pulling him tighter into me as he kisses me back. Pressing him against the length of my body. Feeling his arms tighten around me as his hands drift lower on my back. I hitch a leg up high around his waist and he quickly gets the message, lifting me up and pressing me against the stone wall as his tongue encourages my mouth open and electricity buzzes between our lips, our tongues, our hips.

Our breaths are coming in shallow gasps, my chest heaving into his, as the part of me that is wild and *female* considers inviting him upstairs.

"Do you want—to join me—tonight?" I breathe as his lips find my neck, shivers of pleasure running down my spine in response.

He groans appreciatively against my skin, pressing his hardened length against the inner edge of my hip, like a promise of what he wants to do to me.

"There's nothing I want more..." he starts to say, but he lowers my feet to the ground now and gently untangles my fingers from his hair.

He gives me a soft kiss. Slow and intimate, one hand keeping my chin lifted toward him. "But I don't want to take things too far too soon. I want to take things slow. I want you to be *sure* about being with me... and not just because you haven't been with a male in years."

My eyes open wide in shock. "That's... incredibly *old world* of you," I manage to say.

He smiles at me, his eyes taking in the details of my face.

"I want to be the male you deserve. As much as I want you *now*, I know it will be better for both of us if we wait."

He leans in and gives me a final kiss, this one deep and sensual. Teasing. Taunting. It's my turn to groan as an ache burns between my legs.

"You better leave right now before I force you to come up," I mutter against his lips. He chuckles.

"Does that mean I get a second date?" he wonders, his lips finding my neck again.

I sigh in response. He chuckles again.

"Then goodnight, sweet Fiana," he says, before dissolving into thin air, leaving me alone in the light snowfall, blazing hot and utterly worked up.

I practically run upstairs to continue where he left off.

8

Over the next few weeks, I get quite good at deluding myself into thinking that I'm still seeing Calimo for the purposes of gaining intel on The Cave.

While Calimo's explanation that a different set of spells protect each prisoner *is* news to me, it's not all that helpful. I don't have magic to break said spells, nor magic to even identify what they are.

And I'm not optimistic that he has anything else to share. Plus, I have a Havoc-born High Guard who has essentially threatened to torture me the next time I break in.

Still, it's been over a month since my last break in. I'm starting to feel antsy, and the familiar feeling of guilt keeps creeping into my gut.

So I'm seeing Calimo again tonight.

But I can't even pretend it's for the right reasons.

I just need a fucking distraction.

The door knocks. I smooth my dress and fluff my curls knowing damn well they'll be a mess in a matter of minutes.

He greets me with a light peck on the lips, and electricity is already buzzing between us at the simple touch. I groan, pulling him tight against me, deepening the kiss, letting myself forget about the guilt I've been stewing in for days.

Letting myself forget about the ache in my heart, and focus on the ache now growing between my thighs.

Letting myself *live*, if only for a few moments.

I feel selfish for that. I *am* selfish for that. But it has been *seven years*.

Not months. *Years*.

Seven. Fucking. Years.

An annoying voice reminds me that's also how long my father has been incarcerated, but then Calimo bites my bottom lip and I force that thought out of my mind.

He nibbles a little harder and I moan at that, eager to lose myself in sensations and pleasure. He chuckles at my reaction and gently pulls away from me just enough to get a good look at me.

"You look divine," he says, his voice rough with the fire blazing between us.

I lean back in and kiss him again, keeping my focus on the physical. Not wanting my mind to drift back to darker places.

I lead him over to my bed.

I push him down, and he goes willingly, sliding toward the center as I mount him. Kissing his lips, his face, his neck. I forget everything but the taste and feel of his silky skin.

With speed that might have been immortal, or more likely due to his powerful bloodline, he flips me onto my back and starts mounting *me*. Kissing *my* lips, *my* face, *my* neck.

And as I feel his hot breath against my collarbone, it becomes so much easier to forget.

I feel him harden against me and my hands stroke the length of him as an appreciative groan escapes his throat. His hands slide up my stocking-clad legs and underneath my dress. I hear a little gasp as he realizes my stockings end at mid-thigh. His fingers slide up higher to the nakedness awaiting his touch.

A gentle exploration with his fingers reveals the wetness there and he begins stroking me in a way that makes my back arch. He massages and teases the places that Tarletan hadn't really known about... the places that make my toes curl... the places that make me moan.

And I *do* moan as he traces little circles, around and around. As he kisses my neck, my legs opening wider to give him more access to me. And I can feel it building—the pleasure that Tarletan could never give to me. Building toward a release.

"I want you inside of me," I find myself gasping, and he pauses his movements to obey, unzipping his pants and kicking them to the floor. I rip off my own dress and the garments underneath, keeping the stockings in place as he uses his knees to spread me open wider, his rock hard shaft proudly preparing to enter me.

He slides in slowly at first, giving my initial tightness time to soften around him, letting his impressive size stretch the muscles that have been all but forgotten.

I breathe as he plunges into me. Languidly at first... and then deeper. Faster. Feeling my body open to him with each delicious thrust.

We tangle together, our breathing hot and wild, as the connected parts of us find a rhythm that riles both of us up. That drives us closer to the edge. His fingers stroke me again as he continues to drive into me, as electric sensations cause goosebumps to erupt all over my bare skin.

It feels so damn good to forget.

Between our entangled bodies there's no obligation to free my father. No wicked patriarchy. No fucked-up King.

There's just skin against skin.

Flesh against flesh.

Lips against lips.

Teeth against teeth.

There's just him, and me, and this all-consuming pleasure that can't possibly get better—and then somehow, it does.

Another thrust, another stroke.

My heart is beating wildly.

I feel out of breath, out of control, and yet I don't want to leave this delicious chaos. I want to drown in it.

I bite my lip, my eyes fluttering closed as the chaos consumes me. Ripples and waves of pleasure beyond anything I ever felt with Tarletan... or even with myself.

I let myself sink, let myself drown, let myself dive into the pleasure. Until nothing but breath and ecstasy remain. Until my throat hurts from screaming, and my body aches with carnal bliss.

And he must have found his release as I did, because I watch his eyes roll into the back of his head. I watch him drown in his own pleasure, drown into me, sink into the chaos of skin and friction and heat.

His fingers coax another release through me, and my body eagerly obeys.

When the chaos fades to blissful calm, he lays there on top of me, his chest breathing into mine, our limbs still completely intertwined.

We let our heart rates slow, unwilling to part just yet.

Later, when my thoughts drift back to a darker place, I roll back over on top of him.

And we drown all over again.

My next tavern shift interrupts our... activities.

It's busy tonight. The bar is full and the couches are overflowing. It smells heavily of tobacco, more so than usual, and a thick cloud of smoke obscures the view of the tables at the back.

Mila and I are running around chaotically trying to fulfill all the orders. My pockets get stuffed by ten o'clock, and the tavern shows no signs of slowing down. My feet are already aching and there's a sheen of sweat on my forehead. It's going to be a long night.

There's a few faces in the bar I haven't seen before, but Mila seems to know them quite well.

One is all muscle and over six feet tall, and looks even more ripped than Evander. He's dressed in black but not like a High Guard—just casual pants and a long sleeve shirt that's pushed up at the sleeves, exposing muscular forearms that are littered with dozens of scars. His black hair is long and pulled back in a knot at the nape of his neck.

But the most striking thing about him are his greenish-blue eyes. They should be beautiful, but there's something off about them. There's no light in them. Only—*pain*.

Like he was swallowed up by grief years ago and never fully recovered.

The other is much more slight with short, inky black hair and golden skin. While the bigger one seems like he's in perpetual pain, this one appears to be perpetually *aware*. Like he's reading something in the liminal spaces that no one else can see.

As soon as they approach the bar, Mila serves them a few jads and exchanges meaningful looks with them, yet none of them speak.

"Who are they?" I ask her once the two slink away. They disappear into a cloud of smoke near the back tables.

Mila shrugs as she wipes down a section of the bar. "They've been coming here for years. They're not regulars but I see them sometimes."

"I haven't seen them in the village before," I mention.

She gives me a sidelong glance, her jaw tense. "They live in Parley. They only come to Ador occasionally."

I snort. "What for? Parley is way nicer than Ador." So nice that there's an actual school there for the village children. Adorian children have to travel to neighboring villages like Parley or Veliathon, or they get homeschooled.

She sighs tossing the towel onto the back bar. "I haven't the slightest idea, Fiana. I don't keep up with the lives of all of our customers."

I stare at the back of her blonde head as she quickly moves to the other end of the bar where the slight one has reappeared. He's saying something in a low voice that I can't discern over the noise of the tavern, but his expression is clearly strained.

"Can I get a drink, Fiana?" Evander says from right across the bar. I jump, not realizing he'd come in.

"Oh. Sure," I say, still glancing toward Mila and the golden skinned male.

Evander follows my gaze. "Oh for fuck's sake," he says under his breath.

I whip my head back to face him. "Do you know him?"

His jaw tenses. "Koa Zell, likely here with—yup. Warren Volkov. I'd tell you to stay away from them, but we know how well that worked with Calimo," he says drily.

I cut him down with an icy glare. "You seem to enjoy telling me to stay away from damn near every male in this village."

He shoots me a grin. "All except for me."

I roll my eyes. "Isn't the fact that I'm sleeping with Calimo enough to turn you off me yet?"

His grin falters and he smacks his fist on the bar with enough force to rattle the glasses on the far end. My eyes widen.

"I beg you not to remind me of that again." His eyes are intense, his mouth pressed into a thin line.

The entire bar is looking at us now. Mila shoots me a nervous look as Koa's gaze darts between Evander and me, his mouth curving into a thoughtful frown.

My heart is pounding as Evander stares me down, his power tinging red as anger tenses his muscles.

"Fine," I say finally. I roll out my neck, attempting to loosen the tension there. "Let me get your drink."

"No need," he counters, his voice clipped. "I'd rather drink at home tonight." He dissolves away instantly, without even bothering with the custom of leaving the tavern first.

The whole bar is still staring at me.

Mila approaches me. "What was *that* about?" she asks in a low voice.

"I must have hit a nerve," I say. I feel like I'm in a daze collecting a few stray tips on my end of the bar. I take a deep breath, focusing intently on the scent of beer and smoke.

"What did you say to him?" Mila presses. She's adjusting her blonde ponytail with bright, curious eyes.

"I just told him that I'm sleeping with Calimo and he lost it," I admit. "I guess I shouldn't have pushed him like that."

Mila's eyes appraise me. "He really has it bad for you, huh?"

I shake my head. "He just wants to sleep with me. It's not anything deeper than that."

Mila glances down the bar at Koa again, which makes me follow her gaze. He has the most curious look on his face. Like he's found something he's been looking for.

And he's looking directly at me.

The bar stays busy until early in the morning. Mila goes home around two—shortly after Koa and Warren depart I notice. I'm closing up at four in the morning when it hits me like a stab wound to the heart—*something* is in trouble. A smaller animal, by the feel of it. It's close, too.

I clutch my chest and follow the stabbing pain, which leads me through the alley toward the back of the tavern. It pulls me like a thread toward the thick grove of aspens. I bend to reach inside my boot for my dagger before I enter the woods, an eerie chill snaking down my spine as I straighten up.

I get about fifty paces into the forest when I see a male crouching over the poor creature. It's Nasgardo, I quickly realize as I recognize his short blonde buzz cut. I hide behind a fluffy evergreen and deliberately try to slow my breath. The pain is so intense I have to brace myself against the tree.

He's chanting something. It isn't in modern elven, nor even in old elven. It sounds—dark.

The words are guttural and grating. It triggers an unexpected memory, a night over twenty years ago. The night the demon came for my mother.

I tense, remembering the book he got from the bookshop. *Rituals and Spells of the Shadow Realms.* At the time, I thought it was for defensive purposes. It's not odd for the High Guard to study such things.

But this definitely doesn't look defensive.

The chanting stops, and I hold my breath as Nasgardo stands, his head and heart opening upward as his back begins to arch.

A clicking sound—much like the language he was chanting, but deeper in tone—begins channeling from the space above Nasgardo's chest and face. There's a *crack*, and then black light channels from some unknown source directly into his energetic crown, his forehead, his throat, and his heart. He shudders as the energy enters his system, then he sends a dark wave of energy rippling out in every direction, staining the realm with the curse of this dark magic.

Demonic—this is *demonic.*

The animal is still writhing in agony and I'm gritting my teeth to avoid crying out myself.

He needs to *leave* so I can save the poor creature.

My thoughts begin to cloud as the animal's suffering intensifies, and I start begging the Maker to make Nasgardo go.

My breathing is more like ragged gasps now, and I'm counting the seconds.

Waiting.

I shut my eyes. The pain is too much. Too debilitating.

Seconds or minutes later—it's impossible to tell—another *crack* sounds. I open my eyes. He's gone.

And there she is, in the snow, mangled and trembling, her white fur stained a horrific shade of red. A snowshoe hare clinging to the final threads of life.

I run to the hare, a lump forming in my throat as I reach her. I collapse to my knees, feeling the cold snow seep through the fabric of my pants. I pull out a rag to staunch the bleeding.

I curse Nasgardo under my breath as I feel the fullness of her wounds, both under my shaking hands and under my own skin.

Heal her. Maker please—*heal her!*

I press my fingertips against her jugular, trying to feel a pulse. It's there, but weak.

I need something to stop her bleeding before she loses too much blood. I desperately scan my surroundings as the hare's pulse weakens further underneath my fingertips.

She's got mere minutes left. Seconds, even.

Tears prick at my eyes as her suffering starts to fade. She'll be gone at any moment and I'm just watching her *die.*

There's a whooshing sound and I look up, gasping as Haldric nosedives toward us, a parcel clutched in one of his sharp talons. He drops it into my lap and then swoops upward to land on a branch overhead.

My bloodied fingers shake as I open the parcel. It's a glass vial. I check the label and feel relief wash through me. It's one of my yarrow tinctures, embedded with Curic magic. I carefully remove the stopper and gently dribble the greenish yellow liquid over the hare's wounds, which sizzle before beginning to close.

It's slower than having an actual Curic, but a few minutes later, the hare's flesh is knitted back together, though her fur is stained all kinds of sickly shades of burgundy, green, and yellow.

She shudders in the snow and then leaps into my arms. I hug her tight to my chest, wrapping my cloak around us both, letting my body heat warm her.

"You're okay now. You're okay," I breathe.

A *crack* interrupts the silence somewhere nearby and I bolt to my feet. Did Nasgardo come back?

I squint through the dark, but I can't see anyone. I shoot a look to Haldric, who looks slightly ruffled but doesn't seem to be fixating on any one spot.

Let's get the hell out of here.

I don't say it out loud, but Haldric still somehow understands.

9

Disturbed is what I am the next day as I try to interpret Nasgardo's actions. I wish I hadn't seen it.

He was obviously performing a demonic ritual. The chanting, the animal sacrifice, the energetic connection with the Shadow Realms...

He must be siphoning power from the demons.

Is he working *with* them to do this?

Do they even *know* he's doing this?

I'm surprised he even knows the chants. Those aren't listed in the book he bought, for obvious reasons: it's all highly illegal. Treasonous, even. A warning in the book says as much.

It's not like I have any leverage to turn him in, though. Or even any proof that he did what he did.

Last night I brought the hare back to my apartment, bathed her, and let her sleep on a pile of blankets that I set out by the fire. This morning, I foraged some twigs for her to munch on and took her out to relieve herself. She wiggled her nose at me in a gesture that felt like gratitude, then she hopped away with a few twigs still wedged in her mouth.

Her fur was unscarred thanks to the yarrow tincture, so even if I can find her again, there won't be any proof of what I saw last night.

By the time I make it to my tavern shift, I'm still thinking about it. It makes time slow to an arduous crawl.

It's Sunday, and Calimo hasn't come in yet, though the bar is winding down. Evander hasn't come in today. Mila cashed out and left early, citing some family emergency or something. And Credo's already left for the night as well.

Most of the patrons are sitting by the fireplace with a few villagers at the far end of the bar. It's fairly quiet, and I'm getting tired.

I just want to go home.

My mind keeps drifting to the ritual last night, but I force myself to try and think of other things. Like the two mysterious males Mila was talking to, and Evander's strange reaction to them. And his even stranger reaction to... me.

I wonder when Calimo will arrive.

He's supposed to come in before closing. We have plans to spend another night together.

At least I have that to look forward to.

The minutes tick slowly by.

I haven't felt this bored at work since my last day in the bookshop. I shudder at that thought—because it brings my focus back to Nasgardo.

I really need a distraction.

I start pouring another beer from the tap for a stocky old villager male, scanning the bar to see if anyone else's drink is empty, when my eyes stop on a male in black who has just entered the tavern.

My heart stops. It's Nasgardo, here as if summoned by my own fearful thoughts.

He takes one look at me, his dark brown eyes blazing with fury, and launches himself toward the bar.

"I need a word with you, bitch," he growls, pushing a few empty barstools to the ground. They clatter loudly, causing the males on the couch to turn and stare. He glances back at them and then closes his eyes for a beat, undoubtedly intending some sort of spell.

I stand there mutely, my stomach churning, feeling utterly frozen. The dagger in my boot somehow feels too far away. I stare at him with wide eyes, the now full stein of beer shaking vigorously in my hand.

The villager I poured it for bravely steps up next to Nasgardo.

"Nasgardo, lay off Fiana... or you'll have to deal with the rest of us," he says proudly, puffing up his chest, though his eyes are barely level with Nasgardo's chin.

"Palus, did you fail to realize you're talking to a High Guard? How quickly you forget what I can do with a snap of my fingers. Throw you in The Cave, or your mother, just for insulting me," Nasgardo sneers at the male.

Palus shrinks a bit but keeps his chin up. "You need formal charges to throw us in that prison. Last I checked males still have freedom of speech in these realms."

Nasgardo throws back his head in laughter. "You call yourself a male? Drunk son of the blacksmith, struggling to keep your father's business afloat, never bedded a lady..."

Palus grows taller, eyes darkening with fury. "You better watch your mouth."

Nasgardo rolls his eyes. "I will spare you the beating you deserve for now, but rest assured next time I see you we will have a problem. Tonight, I have different matters to attend to." He flexes his fingers as the temperature in the tavern seems to drop.

Suddenly, every patron in the bar pulls out money for their drinks and places it on whatever surface is in front of them, their eyes going blank and lifeless. I watch in horror as each one leaves the tavern in an orderly fashion, without even looking in my direction, Nasgardo's magic compelling them to leave us alone.

Even the one called Palus goes blank in the face, tossing a

twenty note on the bar, and leaving without another word. His fresh beer vibrates in my shaking hand.

Nasgardo's eyes slide toward me now, and I feel magic pin my feet to the ground, binding my legs in place, immobilizing me from the neck down.

I drop the beer stein as the magic hits my hands, and it comes crashing down loudly onto the bar, soaking me with beer. Soaking Nasgardo with beer, too. He swears, shaking his head in disgust, spraying my face with more droplets of the brew. My stomach knots with fear as I understand I can't move—and can't even scream.

And even if I could, no one is here to hear me.

Tears prick at my eyes, and as they fall down my cheeks I feel furious knowing I can't even wipe them away.

"Good, you're listening," he says with a cruel smile. "You seem to have seen something you shouldn't have."

He tosses something on the bar. I can't tilt my head, but my eyes strain to see a glass vial. The one full of the yarrow tincture. My mouth runs dry.

"And you also seem to have deprived my friends of their blood. And not for the first time, I reckon."

I feel magic release my lips, my voice. "I don't know what you're talking about," I snap. Hatred courses through me knowing he's responsible for so many animals' suffering.

Oh, how I wish for magic now—violent, destructive, demolishing magic. Havoc magic. The kind that would mangle his body like he mangled the hare's. The kind that would crumple his bones and rip apart his skin into a thousand deep cuts. The kind that would leave him gasping for air and begging for mercy.

Revenge. *I want fucking revenge.*

"Don't play dumb, female." He rolls his eyes. "Now I *was* going to kill you... but it occurred to me that Evander hasn't yet claimed you as his own."

"What the hell does that mean?" I growl.

Out of the corner of my eye I notice the fire turns an eerie shade of white.

He snorts. "The entire High Guard knows Evander has been lusting after you for months. *I'm* just surprised he hasn't claimed you yet. Calimo or no Calimo, there's no escaping that immortalization." His eyes glint in the white firelight. "I'm not complaining, though. A dead body is a little inconvenient for me. Fortunately, there are other ways to ensure your discretion."

My heart staggers as his magic hits me again, this time bending me over at the hips and anchoring my hands to the bar, my legs being forced open into an unmistakable wide stance. One that hints at what is to come.

Anger and disgust simultaneously swim through me.

He licks his lips as bile rises in my throat. "I haven't immortalized anyone in a while. I killed the last three because I grew tired of them after a few years. Perhaps it's time for a new pet..." His eyes shine with desire now as I fight another wave of nausea.

"If you touch me, Calimo will hunt you down," I warn through gritted teeth. Though even as I say it, a part of me isn't sure.

"It's silly for you to think so highly of Calimo, not even his own father does," he sneers, and he starts to climb on top of the bar, using magic to sweep away the broken glass from the dropped beer.

"Perhaps first we'll wash out that mouth of yours..." he muses, spinning around on the bar so his crotch is toward me, scooting closer and unzipping his pants, my face stuck just a few inches above where he sits.

I will my body to move, but it stays frozen in place. I will my body to scream, but my voice is now silenced again.

Help me! My inner useless intentions ring out in my mind. *For the love of the Maker stop this!*

He's taking himself out now so I squeeze my eyes shut as the bile rises higher and vomit threatens to spew out of me.

Help! My intentions ring out again loudly in my mind, as he laughs darkly at my frozen form. Something presses against my closed lips. "Open up, whore. Or I'll have to make you..."

Please! I clench my teeth together as tightly as I can, as I feel the magic compelling me to open my mouth. My jaw muscles ache as I fight against it.

If I'm forced to do this, I'll fucking bite it off, I decide as I clench my teeth tighter.

No way in hell am I going down without a fight.

But if you can stop this, stop it. Please.

"Nasgardo, what the *fuck* are you doing on my bar?" Credo's booming voice comes from the front door. My whole body trembles —I can't believe my luck. I practically cry tears of joy, though I still can't move, and don't dare open my eyes.

"Credo..." Nasgardo sounds frustrated and guilty and—fearful? I don't believe my ears as I hear him shrink away from me and feel him climb off the bar. I brave a glance as he turns to face the grey-haired giant, still zipping up his pants.

I'm shocked as I notice Haldric perched on Credo's shoulder—but I should have known. Fresh tears pool in my eyes as I meet his yellow gaze.

"What the *fuck* are you doing with your dick out on my bar?" Credo demands. I feel the magic slip off my face, my arms, my legs. I nearly collapse as the feeling returns. I keep both hands on the bar to steady myself, my breath whooshing out of me in a strangled gasp.

"Credo..."

"Enough! You have crossed the line. You are hereby banned from the Ador Tavern and should you ever enter it again, you will die a most painful death," Credo barks, and the whole tavern vibrates with the magic swirling around Nasgardo, binding him to the ban and magically shoving him out the front door. He yelps on the way out, as if he's been poked with something hot.

Credo's eyes are cautious as he approaches me. My legs turn to jelly and I shrink to the ground. Angry tears begin gushing down my cheeks. Remembering he touched my lips, I wipe my mouth vigorously on my sleeve.

"You okay?" he asks gently, his forehead creased with concern. I nod weakly.

Haldric joins me on the ground, butting his head against my arm. I pet the soft feathers on his chest.

"Your bird crashed into my window and wouldn't stop hitting it until I let him in. Practically pecked my eyes out when I tried to tell him to leave. Eventually, I understood he wanted me to follow him," Credo chuckles. "But I'm glad he persisted. I wasn't planning to come back tonight."

I shudder. "Thanks." My voice sounds choked.

"You can head home now. I'll clean all of this up..." Credo says, glancing around at the mess of the tavern. I let out a breath and wipe my eyes.

"No, that's okay. I want to stay here until Calimo gets here to walk me home. Just in case Nas—just in case." I wipe my mouth harshly again. My lips burn from the friction.

Credo nods in understanding. "I can contact him if you'd like. Get him here sooner?"

I nod once. "Sure, that would be fine. Thank you."

Credo closes his eyes briefly, setting the intention for the message to reach Calimo. I wipe my eyes again.

A few moments later, Credo opens his eyes as Calimo dissolves into the bar.

"What happened?" Calimo gasps as he arrives.

"Nasgardo. He's been banned—magically. He won't be a problem again," Credo explains. "Can you take her home? He might still be lurking about. Make sure she gets in safe..."

Calimo nods. "Of course. Fiana—I'm so sorry this happened. Come here."

I sigh a shaky breath and then make my way to the bridge. I duck under and he's right there on the other side, arm outstretched for me.

I take it and we dissolve into black, before appearing in my bedroom. I collapse on the bed, sobs shuddering through me, not even caring that I'm still soaked in beer. Calimo holds me as I cry, stroking my back.

"He won't hurt you again..." he promises. "I won't be so far away next time."

I don't know what he means by that, but I'm too emotional and exhausted to care.

We don't make love that night, but he holds me while I sleep.

Except somehow, I still don't feel entirely safe.

10

I walk with my dagger out to my next tavern shift. I get a few stares from some villagers on my way, but I don't care.

I refuse to be defenseless ever again.

The snowfall is heavy but still somehow soft tonight, and the streets are relatively quiet. Haldric follows me from the sky, and his presence is comforting. Without him, I could have been immortally tied to Nasgardo by now.

That thought turns my stomach, and I stop short as the wave of nausea flows through me. I clutch my abdomen, breathing through my nose, focusing on the scent of fresh snow and pine.

I can feel someone's eyes on me—they're approaching me from behind. I whirl around with my dagger out.

But it's just Evander.

"Are you alright?" he says in a frantic voice. "I heard what happened. I'm sorry I wasn't there to stop it." He stops a few feet away from me, his brow furrowed with concern. "I wish I could have been."

His fingers fidget by his sides as his eyes dart between my face and the dagger. He's in his uniform and uncloaked as usual, his muscles bulging under his armor as snow coats his hair, shoulders, and chest.

I lower my blade. "I'll survive."

"Did he touch you?" His jaw ticks as he waits for me to respond.

My eyes water. I look away from his anxious gaze. "Just my lips." The admission has me wiping my mouth again with my cloak.

I can feel Evander fuming in front of me, but I don't look at him.

"I wish I could kill him," he finally says, his voice tight.

"He mentioned you," I say without thinking. I snort humorlessly then look him square in the eye as anger sharpens my tone. "Said because you haven't *claimed* me yet, he would instead."

Evander's face turns to stone under his beard. "He was going to—"

"Immortalize me, yes." I turn on my heel and start walking back toward the tavern.

Because fuck him, and fuck *that*.

He keeps pace with me easily. "I would never do that to you," he insists. His tone sounds sincere.

But I don't buy it.

"And yet you can't stand the idea of me being with Calimo. So much so that you nearly shatter the bar." I stop walking and whirl on him again, my eyes piercing him like needles. "Why is that?"

His jaw ticks as he thinks of a response. "Calimo is dangerous."

I laugh derisively. "Calimo? The most magic I've seen him do is pull out a chair for me. Unlike *your* friend, who immobilized me and bent me over the bar for his own sick enjoyment."

He's shaking his head, his eyes murderous. "Nasgardo has never been my friend. I ripped his heart out this morning when I learned what he did."

I narrow my eyes. "That doesn't impress me. I'm sure he's all healed up by now."

"Even so, don't underestimate who you're sharing your bed with." Evander says harshly, his eyes intense. "I've seen him use Hypnotic magic on females before. I wouldn't put that past him."

My throat tightens. Hypnotic? As in *mind* control?

"I thought he was a Relic?" My heart hammers in my chest.

He raises a brow. "Yes, and Hypnotic."

Shit.

Something plays at the edges of my awareness. A memory of first meeting Calimo. How he'd held out his hand, practically insisting I shake it.

I sheath my dagger, because I'm really close to stabbing my own eyes out.

Because *what the fuck?*

Did Calimo trick me into liking him?

"Is it activated by touch?" I say through gritted teeth.

Evander's eyes tighten. "Yes."

Shame heats my cheeks, and my eyes burn with unshed tears. I drop my gaze to Evander's chest, too embarrassed and angry to meet his eyes. "Can you undo it?"

His reply is unbearably gentle. "Of course."

I feel him move closer, and I flinch as his fingertips rest lightly on my temple. It's freezing out, yet his fingers are warm. I squeeze my eyes shut.

It's a knife wound to the heart as I feel the illusion start to fall away. A veneer of beauty and attraction melts down like dripping hot wax, revealing nothing but a selfish monster underneath. I gasp as I recall my initial gut feeling—how his smile seemed predatory. How his eyes looked *off* somehow.

I was stupid to let Calimo in. I never used to let males touch me at the bookshop—I knew something like this could happen. And yet I let my own *politeness* in my first few weeks at the tavern put me in this position.

One where I trusted a male who—what was it he said?

Wanted to give his father something *valuable.*

He's never brought me in front of the King, yet that word struck me on our first date. And yet I ignored it. Stupidly.

What else have I ignored?

Is he biding his time until I go for my father again?

Does he realize who I am, and why I'm in Ador?

And worse—why I started seeing him in the first place?

My skin feels like it's crawling with a thousand spiders as the truth sinks in. How much does he know? And what's his end game?

The questions are like gashes in my aching heart.

Then there's the intimate moments. My stomach tightens as I remember them, my body going numb in the memories as they become clearer. The chemistry I imagine fades and distorts into something impersonal and mechanical.

Like I wished I could leave the whole time, but couldn't.

I feel sick.

"Fuck," I say aloud. I open my eyes.

Evander's a sight when I do. All tousled hair and piercing blue eyes. And his lips, parted subtly under his dark brown beard. I hate how beautiful he is.

And how he always seems to catch me in my worst moments.

"Fuck," I say again. My heart gallops in my chest, and I feel like I'm going to hurl. Evander was *right* about Calimo.

And I was horribly, disastrously, stupidly *wrong*.

"Feel better?" he says gently, moving his hand to the side of my neck. The nausea starts to fade rapidly away, and his magic soothes my body's visceral sense of betrayal.

Despite that, I don't answer his question. Because actually, I feel worse.

"And you're not a Hypnotic," I say instead, though it sounds more like an accusation.

He frowns. "No, but Curics can undo Hypnotic magic."

"That's what I thought," I say. I feel disgusting. His hand is still lingering on my neck. It's helping, and yet all I want is to be free of him. Because he warned me this whole time.

And I didn't listen.

I laugh once, and it sounds hysterical. "I wish you did this a month ago."

His eyes look concerned and he grips my neck a little tighter, though it's not at all unpleasant.

In fact, I kind of like it.

"Me too," he says, his eyes drifting to my lips. He clears his throat abruptly. "Will you be late for your shift?"

I glance at the giant clock near the portal station.

"Yes," I groan.

"Want me to get you there faster?" he says with a hint of a smile.

I nod. He pulls me into his arms, and we dissolve beyond the next seven blocks in under a second.

"Thanks." My voice falters a bit as he releases me from his embrace. My eyes collide with his—and there's nothing but warmth and concern there.

It makes me hesitate outside of the tavern.

"You're not all bad," I say, biting my lip.

He pushes his hair back as his lips stretch into a cocky grin. "I can be bad if you want me to be."

Well that was short lived.

I shoot him a glare, pushing the door open. The tavern is fairly empty with a few villagers at the bar and a few on the couches. My footsteps echo in the empty space, and Mila gives me a wave as she sees me come in.

Evander follows behind me closely, and I feel his breath tickle my neck as he leans in to whisper, "I can be *anything* you want me to be, Fiana. Just tell me what you want, and I'm that."

I exhale hotly. "Don't push it. We were having a nice moment." *And now you're ruining it.*

He chuckles. "It's hard for me not to. You're so damn hot when you're mad at me."

I whirl on him, cheeks pink. "Stop it."

He ignores me, his eyes turning playful. "Now that things are over with Calimo, surely that means you need someone else to keep you company at night." His fingers tug down the length of my cloak as his smile turns wicked. "I'd be more than happy to fill that void."

I grab his hand, stopping it near my belly. "Quit while you're ahead, Evander. I hate your guts just a little bit less, that's all."

He throws back his head in raucous laughter. "I'll take it. It's only a matter of time, anyway."

I catch Mila's eye again as I walk under the bridge. She looks stupefied as she listens in on our exchange.

"Until what?" I say, annoyance clear in my tone. I hang my cloak in the back then start gathering empty glasses off the bar and putting them in the automatic cleaner.

"Until you realize you want me," he says, his expression ridiculously confident. Those annoying blue eyes of his have my heart beating too fast.

"I have higher standards than that," I retort.

It doesn't work—he's completely unruffled. "Just a matter of time, Fiana. You'll see." He gives me a wink and then heads toward the door, shooting a dark look at the back of someone's head before he leaves.

I glance down the bar to see who it is and notice it's Warren and Koa again.

Interesting.

I don't have much time to wonder about that though because Mila assaults me with questions the second Evander is gone.

"Did I hear him right? You're done with Calimo?" Her voice is burning with curiosity.

"What? Oh. Yeah, I guess so," I say as my thoughts stay fixed on Evander.

My mind starts to tick off all the times he's helped me. All the times he's proven to me that he's not all bad.

The first night with Raven, and the second after that.

When he healed the doe.

The time he dried my shirt.

And his warnings about Calimo, now known to be true.

"You can't start seeing Evander, though," Mila says as if it's a forgone conclusion.

I stare at her face, which is scrunched up in disgust. "Why not?"

Someone down the bar clears their throat. I look up and see Koa's eyes fixed on Mila. She meets his gaze briefly, then hastily turns back to me.

"Well you *can*, but he's dangerous. Would you really be willing to go there?" Her eyes are wide and expectant. Like it's the most important question in the world.

I stare at the door where he left minutes ago.

"I don't know," I admit.

Mila tenses next to me, but doesn't say anything more. She returns to Koa and Warren, and I see her relay something in a low voice.

For the next ten minutes, the three of them keep glancing at me furtively.

Something about it makes my skin crawl, much like it did with Calimo.

Except this time I'm paying attention.

11

Calimo arrives at the tavern toward the end of my shift. I fight alarming levels of rage as I see him stroll in, dragging melted snow into the tavern with his boots.

He's the same, and yet different.

His skin is still warm, his hair is still short and dark, and his eyes are still black as night. He gives me a grin when he catches my eye, and his smile still appears charming to the untrained eye.

But it's like a veil has been lifted and I can see a darkness underneath the charm. It's so obvious to me now that I can't believe I didn't see it before, and yet I know deep down I did.

It's just his magic blocked me from realizing it.

Mila raises a brow at me from her end of the bar as she watches him approach. I sigh as he sits down in the one empty stool directly in front of me.

"Tough night, baby?" he says, and I see mock concern in his eyes. The difference between his fake charm and the real thing is subtle, but it's there, and there's something in my gut that feels like a warning bell.

"I have to cancel our plans. We won't be seeing each other anymore," I say calmly, yet my stomach braces for his response.

His charm immediately disintegrates as anger contorts his features. "And why is that?"

"I know you did Hypnotic magic on me," I say quietly. Elyon and Palus are sitting to his right, and they shoot me a cautious look.

"You're mistaken," Calimo says sharply. "Who told you that?"

I shrug, raising my chin. "Doesn't matter who. All that matters is you violated my trust and tricked me into liking you. So I'd like you to leave."

"I can't believe you don't believe me," he sneers, his hands tightening into fists on top of the bar. "Why don't we go outside for a moment and talk this through?" he adds, holding out a hand for me.

I stare at his hand, snorting. "Nice try. Please leave or at the very least go sit in the back."

He stares at me, hand outstretched, and I watch the fury bloom in his eyes.

"Cal, maybe you should go…" Elyon says gently, side eyeing him while scratching the stubble on his cheek.

Calimo lowers his hand and levels a seething look at Elyon.

"Fucking bitch," he mutters as he stalks out of the door. He slams it shut loud enough to cause the entire bar to look over their shoulders.

"Can I get anyone anything?" I say loudly, drawing their attention back to me. Three males raise their hands for beers.

I move to the tap and start filling cups.

The night dies down around midnight. Early, for once. I lock up the tavern and tighten my cloak around me as the bitter cold burns my eyes.

The wind is blustering, and the streets are quiet. It reminds me of the night I saved the doe. With Evander.

I pull my hood up, shielding my face from the wind. Thinking of things I really shouldn't be thinking about.

Like how much I liked it when Evander had his hand on my neck.

I snort to myself. He's too charming for his own good. For *my* own good. That's probably why he has dozens of females devoted to him.

I'm three blocks away from my apartment building when a chilly sensation hits the back of my neck. Like someone is watching me. I pull my hood back slightly and look around, but don't see anyone. I reach for my dagger and hold it in a tight grip as I quicken my pace.

Haldric isn't flying about so I don't have a second set of eyes on my back. I glance over my shoulder a few times as I reach the final block, but again there's no one there.

I sigh as I reach my building's stoop, and keep my knife ready as I fiddle with the lock.

My vision begins to blur for some reason, and my hand starts to slacken on the knife. I fight to grip it tighter, but it's like a weakness is spreading throughout my whole arm. My knees begin to wobble as panic overtakes me. Is this a stroke? A heart attack? *What the hell is happen—*

Everything goes black.

"Was knocking her out really necessary?" a familiar voice asks in a concerned tone. It's a female.

"She was holding a knife," a male says, sounding bored.

"I just don't understand why you couldn't have just let me *ask* her to join us," the female complains.

"This is easier," the male argues.

"She awake yet?" says another familiar voice. A male's this time.

"No, and I'm getting concerned. This isn't what Credo and I agreed to."

Credo?

Awareness comes rushing back to me like a jolt of electricity. I open my eyes a sliver.

A blonde—Mila, I realize—has her back to me. She looks tense in the shoulders and is looking at a slight male with dark hair. Koa?

"What the hell is going on?" I say, pushing to a seated position. Mila whirls around, her eyes wide with concern.

I'm on some couch in a dark room with no windows. It's lit only by torchlight. Credo leans against the wall—a giant mostly obscured by shadows, his wiry grey beard instantly recognizable.

Warren is blocking the only door I can see in this room with his massive, muscular form. His dark hair is pulled back into a pony-tail, and looks as if he wishes he was anywhere but here.

The first male I heard is indeed Koa with his golden complex-ion, slight frame, and dark hair. He's smaller than I expected—the same height as Mila—and is radiating superiority and annoyance.

"Sorry Koa knocked you out," Mila says, coming to sit next to me on the couch. Credo lumbers over closer to me, forming a small triangle with the couch and Koa. Warren doesn't react nor move a muscle.

"Where am I?" I say carefully, spotting my dagger on a table behind Koa.

Mila answers. "You're in—"

"We won't be revealing that detail," Koa interrupts.

She whips her head in his direction, eyes scathing. "She can handle it."

"I said no, Mila," Koa says evenly. He scratches the inner corner of his eye then squares a look at me. "You are in a unique position. Evander has taken an interest in you. We are a group of people who can benefit from that, and we want you to help us."

My stomach clenches, but I don't let anything show on my face. "How does it benefit you?"

Mila opens her mouth to speak, but Koa holds up a hand.

"We require information. The kind you might get if you were to form a—*relationship* with him." Koa tilts his chin up higher, so he's staring down his nose at me. "Is that something you would be open to?"

"You haven't answered my question." I sit up straighter and narrow my eyes at him. "How does it benefit you?"

"That's none of your concern. Are you open to it or not?" Koa pushes.

Credo clears his throat, the sound rumbling deep in his chest. "We should tell her why, Koa. She can't go into this blind."

Koa doesn't even grace Credo with a look.

"Answer the question," he repeats.

I sigh. "It depends what it's for."

"For the love of the Maker, just tell her, Koa! She's not going to turn on us. She *wants* more rights for females—don't you, Fiana?" Mila argues, her hazel eyes pleading.

"Of course I do," I say, narrowing my eyes at her. "What is this?" I scan each of their faces. "Are you some sort of resistance?"

Koa lets out a dramatic sigh, as if Mila has ruined his whole day.

Credo interjects before Koa can respond. "It's not like we can have her fishing for information without telling her what she's doing, Koa. We need to tell her what we do."

"I would prefer she have as little knowledge as possible while she decides if she wants to join us or not, Credo. Is that so hard to understand?" Koa barks, pacing.

"You wouldn't turn us in, would you?" Mila says, her eyes pleading again.

"I don't even know what it is you're doing," I admit. "But if it's against the King, I would never try and stop that."

"Not even for personal gain?" Koa says, stopping his pacing

abruptly. "You live in squalor and make a barkeep's pay. Are you certain there wouldn't be a price you'd accept?"

I scoff. "I do *not* live in squalor."

"Agree to disagree. The question was can you be bought?" Koa sneers.

I glare at him, crossing my arms. "Evander has been trying to *buy me* for the past two months. Hasn't worked yet. So what do you think?"

Koa levels another calculating look at me. Finally, he nods once.

"Fine. Tell her, Credo," he concedes.

Credo gives me a hesitant smile. "You're right, Fiana. We are a resistance against the King. We call ourselves the Dissenters. We believe in returning magic back to the females and ending his tyranny, and we want your help in that mission."

Mila chimes in. "We need you to help us gain information on Evander's weaknesses—and the King's. Which, with how much he's obsessed with you, shouldn't be too hard."

"And—" Credo sighs. "We could use your other skills."

"What other skills?" I raise a brow.

"We've been watching you for several months," Koa says flatly. "We know you can sneak into The Cave without being caught."

"Watching me?" I breathe as a chill seeps under my skin. This is so much worse than just Evander knowing. "Even before you hired me?" I say, looking in Credo's direction.

He nods solemnly. "And that's the other part of this."

"What is?" I say as a lump forms in my throat.

"If you are to join us, we need you to give up on saving your father," Koa says curtly.

"Give up?" My eyes begin to burn. I realize my fingernails have been digging into my palms. I uncross my arms, flexing my fingers. "I can't do that."

Mila places a soft hand on my arm. "It is a lot to ask."

"It's too much to ask," I correct. "I can help you, but I'm not giving that up."

Koa shakes his head vigorously. "You cannot do both. If you get caught for that, then they'll interrogate you and if you're working for us, we're fucked."

"If she gets caught working for us, we're still fucked," Warren says from the corner.

Koa snaps his head in his direction. "Even so, we don't need additional risks."

"Well what do you want from me? To help other prisoners escape? I haven't even gotten my father out yet, and he's my priority," I argue.

"No. We don't want you to go back to The Cave. We want you to steal things for us," Koa corrects.

"Like what?"

He snorts. "That's none of your concern. If you agree, we will tell you more information. Until then this is all you're getting."

"And if I decide not to join you?" I press.

Credo sighs. "Then we will need to have Koa wipe your memories of this conversation. For the safety of the movement."

"Wipe my memories?" Disgust swarms my stomach and I'm reminded of Calimo's mind control. "You're a Hypnotic then?"

"One a thousand times more powerful than your ex-lover, yes," Koa responds as if the question insults him.

My heart starts hammering in my chest. "And you two trust him?" I say, looking from Mila's hazel eyes to Credo's golden ones.

They both nod.

"Why do you trust him?" I ask, looking at Credo.

"He only uses his magic for the purposes of protecting our movement or advancing it. Never against us maliciously," he says, shrugging.

"You can trust Koa," Mila agrees, putting her hand on my arm again.

"Can I think about it?" I say, looking between Credo and Mila.

"No," Koa says shortly. "You're in or out now."

"Koa," Credo says, clapping him on the back with one of his

giant hands. He nearly buckles at the knees. "That's not fair. Let's give her some time."

"It's a risk—"

"Everything's a fucking risk, Koa. I'm with Credo. Give her time," Warren says.

Outnumbered, Koa shakes his head once then turns to leave. "Warren, you take her back. I'm done here."

"Fine," Warren says emotionlessly, moving aside for him to leave.

The door slams shut.

"Can I ask you a few more questions?" I say timidly, glancing between Credo and Mila again.

"Definitely," Mila says, smiling.

I let out a forceful exhale. Now that Koa's left it feels like a weight has been lifted. I meet Mila's waiting eyes. "Why do you want to look for Evander's weaknesses? Why not just the King's?"

Her face contorts into disgust. "Evander is the top of the High Guard and has been for over three hundred years. He has *a lot* of secrets to share. And if we find a way to take him out, getting to the King will be *way* easier."

Take him out.

"You mean kill him?" My heart pounds.

Mila's throat bobs as she swallows. "If we need to, yes."

My mouth runs dry.

Warren lurks closer to the couch. "Is that a problem?" His eyes turn steely.

I manage to shake my head. "I just need some time to think— about my father. I'm ready to go home now."

12

For all of his faults, my father was a good male.

I think of him that night before I fall asleep, and all the good times we had. Those came mostly in my earlier years, before teenage rebellion settled in.

He used to rent a boat for us once a month at the Port of Heron and take me whale watching. He knew I loved animals even then, but wouldn't let me have a dog because he didn't think I could handle the responsibility.

We'd always go alone, just the two of us, and we'd somehow *always* see a few whales. They'd swim right up alongside the boat, puffing water up through their blow holes. Sometimes dolphins would show up too, and do tricks in and out of the water.

He'd let me stay there all day, talking to the whales and dolphins. He asked me a few times if they ever talked back, which always made me laugh.

Then we'd come to shore around dusk and we'd be greeted by a swarm of lightflies. They'd practically follow us on our walk back home, dancing and changing colors and lighting our way. We'd stop at the ice cream shop and get a cone to go, eating that instead of dinner on those nights.

For one day each month, I wasn't the sequestered child being privately tutored in the hilltop home with only the occasional visits from my friends.

For one day each month, I was just a kid hanging out with her father.

I was free.

I often wonder if every day would have been that way if my mother had never sold her soul. If my father didn't have the threat of demonic intervention constantly hanging over our heads.

He wouldn't have become so obsessed with protecting me. I could have had a normal life and gone to a normal school. Maybe he never would have met Mr. Mason, let alone killed him.

Maybe we would all three still live together in Abyssia. Or maybe by now I would be married, and living with Tarletan, visiting my mother and father on the weekends. King Vilero would be a far off concept who rarely played much of a role in our day to day lives. We would be happy.

And I wouldn't have to make the choice between joining the Dissenters to bring down the King, or breaking my father out of The Cave for a crime he didn't commit.

He can't *have done it.*

I just know he can't.

The father who never beat me or harmed me, and rarely even raised his voice at me can't have killed anyone. He wasn't perfect, he was overprotective, but he wasn't violent.

Never.

Not even once.

Demonic possession. It *has* to be.

Which means my mother not only broke his heart and abandoned us, she also condemned him to a life in prison. A dark, isolated, crazy-making magical prison.

And he doesn't deserve that.

Which is why I can't give up on him.

Haldric wakes me much too early the next morning, and it's far from gentle; his screeches sound like a cat being strangled.

"*What*, Haldric? Can't it wait?" I plead, covering my head with my pillow.

He flies from his perch by the window and lands on top of me, nicking my arm lightly with his beak.

"OKAY! Okay. I'm up," I groan. I dress quickly in a pair of pants and a thick flannel shirt, wrapping my cloak around myself tightly as I leave the warmth of my apartment. Haldric follows me out.

It's barely light out. Sunrise. He leads me to the stables Evander showed me over two months ago.

I narrow my eyes at him. I haven't tried to ride Sterling yet. I'm not even sure if Evander still keeps his horse there.

"We're really doing this?" I grumble. Never mind the fact that Haldric is an owl and won't be doing a damn thing with Evander's horse.

That's all me.

Haldric's look is fuming. I shake my head. "I swear, if this is some trick and Evander ends up arresting me anyway it will be *your* fault."

I enter the stables through the front; after all, I have the owner's permission to use Sterling. The Guard gives me an inquisitive look but doesn't stop me. There are only eight stalls, each labeled with the horse's name. I find Sterling near the back next to an empty stall.

The stallion is muscled and majestic with a chestnut coat and deeply aware eyes. I approach him slowly, catching his gaze to ensure he doesn't see me as a threat.

Sterling bows his head slightly, a clear signal he is welcoming me. I pat his neck.

"You're gorgeous," I admit. "We're going for a quick ride, Sterling. Sound good?"

Sterling kicks his back hoof in confirmation. I grin.

I lead him out on foot with a quick nod at the Guard, who gives me a bored half wave. I relax slightly at that. Perhaps Evander's offer wasn't a trick.

No—I don't totally believe that.

Maybe his generosity isn't intended to set me up and get me arrested, but it isn't without strings attached.

That much is clear.

We ride northward again with Haldric in the lead. I curse under my breath as we near the same area where we found the doe—right beneath the King's castle. I can't feel any suffering yet, which is odd. I usually feel it at a reasonable distance.

Haldric stops on a low aspen branch at the edge of the trees before the clearing that leads up to the castle itself.

"Why—?" I start to ask but clamp my mouth shut as the King himself strides out of the castle with Evander and six others in black. Behind them is a female a few years older than me flanked by two more Guards, though she isn't cuffed.

"Thank you for your honesty, Beatrice. I understand how hard it must have been to come forward, but you did the right thing," says the King to the female. Three carriages come into view from the left side of the castle, and the King and his Guards begin to climb in.

"What happens now?" the female croaks. It sounds like she's been crying.

The King speaks through the window of his carriage. "We'll be summoning the village for the hearing to—take care of the matter. You are welcome to attend, though I can understand if it would be easier for you to skip it."

"Can one of your Guards help me leave? My husband will be

furious with me. Would you be able to provide me with safe passage to Abyssia? Or Meddia, even?" she asks.

"Evander?" the King says lazily.

"I prefer to be at the hearing, Your Majesty," he says. There's an edge of anger in his tone.

"Ah—of course. Nasgardo then, would you do the honors?"

"Certainly, Your Majesty," Nasgardo sneers. I shudder involuntarily.

Nasgardo climbs out of the carriage and grabs the female's arm. They dissolve in an instant.

"Evander, send word to the sentinel to ring the bell in thirty minutes. We want the town assembled by the time we get our hands on the delinquent," King Vilero instructs as the remaining Guards settle into their respective carriages.

I wait for the carriages to leave, then I shoot a look up at Haldric. "Why did you want me to see this?"

The owl's eyes reveal nothing.

I wait another five minutes or so before starting my own descension.

I struggle to piece together what exactly Beatrice had done and why she would need safe passage out of Syra to get away from her husband. I don't have to wonder for too long though, because by the time I return Sterling to his stall, the giant bell atop the portal station clangs loudly, echoing through the village.

I stay toward the back of the small crowd with my hood up, and Mila somehow still spots me and joins me with a confused look on her face.

"Do you know what this is about?" I ask her when she's close.

She shakes her head.

The last time the village was summoned was in celebration of the King's five hundred and ninety-ninth year of rule. I got spectacularly drunk that night to try to snuff out my anger. It only partially worked, and if Haldric hadn't stolen my cloak in an effort to drag me home, I probably would have given King Vilero a piece of my mind.

A very *inappropriate* piece of my mind.

As he was then, he's standing atop the bell tower of the portal station, looking down on us with disapproving eyes, a chilling smile interrupting the harsh lines of his pale face. His hair is a light copper color and his eyes are black as tar. His cloak, a midnight blue velvety thing, is thick and refined.

He looks nothing like Calimo—other than the eyes—and I am unimaginably grateful for that.

King Vilero scans the faces of the crowd with bland interest. I wonder idly if he even knows any of his own people. Any other than his precious Guard.

By the way he treats his son, I doubt it.

The King straightens up, sweeping his hands out wide as he speaks.

"My good people, I've gathered you here today to witness the judgement of a most serious crime. A crime so heinous, that the punishment for it can be nothing other than death."

He pauses, his face melting into a forlorn frown. "It is such a waste. My dear people, you know how I value life. *All* life. And though females do not have the same rights as males, and rightfully so as many of you agree, it still deeply saddens me when I have to take away a female's life."

My stomach twists, and Mila and I exchange a loaded glance.

"But the law *is* the law. And we have laws for a reason, do we not?" Vilero muses. "For without law, who are we but useless savages?" He pauses, and a sneer overtakes his face. "Of course, some of you *are* useless savages, but at least you do not break the law. That makes you better than those who do, would you not agree?"

Awkward murmurs erupt from the crowd, but the King presses

on. "I learned early this morning that our most important law has been broken. The very law that holds our society together, that ensures we have peace and order. The law that keeps everyone in their rightful place..."

I clench my jaw as a familiar rage heats my insides.

"Please bring the delinquent," the King says to his High Guard. I can't see over the crowd at first, but my heart stops when she is forcibly shoved forward on the balcony next to the King, her tiny wrists encircled with cuffs exactly like my father's had been.

I gasp. Mila looks just as alarmed next to me, and she links her arm with mine.

The whole demeanor of the crowd shifts from one of sleepy annoyance to abject horror. She can't be more than six years old, and even from our distance below the bell tower, I can see her face contorted in fear.

"Maybelle Frost—is it true you still have your magic?" the King says harshly.

The child cries audibly, but doesn't answer. The King waits, staring at her, his expression one of pure evil.

He faces the crowd again, sweeping his arms out wide as if to embrace us.

"My good people, this *criminal* is still in possession of her illegal magic. She is six years old, a full year past the allowable age." He points at her with a stiff arm. "And yet here she stands, mocking every male in these realms, with magic she has no right to possess."

He pauses, shaking his head dramatically as if this child has murdered her own parents or something equally heinous.

It's sick. My whole body is wound tight. Every part of me wants to bring him crashing down. I fleetingly imagine throwing my dagger at his face, but the steep upward angle means the knife likely wouldn't hit the mark. I would probably harm someone in the crowd instead.

The King points down at a male near the front of the crowd. "You, sir, do you think this is *right*?"

The male shakes his head emphatically. "No, Your Majesty."

"Of course it's not. She deserves to be punished. And so she will be..."

Mila pulls me in tighter. I'm fuming. The wind picks up violently, blowing the light snowfall to and fro. It whips the hood of my cloak loudly.

Even the fucking *weather* has a problem with this.

"Maybelle Frost, I am going to take your illegal magic so I may restore order and balance to these realms after your heinous insurrection. Do you understand?"

The child trembles, but she nods her head.

A loud *crack* echoes in the village as King Vilero opens Maybelle's energetic crown. She squeals in pain as flashes of white and pink light leave her, flowing directly into the palm of King Vilero's hand. He presses that hand to his belly, and he shudders a few times as the extra energy seeps under his skin and begins to fill his cells.

The crowd is unbearably silent as we wait for the King to adjust. His eyes are closed. A victorious smile spreads across his face.

"Order is restored," the King says triumphantly, finally opening his eyes. Maybelle shrinks several inches, her spine curving as if she is in tremendous pain.

"Now, who in my High Guard would like to complete the rest of her punishment?" the King says cheerfully. He glances down his nose at the crowd again. "As you all will do well to remember, possession of illegal magic is punishable by death," he adds.

"No!" I gasp, but Mila clamps her hand over my mouth, her eyes practically popping out of their sockets.

"I will, Your Majesty," says a calm voice.

Tears start spilling out of my horrified eyes as I watch *Evander* join the King and Maybelle on top of the bell tower.

Mila's hand still covers my mouth.

"Thank you, Evander," the King says, tilting his head slightly downward.

"I'll take her to the forest. We can't have her poisonous blood staining our streets," Evander adds in a flippant tone. My heart jolts as he grabs Maybelle's arm.

I feel sick. She isn't even fighting him.

And he's going to murder her.

13

I walk back to my apartment in a daze, Mila with me, our arms still linked as we leave the crowd.

Haldric finds us from one of his rooftop perches and follows us back. I don't remember inviting Mila in, but we somehow all three end up in my tiny apartment together.

"Fiana, is that normal for an owl?" Mila breaks our tense silence as she observes Haldric settling into his favorite spot by the window.

"Probably not, but he steals me food sometimes." I slump into one of my kitchen chairs. "Have you seen that before?" My voice is lifeless. I stare at the table.

Mila shakes her head, taking the seat opposite me. She's still wearing her cloak, and I notice she's wearing pajamas underneath.

"No, but Credo, Warren, and Koa all have. The King normally does them in the throne room. He hasn't done one in public in this century," she says.

I meet her eyes. "And Evander volunteered to do it."

She nods, her expression fierce. "There's a reason we want intel on him, Fiana. From what Warren says from his time in the High Guard—he *always* volunteers."

I shudder. "I understand why you all hate him so much." I shake my head in disbelief. "I understood before, but this—"

"This is unforgivable," Mila finishes for me, her hazel eyes steely.

I stare out the window, trying to make sense of everything that has just happened.

"We think you have a good chance of breaking him," Mila says softly. "He seems to have a blind spot where you are concerned."

I snort, crossing my arms. "Why do you think that is?"

Mila pushes a long lock of blonde hair behind her ear and sighs. "Koa thinks he just likes the challenge. Evander *lives* for challenges."

"And what do you think?" I counter.

She laughs. "I think when you went out with Calimo instead of him, it struck a nerve. A rather deep one, I'd bet."

"So you think it's just ego?" I bite my lip. Of course I believe that on some level, but it still hurts to say it out loud.

"Nothing blinds a male more than his ego," Mila says with a shrug. She pulls her cloak tighter around her pajamas. "I know it's dangerous. I know we're asking you a lot. But I also know you're not a stranger to doing dangerous things for the people you love."

"I'm not worried about the danger—you know I'm not, Mila," I argue. I kick out of my chair and go over to Haldric, stroking his chest plumage to avoid looking at her. "It's the fact that you want me to give up on my father. I don't know if I can do that."

I don't want to do that.

Her chair scrapes against the wooden floors and I feel her come up behind me. I tense, but she doesn't touch me.

Her voice is gentle. "Haven't you already given up on him? When was the last time you broke in?"

The words are like a stab wound to the heart. "I haven't given up on him," I disagree.

Her hand rests lightly on my shoulder, and I flinch. She quickly removes it, and instead sidles up next to me. I keep my eyes fixed on Haldric.

"Do you want to know why my father joined the Dissenters and died for our cause? And why, after his death, I joined too?" Mila asks me.

I glance briefly at her. I hadn't realized her father was involved. Or dead.

"My mother was executed just like Maybelle was," she continues. "Except her blood *did* 'stain our streets.'"

My stomach churns. I face her fully. "I'm so sorry, Mila."

Her eyes are hard. "She didn't even have magic. Her big crime was refusing to leave my father and me and become the King's next whore."

My jaw drops. My thoughts flicker to my own mother.

"How old were you when you lost her?"

Her jaw ticks. She looks out the window and her voice shakes a little as she responds. "I was nine."

I reach for her hand and squeeze it. "My mother walked out on us when I was four."

Mila jolts. "She left you?"

I nod. "At least yours died refusing to leave you. Mine just didn't want me anymore."

The look of sympathy in Mila's eyes somehow reaches all the way into my chest and cracks open my heart.

"I understand why you want to break your father out," she says quietly.

A tear runs down my cheek, and I wipe it swiftly away.

"I understand why you want me to help you bring down the King," I admit. "Believe me, I want him dead and gone, too. I just don't know if I—" the words die on my tongue as a sob rocks through me.

She places her other hand over both of ours. "You don't know if you can let your father go just yet."

I nod. She pulls me into a hug and then pulls back to look at me.

"You have a chance to make a *real* difference, Fiana. The Dissenters haven't had an in with Evander since our inception. He's the *top* of the High Guard. Gaining intel on him would be infinitely valuable to us."

Something in her words turns my stomach, but I also know she's right. Especially after what I witnessed this morning.

"I need some time to process all of this," I admit.

She nods. "I get that. I do. But just remember every moment you spend making up your mind about whether or not you'll help us, another child is at risk of dying."

My heart feels like it's been singed.

I glare at her, jerking away from her hold. "You say that like it's *my* fault that this is even happening! Did you forget the fact that you only pulled me into your little rebellion hours ago?"

Her face falls. "You're right. You're right—I'm sorry. I shouldn't have phrased it that way."

"No, you shouldn't have," I bite.

She sighs, pulling her cloak protectively around herself, edging toward the door. "I think I'll give you your space now."

"I think that would be best." I take a deep breath and then soften my tone. "I am glad you found me in the crowd this morning, though."

She gives me a half smile as she opens the door.

"Think about what we talked about. Take your time—as much time as you need. But don't avoid this. Because we really need you," she implores. "I'll see you at the tavern tonight."

She leaves, pulling the door shut behind her.

I stare after her, feeling stuck between conflicting feelings.

I could do it.

I could get closer to Evander and learn all of his secrets. I don't think it would be that hard either, considering his infatuation with me, however ego-driven.

I could feed the information I learn to the Dissenters and help them undermine Vilero's rule.

I could use him for our gain—much like I tried to use Calimo. And with that, I could make a real difference. Not just for me, but for all of the females.

And I *should* want that, especially after what I witnessed today. Even if it means giving up on breaking out my father.

Which—to Mila's point—I haven't made progress on since Calimo.

It should be an easy yes for me to join the Dissenter's efforts. It should be an obvious choice to give up on my father and join the rebellion.

And I shouldn't feel any type of guilt at the thought of using Evander in the process. Especially when thinking of his cavalier attitude toward his immortal females. And worse—seeing him volunteer to murder a child.

Because it's as Mila said.

Unforgivable.

And yet despite everything that seems so clear and true, I still feel a desperate need to cling to my father's innocence.

To not give up on him. To find a way to break him out.

But that's not even the part that disturbs me the most.

Because there's another male's innocence I find myself wanting to cling to.

And that makes absolutely no sense.

November bleeds into December with Maybelle's execution occupying a large part of my mind as the days pass by. As horrible as it seems, I find myself wishing I could just forget about it.

I try to avoid Mila. Even at work, despite her many attempts to apologize. It's not that I'm still upset with her; I just haven't made a decision yet.

On the nights when I get off work at a decent hour, I find myself riding Sterling down to The Cave. I don't break in. I just stare at the entrance as if it will give me answers that don't exist.

I try very hard not to think about the fact that Maybelle's killer is the source of my transportation; I need the escape too badly to feel guilty about it.

It's stupid. And reckless.

But I'm feeling that sort of way these days.

Haldric came with me in the beginning, but after he realized I was just sitting in the cold until I was practically numb, he started staying back at my apartment.

I don't blame him. I can't stand the suffering of animals. Maybe he can't stand the suffering of elves.

In the dead of night, under blankets of snow, in the bone-chilling cold, somehow the pain recedes just enough to where I can get to sleep in the early hours of the morning.

Tonight, I'm still a long way off from that point.

A *crack* rips in front of the entrance, and I jump at the sound. There haven't been reports of any new prisoners coming in. I hop off Sterling and approach the edge of the evergreens, catching a glimpse of a lone Guard in grey entering the prison.

I don't think, I just follow.

I make it to the first enclave easily enough and do a mental calculation. It was just after eleven when I rode down here. Has it already been a whole hour?

Normally I notice when the night shift leaves, but tonight I've been so lost in my thoughts that I can't be sure. I wait four hundred seconds, just in case, and then set off toward the passageway that leads to the cells.

I make it down the hall and to the right, down another hundred feet or so and a sharp left followed by a right turn, past a lit section and into the darkness that follows. I make it to the first wing: the cells numbered one to one thousand.

Strange noises come from those cells. Whimpers and heavy

breathing. Even snoring. From a thousand different males. And Maker knows what else.

I ignore the discomfort I always feel being so close to the prisoners and start the long trek to the next wing. I'm being sloppy—I know I am, but I don't care anymore.

If *children* are dying, is this really a world I want to keep living in?

I make it to the four hundreds when a torchlight appears a hundred feet ahead of me. I freeze. It's someone in black.

Shit, shit, shit!

I back against the wall and crouch down, trying to make myself as small and invisible as possible, though there isn't much to hide behind.

A split second later, a pair of heavy black boots skid to a stop inches from my face as an iron fist grabs my forearm and yanks me to a standing position. I whimper, but a firm hand covers my mouth before much sound can escape. I look up in alarm, seeing his thick beard before meeting his eyes.

His beautiful, murderous eyes.

He pulls me into his arms and like Maybelle, I don't even fight him. He can't dissolve in The Cave, but he races us through the passageways so fast that I shiver at the wind tunnel effect. He pauses at the gates—even immortal speed can't make those move any faster—then launches us out into the night.

He isn't going to imprison me, then. He's going to kill me. A part of me longs for the eternal peace of death.

"Are you *fucking* insane?" he growls in my ear once he's run us halfway up the mountain, leaving Sterling and The Cave far below us.

He sets me down roughly onto a pile of fluffy snow at the base of a giant aspen. While the landing is soft, the breath is still knocked out of me.

He paces now, so fast that his form is a blur of black tinged with the subtle glow of his magic. He stops suddenly and looks me in the eye, seething. "What *exactly* were you planning to do when you made it to his cell? How were you planning to get the door open?"

I disregard the fact that he must have figured out I was there for my father. Instead of answering him, my thoughts drift to Maybelle.

"Is this where you did it?" I subtly reach my fingertips to my boot, letting them rest on the hilt of the dagger.

He ignores that, pacing again. "I have given you *every* opportunity to not get caught, Fiana. Are you *trying* to get yourself killed?" His power tinges red, exuding white hot rage.

But it's nothing compared to mine.

I jump to my feet, yanking the dagger out in the same move. I stalk toward him, head held high, blade outstretched. I'm completely void of fear, numb from grief and the bitter cold.

He scowls at me. "What the fuck are you doing?"

I look him dead in the eye. "I'm going to stab you."

"The fuck you're not, Fiana," he snaps.

I ignore him, edging closer.

He narrows his eyes. "First of all, I'm immortal. Second of all, you know you won't win this fight."

"Who says I want to win?" I say as my blade inches toward his throat. "Maybe I just want to provoke you."

His nostrils flare. "Put down the knife."

"Or maybe I just want to watch you *bleed*." My blade makes contact with the bare skin of his neck. His hand grips my wrist in a blindingly fast movement, locking my hand in place, preventing my knife from sinking into his flesh.

His eyes go hard. So does the set of his jaw. "You are the most reckless female I have ever met."

"At least I'm not a *child murderer*," I hiss through gritted teeth.

He doesn't shrink under my gaze as I expect. Instead, his eyes darken. "I didn't have a choice."

I laugh without humor. "Bullshit. You could have led Beatrice to her escape. But instead you convinced the King to let you stay for the trial."

He curses under his breath. "You saw that?"

"Yeah, I fucking saw that."

He shakes his head in disbelief. We're silent and still for a long moment, just fuming at each other.

"I didn't do what you think I did," he says finally, so quiet I'm not sure I hear him correctly.

I snort. "Nice try, asshole."

"Fiana," he says harshly, pulling my hand away from his throat. I grip the blade harder, but I can't fight against his impossible strength. "I have no reason to lie to you." He pauses for a moment, then adds, "I *don't* lie to you."

"I don't believe you." My heart rate quickens. "I have *no reason* to believe you."

Evander's eyes darken. "Do you know how many times I could have arrested you? Did you forget the fact that I've lent you my thoroughbred, no questions asked? Or how about the fact that I just stopped you from getting caught by someone worse *yet again*?"

"Yes, and why do all of that? Why do you want me indebted to you, Evander?"

"*Indebted* to me?" He shakes his head, his eyes disbelieving. "I'm trying to protect you."

"I don't need protection," I fume.

He softens at that, surprising me. "No, in some ways you don't. But in other ways—" he pauses, removing the knife from my grasp and tossing it onto the snow. It lands with a dull *thud*. His voice is pained as he continues. "You wouldn't have been able to save him, Fiana."

"How the hell do you know that? You stopped me before I had a chance!"

I try to yank my wrist out of his grip, but his fingers tighten like a vice. I put my free hand on his chest, driving a knee toward his crotch. He deflects it easily with his own leg, grabbing my thigh with his free hand and launching me toward the ground.

The landing is brisk, air whooshing out of my lungs. He climbs on top of me, pinning me down against the snow. His thighs squeeze my waist as he grabs each wrist and pins them down by my face.

I buck my hips up hard, trying to shove him off, but the snowdrift is too deep that I don't get him very far. It's enough to free my hands though, and he grunts as he catches himself above my head.

I'm still stuck underneath him, so I fumble my hands to the sides, searching the snow for my dagger.

I close around the hilt at the same moment he mounts me and pins my arms down again.

"Stop fighting!" he growls in my face as I writhe underneath him, trying to free my hands again.

"No!" I try kneeing him in the lower back but his foot kicks my leg back down.

"Enough!" he shouts. "Your father is dead!"

I freeze.

I stare at him blankly, still catching my breath.

Your father is dead.

He waits for me to respond, his own breathing labored. My body sinks deeper into the snowdrift underneath his weight. I shiver as the cold creeps through my cloak.

Your father is dead.

I still can't speak.

Your father is dead.

The words don't make sense.

"He died this morning," he says in a softer tone. "Another prisoner killed him."

He died this morning.

I study his eyes, looking for the lie. But all I see is sincerity and —sympathy.

"Let me up," I finally choke out. A lump is rapidly forming in my throat.

He died this morning.

He quickly backs up on his knees.

Another prisoner killed him.

I sit up slowly, still clutching the dagger.

"Who killed him?" I say mechanically. There are difficult emotions brewing somewhere inside of me, but at the moment they feel very far away.

"Another elf," he says gently. "Vito Stargrove."

He died this morning.

"How did he die?" I slide the dagger into my boot. Evander follows my movements with his eyes.

He clears his throat. "Strangulation."

I push up onto my feet, dusting off the back of my cloak.

Another prisoner killed him.

"What was the motive?" My voice sounds surprisingly calm. And very far away.

Evander stands up with me. "Unknown." He takes a step closer to me, his eyes pleading. "I'm so sorry, Fiana. I didn't want to tell you this way."

"No, I'm glad you told me," I breathe. Grief is bubbling up like acid, but I force the emotions down. "So are you going to arrest me, or kill me? Or can you take me home?"

His eyes look bleak. "I'll take you home."

He takes another step toward me, wrapping his arms around me as he dissolves us back to the village.

Your father is dead.

He died this morning.

Another prisoner killed him.

Strangulation.

My next breath is a strangled gasp against Evander's chest.

I can't help it.

The close contact unleashes my tear ducts.

I'm full on sobbing by the time we land in town, my whole body convulsing as tears gush down my cheeks. I try shoving out of his arms, but he won't let me go. He holds me tight, guiding me toward a bench and pulling me onto his lap.

I'm too distraught to fight him further, so I let myself forget whose arms I'm in. I let myself be comforted by the way he rubs my back. By the warm, woodsy scent of his skin. By the radiating heat that keeps the cold at bay. From his own flesh or from his magic, I don't know.

He holds me, and I cry.

And cry.

And *cry*.

Your father is dead.

The grief crushes me and punishes me. It steals my breath and stabs my heart and wrenches the very life out of my flesh and bones.

Another prisoner killed him.

A hole has been carved through my chest, and I can't get enough air in no matter how hard I try. My body shakes as I gasp for breath, and terror rises within me.

Strangulation.

I feel Evander's hand slide up to the back of my neck. It's unbearably warm. There's a soothing pressure as his magic flows underneath my skin.

It doesn't take away the grief, but it helps me take a deeper inhale.

The panic fades and a sense of calm slowly returns as oxygen hits my lungs in long, steady increments. I lean my head against his throat, soaking his neck in tears.

His arms tighten around me and I feel his lips brush against my forehead.

A soft, chaste kiss.

One meant to comfort and soothe.

I hate it, and I love it.

It kills me, and it saves me.

Because somehow in his arms, I feel safer than I have in years.

14

The next day my eyes feel tired and raw. But my mind is made up.

I'm joining the Dissenters.

Because if my father is dead, then I have no reason not to.

That thought sends a throbbing sensation into my heart and a lump into my throat, but I fight like hell to ignore it.

I don't want to cry anymore.

After holding me on the bench for Maker knows how long, Evander eventually carried me back home, somehow knowing exactly where I lived and which unit was mine. He tucked me into bed before dissolving away.

The sobs continued for two more hours.

I slept for four at most.

It doesn't escape my notice that he had every opportunity to take advantage of me, to kill me, to arrest me, to abuse me.

But he didn't.

I'm desperate to believe what he alluded to about Maybelle— that he *didn't* kill her.

But if that's true, then he's directly defying the King right under his nose.

Could I really believe he would go against him?

I'm not fully sure.

But I sure as hell am going to find out.

And I may as well help the Dissenters in the process.

I get to the tavern around midday—hours before I'm expected for my shift. I recognize the day bartender. Lark, I think her name is. She raises a brow as I walk in.

"Is Credo in?" I say calmly. Her lips twitch, but she nods.

I duck under the bridge and knock twice on his office door. His footsteps shake the walls as he lumbers to answer it.

"Fiana," he says, his golden eyes knowing as I slide inside his office. The space is small and sparse, with a desk and chair and a long blue couch along the back wall.

There aren't any windows. He shuts the door behind me.

"You've decided," he predicts.

"Yes." I turn around to face him. "I'm going to help you."

He stares at me for a long moment, with something like worry in his eyes.

"What made you change your—"

"My father was killed. So there's nothing stopping me from helping you anymore." I pull my cloak tighter around my body, though his office is quite warm.

His wiry grey beard twitches as his face falls.

"I'm so sorry, Fiana," he says, his eyes concerned. "I'll let Koa know," he adds, closing his eyes to send the magical message.

I swallow thickly as I wait. Seconds pass before Koa and Warren arrive with a *crack*.

"You're joining us?" Koa says. His dark gaze scans my face. Noticing the red eyes, splotchy cheeks, and dark circles there.

"As Credo said," I say emotionlessly.

Koa nods once. "Though the circumstances are regrettable, we are glad to have you."

I don't respond. Credo clears his throat.

"And you're willing to spy on Evander?" Warren asks. His hair is down today, hanging like a thick black curtain to his shoulders.

"As Credo said," I repeat, keeping my face neutral.

Koa nods again. "Good. Very good. Warren—let's go ahead and mark her."

I raise my brows. *Mark me?*

Warren throws a look at Koa that indicates he disapproves. "She's supposed to get close to *Evander*. No way we can mark her, he'll find it in an instant."

"We'll hide it with magic of course," Koa argues, wiping his brow with one of his knuckles.

Warren clenches his massive hands in fists by his sides. "He's still going to find it."

"Every Dissenter gets marked. It's how we ensure our loyalty." Koa looks down his nose at Warren, which is an impressive feat considering Warren is a whole head taller than him.

"What mark?" I start backing toward the door.

"A binding mark," Koa clarifies. "You pledge to do everything we say—on your life."

I gape at him. "Everything you *say*? I thought this resistance was about returning power *back* to females."

Warren moves his body between me and Koa.

"We can't bind her to that. That's extreme, and you know it, Koa," he argues. "At most, we can bind her loyalty to taking down the King."

Koa shrugs. "It's the same thing."

Credo shakes his head. "I have to agree with Warren."

Koa scoffs. "Are we forgetting the missions we have planned for her? She's known to go off script even in her *own* illicit activities. We can't be sure she won't get caught if she's not bound to follow our every command."

I back myself against the door now, and I can feel my cheeks turning red. "If you want to bind me to following your *every* command, you can forget it. I'm out."

I start to twist the nob, but it's locked.

Warren whirls around to face me. His green-blue eyes are earnest. "Are you willing to bind yourself to a lifelong commitment to take down the King?"

"That's not good enough," Koa complains.

"Enough, Koa," Credo says, his voice stern.

"Are you willing, Fiana?" Warren repeats.

My heart pounds in my chest. "What happens if I don't?"

It's Credo who answers me. "We need to bind you with something if we are going to let you into our meetings. Otherwise Koa will wipe your memories of the Dissenters, and I'll have to fire you."

"Fire me?" I ask, meeting Credo's golden eyes.

He nods once, his face apologetic. "Seeing us every day might trigger your memories even after he wipes them."

"You never told me this was part of it," I argue. "You just said you wanted me to steal things and get close to Evander."

"But we need to know you won't turn against us, Fiana," Koa says, annoyed. "*Especially* as you get close to Evander."

"I never agreed to this," I complain, trying to twist the doorknob again. It won't budge.

Warren takes a deep breath and then looks me in the eye. "Do you want to see the King fall? And are you willing to pledge your life to that cause?"

"In theory, yes," I say hastily.

"That's all we're asking for," Warren insists.

"We *should* be asking for more," Koa counters.

"Quiet," Warren says over his shoulder. He fixes his green-blue eyes on me again. "Are you in agreement?"

I swallow thickly. "Yes, I'm in agreement."

"Lift up your shirt," Warren says.

"Excuse me?" I narrow my eyes at him.

"Her hairline would be better," Credo suggests. "You won't even need magic to hide it."

"Evander can't detect Hermetic magic," Koa argues. "Almost no one alive can."

"Don't underestimate him," Warren snaps. "Pull your hair up and turn around. I'm going to do it just under the thickest part of your hair."

"Okay," I breathe, gathering my curls up into my fist and turning around to expose my neck to him.

Warren places his fingers on my scalp, just above my brain stem. There's a warming sensation as he intends the binding. "Do you, Fiana Willowbark, pledge on your life to do whatever you can to take down the King?"

I take a deep breath, pushing down the fear that bubbles in my gut. "Yes."

I feel the mark tattoo my scalp like a shallow scrape against my skin.

"It's done," Warren says, removing his hands from my head. "You can hardly see it."

"Whatever," Koa laments. "At least it's done."

"Our next meeting is in two weeks. I'll have Mila come and get you," Credo advises.

I touch the back of my head where the fresh tattoo is hidden.

"Fine."

"Stay out of trouble until then," Koa instructs, dissolving away before I can respond.

Warren gives me a curt nod before doing the same.

I level a look at Credo.

"You trust them?" I say pointedly.

Credo gives me a crinkly-eyed smile. "I've known them a long time."

I nod once then try the doorknob again. It's unlocked.

Haldric lands on my shoulder the second I'm outside. I jump at his sudden touch.

I make it outside of my apartment building and am climbing the stairs when it occurs to me.

Credo never really answered the question.

And I just bound myself to the Dissenters for life.

Later that night, the tavern is absolutely swimming with the Guard by the time I arrive. There're dozens in grey and even a relatively large group in black.

"Winter solstice. It's a major holiday for the Guard," Mila tells me when I duck under the bridge. Once I'm behind the bar, she gives me a knowing look as she scratches the back of her head. I give her tight smile.

"I'm proud of you," she whispers as she slips past me to get to the register.

I don't respond. Because I'm still not sure how I feel about what I've agreed to.

I busy myself with filling cups, as clinking glasses and boisterous conversation fill the space. Thirty minutes into my shift, a Guard in black catches my eye at the back of the tavern.

His hair looks more disheveled than usual, and there are purple circles under his striking eyes. Despite that, he's still more beautiful than any male I've ever seen.

He lifts a glass of jad to his lips, throwing the rest of it back. He slams the empty glass gently onto the table, wiping his mouth with the back of his hand.

He's listening intently to the Guard across from him, his immortal females missing for once.

I hate that I notice that.

Just then, his eyes shoot up to meet mine, and it's like he's checking me over to see if I've been crying. He holds my gaze across the room. Dozens of Guards pass between us, yet somehow our sightline never wavers.

I'm going to figure you out, I think to myself.

And not for the Dissenters.

For me.

I want the truth.

If he saved Maybelle. And if so, why?

Why he healed the doe. Why he still hasn't turned me in.

Why he held me while I cried last night, and didn't try to take advantage of me. Not even once.

He dips his head slightly, still holding my gaze.

As if he somehow knows we're about to play a brand new game.

A few days into January, I'm with Mila and she's yanking on my arm, pulling me faster toward the edge of town.

"We're going to be late," she murmurs. "Koa hates it when we're late."

"Seems like Koa hates just about everything," I mutter.

She snorts. "Keep those comments to yourself when we get there."

"Noted," I sigh.

We pass the stables where Sterling is kept, and I notice Haldric perched on the roof, his eyes curious. I give him a half smile and he flaps his wings once.

Here if you need me, he seems to say.

We pass the last few buildings and she leads us into the trees. We walk twenty paces in before I see Warren up ahead, leaning against a tree, looking annoyed.

"You're late," he says flatly.

"Yeah, yeah," Mila dismisses, but she shoots me a look.

He holds out an elbow for each of us to grab. I grip it tight.

We land in the same room as before with a *crack,* except this time the door is open. Both of them walk through it, Mila giving me a look over her shoulder beckoning me to follow.

The door leads immediately into a bigger room with a large table at the center, with a dozen elves seated on each side. Koa paces at the head of the table farthest from us, deeply engrossed by some unknown stressful thought.

He stops short when he sees me.

"Everyone, please welcome Fiana Willowbark to the Dissenters," Mila says from the other end of the table, wrapping an arm around my shoulders.

Every head turns to face me.

"Willowbark?" says an ice-blonde female with a pixie haircut and a pointed nose. "The one who's been sneaking into The Cave?"

Guess everyone knows, then.

"Indeed," Koa says with a sharp look at the blonde.

She shifts awkwardly in her chair.

Mila leads me quietly around to a pair of empty chairs near our end. We sit.

"Paul, where do we stand with the Port of Heron?" Koa looks to a buff dark-skinned male with striking cheekbones and a shaved head.

Guess the meeting has officially started.

My heart skips at the mention of my old home, my curiosity sparked.

"We have everything in place to intercept the latest shipment," he says with a curt nod. His air is one of a military general—stark, emotionless, and duty-bound.

"And after?" Koa says, lifting his chin slightly.

"The network is ready to receive the goods, sir," Paul assures him.

"No leaks?" Koa narrows his eyes.

"None, sir." Paul meets Koa's gaze unflinchingly.

"Good. And how are the replacements coming, Blaze?" Koa shifts his eyes to a pale blonde male with a sharp nose and tilted brown eyes.

"They're ready. I spoke to Aludo moments ago. Totally indistinguishable from the real thing," Blaze says with a wide grin.

"Yet they fail with shielding techniques—yes?" Koa presses.

Blaze nods. "Naturally, sir."

"Very well. That leads me to our last order of business for this meeting. We've asked Fiana to join us for two reasons. The first is that—as many of you know—she possesses a skill many of us are lacking up north," Koa explains. His mouth turns up into something that could resemble a smile.

But only if you squinted.

And then shut your eyes entirely.

"Stealth," he continues. "And we'd like her to start her service to our cause by stealing something from the King."

"What is she stealing?" asks the blonde female, pushing a short lock of hair behind her ear.

"A golden dagger. It is an extremely powerful weapon that will aid our efforts tremendously," he explains.

"What's her other purpose?" a redheaded female with plump cheeks asks.

"To gain intel on our biggest hindrance," Koa says with an air of boredom. "Evander."

The whole table erupts in shocked murmurs as people dart their eyes between me and their neighbor.

"How's she going to do that?" A raven-haired beauty asks with disdain. I realize with a start that I've seen her in the tavern before.

With Evander.

My stomach clenches. But if she was *with* him... isn't she *bound* to him?

"He's totally obsessed with her. It's *weird*," Mila says, snorting.

"Excuse me?" I say to her, in a relatively low voice.

"I don't mean it's weird that he likes *you*." She turns to me, raising a hand in defense. "I mean it's weird that he's obsessed with any female at all. We've been trying to crack him for centuries. He's impossible to please. He typically loses interest with one of our plants within a few weeks and since you've started working at the tavern, he only agrees to seeing them for a single night."

"*What?*"

Was every female I witnessed with Evander a Dissenter *plant*?

"Yeah something changed when you arrived," Mila says, shrugging.

Credo chuckles from the other side of the table. "It's true. I've known Evander since he was a boy. Generally, the ladies chase him. You're different."

"Can we focus?" Koa says, pinching the bridge of his nose.

Real inspiring leader they've chosen for their movement.

"You are to start growing closer to him, but do not make it obvious. It should be a natural progression from wherever you stand now," Koa instructs, his eyes severe.

"Where *do* you stand now?" Mila demands.

Good question. "We're—on speaking terms."

The dark-haired one snorts. "*That* sounds promising."

"Enough, Collette," Koa bites. "Become friends. And then closer. But keep it gradual."

"What about training?" Warren says as Koa moves to dismiss the meeting.

Most at the table exchange nervous glances.

"We don't need her to be able to fight," Koa dismisses.

"She will if she gets caught. You really gonna leave her defenseless?" he argues, raising a thick brow.

"Everyone gets trained, Koa," Paul chimes in.

Koa shakes his head once. "Evander will notice if she suddenly has bumps and bruises all over her body from training. Not happening."

"Evander might turn on her," Warren counters. There's no yield in his tone.

Koa stares down his nose at him. Warren looks virtually unthreatened.

"Fine." Koa starts leaving the room. "In the mornings, before your tavern shifts."

Once he's out of view, the whole room relaxes.
It bothers me, how tense he makes everyone.
Because he's supposed to be our freedom leader.

15

"Show me what you already know," Warren says. His mouth is pressed into a thin line, his forehead creased. His dark hair is knotted at the nape of his neck, and he's dressed in an armor that suspiciously reminds me of the High Guard uniform.

We're in a small clearing at the bottom of Parley, the mountain to the east of Ador. Towering evergreens surround us on all sides. Though we're protected from the wind, it's somehow colder here, and my lungs burn with each breath.

"Basic self-defense stuff. And where the major arteries are." My fingers brush against the sheath at my thigh where my dagger is housed. After the meeting last night, Mila sent me home with fighting leathers and a whole host of new weapons.

"Show me," he says again, his green-blue eyes lifeless.

I take a painful breath then rush at him, gripping his arms to do the same maneuver I did with Elyon in the bar. He moves in a flash grabbing one of my arms and twisting me around so my back is to his chest. My shoulder aches at the unnatural angle, like it's at risk of dislocating any second.

I kick my foot back aiming for his crotch, but he turns his hips sideways and catches my ankle. He releases my arm, yanking my leg higher so I lose my balance and fall face forward into the snow. I gasp for air against a flurry of powder, my face burning from the cold.

He pins me down from behind. I reach for a knife but two massive hands grip my wrists and stop me before I reach it.

"Yield," he says emotionlessly.

I cough against the snow. "Yield," I choke out.

He releases my wrists and slides off me, getting to his feet and reaching for my hand to help me up.

"Charging a bigger opponent isn't your best strategy, though I admire the bravery. You want to wait for them to show their hand. And react quickly."

He eyes me for a moment, seeing if I'm ready to go again. I give him a nod.

He rushes at me, aiming a fist at my stomach. I dart to the left, jamming my foot behind his knee. He falters but quickly recovers, spinning around to throw another punch toward my face. I duck, ramming my shoulder into his gut and pushing him backward with all of my weight. He backs up, his feet sinking deeper into the snow, but doesn't fall.

He's too damn heavy.

"Good, now pause here," he says, and I stop pushing but stay in position. "Grab my hips and drive your knee toward my groin. Gently, please," he instructs.

I do as he says, barely brushing my knee against him.

"See in this position it's harder for me to block that if you move quick, since you're forcing me backwards and I need my balance. So now I react," he doubles over, pretending I've hit him. "How do you finish me?"

I push the heel of my hand up against his nose at the same time I pull out my knife and aim for his throat.

"Nice. Let's go again," Warren says with a nod.

The weeks pass quickly as my days become utterly consumed by training and work. By the time Warren takes me back to Ador after each session, I'm always freezing, tired, and sore. And I typically still have a closing shift at the tavern to look forward to.

I don't hate the endless activity. It keeps my mind off my father.

My now dead father.

I can't believe it's already been two months.

I haven't seen Evander since the winter solstice, but Mila said that's typical. That the King typically keeps his Guard on a tighter leash after the holiday.

I notice his absence more than I should.

I tell myself it's because I'm supposed to be gathering intel on him and he's nowhere to be found.

I don't let myself dig any deeper than that.

Today's session with Warren is brutal, but I relish the pain. At least until he dissolves us back to the forest, at the far edge of town near Sterling's stables; I realize when we land that I can barely walk.

Haldric is there waiting for me as usual, perched on an aspen branch. His eyes are wary as he watches me hobble through the cobblestone streets back home. Nearly two months of back to back training days have eviscerated my muscles, and every movement feels like pure agony.

He hovers closely, concern emanating from his plumage, seemingly sensing my weakened state.

I desperately need a hot shower and a hot meal. And maybe a shot of jad to boot.

Before I leave my apartment, I eye the two bottles of yarrow tincture I have left, tempted to gulp a small dose to heal my sore muscles. I sigh, forcing myself not to.

Better save them for worse injuries.

Mercifully, the bar is completely dead for once when I arrive for my shift. Mila smiles at me as I hobble in.

"Rough session today?" she says, amused.

I glance around. There's literally no one here. The only sounds are the crackle of the fire and my leaden footsteps.

"Where is everyone?" I ask as I move under the bridge.

It's an effort not to drop to my knees and crawl.

"I think a lot of our regulars traveled to Veliathon for the annual Elven Beer Fest. We've had a few pop in and out, but I expect tonight will be slow," she shrugs.

"Gotcha." I pour myself a shot of jad. "Want one?"

"Sure, why not?" She grins.

We take our shots, our faces scrunching up at the burn of the liquor.

"I don't know how people drink eight or ten of these. Like three and I'm done," she giggles.

I snort, but don't respond. My thoughts are still on my morning training. And the carefully choreographed sequences Warren guides me through.

He's too proficient at fighting. It's somewhat alarming.

"What's Warren's deal, anyway? Why does he seem like a High Guard warrior?" I ask, leaning against the back bar.

My legs *ache*. And my *ribs*.

"He was," Mila responds, covering her mouth as she coughs. "He watched his divine feminine get tortured and executed by Vilero. After that, he was done."

I gape at her. "When was that?"

She shrugs. "Fifty years ago or so. He doesn't talk about it. I only know because Credo told me. They were a real divine union, too. With the telepathic thoughts and everything. Credo says they loved each other very much."

"Damn." Sadness comes over me. "That must have crushed him." Suddenly the pain behind his eyes makes total sense. "So everyone in the Dissenters really does care about females?" It's the first chance I've gotten to talk to her privately about it all.

Mila's eyes widen. "Oh yeah. Definitely."

She sounds convinced.

"How long have you been a part of it?" I ask.

She sighs dramatically, adjusting the blonde bun atop her head.

"Since I was your age. My father wouldn't let me join until then," she muses. *So five years.* She pours us both another shot. "He was the old leader before Koa—before he died."

My heart clenches. I try to swallow around the lump in my throat.

"I'm sorry," I breathe. She knocks back a shot, wiping her mouth with the back of her hand.

"It is what it is. We know what we signed up for," she says evenly, though there's a hint of grief behind her eyes.

I wipe mine.

My grief is a prisoner in the pit of my stomach. Shouting for attention. Clawing at my insides. Pulling me out of the now, and dragging me into the pit with it.

I take a deep breath and try to pull myself back out.

"Are you okay?" Mila says, concerned, her eyes flitting all over my face.

I nod quickly, looking away. I stare at the fireplace. The flames are a deep navy blue tonight.

"It's your father—isn't it?" she asks. Her tone is gentle.

I exhale sharply, shoving my feelings down deeper. "It's still a shock, that's all. I've been trying not to think about it."

"I'm sorry," she says, resting a hand on mine.

I snort. "Don't be. I probably wouldn't have joined the Dissenters if he was still alive."

Mila pulls her hand away, her expression uncomfortable.

"I'm still sorry," she says quietly, looking at the ground.

There's an awkward silence. I pour us both another shot.

We drink it down.

My thoughts drift back to Mila's earlier remarks.

"Why did Koa take over after your father? Did he name him as the successor?" I wonder. I just can't imagine anyone nominating *him* into such a position considering his temperament.

Mila clears her throat. "No, he just convinced us all that he was the best fit. It makes sense because if he ever gets caught, he can just wipe the memory of whoever catches him and escape. That way we have stable leadership no matter what."

Stable, uninspiring leadership that is.

"Ah." I pour myself a glass of water from the tap. I take long pull then set the glass down. The sound echoes in the empty room.

"And what about the other females you've... planted? With Evander. What have they done exactly?" I ask, trying to sound casual.

She snorts. "Apparently decades ago—he was a *huge* rake. It was kind of a thing amongst the females of Syra." She rolls her eyes. "Everyone wanted to see who would end up with him. He's stupidly rich, of course. And more than that, powerful. I don't know if he immortalized them all or what, but I hear stories of females from back then that are *still* not over him." She shakes her head as if they're all idiots.

"But like twenty years ago or so he calmed down a lot," Mila continues, "and no one in the Dissenters knows why. I don't think any of our recent plants even made it home with him."

The door opens, causing us both to whip our heads to see who it is.

Speak of the devil.

My chest loosens as his eyes find mine, and I feel like I can take a full breath for the first time in months.

That revelation quickly makes me turn beet red, and I grab a towel and start wiping down the sparkling clean bar surface just for something to do.

"Quiet night, ladies?" he says with a cocky grin.

A part of me wonders if he heard everything Mila just said with his immortal ears.

"Beer Fest in Veliathon," Mila explains, shrugging. She gives me a quick look and then adds, "And I think I may take off. Fiana's got you from here."

I snap my head in her direction. "You're leaving?" The words sound strained.

She fights a smile as she pulls on her cloak. "See you tomorrow, Fiana. Bye, Evander."

I watch her leave with my mouth open in shock.

Guess my intel gathering starts now.

"Can I have one of those?" Evander says, jerking his chin to the bottle of jad still on top of the bar as he takes a seat.

I take a deep breath and refocus on him.

His eyes look softer than I remember. Like part of the mask has slipped. Like he can no longer hide from me.

Or no longer wants to.

"Yes," I say finally, fighting to emerge from the daze his eyes throw me into.

And that beard.

The male somehow makes facial hair attractive.

I pour his shot and another for myself. He arcs a brow as I pick up the glass but clinks mine before we both knock them back.

"Want to sit?" he says, tapping the bar stool next to his.

It's still just us in the bar.

My aching legs quiver at the suggestion.

"Fine." I duck under the bridge. He's standing again, pulling the chair next to his out for me. I'm hyper aware of his proximity as I sit. He scoots me in, angling my chair slightly toward his, then does the same with his own chair.

"I haven't seen you in a while. Not since—how have you been holding up?" he asks quietly.

Kindly.

It cuts me deep, reaching the places I hadn't let Mila see. And hadn't let myself see, even. Not since that first night. It slashes my heart into a million different pieces.

How can kindness be such a vicious blade?

I shake my head quickly, fighting to keep the tears back.

"Let's talk about something else. Anything else."

He puts a warm hand over mine. The magic flows into me, and my breath deepens as the edge of panic recedes.

"Thanks," I breathe. An involuntary shudder moves through me. He squeezes my hand.

"Do you like dogs?" he asks randomly.

I meet his gaze, confused.

"Of course." I somehow make it sound like an insult.

He fights a smile but nods. "I figured considering your owl friend. You seem to love animals."

"Always have," I admit.

"So when I was a kid, eons ago, we had a family dog named Lucy. She was a sweet dog. A Cavalier. And she *loved* butter. I used to sneak her little pats of it at the table," he says, chuckling. "One time, my parents were out in the garden doing something. I was probably three or four at the time, and I knew where the butter was, so I got some for Lucy. And then I had the inspired idea to just slather it all over her face. And then eventually, the rest of her," he says, laughing.

I fight a smile, picturing it. "Bet your parents were furious."

He grins. "My mother comes in and catches me in the act— Lucy is buttered up like a piece of toast at this point—and she's like 'Evander! What have you done to our poor dog? You're getting a time out for this,'" he says, imitating a feminine voice. He laughs again. "And I just look her square in the eye, at all but four years old, and say '*Fuck you.*' Then I *really* got a time out."

I explode in laughter. He watches me crack up, his eyes admiring, a playful smile still on his lips.

"My father gave me a whooping of course," Evander continues, pouring us both another shot. "It wasn't for Lucy's sake, though.

He always made sure I knew I was wrong to disrespect my mother."

I drag the shot glass toward me. "Really?"

He nods. We clink glasses again and I knock mine back more slowly this time, keeping my eyes fixed on his face.

"How did you end up in the High Guard?" I ask once I finish my shot. I shudder as the alcohol burns my throat.

Evander shrugs. "You're too young to know this, but in the first few centuries of Vilero's rule, the whole culture around males taking female's magic was driven by fear of war with the Shadow Realms. Males were better equipped for battle and many *wanted* to fight—whereas most females did *not* want to fight. Females in the 100s and 200s were somewhat willing to sacrifice their magic if it meant that their fathers and husbands would fight to protect them and their children."

He pauses, pouring us each another shot. I'm feeling the liquor, but I still pull it toward myself.

Evander continues. "That was the narrative they were sold, and most bought into it without questioning it. Or even thinking through the larger implications..."

I hadn't known that.

Could it really have been that easy to convince multiple generations that forcing females to give up their birthright was a *good* thing?

I shudder, already knowing the answer.

Yes, it could be.

Because yes, they did.

I take a small sip of my jad.

Evander's eyes follow my movements. He clears his throat, and then continues.

"I was born in the early 200s—and even then many females weren't opposed to sacrificing their magic for what they viewed as the 'greater good'. At that point, we'd already had two wars with the Shadow Realms, so the threat felt much more imminent."

A small part of me wonders if Vilero hadn't instigated those wars on purpose, just to have a logical reason to push his agenda. And then, over the centuries, he eventually dropped all pretenses.

By that point, he wouldn't have had much opposition even if his reasoning changed. Because taking magic from females would have already become the cultural norm, so much so that resistance would have become futile.

Evander's lips curve into a half smile, his eyes almost apologetic. "I share this because when my parents sent me for training, it was a much different time. It was one thing to want to protect our realms from war—that I could get on board with. I *wanted* to be a part of that, even as a child. That's what drove me to train as hard as I did. I couldn't imagine our people being possessed, haunted, or killed by the filth in the Shadow Realms."

My thoughts unwillingly flit to my mother. "That does sound like a noble reason. Or at least a logical one," I admit. "Why did you end up staying, though? As things changed?"

It was the wrong question to ask. His eyes tighten and he looks away abruptly. I watch his throat bob as he swallows.

"I have my reasons."

My mind jumps to Maybelle. Intuition strikes. "You were telling the truth in the forest, weren't you?" My heart hammers steadily in my chest as I wait for him to respond.

He softens, meeting my gaze again. "I always tell you the truth." And then his face contorts into a wicked grin. "Want me to teach you how to detect lies like a Premonic?"

I stare at him blankly. "I don't have magic, Evander."

Something lights up in his eyes but he quickly shakes his head. "That doesn't matter. You have Premonic in your bloodline—it leaves a trace in your body's signals."

"A trace?" I raise a brow skeptically.

"Like an inkling. A feeling. For me, lies are more like a punch to the gut. It's like alarm bells—not subtle at all. Like when you lied to me about stealing Raven," he says, his eyes twinkling at the memory.

I look at him like he's crazy.

"Want to test it out?" he encourages.

I scoff. "How?"

An evil glint fills his eyes. "I'll tell you three statements, and you tell me if any of them... set off your alarm bells..."

I sigh. "Okay fine. Try me."

He fights a smile. I squirm in my seat as I wait for him to speak.

"I *don't* think about you naked every night before I go to sleep..."

I immediately smack his arm. "Come on!" I can already feel the blush creeping into my cheeks.

"No, you come on! Tell me. Truth—or lie?"

I grimace. "I don't know!"

He smirks. "Listen again. And listen with *your body*. I *don't* think about you naked every night before I go to sleep..."

I close my eyes, if only to stop looking into his taunting ones. I bring my awareness into my body and wait.

"I *don't* think about you naked every night before I go to sleep..." he repeats.

And then I feel it. A twinge of fear, a tightening of my belly. "Lie," I say, eyes still closed. Blush still growing furiously in my face.

"Good! Now what about this one—I promise *never* to lie to you. Truth or lie?"

I keep my eyes closed, keep my awareness inward. Waiting for that twinge, that tug at my gut. But my stomach feels light. Spacious. Open.

"Truth..." I say cautiously, not quite believing myself.

"Correct again! Okay last one... I have an incredibly, *disastrously* small penis."

I burst out laughing at that one, and the tug at my gut is *major*, which has me blushing like crazy again. I open my eyes to glare at him. "I think you're wrong about the whole 'it leaves a trace' thing, because my gut said that one was a *lie*..."

He smirks at me, completely unruffled. Like a male with a massive... "Your body knows the truth, even if your mind can't handle it yet."

"No, I stand by what I said. It can't be accurate." I bite my lip, fighting to keep my attention off the part of *me* that is suddenly... intrigued...

"All jokes aside, use that to your advantage. Just don't tell anyone I told you about it," he says with a crooked smile.

My stomach clenches as I realize the implications of his words. And the implications of the tattoo seared onto the back of my head.

I pour myself another shot, feeling like a horrible person.

He sees my face fall. "What's wrong?"

I force a tight smile. "Nothing." He knows it's a lie, but he doesn't push it.

Instead, he clears his throat, resting a hand on my knee. "Don't you want to ask me about Maybelle one more time? Now that you know how to detect the truth?"

My breath catches. "Did you save Maybelle?" It's barely above a whisper.

"Yes. I did," he says quietly.

I check my gut—it's calm. Open. Spacious.

The truth.

Tears pool unexpectedly in my eyes.

"Good," I say, my voice breaking.

16

The rest of February passes like a blur with too many hours spent working and training. Koa doesn't call us back for any meetings until mid-March, citing a lack of activity with the weapons shipments.

I welcome the delays.

Because I don't want to share a single morsel of information I've gathered about Evander.

I tell myself it's because he's not nearly as bad as I believed. He joined the High Guard to protect the kingdom, and he didn't murder Maybelle. But he also didn't tell me where he took her or what he did with her.

I tell myself that, and yet I know it's not *that* at all.

I'm somehow already too invested.

I don't want to betray him.

Not even to bring down the King.

The thought makes me sick.

The bruises aren't just emotional, either.

Warren's daily training sessions have taken a toll on my body.

I'm building muscle, which is nice, but I'm always wiped by the time I get back from the tavern.

I have gotten better at defending myself, though.

In recent sessions, I've been able to pin *him* down for a change, which is a welcome improvement.

The meeting is in the same room as before, which is located in Parley. Or at least that's what I've been told.

We never go outside, though, so I don't know for sure. Warren always dissolves us directly into the room.

Tonight, Koa is already pacing at the head of the table. Mila sits next to me, anxiously bouncing her legs. Warren sits on my other side, and despite his dark moods, I've come to like his presence. Credo is absent today for some unknown reason, but the rest of the Dissenters from the first meeting are here.

"The latest swap was a success, sir," Paul says the moment Koa lifts his eyes to start the meeting.

Koa nods. "And our network?"

"They're moving them northward as we speak." His jaw twitches as Koa stares him down.

"When's the next shipment?"

Paul runs a hand over his shaved head. "Don't think they're ordering more until April," he says, looking uncomfortable. The whole table tenses.

Koa's lip curls. "That's weeks from now," he complains.

"Sorry, Koa," Paul says with a shrug. "Outta my hands."

Koa's nostrils flare. He begins pacing again, seemingly deep in thought.

I glance at Mila, who looks utterly bored. As if these tantrums are normal.

"Alright. That's a setback. Fiana, what's the latest on Evander?" He meets my gaze.

It's an effort not to shrink under it. "He hasn't spent much time in the tavern the last several weeks, and the few times he's come in we've been busy," I say, shrugging.

Mila shifts in her chair. I force myself not to look at her.

"Nothing?" Koa asks, glancing between me and Mila.

"Nothing of consequence," I say firmly, sitting taller.

His eyes darken a shade. "Then we need to use your talents elsewhere for the time being."

"She's not ready," Warren speaks up. "She still reacts too slowly."

I shoot him a glare.

"I don't care." Koa lifts his chin. "The King's golden dagger is being removed from its vault for inspections and cleaning tomorrow night. This is our best chance to get it before it's locked up for another three months."

"We can wait three months, Koa," Warren says flatly.

Koa clenches his hands in fists. "No. We cannot."

They stare each other down.

"Fine. Then I'm going with her," Warren concedes.

Surprised, I turn to look at him. His face is as expressionless as always.

But I'm touched.

"Fine," Koa says flatly. "You'll need to create a diversion for her anyway. You'll enter through the tunnels. It will be in the antechamber to the vault, which is in the eastern wing of the dungeons. Show Fiana the maps tonight so she can prepare for tomorrow. I've already spoken to Credo—no work for you tomorrow."

My heart flutters in anticipation. "What kind of diversion will you be making?" I say, glancing at Warren.

He shrugs. "You'll see."

Mila is tense on our way back post meeting, but to her credit she waits until Warren dissolves away after bringing us back to Ador.

"Why did you lie about not spending time with Evander?" she

snaps, frustration evident in her tone. "What about that night during Beer Fest last month?"

"It's complicated," I say edgily, cognizant of the fact that we're still on the streets. "We can't talk here."

She rolls her eyes and pulls me by the arm to an apartment building two doors down from the stables.

"This is me. You're coming up so we can talk," she announces as she unlocks the door.

Her unit is on the second floor and is as sparse as mine with one glaring exception. Her walls are covered ceiling to floor with papers, though none of them are art.

They're words.

Poetry, it looks like.

"I write when I'm angry," she says flippantly as my eyes catch on one at eye level near her front door.

sometimes when i first
wake up in the morning
i feel like i might
actually
be

dead

and then
after a cup of coffee
and careful consideration
i realize i might
actually
be okay

at least
until the end of the

cup

or
if i'm lucky
until the end of the
next

I fight a smile as I meet Mila's eyes again. "These are really good."

She shrugs, nonplussed. "We're not here to talk about me," she complains. "You lied," she says again, prompting me.

"It's true that I didn't learn anything of consequence, though," I explain. "He just talked about silly things, like having a dog growing up and getting in trouble with his parents."

"You should still tell Koa everything you know," she counters. "Why didn't you?"

I repress a sigh. "Because Koa hasn't proven himself trustworthy to me yet."

"I trust him—isn't that enough?" She crosses her arms.

I shake my head. "No, sorry."

She groans. "Why do you have to be so difficult about all of this?"

"Why do you want me to just fall in line?" I counter.

She appraises me for a beat before sitting at her small kitchen table. She gestures to the open chair and waits until I sit to speak.

"When my father died, it's because he was captured by the Guard on one of his missions. His mental shields were exceptional, so the Dissenter network remained hidden. But no one can hide their own daughter in their mind."

My pulse quickens as I watch Mila's face contort with rage.

"It was going to be a public execution just like my mother's, so the King could make an example of me. But Koa stayed with me until they arrived and wiped all their memories of the King's orders before they even had a chance to read my arrest warrant. Then he went back to the castle and did the same to the King and the whole Guard."

"And it worked?"

Could Koa really be that powerful?

Mila shrugs. "I'm still here, aren't I?"

My stomach turns. "Did he wipe Evander's memory too?"

"No," Mila sighs. "He was on leave at the time, and his mental shields are really strong according to Koa."

"So Evander might know that you were meant to be executed?" My chest tightens as anxiety surges through me.

Mila shrugs. "It seems unlikely considering I'm still here and his proclivity for killing innocent females, but we don't know. That's another reason why we want you to get close to him. He hasn't tried anything against me in the years since, but what if he's been watching me this whole time? He certainly comes to the tavern a lot. What if he somehow knows about the Dissenters and has been building a case against us, and we're all just sitting ducks?"

Her fears are valid given what she knows about him, and a part of me wants to tell her about all that he knows about me, and how he didn't take advantage of me the night I learned my father died.

But I don't.

"None of your plants were able to find out anything?" I ask instead, tempted to grill her about all the females he's been with in the tavern.

"No," she says, leaning back in her chair and crossing her arms over her chest.

"But you said before, that they were his immortal females..." I press.

She snorts. "I was trying to protect you. Steer you away from a male who looks rich and handsome and powerful on the surface, but is really a monster underneath."

"Right," I breathe, remembering that she still thinks he killed Maybelle.

She stares at me for a long moment. "You know you can tell me anything, right?"

I tense. "Sure," I say quickly, fighting to keep the guilt off my face.

She sighs, sensing my hesitation. "I'm your friend, Fiana. I know I kept my distance in the beginning and said some horrible things when you were still deciding to join us, and I deeply regret that."

"I know," I say quietly, averting my eyes.

"And I get the feeling you're not used to trusting people," she goes on. "But you don't have to shoulder everything alone. And if there's something you want me to keep to myself—" she sighs, and it seems like she's deliberating. "I'll do it."

I lift my eyes. She looks sincere.

"Thanks for saying that."

"So is there something you want to get off your chest?" Mila prompts.

I shake my head.

She sighs, clearly disappointed. "Do I need to worry about you with Evander?"

I meet her hazel eyes and let out a silent exhale.

"I promised to help you bring down the King," I say, hoping she won't force the issue. "And I will."

Later that night, there's two hard knocks on my door. I let Warren in. He's dressed in his typical black shirt and pants. There's snowmelt staining his shoulders, his black hair is pulled into a low bun at the nape of his neck, and his green-blue eyes look blank and lifeless.

"Thanks for agreeing to come with me," I say as he glances around my apartment. He notes the stolen table, the contraband potions, and the snowy owl perched by my window.

"Sure," he says, spreading a map out on my table. He sits, then lifts his eyes to mine. I sit too.

"The golden dagger is kept here," he points his index finger to a small square vault at the eastern corner of the dungeons. "This tunnel here," he drags his finger across the map, "connects to the jail. It will be empty. This tunnel here," he drags his finger down a tunnel that leads down to another, deeper one. "Leads out of the castle."

"Seems simple enough," I remark.

"From what I've seen, you'll do fine," he says. "We have this," he pulls a sheathed golden dagger out of the waistband of his pants and places it on the table. "It's a perfect replica, less the magic of the true golden dagger. I'll create a diversion that will draw the cleaners away, and then you'll swap 'em. Don't get 'em confused," he says, his eyes stern.

I take the knife. "I won't. What happens if someone sees me?"

"We'll shield you. And you could take some of that essence of repulsion you've got over there," he says, a hint of a smile playing at the corners of his lips. "So it shouldn't be an issue."

I fight a sheepish grin. "Right."

He stares at me for a moment before clearing his throat. "Now that we've gotten the logistics out of the way, you want to tell me what was going on between you and Mila at the meeting?" He lifts a black brow.

I swallow, and my throat feels tight. "Mila believes I should have shared more about Evander, but she was wrong. There's nothing to share that will help us kill the King."

Warren stares at me, his face immovable as stone.

"I can tell you're not lying, but I can also tell that isn't the whole truth," he says finally.

"If it's not relevant to killing the King, I don't see why I have to share it with anyone," I say, shrugging.

"Hmm," he says, pushing up his sleeves.

There's another long silence as we stare at each other.

"Are we done here?" I prompt when he doesn't speak for several moments.

"One more thing," he says, gathering up the maps and tucking them somewhere in The Ether. He gets to his feet and heads to the door, before whirling around to look at me. "I'm going out on a limb for you by training you and coming with you on this mission. I've stood up for you behind closed doors with Koa, and you've seen me stand up for you at other times, too."

My chest tightens. "Yes."

"I have this feeling," he says, and there's an edge of emotion in his voice. "Call it a hunch. I just think that one day you're going to fuck us all over." I start to speak but he holds his hand up to stop me. "Except I don't think it will be for the wrong reasons. And so if that day comes," he says, lowering his head so we're eye to eye. "I want you to remember that I've been sticking up for you."

My heart feels heavy in my chest. I nod once.

"And I want you to give me a chance to be on your side—as you've seen me be—before you decide that I'm your enemy."

I swallow thickly. "That sounds fair." My voice is rough.

He nods once then turns around. "It is." He opens the door. "See you tomorrow, Willowbark."

It's the next night. Warren points out the opening into the tunnels, hidden under a small overhang blanketed in snow. I pull out the vial of essence of repulsion and down two gulps of it. Enough for an hour.

Warren stares at me as the potion takes effect.

"Good. I'm going to shield you, too," he whispers, and I feel the heat of his magic snaking over my skin.

It's an optical illusion; I'm not entirely invisible. Energy just barely cloaks me from view, though my shoes are fully exposed. A necessary risk, because if I touch anyone or anything hard enough, it will break the energy seal and disrupt the integrity of the entire shield.

It's impossible to not touch the ground, though.

"Go in quick, wait for the diversion, swap the daggers, then get the hell out," he instructs.

I nod once. It's the *get the hell out* part I'm most worried about, but I keep that to myself.

On the way in, I can lie through my teeth any number of ways if I get caught. On the way out, with the King's golden dagger on me —not so much.

Warren nods once at me, encouraging me to get moving.

I take a deep breath then carefully creep across the open space to the tunnel's entrance.

Once I'm inside, it feels eerily similar to my midnight treks through The Cave. That relaxes me slightly as I make my way deep underneath the castle. I'd broken in tons of times and never gotten caught.

Only Evander has ever been able to catch me.

I wonder briefly to myself what he might do if he catches me this time. It sends a shiver down my spine.

I can't tell if it's a thrill or fear that drives it.

Perhaps with him, I enjoy getting caught.

He's lulled me into a sense of safety. One that naturally has me wanting to test his limits.

Because it's clear to me that his loyalty is not with the King, despite his post.

Despite his masks.

But where exactly *do* his loyalties lie? That part is still unclear.

I make a left at the first fork in the tunnels and freeze—torch-light is visible up ahead. I wait an agonizing thirty-five seconds until it disappears from view, down another passageway.

I keep walking, careful not to bump into the cavern walls and disrupt my shield.

I make it to the second fork—a right this time based on the

map. The path starts sloping upward as my heart pounds against my ribs. Pretty soon, I will no longer have the dark to comfort me.

I curse under my breath as I climb the stairs and approach a trap door, which is squarely shut. I could attempt to kick it open, but the angle makes it difficult. I'm not sure if I can get my foot that high without falling backwards.

I could try a light touch with my fingertips and hope my shield doesn't break. But if I'm wrong...

I let out a breath and try working my foot up. All I need is one good kick.

I strike upward with my foot and the trap door flies open, streaming light into the tunnel and crashing with a *clank* against the stone floors above. I cringe at the sound.

I pause for thirty seconds, hear nothing, and creep up the final steps into the dungeons.

There aren't any prisoners kept here anymore, but I still feel like the cells are full of watchful eyes as I snake my way through the maze of iron bars.

My breathing is shallow and much too loud, but so far I haven't encountered anyone since the torchlight down in the tunnels. I forge ahead, wondering exactly how I'll know that Warren has done his diversion.

I round the corner at the last pair of cells and stop short, holding my breath.

Less than twenty feet away, Nasgardo has his hands all over a dark haired female. She's pressed against the wall, her face hidden by the shadows, but her voice strikes me as oddly familiar.

"You know I love you, it's not that," she says quietly.

"I can't keep sharing you with him," he groans.

"That's not your choice to make," she admonishes. She grabs his chin and pulls his eyes down to meet hers. "All I want—all *we* want—is for me to have more freedoms. I don't want to leave him. I love him, too."

Nasgardo sighs, and I can't believe my eyes.

He's really *submitting* to this female.

"All we need is for you to gain a bit more favor with our *friends*," she says, the last word seemingly loaded with deeper meaning.

"I'm working on that," Nasgardo gripes. "I've *been* working on that."

She strokes his cheek. "I know my love. But they're not happy about your recent foibles."

"That's not my fault and you know it," Nasgardo counters. "But I hear you, and I'll keep working on it." He steals a kiss, but she pushes him away.

"Just take out this Fiana Willowbark and be done with it. We don't have time for distractions," she hisses.

I force a silent breath as panic jolts through me. My mind flits to the doe and the rabbit.

Are their 'friends' the Shadow Realm demons?

"No," Nasgardo says firmly, and my invisible eyes widen in shock. There's even an edge of fear in his tone.

"Why? Because of this Evander?" she snorts. "Kill him too, if you must. He can't be that big of a threat to you. Or convince him she's a threat to the King."

"That won't work," he argues.

"Why not?" she demands.

He sighs, shaking his head. "Just trust me. It won't. Besides, I don't want to."

"Kill him?" she asks.

"Kill her," he clarifies.

I stifle a gasp.

Where is the Nasgardo that had his dick out on the bar? That shoved it in my face? That wanted to bind me to him forever?

Why *wouldn't* he want to kill me?

"You're weak," she says, pushing him away. If she pushes her hair back from this angle, I might be able to see her face.

Just then an earsplitting *crash* echoes through the tunnels, coming from the western corner of the castle. It sounds like an entire tower is collapsing, and the structure shakes as both the female and Nasgardo whip their heads in the direction of the sound.

"I need to get you back," Nasgardo shouts. They dissolve away before the female has a chance to respond.

I sprint down the tunnel, skidding to a stop as I see the cleaners scrambling out of the vault. I glance down, and I'm still invisible, so I stay frozen in place while they race down the opposite hall and up the stone staircase.

I sprint the last of the way, seeing the golden dagger perched on its stand, centered on a tall table in the middle of the vault.

I glance down the two tunnels that intersect at the vault, knowing the second I grab this thing my shield will disintegrate, though the potion will still keep me somewhat faceless.

No movement. No torchlight.

As good as it's going to get.

I grab the dagger and its golden sheath, tucking it into the waistband of my pants and putting the forgery in its place.

I'm fully visible now, so I haul ass back the way I came, sprinting through the torchlit section, the empty prison cells, and toward the trap door. I seal it shut and let out a relieved exhale before jogging down the stairs and through the forking tunnels.

I make it to the entrance and squint through the darkness. No Guards in view, but there's another intense *crash* that shakes the whole building.

Guess Warren is putting his Havoc magic to good use.

I race across the open space with my hood up, pausing in the trees where Warren is supposed to meet me.

I wait sixty seconds but then start to get nervous as Guards start rounding the corners and patrolling the grounds again.

Sorry, Warren, I think as I back my way down the mountain.

He dissolves right in front of me the moment I think his name and grabs my arm, dissolving us both away to our escape.

We land outside of my apartment building and I quickly open

the front door and move inside, holding it open for Warren to join me.

"Get upstairs," he says, backing away from the door.

"Don't you want—?"

"I might get visited by the Guard tonight so no, you keep it. Give it to Koa at the meeting tomorrow," he whispers tensely, pulling the door shut.

I give him a wave, feeling guilty that I almost left him there. Especially after our conversation last night.

He waves back, eyes pained and blank as usual, before dissolving away. The snow swirls around the space where he disappears.

I hesitate for a second, my stomach knotting as the horrible thought occurs to me that this could all be a set up.

I shake my head, unwilling to entertain that thought further and race up the stairs to my unit.

17

I crash as soon as I get in bed, and the sleep feels heavy and comforting after my long night. It's a dreamless sleep. True blissful unconsciousness.

So when there's a pounding at my door, my heart jumps into my throat as I startle awake.

Haldric hisses from his perch by the window, shooting me an apprehensive look as I grab the golden dagger off the kitchen table and approach the door.

"Open the damn door, Fiana," Evander growls from the other side. "Before I reduce it to a pile of splinters," he adds in a lower voice.

"Why the hell are you here at—" I glance at the clock, "five in the morning?"

"Take a wild fucking guess," he says, and my mouth runs dry. He lets out a forceful exhale. "I'm here unofficially. Just let me in."

"Unofficially," I whisper. I open the door, keeping the dagger hidden behind it. "You *know*?"

He looks at me like I'm stupid and pushes his way in.

"Your scent is unmistakable," he says.

"To you or to everyone else?" I ask.

He stares at my unmade bed for a moment before turning back to face me. "What do *you* think?"

My breath catches as his gaze meets mine, then flickers downward. He notices the scrap of lace I'm wearing and my body heats under his wandering gaze. Then it drifts to the hand that's still gripping my contraband.

Too late to pretend I don't have it. Shit.

He snorts, his eyes unreadable. He starts scratching his beard, eyes a million miles away. Eventually, he shakes his head, as if to clear it.

And then he *sits* on my *bed*. He leans back on his hands, staring at me.

"I don't remember inviting you to sit," I growl.

"Considering you're holding one of the King's most prized possessions in those thieving little hands of yours, I'd suggest you rethink your attitude," he counters, raising a dark brow.

On my *bed*.

"So what, you want me to fuck you to get myself out of this?" I accuse.

He throws his head back in raucous laughter. "Oh trust me, I want you to fuck me. But I don't do sexual blackmail so keep your panties on for now." His eyes drop to the hem of my night gown. "That is, if you're even wearing any..."

An ache erupts between my thighs at the same time embarrassment heats my cheeks.

He's always catching me in compromising positions, and yet he never takes advantage of them.

I bite my lip. "So what's my punishment then? Are you going to take the dagger back?"

He snorts, lying back on my bed, dangling his feet off the edge and resting his head on my pillow. He folds his hands over his stomach.

Like he fucking owns the place.

"Well?" I urge, crossing my arms over my chest, the golden dagger sticking out underneath my arm.

He inhales deeply, closing his eyes. "If I take it back, you'll just steal it again."

I cock a brow. "So you're going to let me keep it?"

His eyes open a sliver. "For now."

I exhale in relief, putting the dagger back on my kitchen table. Haldric eyes me suspiciously, but doesn't make a sound.

Evander is still laying in my bed. Fully clothed and yet visibly relaxed. I stare at him for several seconds, waiting for him to say something else.

He doesn't.

"So why are you here then?" I grab a sweater from my wardrobe and slip it on over my night gown.

He sighs, but doesn't open his eyes. "I'm trying to decide what to do with you."

My lower half suddenly feels far too exposed. I hastily grab a pair of leggings and slide them on before I do something stupid.

Like mount him right there on my bed.

He's still just lying there.

And I'm getting impatient.

"Can't you decide what to do with me in your own bed?" I suggest.

He grins, and opens his eyes a sliver again. "Aw, you changed. Such a damn shame." He folds his hands behind his head, opening his eyes fully now. "Here's the thing, Fiana. I need you to stop sneaking into places where you shouldn't be, and taking things you shouldn't have. I can't keep covering your tracks. People will start to notice."

I snort. "I never asked you to cover my tracks."

He crosses one ankle over the other, still a picture of ease.

In *my* bed.

"Even so, I have to. And I'm risking a lot every time I do." His expression grows serious. "And so are you."

I'm past impatience. I'm annoyed. "Why *are* you covering my tracks? Clearly you're protecting me for some reason. So what the hell is it?"

Tell me something real.

He narrows his eyes at me. "For the same reason you stole *that* particular dagger." He jerks his chin toward my kitchen table.

My mind goes blank. Koa and Warren never explained *why* the Dissenters need it. My heart starts racing as I wonder if Mila was right and Evander already knows all about the Dissenters.

He watches me process and when I don't respond he lets out a short laugh. "Don't tell me you don't know what that's for." He raises his brows.

I swallow thickly. "No," I admit. "What's it for?"

He jerks to a seated position, eyes blazing with incredulity. "You're telling me you snuck into the King's palace and stole *that* exact dagger and you don't even know *why?*"

I shrug, but don't say anything.

Awareness dawns on him. "You didn't steal it for yourself, did you?"

My heart starts sprinting. He'll know if I'm lying.

"I stole it because it's obviously valuable. Just because I don't know *why* it's valuable doesn't mean I don't know that it is," I say quickly. "But *you* obviously do. So why don't you help a thief out and tell me?"

He launches to his feet. "No way. She's clueless!" he says with a shocked look at Haldric, who clicks his beak in response.

"*Excuse* me?" I gasp, advancing a step toward him. "You do *not* insult me in my own home after lying in *my* bed to *my* fucking pet!"

He crosses the short distance between us in a split second, gripping the back of my neck, staring me down with steely eyes. My breath grows shallow as he lowers his face just inches away from mine. I catch a hint of spearmint on his breath combining with the delicious woodsy scent of his skin.

"Do us both a favor and don't give that to whomever you stole it for. Keep it under lock and key. Tell them that you failed. I'll ward your home against Possessic magic for now, and we'll figure out what to do with it later. Do we have an understanding?"

My body is hyper aware of how close he is to me. His lips, his chest, his hips. They radiate heat and invite me closer. My body starts leaning toward him of its own accord.

I take a deep breath, trying to focus. There's no lying to him— he'll know it if I do.

But I also don't want to let the Dissenters down.

"I can't do that," I confess. "Not unless you tell me *why* I need to do it your way."

His jaw drops a centimeter, his eyes disbelieving. "You really don't know," he murmurs.

He's too close to me. The heat of his breath warms my lips. And I can't breathe.

He shuts his eyes, and for a second I think he's going to kiss me.

"That dagger is one of a kind. It's used for a specific purpose, one that no other dagger can be used for." He opens his eyes again. "Is that enough of an explanation for you to do as I say?"

His ocean eyes hold my gaze. There's no pretending in front of him now.

"No. It's not," I admit, taking a shaky breath.

He's frustrated. I can feel it in the way his body tenses. He pulls me closer, bringing my ear to his lips. He whispers, sending chills down my back, and it's an effort to keep my wits about me.

"That specific purpose—it's one the King would level entire cities for. You give that to the wrong person and the entire Kingdom is at risk." He pulls back to look into my eyes. "Are you willing to risk the entire Kingdom? Or will you do as I say?"

He's got me there.

"If it's that important, why don't you just take it back?" I suggest. Suddenly having it in my possession feels like *way* more than I bargained for.

"The Guard is warded against touching it. The King takes many precautions with the ones closest to him," he says, as his eyes go bleak.

I let out a ragged sigh. "I will keep it for a few days. After that, no promises," I say truthfully.

He stares at me for a long moment.

His gaze lowers to my mouth. My heart jumps.

"Would you have fucked me to get out of trouble?" he asks with hooded eyes. A jolt of pleasure hits my core.

My lips part. "N-no."

He grins. "You are such a liar."

He moves the hand at my neck around to cup my cheek. His thumb grazes over the flesh of my bottom lip. My breath is all steam, and my pulse runs wild.

His voice is low and guttural. "When you fuck me for the first time, it's going to be because you *need* me. And I don't mean need me to get yourself out of trouble."

I gasp as his other arm snares around my waist, pulling me flush against the length of his body.

His hard, warm, insanely muscular body.

"You will need me like you need oxygen. The need will consume every cell of your being. It will keep you up at night and torment you all day. Until your lips, your skin, and every little bit of you is aching and craving and *begging* for the feel of me. Then— and only then—will you get the chance to fuck me."

He releases me then and I stumble back, my chest heaving with chaotic breath.

His smile is deadly as he backs toward the door. "Get some rest, Fiana. I'll ward your home from outside."

He leaves then, gently shutting the door behind himself. I collapse on my bed as I feel his magic seep into my space. A scent of palo santo and smoke envelopes me as I pull the covers over my head.

His scent. He's all over this damn bed.

I groan because now I know *exactly* why he laid here. I inhale deeply, my core already tensing with senseless need. I kick my leggings off and rip off my sweater. The nightgown comes off too.

I close my eyes and slide my hand between my thighs, gasping the moment my fingers make contact. My flesh is so sensitive, so heated.

It fucking aches.

I need friction, now.

I give my body the touches I wish were coming from him, my feet tangling in my sheets as pleasure ripples through me.

Once, my back arches.

Twice, my toes curl.

As I catch my breath, I know I'm done for.

Because I make myself climax six times just breathing in his scent.

And I'm nowhere close to feeling satisfied.

18

I meet Warren and Mila at the edge of town for our next Dissenters meeting. By the way Warren looks at me, I feel like my betrayal is branded on my forehead.

I don't have the dagger with me.

I'm still not giving them a speck of intel on Evander.

And I spent the better part of five a.m. writhing in pleasure at the thought of the male I'm supposed to be undermining.

It's dangerous territory considering the binding I've agreed to. The one tattooed on the back of my head—the one that can take my life if I step too far out of bounds.

But I *can* conceive of a reality where Evander might not be a hindrance to our efforts.

He could be an asset.

That's what I've convinced myself of, at least.

It might be wishful thinking considering my new... proclivities. But I refuse to betray the male who's earned my trust for the past five months without knowing his whole story.

We are all silent as he dissolves us to the meeting.

The room is empty except for the three of us and Koa. I glance at Mila nervously, but she seems unsurprised.

"The dagger, Fiana?" Koa immediately asks.

I glance at Warren, who looks bored.

Here goes nothing.

"I need to know what it's used for before I give it up," I say calmly, keeping my back straight as a rod.

Koa stares at me blankly, his lip curling. "You don't have it with you?" The fire crackles loudly behind him, bathing the room in a warm red glow.

"Tell me what it's used for, and I'll give it to you at the next meeting," I say firmly. That gives me time to check with Evander on whether that's a good idea, too.

"No. We're going back to your apartment right now," he hisses, coming around the table with an arm outstretched. I back up, circling around to the other side of the table as he pursues me.

"I have a right to know what it's used for. I'm part of this resistance," I argue, pulling my dagger out of my thigh sheath.

Koa keeps advancing. "You aren't part of *anything*. You are our resident thief and whore, whose sole purpose is to steal what we tell you to and to gain intel on Evander by opening your fucking legs. You are not here to *think* or to *know* a damn thing!"

"Koa! That's enough," Warren growls, moving his body between Koa and me. "What the hell is your problem?"

"My *problem* is that you and Credo screwed up with the binding on this one! We want *obedience* in the Dissenters," he argues.

"No, Koa. We don't—and you damn well know that. Or you used to." Warren grabs Mila's arm and backs up, grabbing mine. "And until you get your head on straight, consider the three of us—and Credo—out."

He dissolves us back to the forests of Ador with a *crack*. We're miles away from the village, I notice. Presumably to talk freely.

"Damnit, Fiana—what the hell was that?" he asks the moment we're back.

My breath is coming too fast. "Evander caught me last night," I say. Koa I don't trust for a second, but Warren and Mila have earned my confidence.

"He did?" Mila's eyes widen. "Why didn't you say anything before?"

"Because he's not evil like you all think. He's caught me several times before—when I broke into The Cave. When I've stolen other things here in the village. He never turns me in." I sheath my dagger. "But I don't trust Koa. And based on what we just witnessed, I don't think you guys should trust him either."

"I've never seen him act like that," Warren admits quietly.

"This is supposed to be a rebellion for female rights and yet that's the nastiest thing a male has ever said to me," I say. "I know you've known him for decades, and I know he saved your life, Mila. But I don't trust him."

Warren's brow furrows. "He was different in the early days. That's why we agreed to follow him in the first place," he explains.

"I thought Mila's father was the leader before?" I say, glancing in her direction.

She sighs. "He was, but Koa always had a leadership role as well, right?" She looks to Warren.

"Yes, always. He just preferred someone else being the face of leadership. He thought others would be better to inspire the Dissenters into action, all while he pulled the strings behind the scenes. But when your father died—he immediately stepped up." Warren rakes his hands through his long black hair. "This isn't good."

"Are you both bound to do everything he says?" I say, my heart racing in my chest.

Mila shakes her head, looking puzzled. "No, we're bound to taking down the King."

"Then why did he want *me* to be obedient?" I snap, looking at Warren. "What's different about me?"

Warren looks at me and sighs. "Koa thinks there's something

unique about you. That you're more connected to the King than the rest of us somehow."

"Why would he think that?" I demand.

Warren shrugs. "He wouldn't say." I quickly check my gut at that. It's the truth.

I scoff. "What a fucking mess."

"Why do you think Evander hasn't turned you in? Could that have something to do with what Koa thinks?" Mila wonders.

I shrug, blush creeping into my cheeks. "It could be just because he wants to sleep with me." But a part of me knows that's not the whole story. "There's more about Evander—something I cannot share with anyone. Something that makes me think he might somehow be on our side."

"On *our* side?" Warren says with deep skepticism. "I worked with him in the 540s. The male is ruthlessly committed to the King's causes. He volunteers to execute the child every time a girl comes in with illegal magic."

I swallow thickly, holding back the urge to tell them about Maybelle. "I'm telling you, there's something about him that makes me think differently."

Warren stares me down for a long moment. Finally, he nods.

"I believe you," he says.

Mila lets out a forceful exhale. "What the hell are we going to do about Koa? And the rest of the Dissenters?"

Warren scratches his forehead. "Credo may have some thoughts. We should get to him before Koa does." He holds out an arm for each of us, and we dissolve into Credo's office directly.

Credo jumps out of his chair with a start, his sudden movement making the floors shake. "What the hell?"

"Sorry to intrude, but it's an emergency," Warren says, leaning against the door and crossing his arms over his chest. He nods his head toward Mila, encouraging her to fill in the rest.

Mila sighs and goes to sit on the couch. "Koa lost it on Fiana. Got super disrespectful. And—Evander knows Fiana took the dagger," Mila says, darting her eyes between Credo and me. "And Fiana didn't give the dagger to Koa, so he snapped. So then Warren got us out of there and said we were out."

Credo blows out a whistle, smoothing his wiry grey beard. He thinks for a moment, looking at me with curious eyes.

"Evander didn't take the dagger back, though?" he asks, his forehead creased.

I shake my head.

"Oh yeah—and Fiana thinks Evander might be on our side somehow, but she won't say how," Mila adds, turning her gaze on me while arching a brow.

"Hmm," Credo says, settling back into his chair. I back up and lean against the wall behind me, so all three of them are in view. We wait as Credo processes everything.

"I have wondered about Evander," he says finally. "Especially after he started tipping you," he adds, pointing a thick finger at me across the room. "He didn't slow down ever, did he?"

"No. He didn't," I admit. The giant stack of cash under my mattress right now is proof of that.

"But you don't trust Evander," Credo says, pointing the finger at Warren now.

"He was an asshole in the Guard," Warren grumbles. "Tore out our throats every other week if we didn't obey everything he said, or if we gave him any sort of attitude. And he stood by and watched Lorina—" He clears his throat and looks at the ground.

"And he kills the kids—right?" Credo presses, his tone more gentle.

Warren nods.

I want to say something, but I hold my tongue.

"How does he kill them? Is it vicious? Or quick?" Credo asks.

My heart pounds unsteadily. I press my lips together tight.

Warren shrugs, rubbing his eyes with his fists. "Never saw him do it. He takes 'em to the forest and brings back the ashes."

The room is silent for a beat. I blow out a silent exhale.

"So it could be that he does it quick. He's a Curic, too. What if he anesthetizes them? He wouldn't want to do that in front of the King," Credo muses.

I cross an ankle over the other, biting my lip.

"I never thought of that as a possibility," Warren admits. He turns to me. "You trust him?"

"I've had to," I explain. "He's caught me breaking the law three or four times already. He even caught me in The Cave and rushed me out before someone else found me."

Mila's jaw drops. "He caught you *in* The Cave? Not just on your way out?"

"He rushed you out?" Warren adds, eyes incredulous.

I nod once. "Yes. At immortal speed no less."

"That doesn't sound like the Evander you know, Warren," Credo points out.

"No. It definitely doesn't," Warren agrees. "But he's the lead of the High Guard. We can't exactly bring him into our meetings."

"I thought we weren't going to meetings anymore," Mila counters.

"Even so, Warren has a point," Credo says. He studies me. "You need to get closer to him. Find out what's real and what's fake."

I let out a breath. "I will."

"What about the dagger?" Mila asks.

"Evander warded my home—I imagine it's safe there?" I supply.

Credo thinks for a moment, then nods. "Should be. It's curious that he didn't take it back, isn't it?"

Warren shakes his head. "No, it's not. That thing is warded against the Guard."

Credo raises a thick grey brow. "Is it, now?"

"What's it for, anyway?" I ask, looking between Warren and Credo.

Their eyes meet for an infinite moment and then Credo nods once.

Warren is the one who answers. "It's for killing the King."

Mila is tense during our shift that night. She keeps looking at the door with anxious eyes as if she expects Koa to come storming in to attack us.

Or maybe it's Evander she's worried about.

I'm on edge too, but for an entirely different reason.

Calimo is back at the bar.

I catch him staring at me every now and again, but he doesn't try to talk to me, and Mila handles his orders.

At least until she gets cut at eleven.

It really sucks being the closer sometimes.

"Can I get you another?" I say to him after seeing him swirl his ice in an otherwise empty glass for the past ten minutes.

"Sure. Thanks, Fiana," he says.

I pour him a double shot on ice and slide him the glass.

He takes a long drink then pulls out a pipe and starts packing it with tobacco.

"You smoke?" I lift a brow.

"When the mood strikes," he grumbles.

Ugh. I'm getting sucked in, I can feel it. I bite my lip, forcing myself to keep my mouth sealed shut.

He lights up, takes a drag, and blows smoke directly in my direction. I cough, backing away from the cloud, glaring at him.

"That's fucking rude," I snap.

He snorts, pushing his black hair back away from his eyes.

"So is breaking up with someone without giving them a chance to explain," he retorts.

A peal of laughter echoes from the back tables. I glance back there then refocus on Calimo.

"Why'd you do it? Why not give me a chance to fall for you without using magic on me?" I ask.

Calimo takes another pull on his pipe then exhales, blowing the smoke up this time.

"Would you have?" he sneers. "Think I don't see how you look at Evander?"

I shake my head. "I wasn't interested in him when you asked me out."

He pulls on his pipe again. "And now?" he says as smoke flows out of his mouth.

I shrug. "I don't know."

He kicks his boot against the bar. "It's okay, I'm used to it. Dear old dad prefers him, too." He knocks back the rest of his jad.

"Did something happen with your father tonight?" I take his glass and refill it.

"What do you care?" he snaps, tapping his pipe once against the bar, his magic instantly snuffing it out.

I stare at the pipe, watching the remaining smoke evaporate.

"Your father is hated by far more people than just you, Calimo." I raise my eyes to meet his. "Surely you must know I empathize with you even if I don't want to sleep with you anymore."

He studies me, and a calculating look comes across his features. It makes my stomach tense.

"You were supposed to be my ticket back into his good graces," he admits.

My heart races. "Why?"

"Give me another chance and I'll tell you," he says, leaning across the bar. "We were good together."

I back up out of his reach. "It was a lie, Calimo."

"Not all of it was. Not on my end," he admits.

I shake my head. "No."

He laughs without humor, tucking his pipe back into his cloak pocket. He gulps down the rest of his drink, placing a few notes on the bar as he stands up.

"The irony is, Evander is probably using you for the same reason I was," he says as he heads toward the door.

"What's that?" I snap.

He glances at me over his shoulder at the door, hesitating.

"Give me another chance and I'll tell you," he repeats.

I shake my head again as rage builds underneath my skin.

"Tell me and I'll consider giving you another chance," I counter, pushing up my long sleeves as the anger makes me feel too hot.

He laughs, wiping liquid from his eyes. "I'm not Premonic and even I know that's a lie." He opens the door, pausing halfway out. "If you keep swimming in the deep end, Fiana, one day you're going to drown."

"What the hell does that mean?" I call after him.

But he's gone.

19

I dream of Calimo that night. It comes out that he never did any Hypnotic magic on me. It was all an illusion, and Evander was the one who tricked me.

I run away from him, disgusted by his trick, and run right into Calimo's waiting arms.

And the makeup sex makes my head spin.

His hands are clutching my hands, pressing them against the bed as he drives into me on a deliciously slow rhythm. I open up to him, our bodies becoming one, tangling together in twisted sheets as we both glisten with sweat.

Sweat that seems to get wetter by the minute... as *I* get wetter by the minute. It soaks both our hair, soaks the bed itself. It's dirty and wild and I love every second of it. And then he pulls out of me, twisting me around, his lips finding the spot he just left as his legs straddle my face, his rock hard shaft taunting me.

I take him into my mouth, relishing the taste of *me* layered with the taste of *him* as his tongue edges me closer... and closer.

He drives his shaft down into my mouth now. Harder... harder...

Too hard now as I struggle to breathe, my chest feeling

restricted by his heavy body, my mouth still full of him. I try hitting him, to signal he needs to back off, but he's too heavy, too wet, too slippery, not even solid, really... my blows go right through him.

I struggle to breathe, even struggle to scream as his body continues to suffocate me. I reach for a way to get him off me, my hands running helplessly through him, like he's made of water.

My eyes fly open then and I realize I am *under water*. My apartment is completely flooded, papers and pens and lacy lingerie and teabags floating, while my furniture is in complete disarray on the ground.

Chairs are toppled over. My bookcase is feet from where it should be. Books are scattered everywhere. My bedside table is so lightweight and cheap that the base of it floats ever so slightly off the ground.

Everything is out of place in a giant fish-tank of death, save for the bed and the iron table.

I hurriedly swim to the table, pushing up off it and gasping as oxygen finally hits my lungs, my face a mere two feet from the ceiling as water continues to fill the room from some unknown source.

I cough and splutter, trying to get the water out of my chest. Taking desperate breaths as the water level rises another inch.

Haldric is yelping, flapping his wings frantically, trying to keep himself out of the water.

I take a huge gulp of air then swim to the door, forcing the lock open and pulling it toward me with all my might—pulling and pulling, though it won't budge.

I dig my heels into the wall next to the door, pushing with all of my force against it as I continue to pull on the door. Nothing happens, and I'm out of air.

I give up on that and push back up toward the top, taking a quick breath and then diving back under to try the window. I grab a frying pan off the ground on my way, ramming it against the glass, and then feel searing aches in my shoulders as it rebounds back, though slowly because of the water.

The window remains unbroken.

Panic rises within me as I hit the window again.

And again. And *again*.

Not so much as a crack. I shoot back up to the top with only a foot left to take a breath now. Haldric is flying in frantic circles, fighting to stay above the water line. I dive back under to try the other window, not really believing it will be different, but trying it all the same.

I let go of the frying pan finally and it sinks slowly to the ground. I swim back to the table and push off to gather another breath. Haldric is partially submerged now, flapping toward me unskillfully, trying to keep his head above water.

I swim to him, pulling him under with me and diving for the fireplace. He thrashes violently in my arms as his head goes under, scraping at my skin. I quickly make it to the chimney, thrusting him up above the water level toward the sky above.

He flaps as he clears the water line, and I can hear the muffled sound of his yelps from under water. I kick my legs, pushing against the sooty walls of the chimney with my hands. I get halfway up then the chimney narrows, and I'm forced to use my feet to keep climbing. I suck in breath the second my head clears, but the opening is too narrow for my shoulders to go any further.

Haldric gives me a look of pure panic. Like he doesn't want to leave me.

"Just go," I insist, my voice breathless as the water rises another inch. "I'll find my way out."

He gives me one more look then bolts away in a mad dash, water dripping from his wings as he flees. I can't get high enough to see where he goes, so the second he's out of view, I force my way back down the chimney.

I'm back in the main room now, pushing off the table to gather another breath. The water is only a few inches from the top.

I breathe, pulling on the beams to keep myself up, my nose pressed tight against the ceiling. My panic intensifies as tears stream down my soaking wet face.

Adding more water to my eventual tomb.

Please don't let me die this way, I beg silently. Using my old mind trick as a salve for hysteria. *Please help me find a way out of this. Please.*

The water reaches the top now and I reluctantly release the beams, letting myself float.

Letting myself drown.

A final sob rocks through me, and then abruptly the panic settles, and an eerie calm comes over me.

The water seems to still.

The world goes quiet.

Even my thoughts go quiet.

My chest burns with the lack of oxygen.

It won't be long now.

There's a muffled cracking sound at the window, though I may be hallucinating, because it looks like Haldric is ramming his beak into the glass. I swim over to him with what little strength I have left; my heart aches to see his yellow eyes one last time.

But something's wrong, because his eyes are a vibrant blue. And it's not Haldric's beak ramming against the glass. It's a pointed dagger.

Another hit shakes the window, but the glass won't budge. Whoever is holding the dagger can't break it any more than I could.

I watch the blue eyed stranger wondering idly how he made it up to the fourth floor. I don't see wings, but perhaps he was strong enough to climb.

My vision starts to slip as the stranger does something impossible. He's clawing bricks out of the wall with his bare hands. Water gushes out of the small openings he's able to make. He's calling my name now, and it's the most beautiful sound I've ever heard.

Yeah, I'm definitely hallucinating.

At some point the opening is big enough that a calloused hand reaches in and grips my upper arm.

A second later, everything goes black.

I cough and vomit up water for what feels like hours... Though it was probably only a few minutes.

I spray his dark wood floors again and again with saltwater. And vomit, tears, and snot.

I can't stop crying. Or coughing.

I'm vaguely aware when my rescuer wraps a thick fluffy towel around me and guides me toward what must have been the living room.

He pulls me into his lap on a blue velvet couch and wraps his arms around me. His magic seeps under my skin and soothes the burn in my chest and throat.

It feels so good that I find myself pressing my face into the crook of his neck. He smells like palo santo and smoke, and his arms are so warm. I'm crying against his throat now, and I know instinctively I've been here before.

Not to this place, but in these arms.

The ones where I always feel safe.

I'm vaguely aware when he offers me dry clothes, and when I don't respond, he uses magic to change me. I never am naked... the clothes just switch. They're soft and dry and warm.

At some point, he takes the towel away and replaces it with a furry blanket. He wraps me up tight again, and I burrow into his neck. He presses a light kiss against my forehead as sobs continue to rock through me.

We stay like that late into the night.

At some point, the sobs finally begin to stop. The fire is in embers now. Pretty soon it will be in ash.

He tries to unravel me from his arms so he can bring me some food and water, but I won't let him go.

So he stays.

Eventually... I must have fallen asleep. And he must have carried me to his bed. Because when I open my eyes, he's lying there next to me, daylight streaming in through the windows along his naked back.

20

I bolt upright, feeling my body. Making sure I'm fully clothed. I am—in thick sweats no less. *Thank the Maker.*

There's no ache between my legs, only a dull ache still in my chest and throat. I lift the sheet cautiously and sigh in relief when I see he's wearing sweatpants.

I glance around, trying to orient myself. But I've never seen a room like this.

The bed we're lying in is a sea of black silks and velvets and is far more comfortable than any bed I've ever owned. In front of it, there's a plush couch atop black fur rugs, and a stone fireplace blazing with flickering silver flames. To my right, there's so many side by side windows that they somehow form a seamless wall of glass. A huge terrace extends beyond the glass wall, and the view—

It's fucking spectacular.

We're somehow higher than the village, because I can see it way down below. The whole room seems to extend out from the cliff. Like the only thing stopping it from crashing down the mountain is magic.

Evander stirs awake. "Morning," he says sleepily. He rolls

toward me and drapes a heavy arm over my legs. I scurry away from the touch, curling my knees up to my chin.

"Why am I in your bed?" I say tensely, hyper aware of the many, *many* muscles exposed in his back.

And his shoulders.

And his biceps.

And his forearms.

Fuck.

"You wouldn't let go of me," he says, flipping over onto his side. My eyes catch on his pecks.

And his abs.

And lower.

Fuck.

"So I brought you to bed so you could get some sleep," he adds, his face the picture of innocence.

"Nothing happened?" My voice is terse.

He cocks a brow. "If you don't count the fact that you almost drowned to death in your apartment and someone stole the golden dagger in the process, then sure, nothing happened."

"Shit—the dagger's gone?" I say, my heart pounding.

Evander lifts a shoulder, then lowers it. Unbothered. "I'm certain I can find out who has it."

We're silent for a moment. My eyes drift down the length of his abdomen again.

"We didn't—?" I lift a brow.

He snorts. "Trust me, you'd remember if we did."

My cheeks heat, but I have too many questions to sit in embarrassment. I climb out of his bed and start pacing. "What the hell happened?" My voice is raspy, and it hurts my throat every time I talk.

"I need to figure that out." He sits up, scratching his beard and letting out a colossal yawn. "There wasn't an energetic signature on the flood. Did you piss someone off recently?"

Koa. Calimo. Nasgardo. You.

My heart stops.

"Did you do this?" I whisper. "So you could rescue me and make me fall for you?"

His face contorts in bewilderment. "You have *got* to be fucking *kidding* me, Fiana!"

"I'm not. Did you do this?" I say, crossing my arms over my chest. "How did you even know I was in danger?"

He lets out a humorless laugh then gets out of bed. He's walking toward a door that looks like a bathroom.

"Where are you going?" I complain.

"To wash off all the bullshit you're spewing at me. It's too fucking early for you to insult my character. Especially after I just ripped apart your building to save you." He opens the door and seconds later I hear his pants fall to the floor. The shower starts running, and I hear him step inside.

I edge toward the bathroom, averting my eyes as I pass the partially open door.

"Haldric crashed into my window and woke me up, that's how. Poor thing had ice on his wings and could barely move," Evander explains over the spray of the shower. His tone is annoyed.

I pause, keeping my back to him. "Is he okay?" I hold my breath.

"He's fine," Evander assures. I exhale in relief. "He'll be in the weapons vault on the ground floor. Two floors down. Go see for yourself."

I risk a glance over my shoulder and my heart leaps into my throat. His back is to me, but I can see every line of his muscular form, steaming hot and dripping wet.

The male is a fucking god.

I swallow, and it burns my throat but I use that to tear my eyes away. I let the pain replace the *other* feelings as I open a door that leads to a long hallway.

There's five other doors lining the hall, and each one is propped open slightly. They're all bedrooms.

I scurry past them quickly, unwilling to run into some other female. I jog down the stairs, then down another flight.

The weapons vault is overflowing with swords, bows and arrows, knives, spears, and other instruments of torture I don't even have the name for. There's no windows in this room so it's dim, with only a wide fireplace casting a light. I scan the room quickly, my heart aching as I search for him.

Relief washes through me as I finally sight Haldric. He's perched on a work bench littered with dozens of knives, his yellow eyes glowing in the shadows.

I hold out my arm and he flies to me, perching on my forearm. I rub the silky plumage at his belly as tears drip down my cheeks.

"You saved me again," I whisper. "I don't know how, but you did."

He clicks his beak in response. I kiss the top of his head.

I carry him on my arm up to the main floor, where he flies away to perch on a cloak rack near the front door.

The house is sprawling.

I recognize this space as where Evander first brought me last night. There's the blue couches, the white fur rugs, and the white stone fireplace with light blue flames. I didn't realize it before, but this room also has a wall of glass flanking either side of the fireplace. Impressively, it doesn't end at the ceiling, and there's a diagonal sloping window in lieu of a roof for the first fifteen feet or so.

Snowflakes cake the top, giving the room the feel of giant icebox.

I walk over to the windows in a daze, mesmerized by the snowfall—which is fast and windy at the moment, obscuring much of the sun's morning light. Outside, it would be horrible to walk through, with cold flakes piercing your face like tiny daggers. Inside, it's a thing of beauty, and I admire it for several minutes.

"Told you my story would check out," Evander says from behind me.

I turn around slowly. He's mercifully covered up in his black uniform, and the sight of it is both a blessing and a curse. His hair and beard are still damp from the shower, his skin subtly flushed.

"I have to get going soon. I need to investigate your apartment. There's coffee and food and anything else you could want here," he says, angling his head to the back part of the massive living area, which transitions seamlessly into a kitchen.

Just past the couches there's a long table and chairs, each made of a similar dark wood as the floors. A single crystal vase sits in the center of the table filled with bluebells—kept alive by magic, no doubt.

Beyond the table, the kitchen counter looks smooth and is made of a white marble. Brown leather bar stools line one side, with the icebox, stove, and oven along the wall behind it. There's also a glass door in the far corner, with what looks to be a wine cellar.

"If you'd like to bathe, just pick a room upstairs. There are clothes that will fit you in the first bedroom, so maybe that one's best," he adds.

"Whose clothes are they?" I ask, shifting my weight from foot to foot.

"No one's." He shrugs. "They can be yours. And you're welcome to stay here as long as you'd like. You can keep your own quarters, of course."

As long as you'd like.

"How long until my apartment will be ready again?" I feel queasy as I wait for his response.

"I think it would be better for you to stay with me. At least until we know who did this to you," he hedges.

"I can find someone else to stay with," I counter. His face falls, so I hastily add, "Thank you for saving me, but I don't think it's a good idea for me to stay here."

"Why not? There's plenty of room. It's just the two of us in this giant house." His tone is carefully controlled, but I detect a hint of defensiveness in it.

Just the two of us.

Interesting. Relief unexpectedly rushes through me.

And joy. Random, unexplainable joy.

"I'm afraid you might cross a line if I stay," I explain despite that revelation, blushing.

Or that I might be the one to cross it, I neglect to add.

He smirks, reading me too well.

"So you liked waking up in my bed, did you?" His teeth scrape across his bottom lip. "If you draw a line, Fiana, I promise to stay on *my* side."

Somehow those words send a jolt of pleasure through my core.

"I'm still going to find somewhere else to stay tonight," I say, my voice shooting up half an octave.

He stares at me for a long moment with his beautiful, penetrating eyes. "You still don't trust me, do you?"

My lips part, but no words come out.

"I thought we'd turned a corner last night, considering you didn't want me to leave your side. I thought we were friends," he says, pushing his damp hair back.

"We are," I say, my heart thudding at the admission. "But friends don't sleep together and if I stay here—"

His cheeks lift under his beard as he grins. "You're afraid you won't be able to resist me."

I blow hot air out through my nose, crossing my arms, glaring at him. "The point is, I think I'm better off staying with Mila or something."

He lifts his brows, then nods once. "If that's what you prefer. I have to go. I'll arrange a carriage for you to take you back to town—what time do you have work?"

"Five."

He nods. "Carriage will arrive at four thirty. And while you're here, help yourself to anything—seriously."

"Thanks." I offer him a tight smile.

He gives me a wave then dissolves away.

I stare at the empty space where he just was, feeling every emotion under the sun.

Anger, because my home is under water.

Fear, because I almost died.

Anxiety, because the King's golden dagger is gone.

And a bunch of other vastly inappropriate feelings about the one who saved me that I don't want to touch.

Not with a ten-foot pole.

Not even with a million-foot one.

Especially considering there aren't any immortal females living here. Maybe all the ones at the tavern really *had* been Dissenter plants.

Maybe Evander is unattached.

Maybe he has been this whole time.

And maybe he is actually, truly a good male.

One I can't stop thinking about all morning.

21

After helping myself to some coffee and buttered toast, I venture back upstairs to bathe. I hesitate for a half second outside of the first bedroom's door, as if I'll be disturbing someone by going inside.

Which is silly, because I'm the only one here.

I push the door open.

Like the lower level, the room is beautiful. The entire back wall is made of windows again, a small balcony beyond the panes of glass overlooking the snow. From this vantage point, I can see the other mountains of Syra easily, tiny villages peppering them at similar heights to Ador.

The room is large—obscenely so compared to my old apartment. Fluffy rugs in a rich violet cover the wood floors, and a small fireplace lit with pale pink flames sits across from a white velvet couch covered in thick, woolen blankets. Beyond the couch is the bed, a sea of white velvet blankets, pillows, and matte white silk sheets.

I notice it's a bit smaller than Evander's, and then I blush furiously as I remember I woke up there this morning.

He *is* comforting, though.

I don't know if it's his Curic magic, or the scent of his skin, or the warmth that radiates from him when I'm folded in his arms.

Whatever it is, it's a drug.

And I'm starting to get addicted.

I sigh, moving to the door that looks to be the bathroom. It is. I wash myself, annoyed at the opulence and beauty everywhere I look. I know the High Guards are handsomely paid... but this seems excessive.

The fixtures are made of gold and the tile looks imported from Meddia, likely made at the hands of the expert artisans that live there.

The shower is against another giant window overlooking the valleys and mountains. Magic keeps the glass perfectly clean, even as the shower sprays it. The water drips to the tile floor, no trace of its path left visible on the glass.

It's stunning, and I hate how much I love it.

I get out of the shower and towel dry my hair, tying it up into a messy knot, ignoring the iron stashed conveniently on a shelf beneath the sink. I do wish for makeup though, as I notice the purple circles beneath my eyes. I open a drawer, half hoping I won't find any so I can find at least one thing wrong with this house. It's full to the brim with makeup, also imported from Meddia, no doubt.

Of course.

My annoyance grows as I apply the face powder and watch it melt flawlessly into my skin. The brow pencil matches my dark brows, the eyeshadow brings out the green in my eyes, and the stupid lash enhancer is the best I've ever used in my life. It makes me want to scream.

But no one but Haldric will hear me.

I go back into the bedroom and toward the other door, wrapped in nothing but a towel. I open the door to the closet and nearly pass out.

It's as big as the bathroom with racks and racks of well made, expensive-looking clothes. There are fur coats, woolen pants and skirts, cashmere dresses and sweaters in every color... all somehow in my exact size.

There's even a warm weather section on one side full of sleeveless tops, short skirts, and slinky, silky dresses that promise to show a lot of skin if worn. I can't imagine why Evander would buy them. Ador—and Syra for that matter—never gets warm enough for the snow to melt.

I push aside the fancy feminine items and find a pair of black pants and a black flannel shirt. It fits tight to my body, but not too tight. The fabrics feel thicker and warmer than any of my own.

I curse under my breathe as I realize my sweaters are now all likely ruined after more than twelve hours under water.

And then I groan, remembering the thick stack of cash underneath my mattress, now waterlogged and soggy. It's enough to move into a new place if needed, but would drain every note I have.

It would be better to stay with Mila, if I can.

I vow to ask her tonight.

Either way, I'm not coming back here.

Mila's eyes are as wide as saucers when I make it into the tavern at sunset. There's a small crowd at the couches and a few at the bar, but otherwise it's relatively quiet.

"I heard what happened," she says when I make it under the bridge. She pulls me into a tight hug. "Do you know who did it?" Her voice is low and urgent by my ear.

"Not yet. Evander is investigating it," I breathe.

"And he saved you?" She pulls back to look at me, her tone incredulous.

I snort. "Yeah. He clawed the bricks out with his bare hands."

My heart stutters in my chest. "But there is one problem. The thing Warren and I—took?" I lower my voice, raising a brow. "It's gone."

"Bloody hell," Mila curses.

"You don't think Koa—?"

She jerks her head back and forth dramatically. "He's off his rocker but he would never try something so dangerous. He'd sooner control your mind and have you hand it to him willingly, then wipe your memories of the encounter."

That doesn't make me feel much better, but I guess it eliminates him as a suspect.

"Could be Nasgardo. Or Calimo," I muse. "But Evander said there wasn't an energetic signature on it, so not sure how he's planning to figure it out."

A patron down the bar holds up his empty glass and looks expectantly at us. Mila hurries over and starts filling it from the tap. The beer whooshes into the glass like frothy liquid gold.

Credo pokes his head out of his office. "You're alive!" He smiles with crinkly eyes.

I smile back. "Still kicking."

He motions for me to join him in his office. I glance at Mila, who nods, then follow him inside.

Warren is leaning against the far wall, looking stoic and emotionless as always.

"We overheard what you said—that the dagger is missing," Warren says.

Damn immortal ears.

"Evander seems to think he'll be able to locate it," I supply. "And I don't think he will return it to the castle vaults."

"Hmm," Credo says. Warren stares at him. "And you're staying with Evander then?" Credo asks, furrowing his wiry brows.

I glance between the two of them. "Uh—no. I was going to ask Mila if I can stay with her."

"It's better if you stay with him," Warren insists, crossing his arms over his wide chest. "More chances to discover what it is he's hiding." He lowers his chin a centimeter, resolved.

Credo looks at me with kind eyes. "I have to agree with Warren."

My cheeks start to heat as my pulse accelerates. I rein in the urge to throw a full on temper tantrum.

"I would rather stay with Mila. I'm going to ask her right now," I snap, leaving the office and shoving the door shut with my hip.

Mila catches my eye from down the bar. "All good?" she mouthes.

"Can I stay with you tonight? And until my apartment gets fixed?" I ask, joining her at the far end.

She stares at me blankly for an immeasurable moment and then shakes her head. "No—stay with Evander."

"I don't *want* to stay with Evander," I complain, fighting to keep the rage out of my tone.

She scrunches her brow, tossing her long blonde ponytail over her shoulder. "I don't have room for you. I live in a studio if you recall." She walks toward me, pausing to whisper in my ear in a kinder tone. "Normally I would, but we need you *there*, not with me."

I follow her to the other end of the bar where a few Guards have lined up for drinks. "Please, Mila—just for a few nights. Until my apartment is fixed," I beg.

She lines up six shot glasses and pours, sighing. "Look—you're the one that wants us to trust him. Show us that we can. By staying with him." She turns to the Guards, speaking louder. "That will be twenty-four notes, boys."

Bills appear, and she collects them.

"But I already told him I would stay with *you*," I complain, collecting abandoned pints and putting them in the automatic cleaner. It's an effort not to slam the glasses down with force, but I resist.

"Then you'll just have to tell him you changed your mind. That you can't *imagine* being apart from him. That you think about him all day long and *need* to be with him all night," she teases with a wicked grin.

"Who are we talking about now?" a familiar male voice asks from down the bar.

I glare at Evander, who's smiling at me like I just begged him to fuck me against the wall.

"Haldric. We're talking about Haldric," I hiss. I grab a glass and start pouring him his favorite jad.

Always the most expensive one.

"What did you find out about my apartment?" I slide the drink across the bar to him.

He throws it back in one gulp. "You're not moving back in anytime soon," he says thickly, wiping his eyes. "The place keeps refilling itself, even with the gaps in the bricks. It's causing all sorts of problems with the building's integrity, too, because at night it freezes. The walls are beginning to crack, and they've evacuated everyone else in the building."

"Are you serious?" I gape at him.

He taps his empty glass with his index finger. I refill it automatically.

"Dead serious."

"This can't be happening," I groan.

"Pour yourself one, on me," he suggests.

I snort. "Alcohol doesn't solve my housing problem."

"No, but that's already sorted. You're staying with me," he shrugs, a smile playing at the corners of his lips.

"That sounds like a *great* idea!" Mila chimes in. I throw her a death glare. She bites her lip to hold in her giggles.

"I have to get back to work—just came to give you my address," Evander says, slapping a cocktail napkin on top of the bar.

"I'm not staying with you," I insist. He whips out a thick stack of cash, starts counting it, then gives up and just puts the whole thing on the bar. It has to be a few thousand notes.

I roll my eyes and split most of it off the top and lean over the bar, trying to give it back to him. He raises a brow, then turns on his heel.

"What are you doing? You overpaid!" I call as he heads toward the door.

"Extra for your carriage ride tonight. Or your hotel room. Up to you," he says over his shoulder with a wave.

I glare at his retreating form but pocket the money. A hotel room *would* be a good option.

Better than going back to that house.

I exhale sharply and stare at the bottle of jad still atop the bar, next to Evander's empty glass. My eyes catch on the company name in fine print near the bottom of the label.

Deschamps Fine Wine & Spirits.

Apparently that one company distributes most of the wine and all of the liquor in the Elven Kingdom. At least according to Mila. I shake my head, unable to comprehend the level of wealth the owners must have.

It has me feeling bitter, so I pour myself a shot like Evander suggested, slipping the money for both drinks into the register.

I knock it back, cringing at the burn of the jad as it slinks down my throat. Fermented witch's barley hits different than ordinary liquor or wine... it gives you a sort of adrenaline rush in addition to the euphoria.

Males sometimes use it to temporarily enhance their magic. Females sometimes use it to temporarily feel strong enough without magic.

I'm using it to block out the fact that I'm homeless and my best friend won't even take me in.

I try to throw the napkin away, but every time I do it ends up magically back in my pocket. The first time I try I don't notice for ten minutes, until I receive my next tip. I slide the money in my pocket and feel the soft paper of the napkin, pull it out to see what it is and curse Evander's name under my breath.

Then I try ripping it up. But I...*can't*. The papery fabric of the napkin won't rip no matter how hard I try.

I throw it into the fireplace, and a new one appears in my pocket again. I flush it down the toilet, and again there it is.

The worst part is, I've already memorized the address from all the times I angrily find the napkin again, so even if I *could* get rid of it... I still know exactly where he lives.

Eventually I let it stay in my pocket just to stop wasting energy trying to get rid of it. At least I have enough money to stay at the hotel.

Because of Evander.

When the bar finally empties, it's nearly two in the morning. I lock up the tavern and quickly walk the six blocks to the only hotel in Ador.

The female at the front desk gives me an apologetic look when I walk in. "I'm sorry, Miss, we're already full, and I'm closing up for the night..."

I just stare at her for a moment, then turn around and walk back outside into the snow, pulling my cloak tighter around me. I start to walk back toward the tavern, figuring the embers might still be warm and maybe I could stoke the fire by hand to keep me warm for the night.

I get less than a block away when I see Calimo leave his townhouse and head in the direction of the tavern. He looks over his shoulder and I duck behind a lamppost to hide.

When I hear his footsteps getting further and further away, I step out from behind the lamp and sit on a nearby bench. I think through my options as my breath comes in heavy pants, fogging up the air around me in the lamp light.

The hotel is full. Mila refused to take me in. And Calimo is likely checking the tavern for me.

Will he give up on his search when he finds it locked up and empty?

I can maybe wait him out, and still spend the night there?

My breathing abruptly stops as an unbearable stillness seems to surround me. Even the snow seems to slow its pace, suspending in midair, and floating with unnatural lightness toward the ground. Uneasiness has me rolling my neck, as I can't shake the feeling that I'm being watched.

It's too quick for Calimo to be back, but I look around anyway.

I scan the streets, squinting through the darkness illuminated only by a handful of scattered lamps. My throat tightens as I spot him—a few blocks down, and across the street. The butcher—the one who had held a knife to my throat—is staring right at me.

Like it's the luckiest night of his life.

I don't think, I just run.

I bolt back for the hotel and can hear him running after me, so I quicken my pace until I make it and yank the door open. Or try to... but it's locked and the lights are out, the female nowhere to be found inside.

Shit!

My heart is pounding, and not just from running. The butcher gets closer, just one block away now and yet still across the street, while I stay frozen in place with nowhere to hide. I can keep running—but where?

Sterling is probably still in his stables, but I would have to run past the butcher to get back down there. And it's a long way; fifteen blocks at least.

He's directly across the street from me now.

I hear the familiar *clump-clump-clump* of a carriage approaching and, hardly believing my luck, I run out into the street and wave my hands up like a lunatic to flag it down. The driver pulls on the reins and the horses skid to a stop right in front of me.

I quickly run to the side farthest from the butcher. I jump in, locking the carriage doors as he glares at me through the glass window from only a few feet away.

"Where to, Miss?" asks the driver, looking awkwardly at the butcher, who stares for a moment, and then turns and slumps away. Defeated.

Relief floods through me.

"Where to, Miss?" the driver asks again, the tips of his ears twitching with impatience.

I sigh. Feeling in my pocket for that stupid, *stupid* napkin, I read the address of the only place I know I can go and still be safe.

22

The house is dark as we approach. I pay the driver and get out, asking him to wait a moment to make sure I get inside.

I brace myself for the inevitable snide remarks I'm sure to get, and then knock on the door. Loudly, in case he's asleep.

I wait. After about a minute, I knock again, glancing over my shoulder to make sure the driver is still there waiting.

"Tick tock, lady..." he says tiredly, eager to end his shift and go home.

I knock again, with even more force than the last two times. My knuckles ache. Nothing. *Shit.*

I shift my weight between my feet, nervousness stirring in my belly. Is he not home?

Is he... with a female?

Though the back of the house is a wall of glass, the front is solid stone. I can't even see if he's coming for the door.

I turn toward the driver and take a step back toward the carriage when finally, *finally* the door swings open.

Damn. Why does he have to look like *that*?

Eyes tired with sleep, hair and beard a colossal mess, naked

chest taut with muscles that would make a lesser male envious...
and his eyes, blue as a cold lake yet somehow as warm as the sun.

It's impossible to think straight when *this* is how he answers the
door.

"What took you so long?" is all he says, a soft, lazy smile
spreading across his face. He gives a little wave to the driver and I
swear I see an extra bill land in his lap before he whips the horses
into a trot.

Evander gives me a look. "You coming?"

I'm still standing outside.

I cross my arms, setting my jaw. "I'm not sleeping with you."

He rolls his eyes. "You're the one that wouldn't let go of me last
night."

I ignore that. "I'm only coming in here if you promise not to
touch me. No more sharing a bed, and no more showering in front
of each other."

His lips twitch, fighting a grin. "Am I allowed to speak to you?"

I glare at him. "Only when spoken to."

He snorts. "That's hardly fair considering this is *my* home."

I roll my eyes. "Fine. We can talk occasionally."

"Am I allowed to look at you?" he asks, his eyes tracing a heated
line down the length of my cloak.

"Only when absolutely necessary, like to avoid crashing into me
in the hallway," I retort, pulling my cloak tighter around me.

He snorts. "Alright, no touching, no sex, no nudity, no fun. Did I
get it all?"

"You are so annoying," I groan.

"And yet you keep coming back for more," he drawls, holding
the door open wider for me to come inside.

I bite my tongue as I pass, refusing to take the bait.

I make my way up the stairs and into the first bedroom, where I
got the clothes from this morning. Evander trails slowly behind me.

"Bet you're glad that napkin survived..." he teases. I scowl as he
goes back to his room.

~

I sleep deeper tonight, mostly due to pure exhaustion, but my dreams are disturbing.

I keep dreaming of being trapped under water, suffocating second by agonizing second.

Then the dream morphs and Koa is chasing after me. He wants the dagger, and he's going to kill me if I don't hand it over. I outrun him just barely, only to ram right into the King himself, who grabs me, pins me down, and rapes me.

And then I'm under water again, and I can't breathe. I scream and scream but the nightmare plays on an endless loop that I can't escape.

"Fiana!" Evander's voice rings out loud and clear. My eyes fly open and find his, dripping with concern as I drip with sweat, even while in the tiniest of nightgowns—one I'd found in one of the dresser drawers.

He's shirtless again, sitting on the edge of my bed, and as I catch my breath I can't help but stare at his pecks, his biceps, the hard ripples of his abs...

"Are you alright?" His voice is gentle. Soothing.

I tear my eyes away from his naked hipbones, exposed over his low slung sweatpants, just an inch or two from my bare arm. I look up at him.

"I'm okay. I'm okay." My voice is shaky, my breathing still labored.

He doesn't look convinced. "Do you want to talk about it?" The question is gentle, as if he isn't going to push me one way or the other.

"It's the flood." I can feel tears pricking at my eyes but I fight to keep them from spilling. My chest is tight, and I'm hyperventilating. "I can't breathe," I gasp.

He presses a featherlight touch on my inner arm and I feel his healing magic at the same time I gather a full breath. A sense of calm washes over me as I take another. And another.

Evander squeezes my arm. I jump at the change, and he pulls his hand away. "Sorry... no touching..." he says with a sheepish grin.

But that isn't exactly why I flinched.

My heart pounds for an entirely different reason now. I sit up in bed, eager to stop being eye level with his...

"Tell me something. Tell me a story or something," I say breathlessly, needing a distraction.

His beard twitches. "What kind of story?"

"I don't know... something happy, I guess," I say, my heart still thudding erratically.

He thinks for a moment, and then begins.

"Before I joined the Guard," he clears his throat, eyes going distant, "I used to love playing tricks on the grey ones. One time, I set a spell on one that made his pants invisible anytime he talked to a female, except he wouldn't be able to see that they had gone, only the female could. I followed him to the tavern—your tavern—and watched from the windows how many times he got rejected," he starts laughing, his chuckles vibrating the bed.

"He started out strong... all confident as he strutted toward the first one. But the second he opened his mouth to speak, boom—his pants were gone. The female took one look at him and gave him the biggest scowl I've ever seen. A few threw their drinks at him..."

His eyes twinkle at the memory. I giggle with him as I imagine it. "How old were you?"

He shrugs. "Only about ten or so. My parents made me join the Guard a few weeks later."

"Why did they make you?" I wonder.

Another shrug. "They knew I was valuable. The Guard—not my parents. My parents were just glad to be rid of me." He looks at me, his face contorting in a dramatic show of innocence. "I guess they thought I was a trouble maker..."

I fight a smile. "Can't imagine why..." I wink.

His jaw drops. "Is this...? Can it be?" His eyes widen dramatically.

I furrow my brow. "What?"

He shakes his head slowly, theatrically, mouth still agape. "I can't believe it..."

"*What*?" I demand, as nervous flutters fill my stomach.

"In my nearly four hundred years...I never thought..."

My voice grows louder. "WHAT?"

He bursts out laughing. Angry, I push him hard enough that he falls over onto my bed, which only makes him laugh harder, tears pooling in the corners of his eyes. I climb on top of him, pinning him down between my thighs and slap his bare chest—not hard, but just enough to snap him out of it.

It doesn't work. His body continues to shake with uncontrollable laughter, gyrating underneath me, his bare hips bucking against my bare thighs.

"TELL ME!" I shout, crossing my arms. Using anger to hide the turn on I now feel building rapidly between my legs.

He lets out a few more weak chuckles, wiping the tears from his eyes and then finally looks up at me, eyes alight with lazy amusement.

"I just can't believe you actually flirted with me just now." Another chuckle ripples through him.

Now *my* jaw drops. "I wasn't flirting with you!"

His brow shoots up, challenging me. "Please." The word drips with sarcasm.

"I wasn't!" I insist, crossing my arms.

"Mmhmm... please," he taunts.

I glare at him.

But perhaps a different approach...

I run my hands lightly over his muscled chest, tracing a wandering line down the length of his abdomen.

So lightly, so slowly.

His eyes widen in shock, so I lean toward him without breaking eye contact, my hands pressing the bed on the sides of his shoulders as I hover myself a few inches above his body... and then closer.

I'm close enough now to smell the spearmint on his breath and I lean in as if to kiss him, his eyes still wide, his chest heaving toward mine as his breathing speeds up. And then I collapse my body into his, moving my lips to his ear as I feel him harden beneath me. I nibble his ear, feeling his hands wrap around me, clutching my ass tighter against him, now rock hard.

I whisper in my most seductive voice, "No touching."

He groans, pulling me tighter against him for a second and then letting go, his hands falling limp against the bed.

I sit up, my grin victorious, with him still hard beneath my ass.

"What was the point of that?" he drawls, an edge of annoyance in his tone, but his eyes are still alight with excitement.

"That's me flirting. I just thought you should know the difference." I shrug.

He smiles wickedly, sneaking another gyration against my ass. "I'd like to see that more often."

I shake my head. "Nope. Now you know, so there's no point in me showing you again." I bite my lip to keep from laughing. I slide to the side of him, setting him free.

"Now get out," I order with a smirk.

He sits up, but doesn't leave. He crawls toward me, his gaze predatory, and I instinctively back up against the headboard, my heart beating wildly as he advances. His hands press against the headboard on either side of my face.

"I don't have to touch you," he murmurs, leaning in close, bringing his lips near my neck, close enough to where his hot breath teases that sensitive skin, "to drive you *crazy*..."

I'm frozen in place as he blows gently against the skin at my neck... and then my collarbone... and then just above my breast near the lip of my nightgown... goosebumps erupting wherever his hot breath touches... my nipples peaking underneath the lace...

He backs his knees up and walks his hands down to the bed on either side of me, carefully avoiding touching my legs.

His head bows low, near my body but not touching me, blowing hot air against my thinly covered breasts. And then lower, against my abdomen, which tightens with pleasure underneath the lace.

He glances up briefly then dives lower still... his lips nearly caressing the inner edge of my knee. Blowing, hot and damp against the skin there... and then higher, his hot breath slowly climbing up my inner thigh as my legs began to widen of their own accord, giving him space to go a little higher.

And higher he goes, and my back begins to arch, my breath becoming shallow as *his* slides closer to those nerves between my thighs. He tucks his nose underneath the short lace gown, blowing that hot breath gently against my center as ripples of pleasure start pulsing in my core.

He blows, and blows... careful not to touch my now wide open thighs with his beard or the sides of his face. Heating me from the outside... as heat builds within my insides.

I'm getting close, just from that dang breath, just from the sight of him in between my legs.

A little moan escapes my lips and I can't take it anymore, I tangle my fingers in his hair and pull him to me, feeling his lips brush against me, a little flick of his hot tongue right where I want it most.

I'm on the edge and then he instantly pulls back, agony rippling through me as his tongue leaves me... amusement playing in his wicked eyes.

"No touching," he chides. His face stretches into a wide grin. "Goodnight..."

And then he's gone, dissolved back to his room, his disembodied chuckle taunting me from down the hall.

I immediately pick up where he left off, stroking myself

hungrily as I replay the feel of his hands on my ass. My toes curl as I imagine his breath against my naked inner thighs and that slow, torturous climb of his breath higher toward my center.

I grab my breast with my free hand as my release approaches, wishing it was *his* hand teasing my nipples now. I can still feel that single flick of his tongue against that most sensitive part of me...

It isn't long before I climax. Pleasure ripples through me so powerfully that I have to turn my face into the pillow to contain the screams.

23

I'm still wet with desire when I wake up. I fight the urge to touch myself again and peel myself out of bed, making my way to the shower to destroy the evidence.

I wash myself slowly, sensually, replaying the events of last night in my mind as I do. My hands linger on my breasts, gently grazing my nipples, as little shudders of remembered pleasure make me shiver, though the water is scalding hot.

I'm in deep shit.

It was one thing to sleep with a male like Calimo.

But Evander is immortal.

And last night, I came *way* too close to inviting him to stay in my bed.

It was just one little harmless lick, complains a needy, deviant part of me. My breath catches.

More—I want so much *more*.

"No," I say out loud. "No more."

No more flirting. No more breathing.

No more touching. No more licking.

I sigh, ignoring the craving still blazing between my thighs. I shut that part of me off for seven years. I can stay here with Evander and still resist.

I have to.

I quickly finish washing my hair then turn off the water, drying myself roughly. Trying to put out the invisible fire blazing underneath my skin. One that has me biting my lip. And squeezing my thighs together. And desperate for his hot breath against my—

"*No.* I said *no*," I chide my own flustered reflection.

This is nothing like how it was with Tarletan.

Nothing like how it was with Calimo.

Seriously—what fresh hell *is* this?

I towel dry my hair, messily again, and tie it up into a big fat knot. I quickly apply a hint of makeup, glaring at my reflection in the process.

His words come back to me like a taunt.

You will need me like you need oxygen. The need will consume every cell of your being. It will keep you up at night and torment you all day. Until your lips, your skin, and every little bit of you is aching and craving and begging for the feel of me. Then—and only then—will you get the chance to fuck me.

I'm definitely aching.

I'm absolutely craving.

And I'm damn near close to—

"NO!" I turn away from the mirror. It's too much to see the raw need in my own eyes.

To see the truth of how badly I want him.

I need something to hold on to. Something real that will shut down my stupid, deviant, needy self.

A turn off. I need to be *turned off.*

Evander is three hundred and eighty years old. He's too old for me.

No—that doesn't work. He looks five years older than me at most. *Shit.*

Evander has been with three hundred and eighty years' worth of females.

I take a steadying breath. That sort of helps, but then my mind starts picturing him with thousands of females over the centuries, and white hot anger starts coursing through my veins.

But anger is good—anger does help. I can work with anger. It's just enough to stifle the need.

Thank the Maker.

I shake off the intensity of my internal conflict then find another pair of black pants and a black shirt, ignoring the hand-woven sweaters and long, elegant gowns.

I approach my bedroom door, bracing myself for the jokes, and the irresistible pull of his two-toned eyes. I take a deep breath and then open it.

I go downstairs.

Only to find Evander... gone.

A note on the table tells me he left early for work and will meet me at the tavern during my shift later tonight.

I moved Sterling back up here for you to ride down for your shift. There's food in the fridge and books on the shelf in my office... Try not to touch yourself all day just thinking about me... it says.

FUCK!

I blush furiously and then rip it up. It reassembles itself with a new message. *There's more where that came from... all you have to do is ask.* I rip it up again and it reassembles with a doodle—a very *realistic* doodle—of Evander's head between my legs, my back arched against that headboard, my face in an unmistakable expression of erotic delight.

I giggle at the drawing despite myself and then fling it into the fireplace. A new one appears on the table... *That hurt!* it says. I roll my eyes but let the note live this time.

I open the fridge to find it full of every food I could want... I settle on eggs and bacon and pull it out, setting it on the counter while I hunt for a frying pan.

And then I smell the bacon, fully cooked, and I look back on the counter only to see the packages gone, the eggs scrambled, and the bacon still sizzling on a plate that magically appeared beneath it.

I can't help but smile, especially with Evander not here to make fun of me. This bit of magic is... nice.

I feast on the food, hungry from the late night. Hungry from the love I made to myself when Evander left my room in a flash.

I'm still hungry when I finish the plate, and somehow it knows because more appears. I eat it greedily, the eggs still hot, as if they've just been poured onto my plate from the frying pan.

When I'm done I put the dish in the sink, where it floats in midair and washes itself and then returns itself to whatever cabinet it came from. *Nice.*

I lose myself in a romance novel as outside it begins to snow. Haldric is sleeping on a wooden perch in the living room that Evander must have conjured for him this morning. I sit beside him, near the fireplace on the blue couch, sneaking glances at the snowflakes in front of me and above me, every once in a while glancing back at the clock in the kitchen.

Around midday, I decide to explore the unseen rooms of the house.

I start with the wine cellar. There are hundreds of bottles—maybe thousands even—stacked high on individual bottle-sized wooden shelves. It smells like musk and cedar and I let my fingertips brush across the labels, some of them dusty and faded. I read the years on those and notice several are over a hundred years old. Toward the top right corner, there's even one from four hundred years ago.

I venture into the room where the bookcases live—where I'd gotten the novel from. I scan the titles again, some in languages I've never even heard of.

It's Evander's office. A large, dark wooden desk sits facing the windows at the back of the house. I sit in the chair behind it, sinking into its supple leather. I relax there for a moment before opening the top drawer.

There are weapons immediately on top... knives of all shapes and sizes with papers visible underneath. I shut the drawer and try the one to the side, which is set up like a filing cabinet, with more papers stacked between file folders. I scan the labels, all of them seeming random and unimportant to me.

I shut that drawer and try the smaller one just above it, which is empty save for a small black box. A ring box.

I hesitate, curiosity burning within me, but I also don't want to see a ring that was meant for another female. A female who—what —rejected him? Or died?

I shut the drawer without opening the box and stare out the window for a moment. The snow is getting heavier, so much so that I can't even see the villages below.

I wonder idly what kind of work Evander is doing today, as the King's first-in-command of the High Guard. I shudder at the thought.

Perhaps it's better not to imagine it.

I skip the lower level where the weapons vault is, and head back upstairs to where the bedrooms are. I pass mine then look into a few others... bedrooms similar to mine with the only difference being the decor. I check the closets and notice they are all curiously empty...

Maybe all those females truly *were* Dissenter plants?

Finally—there's his room. I pause outside the closed door, not quite ready to intrude upon his private space just yet, even though I woke up in his bed a few mornings ago.

I run my finger over the smooth wooden door as if it's his bare chest... and then my fingers find the knob and with a quick breath I turn it and step inside...

That glorious bed of his is still left unmade. Tempted, I walk over to it, running my hands along the plush velvet duvet. And then

I'm climbing inside, pulling the covers over me, letting the woodsy scent of him envelope me.

The need will consume every cell of your being. It will keep you up at night and torment you all day.

Yes, lying here in his bed without him, surrounded by his scent was a certain kind of torment. I let out a half crazed laugh, remembering how not too long ago, he laid in *my* bed to torture me.

Two can play at that game.

I roll around in his sheets, letting *my* scent leave its mark. I pull my hair out of the knot, and it's still slightly wet. I rub the damp locks all over each of his pillows then stick my nose against them and inhale.

Yup. Smells like me.

Good.

I lay there for a moment longer, just for good measure, and then laze over to the windows at the back.

A huge terrace extends beyond the largest one, and when I brush my fingers against the glass, it disappears completely, letting the elements into the room.

I walk out onto the terrace, admiring the plush white couches that somehow stay magically dry and perfectly clear of the piles of snow that surround it in every direction. In front of them is a large fire pit with silver-white flames dancing with the snow, melting the flakes whenever fire and ice happen to meet.

The view is spectacular, as it is everywhere in this home. I shiver as thick snowflakes coat my damp hair and shoulders. Time to go back inside.

I touch the glass that instantly reappeared when I exited the bedroom, and it disappears again granting me access inside. The floor is magically free of any snow, and the glass is free of my fingerprints.

I marvel at that. Elven males have it so *easy*.

And for a moment, I feel bitter.

It's a half-life we females live.

We get to witness the beauty and ease our magic creates—but never by our own hands. Only by the hands of those who stole it from us, while we watch, bereft, from our empty shells of existence.

It's why I joined the Dissenters to begin with, but now everything is so much more complicated. Last I heard Credo and Warren haven't heard from Koa, and the rest of the group isn't speaking to any of them.

And now the golden dagger is gone.

The one that, according to Credo and Warren, is used to kill the King.

Meanwhile, I almost drowned two nights ago and now I'm living here. Practically sleeping with 'the enemy.'

Not literally, of course.

Despite what my body wants.

Needs. Craves.

Will the Dissenters still be able to bring down the King without the golden dagger?

Did I just ruin a centuries' long resistance by not giving it to Koa right away?

Koa was unkind to me, but I can see now why he might have felt that way. If the dagger is the only way to bring the King down and I lost it—which I did—I can understand his anger.

And yet... I still don't trust him.

But I trust Evander, a part of me decides. I don't know where the thought comes from, but it resonates as true the moment I think it.

Still, he has secrets. Big ones.

And now that I'm stuck living with him, I may as well start trying to figure them out.

At half past four, I venture outside to the stables on the left side of the cliffside home. Evander's note doesn't say which way it is back to the village, but when I mount Sterling and nudge him into a trot, he seems to know where to go.

There's a level of comfort between us; Sterling adjusts his speed to my liking automatically and slows his pace when the wind whips into a frenzy. He even leads us right to the stables in town without me so much as directing him.

I hop off him and give him a kiss just above his muzzle. He nickers lovingly back.

Animals are simple. Pure. They meet kindness with kindness, love with love. If you hit them, they bite back. Call and response always in perfect harmony. You get what you give, and they give what they get.

It seems the norms of the animal kingdom don't apply to elves, though. Otherwise King Vilero would have met his end by now.

How could evil reign for so many centuries?

Even with an organized resistance like the Dissenters?

I shiver as I leave the stables, Sterling safely tucked into his stall.

It's an upside-down world we live in, and yet nature already has it all figured out for us. All we have to do is observe. And listen. And learn from the perfection that already exists.

And yet it seems like no one else is even paying attention.

The tavern is busy tonight, the usual players filling the bar stools, the couch near the fireplace overflowing with nearly a dozen Main Guards.

It's Mila's day off, and my shift passes quickly as I rush around by myself, filling cups, taking money, pocketing tips, and smiling at the customers.

Credo is spending a rare moment outside of his office, circling the tavern, talking to customers, towering high above them all. He truly knows everyone.

I find it strange that such a public figure in Ador could fly under the radar with the Dissenters for so long. But maybe that's Koa's doing. Maybe he controls minds and wipes memories more often than not.

"Where is she? Where's Fiana? Is she alright?" The frantic voice comes from behind Credo's giant frame.

My stomach drops. It's Calimo.

I want to shrink and hide, but I'm the only bartender on duty and—too late. He peers around Credo and catches my eye.

"You're alive," he gasps, and there's true relief in his eyes.

I lift a brow. "Yes, I am."

He runs a hand through his smooth dark hair. "I just found out about the flood. Do they know who did it?" he questions, his eyes wide with fear.

I narrow my eyes at him. "Not yet."

"Got it, got it," he says, exhaling rapidly. "Well do you need somewhere to stay?" he asks.

I crumple my brow. "No thanks. I'm staying with Evander." I grab a couple of empty pints and put them in the automatic cleaner. When I straighten up, my breath catches.

His eyes are dark, and his whole body has gone tense. "You what?"

"I'm staying in one of Evander's spare bedrooms," I clarify. Not that I owe him an explanation, but by the way his lip is curling it feels like it might be wise to try and deescalate.

"Are you sleeping with him?" His nostrils flare.

I scoff. "That's none of your business."

"Just answer the question, Fiana," he seethes.

I glare at him. "No! You don't own me, and I owe you nothing."

He snorts, climbing on top of an empty barstool and kneeling so he's face to face with me. He speaks in a quiet, grating tone. "I licked that foul pussy of yours enough times to earn the truth. So how much did he pay you before you got on your knees before him? Or was giving you a place to stay payment enough for a whore like you?"

My hand moves in flash before I can stop it, slapping him *hard* across the face. My palm stings, while a satisfying hand print turns rosy on his cheeks.

The whole bar goes silent as it hits me. I—a female—just slapped one of the King's sons in a bar full of a dozen Main Guards. My heart thuds in my chest as panic builds within me.

Calimo looks stunned, and then his face burns scarlet as he moves to launch himself across the bar at me. Before he can reach me, a black sheathed arm appears out of thin air and throws him backwards, sending him and the barstool clattering to the floor.

Evander, livid, takes one look at me and for a split second I think he might arrest me. But then he launches the full force of his magic on Calimo, breaking his legs, his arms. The tavern is dead silent other than the crack of his bones and his agonized screams.

Holy—!

"First of all..." His voice is calm. Too calm. Hinting nothing at the monster beneath. "... Fiana's pussy is *delicious*. And since you will never have the pleasure of tasting it again, I don't see any reason for you to keep your tongue..."

I stifle a half-crazed giggle as Calimo screams, the sound becoming distorted as Evander does whatever he is doing to his tongue.

"Second of all..." Still calm. Still quiet. "... since I have now proven you flooded 47 Glacier Pass, and we've now confirmed that you ruined it beyond even *magical* repair, I *should* be throwing you into The Cave. But since you are the King's son, you have immunity. Therefore..."

He positions his foot lightly over Calimo's crotch as his eyes widen in terror. "I'll settle for this." He stomps down, and *that* bone cracks.

Every male in the tavern reacts by covering their own crotches, collapsing over themselves as if they've suffered the injury personally. Tears stream down Calimo's now sweaty face, as haggard sobs escape his tongueless, bloody mouth.

"Finally..." His voice is a cruel whisper now, an angel of death ready to claim his victim. "... if you ever—*ever* try to harm Fiana again..." He pauses to let Calimo anticipate what could possibly come next, little whimpers choking out of him. "These wounds will remain permanent."

Calimo's skin erupts into a thousand gashes, blood gushing everywhere. A few males in the bar vomit as Calimo's screams become deranged.

Evander stares at him for a breath, watching the pain contort his face, watching his skin turn pale, watching the light threaten to leave his eyes.

And then he bends down and places a hand on his leg and heals him.

Bones snap back into place, his legs no longer jut out at unnatural angles. The oozing gashes begin to close, starting with his legs and working their way up. Calimo winces as his crotch presumably heals, his mangled arms twitching.

Evander stands up abruptly then, hoisting Calimo to a standing position from his bloody shirt. Calimo's arms hang limp and distorted by his sides, Evander apparently choosing to leave those broken.

"And don't you ever call her a whore, or next time I'll keep your tongue. Are we clear?"

Calimo's eyes, crazed and terrified meet Evander's and he lets out an emphatic, though clearly torturous, nod. "Go see the healer for the rest," Evander says coldly, shoving him toward the door.

Calimo stumbles out of the tavern, the sound of him retching violently echoing in the valley as he leaves.

No one speaks for a moment, the entire tavern afraid to move—afraid to breathe—with this trained killer still in their midst.

"Sorry about the mess, Credo," Evander says smoothly. A split second passes, and then the blood and vomit disappear.

Credo shakes his head slowly. "Remind me to stay on your good side..." he says with a nervous chuckle. His eyes meet mine for a split second as if to say *good luck with that one*.

"Shall I get the next round? Shots for everyone. On me." Evander holds up a giant wad of cash and the bar erupts into merriment again.

He grabs the barstool off the ground and rights it, finally meeting my gaze. I instantly shrink to the ground, my knees going weak as those icy eyes meet mine.

Credo approaches the bar, seeing me withering on the ground and says gently, "Why don't you take the rest of the night off, Fiana? In fact... take the whole weekend. I'll get those shots for everyone."

I nod once and Evander dissolves, appearing on my side of the bar, scooping me up into his arms. I wrap my arms around his neck, noticing the concern evident in his gaze.

He looks cautious as he speaks, "Can I take you to dinner, Fiana?"

I nod once more and in a *crack*, we're gone.

24

We land in the snow now on the north side of town, outside Rosemary's, the nicest restaurant in Ador. I've only ever been inside once, to ask for a job. I never imagined being able to eat here as a guest.

He's still holding me. "Are you alright?" His voice sounds half-strangled. "I'm sorry you had to see that... but... I couldn't help myself." It sounds like a confession.

I take a breath—maybe the first one since Evander appeared. I shake my head slowly. "No..." I start to say, a smile threatening to ruin it, "... touching."

And then I burst out laughing. Like a lunatic.

Concern shifts to humor and then to annoyance as he watches me laugh and laugh, my body shaking violently in his arms. He slowly sets me down on my feet, pausing a beat to make sure I'm steady, and then pulls his arms away obediently. Crossing them. With a smirk.

"Come on... it's *funny*," I insist, bending over with laughter now, my hands on my knees as my back ripples with every cackle. "No, it's *hilarious*," I amend. A new wave of laughter hits me.

I straighten up slowly, body still shaking, wiping the tears that now fall from my eyes.

"You're insane," Evander drawls, rolling his eyes at my spectacle. "But I love that little laugh of yours," he adds, with a smile that touches his eyes.

"Let's eat..." I say between the giggles that remain.

He gestures for me to lead the way and I saunter inside, head held high.

The restaurant is empty save for the waitress. She takes one look at Evander's black uniform and leads us to a candlelit table near the back.

He pulls out the chair for me and I sit down, letting him scoot me in. He sits opposite me, his face unreadable, and stares at me instead of reading the menu.

I ignore him, looking down at mine. Seeing exotic meats and delicacies I have never tasted.

Seeing the prices.

"It's on me tonight," he says casually, correctly reading the concern on my face.

"This isn't a date. I'll pay for myself," I say curtly.

Disappointment flashes across his face, and then he hides it beneath a smirk. "Are you upset I broke your lover's penis?"

"Ex-lover. And no, that was actually quite satisfying," I say, unable to keep an evil grin off my face.

His eyes are admiring... and wicked.

"Good. I endeavor to keep you satisfied."

I bite a lip to keep from smiling.

At that moment the waitress appears. Evander orders a bottle of wine that costs triple what my entree costs... which will clean out my tips from tonight. I sigh.

The waitress leaves and promptly returns with the wine, then leaves again. I take a small sip. Layers of blackberry and spice with a silky, full bodied texture and a mile-long finish dance across my palate.

It's delicious. *Of course.*

Evander breaks our silence first. "If this isn't a date... what would you call this?" He arcs a brow.

I shrug. "Dinner. Between friends."

"Friends," he repeats, eyes glinting in the candlelight. "You know friends sometimes buy each other dinner," he says, a look of innocence crossing his face.

"That's true, but not tonight," I insist, unfolding the cloth napkin and setting it in my lap. He does the same.

"And I know you have your rules," he starts, leaning across the table toward me with a hungry look in his eyes. "But every once in a while, really, really *good* friends do get naked together." He leans back, grabbing his wine and taking a large sip, his eyes never leaving my face. "People say it brings them much closer. As *friends*, of course," he adds with a smirk.

"Is that so?" I squeak, and my stupid voice betrays the effect he has on me. I hastily take a sip of wine as blush creeps into my cheeks.

He chuckles, his piercing blue eyes catching every bit of my embarrassment.

"I meant what I said by the way... you are *the most* delicious thing I have ever tasted." He licks his lips in emphasis.

Underneath the table, my thighs squeeze together. "You hardly had a chance to determine that," I counter.

"Would you like me to try you again tonight? Take my time to appreciate you properly...?" he asks, as if I'm a fine wine he's only tasted just once. His voice is velvety, eyes alight with craving. I squeeze my legs tighter.

"There was something else you said tonight... Calimo flooded my old building?" I hedge.

The wildness doesn't leave his eyes, but it dims ever so slightly. "Yes... that."

The waitress returns briefly to give us our food and then disappears just as quickly. Perhaps sensing the intensity between us.

"Well?" I prompt, starting to cut into the elk meat on my plate.

Evander's expression is grave. "We traced it back to Calimo. He definitely started the flood. As far as the stolen property," he says, his eyes full of meaning. "Still undetectable as of now."

Damn. No golden dagger.

I cut into my meat again, feeling frustrated. "But for what motive? We haven't been together for over a month," I complain. "And I almost *died* in that flood," I add a little quieter. I take another sip of wine.

Evander sighs. "Calimo doesn't like it very much when I take his things. Not that you ever really belonged to him."

"Why would he think that we're together?" I argue, cutting my meat again with more vigor.

He shrugs, a cautious look in his eyes. "He may have seen us together one night. On the bench." He clears his throat.

I drop my fork. "That's it? He sees me crying in your lap and thinks I'm yours, then bewitches my home to drown me in my sleep?" I shake my head, disgusted.

Evander catches my eye. "Yes, his impulse control is rather weak."

He hesitates then, looking as if he wants to say more, and I feel a sound shield rise around us. The crackle of the fireplace fades away, and the clinking glasses at a neighboring table are somehow silent. I widen my eyes at him.

"We can't discuss this fully tonight, but considering you *did* almost die I figure I owe you more of an explanation," he says quickly in a low voice. "Calimo might not have tried to kill you just for being with me. He has always been envious of me, but I have to admit that isn't a strong enough motive for murder."

I grip my napkin in my lap. "So what is?"

"When your father killed your tutor—what was your first thought?" he asks, his eyes penetrating.

"What?" I'm thrown off by the direction this conversation has taken.

"You thought he was innocent—right? That's why you tried to break him out?" he urges.

"Right," I say, still lost.

"And if he was guilty—which we have every reason to believe he was—why would he have done it? If it was so out of character for him, what's the one reason he would choose to commit such a crime?" he presses.

"To protect me somehow," I say, thinking of his constant fear of me being taken by the demons.

He nods. "Exactly. And it makes sense considering the other ways he's protected you."

I look at him blankly. "What other ways?"

His eyes widen. "He really didn't tell you." He laughs once. "In a way, it's brilliant."

"*What* is?" I demand.

He leans toward me, brushing a strand of hair behind my ear. His hand lingers there, cupping my cheek. My heart—which is already racing—climbs at the contact.

His voice is soft when he speaks.

"Fiana, you're absolutely *drenched* with protection magic. And I'd wager your father is the one who did it."

Back at his cliffside home, I'm angry. "I had enough for my meal," I insist, holding the wad of cash I earned at the tavern earlier tonight.

He laughs. "I don't want your money. As I said, *friends* pay for each other sometimes."

"Then I'm buying next time," I demand. Another chuckle. "NO LAUGHING!" I shout, which only makes him explode.

I start smacking him hard on his back, my hands growing tired long before my blows seem to affect him. After a while, he spins around and grabs each of my wrists lightly between his fingertips.

"I know, no touching, but you're going to hurt yourself if I don't stop you," he says breathlessly, the humor still evident in his eyes.

I huff. "You're so *annoying*." I pull my hands away, and he lets them go willingly.

"Are we going to finish our conversation from before, or are you going to keep expressing yourself through violence?"

"You want violence? I'll show you violence," I growl, jabbing him in the shoulder *hard* and hooking my foot around the outside of his leg. I yank my foot against the back of his knee, pushing with all my might against his behemoth chest. His knee buckles, and he crashes to the ground, landing on one of the rugs as I throw all of my body weight over his chest.

He laughs harder and starts lazily stroking my back, sending a jolt of electricity up my spine.

"If you wanted to lay on top of me, all you had to do was ask," he murmurs, his voice muffled against my shoulder. He kisses a bare section of skin at my collarbone.

I jerk upright, away from his lips. "I just kicked your ass!"

He lifts a brow. "I'll admit, I didn't see that one coming." He rolls us over once, and now he's the one on top. "But you didn't finish me off, did you?" He pins my shoulders down.

I don't know if it's the alcohol or the pleasant feel of his weight on top of me, but suddenly the fight leaves me.

And all I want to do is *submit*.

I ignore him, and that inappropriate desire, and reach deep in to the well of anger that's been brewing since he lowered the sound shield in the restaurant.

Exactly three milliseconds after he told me I was '*drenched in protection magic.*'

"You can't drop a bomb like that on me and then force me to shut up about it for the rest of the meal," I complain.

He fights a smile, loosening his grip on my shoulders. "You're right, that was very, very rude of me."

"The rudest!" I snap.

He sits up, but I'm still pinned beneath his legs. "Hermetic magic isn't easy to detect—that's part of why it's so effective. But if you're familiar with it, or if you're a Relic, it becomes recognizable. I've never seen anyone so well protected," he pauses, eyes watching me closely, "other than myself."

"But what am I even protected from?" I study his eyes. "I was nearly raped, I nearly drowned, you've caught me breaking the law nearly a dozen times…"

He slides off me and offers me his hand. I take it and he guides us to the couch. We sit angled toward each other. Our knees are close, but not touching.

"I don't think it's the 'from what' that matters. I think what matters is *why*. And not just *why* you're protected with magic—but *why* your father was willing to kill someone close to you to further protect you."

My chest feels tight. "He was always worried that the demon that took my mother would come back for me. Or that she would," I admit. "I didn't even know we had Hermetic in our bloodline."

Evander looks puzzled for a beat but then nods. "It's not super expressed from what I've researched. Your father must have worked very hard to access it to protect you."

I widen my eyes. "You've researched my bloodline?"

He blinks. "Yes."

There's a big old *why* hanging in the air between us, but I ask a different question instead.

"You said you're protected too?" I question. "Why?"

His cheeks lift into a half smile. "Take a wild guess."

I think for a moment before it comes to me. "Maybelle?"

He nods. "I have to be able to lie at work—for her sake. But the High Guard especially have some of the best Premonics in the Elven Kingdom. So when I decided to save them, I knew I had to be protected. So that *they* could be protected, too."

I watch him carefully, listening to my gut. "But you *don't* lie to me?"

He shakes his head. "Never, as I promised you."

"But you *could*..." I raise a brow.

"But I *don't*," he says evenly. He looks sincere.

And my gut is clear and open.

I scoot back on the couch to lean against the armrest so I can fully face him now, kicking my shoes off and propping my legs up, creating a barrier with my knees between us.

The small distance helps me keep my focus. My thoughts drift back to the original question—one that seems an eternity ago now. And one he still hasn't answered.

"Why are you telling me all of this? And what does it have to do with Calimo trying to kill me in the flood?" I cross my arms.

He scoots an inch closer to me on couch. "Calimo is always looking for the next thing to win him favor with the King. And since Calimo has a strong Relic concentration, he may have sensed the magic on you and realized you were valuable."

My stomach clenches. "He said the other day that I was his 'ticket'. Like he wanted to use me as some sort of prize for the King."

Evander swallows, his throat bobbing. "I think it would have ended in a more sinister way, but yes."

"But instead, he chose to kill me?" I press.

Evander tilts his head slightly. "That part does still seem a touch extreme, but if you combine it with the fact that he saw us on the bench, maybe he simply... didn't want anyone *else* to have you."

"Because I'm *valuable* somehow," I say. My heart suddenly feels unsteady in my chest as I remember Calimo's words.

The irony is, Evander is probably using you for the same reason I was.

I narrow my eyes at Evander. "Are *you* planning to give me up to the King?"

He rolls his eyes. "No." It's the truth. "But I am in favor of figuring out what your father believed was so important to hide, and I'm not convinced it was just to protect you from demons. Or your mother. Aren't you curious too?"

I swallow thickly, the grief for my father still very much alive for me in this moment. I try shoving the feelings down and backing the tears up. A single one falls, and I quickly rub it away.

"Of course," I croak. "But why do *you* care so much? What's in it for you?"

He sighs dramatically. "If I tell you—if we go there—" He rests his hands on my feet. "You can't keep doing stupid shit. Like sneaking into the castle to steal things. I know you likely won't go back in The Cave now, but I thought when that was over you would be safe and now—"

"I'm still doing stupid shit," I finish for him, and the brand on the back of my head feels like it's on fire.

"And you can't be doing that if I let you in on all of my secrets. There's too much at risk," he pleads.

I understand what he's saying—even if he doesn't know the full extent of it. He's asking me to choose. Between the Dissenters—and him.

My heart starts to ache, like I'll lose something huge if I make the wrong choice.

But haven't I already chosen?

I've renounced Koa's leadership.

And I've already been keeping Evander's secrets, even from Credo and Warren. Even from Mila, my one true friend.

And for even longer—he's been keeping mine.

"Is this just about my secret then?" I say, my heart pounding so intensely I can feel the pulse in my ears.

"What do you mean by that?" Evander asks, furrowing his brow.

"Do you keep me around to learn my secret? Do you care just because I'm some mystery, and I might be valuable?" My chest feels raw and exposed as I speak, yet I know I need the answer before I can tell him my decision.

His eyes soften, and he squeezes my feet. "You're the one that drew the line, Fiana. I've been standing over here, panting after you like a rabid beast, yet restraining myself for your sake. So no. It's not just about the *mystery* for me."

My heart flutters at the admission, and then his words fully sink in and I'm laughing.

"This has been you *restraining* yourself?" I say, thinking of his game last night. And his remarks at dinner. And his words in my apartment, after he laid in my bed.

"Unequivocally yes," he says, his eyes blazing with heat. He scoots closer to me on the couch, pulling my legs over his, and then pulls me into his lap. I let him.

His breath tickles the shell of my ear as he murmurs, "See when I told you that you would need me more than oxygen, I was speaking of *my* need."

He wraps his arms tighter around me, pressing me against his overheated chest. My stomach coils as I become aware of every place where our bodies are touching.

"When I told you that the need would keep you up at night, and torment you all day," he whispers, pausing for a beat to lay a gentle kiss on my neck. I shiver. "I was speaking of the exquisite torture it is to be around you, and still not have you be *mine*."

One of his hands slides up the inner edge of my thigh.

"When I told you that your lips," he plants another kiss on my neck. "Your skin," another, and I shudder in his arms. "And every little bit of you," he squeezes my thigh. "Would be aching," another kiss. "Craving," another squeeze, "and begging for the feel of me..." He presses a firm hand over my core, and I convulse in his arms. "I was speaking of the harrowing need that *I* have for *you*."

Every cell of my body is alert and hungry for his touch. He still has that hand pressing against my center, and I find myself grinding into it just to get a some friction, even with my pants still squarely on.

"That's it," he encourages, planting another heated kiss at my throat. I grind into his hand deeper, and a moan escapes my lips.

"So you see, Fiana," he murmurs in a deadly voice against my neck. "It's not just a secret that has me wanting to keep you." He scrapes his teeth lightly against my throat. "I am ready and willing to fuck you, ready and willing to make you unequivocally *mine.*"

I'm writhing in his arms now, forcing his hand harder against my center. Friction, I need friction.

And why the hell are our clothes still on?

"That's right, Fiana. I'm willing to give you *everything* you want. Everything you need," he murmurs, sucking the sensitive skin at my neck. He moves his lips up to my ear again, and I shudder as his breath tickles my skin. "Just the moment you cross your own damn line and come and get me."

What the—?

I fall with a *thunk* onto the couch, and for a second I'm completely disoriented.

Because the unfairly hot, muscular male who had his hands all over me... is now nowhere to be found.

And every cell in my body is buzzing with desperate need for *him.*

I lay there in a shocked, overheated silence deciding if I'm willing to give in to his taunts. My hand slides between my legs of its own accord and I don't even care that I'm in his living room with a giant window baring me to the world.

I slip my fingers underneath the soft fabric and soothe the ache he's unfairly created, gripping my breast as I grind into my own hand. Wishing it was *his.*

That fucking tease.

He's right upstairs. I can hear the shower running, now. I can picture that glorious backside and the strong muscles of his back, dripping with hot water and shrouded in steam. My core aches as I imagine it, and a moan escapes my throat.

But I won't give him the satisfaction.

I refuse. No matter how badly my body wants to give in and become *his.*

I won't take the bait.

I won't go chasing after him.

I won't go knocking on his door, or crawling into his bed.

I can hold out. *I will hold out*, I tell myself.

I will fight like hell to cling to the final shreds of willpower—and dignity—that I have left.

At least for tonight.

Tomorrow, all bets are off.

25

I honestly don't know how I went seven years without sex, because when I wake up the next morning I barely last seven seconds before my mind is on him again.

The feel of his lips against my throat is a memory branded into my soul.

And I wake up smelling just like him.

I hate it, and I love it.

I shower, mostly to clear my head. Even with his scent gone, it's still seared into my mind.

When I make it downstairs with damp hair and flushed cheeks, I'm disappointed to find him already gone, but there is a note on the kitchen counter.

If you're ready to give up the stupid shit, don't wear black tonight.

A cryptic note, yet absolutely full of meaning.

Haldric squawks from the balcony and I jump at the sound. He catches my eye then turns his head to the left. I go to the far edge of the wall of windows, pressing the side of my forehead against the glass, craning to see what he's warning me of.

There's a narrow section of path where the trees part and I see a black blur rush by. My adrenaline kicks in and I race downstairs to the weapons vault, grabbing the first sword I see and a dagger. I'm back upstairs when there's a hammering on the door.

"Open up, Fiana," Warren's voice filters through.

I lower my sword onto the kitchen table as relief swims through me.

I open the door, dagger still in hand but hanging relaxed by my side. He's dressed for training with his black armor and dark hair pulled back tight at the nape of his neck.

"Did you forget we have training this morning?" he demands, forcing himself inside.

Damnit.

"Yes—sorry. I did," I admit. "But should you really be in here? Evander might scent you later tonight." I gesture to the still open door.

"I'll clear it with magic. Relax. We need to talk, anyway," he explains. He eyes the sword on the kitchen table then takes a seat. He gestures to the chair opposite him.

I shut the door.

"What's wrong?" My heart is still slowing its rapid pace as I sit. I place the dagger on the table next to the sword.

"Koa has made contact. He wants to apologize to you," Warren says, his forehead creased.

"Is that so?" I press my lips into a thin line.

"And—" Warren hesitates, eyeing my weapons again before meeting my eyes. "He has located the golden dagger."

I swallow around a lump in my throat. "How convenient. Where did he find it?"

"He says after your apartment flooded, he sifted through the minds of everyone in town to find the culprit. He realized it was Calimo before the High Guard even did, and he secured the dagger before they had a chance to get it instead, then wiped Cal's memory of ever even having it," he explains. "Koa cares about you —he was worried that someone was after you. Says he would have killed Calimo for you if he was a nobody, but obviously he's not."

I snort. "I thought I was only of use to Koa when it comes to stealing things and whoring myself out to Evander," I seethe.

Warren lets out a heated exhale. "He regrets his words, too. He was upset when he thought the dagger was lost, but now that it's secured, he wants to regroup."

"Oh! I see! Now that everything is working out how *Koa* wants things to work out, I'm no longer a threat to his control and he can welcome me back with open arms." I push out of my chair and start pacing, too angry to sit still.

What a contrast to how Evander treated me with the loss of the dagger. He wasn't even upset it was gone. He only cared that I was alive.

"Fiana, we need the Dissenters. We split off when he got out of line to protect you, but Koa has the network that actually has the power to bring down the King," Warren insists.

"And the weapon, too. Seems like Koa has everything he needs without my involvement," I retort.

"What are you saying?" Warren says, his voice edgy.

I turn my back on him, staring out the wall of glass. Haldric is watching our exchange with bright yellow eyes. His head twitches back and forth between me and where I assume Warren is standing.

"I'm saying that you, Credo, and Mila can do whatever you want."

I turn to face him. He's standing now, his jaw tight.

"But I'm not going back. I'm not *regrouping*. I don't trust him."

Warren holds up a slip of paper. "But you trust *him*? What is this, some kind of code?" His brows shoot up.

I bite the inside of my cheek. "No. It's a joke, that's all."

"What does it mean?"

"Nothing," I insist, my jaw tightening.

Warren glares at me. "You're not here to have inside jokes, Fiana. You have a job to do."

"Are we going to train, or what?" I hedge.

His green-blue eyes appraise me. He sets the paper back down on the counter.

"Go get dressed. I'll clean up the scent down here and meet you outside," he says.

"Great." I back my way toward the stairs then turn and run up.

Training sucks. It's colder than normal today, and Warren keeps me an extra two hours since Credo gave me all weekend off.

I take my anger out on Warren in our makeshift training ring in Parley, but it does little to chase away the feeling like he's chosen Koa over me.

Deep down, I know they've known each other for decades. But sometimes knowing someone longer can be a blind spot you don't expect.

With fresh eyes, you can see things that others never saw, or became immune to. With routine eyes, it all looks the same to you, and you wonder how anyone could ever see it differently.

We take a break for lunch, and Warren hands me a cold sandwich before bewitching my armor to keep my tired muscles warm.

We eat in silence for a few minutes before Warren finally breaks it.

"So have you given anymore thought to meeting with Koa?" His voice is flat and emotionless.

I finish chewing and swallow.

"I'm not going to. As I said, you, Credo and Mila can do whatever you want, though," I repeat.

Warren sighs, raking his fingers through his hair, which has loosened and mussed from its knot with our sparring.

"Koa needs you. *We* need you," he argues. "And you took an oath."

"To take down the King. Which I still plan to." My tone is clipped.

"What about sharing intel on Evander?" he presses.

I ignore the question, taking a bigger bite of my sandwich.

He watches me chewing, and when it's clear I won't respond says, "Fiana, we're counting on you."

My eyes harden. "Then let me do it my way," I snap.

His nostrils flare. "What *is* your way?"

I scratch my eyebrow. "Look—I've told you Evander might be sympathetic to our cause. If he is, considering his position, you have to know I can't dig too deep without him getting defensive and suspicious. He trusts me. So let me be trustworthy. And when it makes sense to bring you in on it, I will."

He scoffs. "So you're working alone on this now? That's not how we do things—"

"Warren, you all kidnapped me and practically forced me to join your cause, or else I would have lost my memories and been fired. You and Koa are just going to have to deal with the fact that I'm not going to do every little thing you say, in the *exact* way you want me to do it."

His jaw drops a centimeter. "But we can help you—"

"I don't need your help," I counter. "What I need is for you to stop interfering. And then I need you to dissolve me back, because the sun's getting lower and he's always back by dark."

Warren shakes his head then tosses what's left of his bread on the ground for the animals to eat.

He approaches me, towering over me, his eyes fierce. "I meant what I said before—I'm loyal to Koa, but I'm not your enemy. If something happens with Evander and your life is in danger, please tell me so I can handle it for you," he urges. "Even if it means we lose our access to inside information. Even if it means I have to kill him."

The words pierce my heart like a jagged, rusty blade.

"I don't think that will be necessary," I choke out. "But thank you."

I barely have time to bathe when he dissolves me back. He leaves me a hundred feet from Evander's cliffside home, to keep his own scent away from the front door.

I barely have time to dry my hair with the strange magical device I find in the bathroom cabinet. It blows out magically heated air so fast that my strands are dry in fifteen minutes.

I barely have time to sift through the closet and decide which of the slinky dresses I'll wear.

And I most definitely don't have time to think about the fact that I've made my choice, and I'm not going back.

I dress in a long, silky, cobalt-blue gown. One that matches the edges of his irises. One that is decidedly *not black.*

It dips low at my back and low at my neckline, skimming tightly around my hips before cascading to the floor... a single slit up the right side.

It's the kind of dress you wear when you want to be fucked.

And after last night, it's my turn to tease.

I'm perched on a barstool when he arrives with a *crack.* He's in his uniform, muscles bulging beneath his tight black armor.

His eyes immediately light up when he notices the color. Then they linger on my neckline. They drop down the length of the one exposed leg and appreciate the high heel strapped to the end of it. Then they drag all the way back up my body again, eventually landing on my face.

Yes, I certainly chose the right dress for our game tonight.

"I want *you* for dessert..." he finally says, his voice thick with need.

I smirk at him and trace a wandering finger up my bare leg. I will play him like a fiddle after what he did.

He mentions changing and dissolves from the room. I can hear the shower running upstairs. Within minutes he reappears back in front of me, hair still a little damp from the shower. His beard too. My fingers want to tangle in it.

He's dressed in khaki pants and a button down white shirt—something I've never seen him wear before—and the contrast with his hair and eyes take my breath away.

"Not black..." I manage to say, suddenly forgetting my scheme.

He grins widely, his eyes lingering on the parts of me he's yet to see bare.

"Do I need a coat?" I ask, deeply aware of the heat of his sensuous gaze. He shakes his head, a curious little smile forming on his face. He holds out his arm.

I glare at him. "You promise you're not going to let me freeze to death?"

He chuckles. "I promise I will keep you so warm that you may just decide you no longer need that dress..."

I narrow my eyes at him. He grins, and holds out his arm again.

I shake my head, take it, and we vanish in a flash.

"Ooh," I say as we land, my heels sinking into the ground. The first thing I notice is just that—we are standing in damp grass.

Grass! As in *no snow!* I gasp.

"Welcome to Meddia. Have you been here before?" he asks, our arms still linked.

I gape at him. "You brought me to *Meddia*?"

Meddia—the Realm where seasons actually change.

Meddia—the Realm where you can have sun, and rain, and warmth.

Meddia—where all the richest in the Elven Kingdom live.

Where all the best products are made by the best artisans. Where the best foods grow.

Meddia—where the Guard is a distant concept that rarely infiltrates their lands. Where the females are treated not quite as equals, but as close to that as you can get to it within the Elven Kingdom.

"No. I've never been," I say dreamily, taking in the rest of the scenery.

We're standing near the top of a rolling green hill with hundreds like it spanning out in every direction. Some are just green with grass while others are covered in a rainbow array of wildflowers. Nearest us, one is covered in blue. Bluebells I realize... like the vase in his kitchen.

And trees. Green trees, towering high toward the now setting sun. Some with blooms, others ripe with fruit, and still others just leafy, blowing in the warm breeze.

And it *is* warm, as Evander promised, as warm as it was inside his home by the fireplace. No goosebumps appear on my naked arms. No shivers run down my bare back.

The sunset—something I so rarely see in Ador with the near-constant snow—is breathtaking. Oranges and pinks and violets fill the sky, as the sun makes its slow descent behind the hilly horizon, a few clouds adding color and contrast to the scene.

"We'll be having our dinner there," he says, pointing just behind me. I turn, our arms unlinking at last.

At the top of the hill, about twenty paces away from us, lies the most adorable little cottage. A stone path starts just a few steps away from us, leading up to the little house.

Rose bushes and hedges flank the path, with a marble bird bath off to one side. And the house itself: cream colored with a triangular frame, little windows with flowers hanging beneath each one. And a blue door.

Cobalt blue, like the owner's eyes.

He offers his arm again as I start making my way toward the

path, and I take it willingly as I wobble in my impractical—but gorgeous—heels. Crickets begin to chirp as the sun continues to set... and a little tan rabbit hops in front of us between the hedges as we approach.

I giggle. "I love rabbits," I admit.

Evander smiles, but doesn't reply.

We make it inside. It's so different from Evander's cliffside home. Cozy and homey and dare I say it... sweet. And though he looked so out of place in his light attire back in Ador, I can see why he chose to wear it here. He looks like he belongs. Like he's *home*.

"How long have you had this place?" I wonder, my voice layered with awe.

"Oh... about three hundred years or so. I try to come every time I get a weekend off," he says casually, making his way to the small kitchen. "like this one," he adds. An afterthought.

"We'll be staying all weekend?" My tone is cautious. Warren would miss me at training tomorrow.

"There's plenty of bedrooms to choose from... it's bigger than it looks from the outside. You'll have your own space." His voice is even and subtly... resigned.

Does he think I don't want him?

I quickly change the subject. "So tonight, you'll tell me everything?"

His eyes meet mine. Nervous, cautious. "This weekend," he corrects, "I will tell you everything—apart from *one* thing."

"So no... you're *not* going to tell me everything," I accuse.

He rolls his eyes. "I am going to tell you things that go against my better judgement. Things it might be safer if you *didn't* know. But I will tell you the whole truth about all of it."

I narrow my eyes. "So what *won't* you tell me?"

"I'm going to reserve one truth, one part of the story, that is about *me*." His tone is gentle, and yet firm.

"And when will you tell me that?" I press.

"When I see that you're ready for it." He shrugs, his face now artfully blank.

"And let me guess... you're not going to tell me what that thing is—the thing you need to see—to know I'm ready for your final secrets?" I sound exasperated.

He snorts. "Nope. And it's just one secret." His expression turns warm, and yet somehow unreadable. "Just one," he repeats.

I nod. "Okay then, let's hear it." And then my stomach rumbles loudly. Embarrassingly.

He smirks. "Dinner first."

I narrow my eyes, but then smile. "Fine."

26

We eat on the back deck of the cottage, under the stars. And I mean *literally* under the stars—they are all visible. Such an impossible sight in ever-snowy Ador.

The warmth has the animals out and about. Throughout our meal various rabbits, squirrels, and even foxes approach us. I pet a few of the smaller animals as they pass.

Toward the end of the night, even a herd of deer pauses to rest near our table. I ask them how they are and scratch behind their ears. Evander studies me closely, but I ignore his watchful eyes.

The weather is pleasant even with the sun down, and when I shiver a little toward the end of the meal, Evander conjures a small fire pit next to the table out of thin air. The flames match my dress.

The food is exceptional. We feast on lobster and oysters—impossible to find in Ador—and fresh vegetables that taste like they've just been plucked from the garden. The wine is smooth as silk and goes down easy. We finish the first bottle and a second appears in its place. The chefs are somewhere offsite, Evander tells me, and agreed to magically transport the dishes in.

We are just finishing dessert—a chocolate torte of sorts. The animals have all moved along, and I can't take the companionable silence anymore.

I clear my throat, my tone all business. "Tell me what's in it for you—with the protection magic. With me."

Evander takes a long sip of wine, eyes never leaving mine. Observing me. Appraising me. I wait patiently until he sets down his glass and leans back in his chair, clasping his hands in his lap.

"King Vilero wasn't always a tyrant ruler—or at least, he didn't appear to be."

I raise a brow, thrown off by Evander's chosen starting point. And what it could have to do with me.

But I don't interrupt.

For a long moment, the only sounds between us are the crackle of the fire and the singing of the crickets. I have never seen Evander appear so—nervous.

Like he doesn't want to say more.

Or is even afraid to.

I'm getting impatient, but I force myself to wait for him to continue.

Eventually, he conjures a bottle of jad and a pair of glasses and pours us each a shot. He takes his immediately, scratches his brow, and then meets my curious eyes.

"I was twenty-five years old when the King informed me and my brothers—the other Guard recruits—that we were being invaded by the Shadow Realms. My recruit class had never been used in battle, and we weren't supposed to be except in absolute emergencies. We were told this was one, that the rest of the Guard was already in the Shadow Realms, trying to get an advantage on the armies stationed there to try and prevent them from coming here."

My heart rate picks up subtly—I can sense this story doesn't have a happy ending.

Evander pours himself another shot and then continues.

"We were told by the lead trainer of the Guard recruits that a small legion had slipped through the High Guard and Main

Guard's grasp, and we recruits were the only thing standing in between the Shadow armies and the Elven Kingdom—and more specifically, the King."

He downs his second shot, and pours another. I slide my glass closer to me, but don't drink yet.

"We were instructed simply to kill. No survivors. No mercy. The lead trainer explained to us that they had scouted the Shadow army already, that they were clustered in a forest about a half a day's walk down the mountain from town. We were told to dissolve to a specific coordinate—each of us given a slightly different one—so we could form a circle and entrap the group from the outside. Each of our coordinates were far enough away from the other that we couldn't see our brothers when we arrived.

"The lead trainer also told us which way to go based on where we were in the circle, so when I arrived at my spot, I simply started running in that direction. Ready to defend my lands. Ready to kill anyone dressed in Shadow warrior uniforms..."

His nostrils flare in a mix of anger and some other emotion—one I can't quite pinpoint. He downs his third shot.

My stomach is churning, so I join him. The alcohol burns on the way down, but within seconds I feel less anxious.

Evander continues.

"I found the first one within minutes. Beheaded him. The next one came running at me shortly after that, using magic to incapacitate my legs, keeping me rooted in place. But I used my own magic and... boiled his insides. Burning his organs and flesh from the inside out..." He shudders at the memory.

I shudder too.

He shakes his head once, his face contorted in disgust.

"Once he was dead and my legs were free, I took off running again. Feeling *proud* of myself. I knew there were twenty in this group based on what the lead trainer had told us—a one-to-one ratio with our own forces—and I had already killed more than my fair share. I had brief daydreams as I ran of being medaled for this day. For this *great work*."

His eyes look blasphemous.

I refill his glass. Almost reflexively. As if we're still in the tavern. I refill mine, too.

"The next one came at me from above—from up in the trees, but I was too quick. I turned the leaves into razors and watched them slice through his boots, and his feet on the inside. He was brutally injured, but a fighter. He sent flames out of his palms and I remember thinking to myself how much his technique reminded me of my brother Edward's. I shielded against it, creating a wall of glass his flames could not penetrate, and for a moment I paused."

Evander's eyes turn melancholy. My heart lurches at the change.

"This male was clearly a Shadow warrior—dressed in their signature midnight blue and gold. His skin and hair pale as the moon and his eyes blazing red. Their eyes are like that—did you know? They're red as blood. It's terrifying..."

I shake my head in response.

He takes another swill of jad. "My friend—Edward—he had brown eyes. Tan skin. Dark hair. He was built much more rail-like than this warrior. It clearly wasn't the same male. But the move with the flames—that stuck out to me. It somehow... softened my opinion of the Shadow warrior. Because Edward had a wife. And though this clearly was *not* Edward, he made me think of him. And her. So I hesitated.

"But not for long. I had orders, after all, and my glass wall was melting underneath his fiery blaze. So I broke his bones and watched him crumple to the ground, then used my sword to stab his heart. I felt the smallest twinge of sadness as his heart stopped... and wrote it off as my own concern for Edward in this very same battle. I remember hoping I would see him alive somewhere in the forest soon. So I kept running..."

His glass is empty, so I refill it.

"I was growing more concerned as I came upon a fourth Shadow warrior, and still none of my own brothers. Had they all been slaughtered already? It didn't seem likely. These males were all training for the High Guard, so they were particularly skilled in battle, even though we were all untested. I killed this fourth soldier quickly—with a thousand deep cuts, the deepest in his heart. I remember seeing the organ's final pulses and again feeling proud of myself. If these warriors were killing my brothers, I would gladly slaughter everyone I came upon."

Another long pause as he chugs his jad. I've lost count of how many shots he's had, but when he puts down his glass, I refill it again anyway.

"The final three I came upon put up more of a fight, but it was extremely confusing. Because these three were all attacking *each other* as well as me. All four of us, fighting to the death, even as three of them were on the same team. It didn't make sense to me, but with three trained killers coming at me I didn't have time to think too much about it. At one point I was cornered by all three of them. And so I ended them all.

"An electric pulse to each of their hearts—strong enough to stop it. They all three collapsed around me. A triangle of corpses, surrounding me. The killer."

He takes another swill of jad as tears form at the corners of his eyes.

"And then the King arrived out of nowhere. Dissolved to this pocket of the forest. I thought I was going to be medaled right then and there. I had taken out seven of twenty all by myself..." A lone tear escapes. He wipes it away too quickly for me to register the movement.

"And he *did* congratulate me. He said 'Son, you have far exceeded our expectations. I really hope you make it...' and then before I could react, he speared me through the heart."

I gasp. Evander's jaw tightens as he continues. "I woke up several moments later. The spear was gone, but I was still in the forest. Still surrounded by my final three kills, and still covered in the blood of my earlier kills as well as my own. Except they weren't dressed as Shadow warriors anymore. They were dressed like my brothers. And... when I looked at their faces..."

He swallows hard, and shakes his head. He downs the rest of his jad. I down mine, too, shivering as I do. I pour us both another.

He goes on, his voice edged with fury. "The King was ecstatic. 'I *knew* you would be immortal! And an absolute *mercenary* at that,' he said, shaking my hand as if I were his most prized possession. It took me a long moment to understand that it was all a trick. That there were no Shadow warriors. And that I had killed seven of my own best friends. Including Edward."

Another couple of tears escape, and again he wipes them away so quickly all I see is a flash.

"And none of the rest woke back up. I stayed in the forest with the healers. I begged them to try again, to do more, to do *something* to try and revive them. At twelve hours post mortem, they dissolved away. But I stayed. I spent the next twelve hours using every bit of healing magic I could think of, begging the Maker to undo what I had done, and what my brothers had unknowingly done."

We take our next shots together. I'm starting to feel a little drunk. Evander refills both of our glasses.

"At twenty-four hours, the King personally came looking for me. I was still working on my brothers. He saw how upset I was and tried to console me. 'You've been admitted to the High Guard—you'll be my first in command,' he said. As if I *wanted* that honor anymore. As if I *cared* about working for someone who had tricked me—and hundreds before me—into murdering my own friends."

My throat feels clogged. I down another shot.

"Why?" is all I can choke out, my eyes watering at the burn of the jad.

Evander's eyes look dead. "Because the King only wants immortals in his High Guard. And though there are other ways to tell, he wants to know for sure before we're accepted."

I shake my head slowly, feeling absolutely horrified.

"That was when I realized the King wasn't who he pretended to be for the public. At least back then, he pretended. What you see publicly now is pretty close to the truth of his character."

He drains his glass and refills us both. I push my glass away, recognizing I should slow down.

"So then why did you choose to stay in the High Guard? After you learned who he truly was?"

Evander shrugs, his eyes bitter. "At first it was because I was too numb to refuse the King. I had suffered so much emotional pain already... I didn't want to fight with him. And he wanted me badly, so he wouldn't have let me leave without a fight."

I wait patiently for further explanation. He doesn't speak for a long moment.

"And then?"

His eyes focus in on mine. "The King begged me to stay in the Guard for five years. Ten years at the most. I agreed, if only to avoid his wrath if I said no. So I worked with him—for him—with an expiration date in mind."

He hesitates, examining my face, a hint of nervousness behind his eyes.

"You can trust me," I encourage. "I know what I signed up for."

His cheeks lift up into a half smile, though his eyes are still pained. "You don't—not by a long shot. But I do trust you. It's just hard to even say this next part out loud to someone—on the outside. Because I have been keeping this secret for hundreds of years."

I lean toward him, my tone serious. "You know my deepest secrets. And with everything you've done for me—you have my loyalty. We're friends."

His eyes brighten slightly at that. "Mm. Just so you know, most of my *friends* don't get lobster magicked in."

I can feel blush creeping into my cheeks. "Well perhaps I'm your favorite friend, then."

"Oh you're definitely my favorite," he agrees, a true grin stretching underneath his beard.

And then abruptly, his expression turns sour again.

"War broke out again a few years after I agreed to join the High Guard—that was the Third War of Crimson Eyes. As much as I hated the King at that point, I hated the idea of letting others die for me more. Especially when I could easily be revived. I didn't want more blood spilt in my stead."

I nod, understanding.

"Fifteen years that lasted. We lost a lot of good people in that time. The High Guard was halved. It was the first war where vampires actually joined the Shadow army." He shakes his head slightly. "Their venom can be fatal—even to us."

"Like you can't be revived kind of fatal?" I lift a brow.

Evander nods. "Vampire venom, fire, and a ticking clock... an immortal's three mortal weaknesses." He snorts, his eyes going dark. "It was the deadliest war yet. And yet there were some moments—many moments—where Vilero could have ended it with diplomacy. I begged him to in the third year, and the seventh."

"Why didn't he want to?" I wonder.

"I didn't realize it at the time, but Vilero wanted to weaken our population. He wanted to put our people through so much trauma and bloodshed that when it finally did end, they would be so broken that they wouldn't fight him on his domestic measures. They'd just fall in line."

"I've wondered that before—if he started the wars on purpose," I admit.

He shrugs. "I don't know if he *started* them per se—every single one began as an attack from the Shadow Realms on us. But he certainly made no attempts to end them. And knowing what I know now—I wouldn't put it past him to have found a way to orchestrate the attacks from the shadows. Because it was during the Third War—in the early 260s—when it finally became law to steal magic from females. A war time measure that virtually no one opposed."

"I hate how much sense that makes. And how everyone just fell in line," I say bitterly.

Evander drains his glass. "Would you believe me if I said that it was all so gradual? That it took centuries and centuries of slowly shaping the culture and multiple wars before most of us realized where we were headed—and by then, we had already arrived?"

I shudder. "I do believe you—that's the problem. I can see how fear of the Shadow Realms could force people into submission. Fear of any kind, really. When you're fighting for survival and someone offers you a solution... and goes to great lengths to sell that solution as *the* solution, even if it seems extreme—"

"You still take it," Evander finishes for me. "Willingly. Gratefully, even."

"I mean—I just spent the last year of my life trying to break my father out of The Cave. And when I think back on that now, that never made any sense. How did I *really* think that was going to help me—or even him? Even if I had succeeded in breaking him out, then what? We would have been caught within hours." I take another shot, my eyes watering. "But that was the solution I sold *myself* on. I really believed if I was able to save him—"

"You'd somehow save yourself." His voice is softer now.

I look away, eyes watering for a different reason now.

"Exactly." I wipe my eyes.

Evander continues. "So you asked me before—what's in it for me. With you—with the protection magic. And we'll get to that piece in a moment. But I shared all of this because I want you to understand how serious I am about my role in this."

I meet his gaze again, noticing he looks sincere. Steady. Certain.

"Fiana..." He hesitates, and it seems like he's having trouble finding his words. "I've stayed in the High Guard all of these years, despite my hatred for the King and his policies, despite the First

Death and all the bloodshed I've been a part of over the centuries —for one reason only."

I'm gripping the table, I realize, and my heart is racing. "And what's that?"

Evander's eyes are intense, blazing with conviction. His power swells slightly, causing his eyes to almost glow. I feel an instinctive hit of danger at the sight of his barely leashed magic.

His voice is low when he finally speaks.

"I stayed close to the King for three hundred and fifty five years because when the day came that I finally had a way to overthrow him, I wanted to know all of his secrets, so we'd actually have a fighting chance."

I'm hardly breathing.

Does this mean he knows about the Dissenters?

"And what does any of this have to do with me?" I say carefully.

"Fiana," Evander leans in closer, his voice barely above a whisper. "I think you still have your magic. And I need your help to overthrow the King."

27

I'm too drunk. I have to be. And yet I take another shot.

"I don't understand," I admit after I set down my empty glass. There's half a million thoughts going through my mind now.

"Think about the protection magic—everything your father did. And the fact that he murdered your tutor, perhaps one of the closest people to you in your life besides him. What could he possibly be protecting that was so important that he would *kill* for it to stay hidden?" Evander muses.

I'm definitely too drunk.

"No—no. I don't have magic. I can't do anything and believe me, I've tried," I complain.

He clasps his hands on the table, leaning toward me. "I don't know about that, Fiana. Haldric is unnaturally loyal to you. You might even say... magically."

"No, I helped him break his wing free from a shingle. He's loyal because I saved him from being stuck there for Maker knows how long." I cross my arms.

"But you also *feel* the suffering of animals, don't you? Like the doe?" Evander presses.

"Yes."

"What if you're not really *feeling* it though? What if those feelings or inklings in the body are your way of interpreting their communication with you?"

I snort. "Communication? You're crazy. Or drunk..."

He ignores that. "You could be a Natric, Fiana."

I shake my head. "I was wrong. *I'm* drunk."

"Fiana," his voice is more urgent now. "Why else would your father go to such lengths to protect you? And not from harm or magic or getting in trouble. No, his magic is designed for one purpose only."

I shake my head again, but he continues. "His magic is there to guard a secret. Your secret. That you still have your magic."

I look at him dubiously. "Even if I do—and I don't—why would the fact that I still have magic lead you to believe that you need my help overthrowing the King?"

Do you know about the Dissenters or not?

"I'm pretty sure Havoc magic is much more useful when staging a coup than talking to animals," I add, my voice full of sarcasm.

Evander nods. "You're right, and I could have killed the King a thousand times over the years. But if *I* kill the King, the magic he stole from females dies with him. If *you* kill the King, the magic he stole returns to the females."

"I don't understand..."

"Fiana, you are the first female who has made it to adulthood with her magic still intact since the Third War of Crimson Eyes. Legend has it that only a female who still has her magic can kill the King to restore balance to the Elven Kingdom."

My stomach tightens in knots as a worrisome thought occurs to me. "Do you think others know?"

Does Warren?

Credo?

Koa?

Is that why they kidnapped me and asked me to join them in the first place?

Evander shakes his head. "You are already unbelievably well protected. Calimo likely knows you have the Hermetic on you, but he's not clever enough to figure out why."

I swallow thickly. "What about Credo—isn't he part Relic?"

Evander's jaw ticks. "He hasn't given me the impression that he does. Why—has he said something?"

The truth wants to come out. I can feel it on the tip of my tongue. I bite back the urge and shake my head.

"No. I was just worried he might," I say quickly.

Evander's eyes look tense. "That was a lie, Fiana."

Shit!

The booze has softened my edges, has weakened my ability to think.

"I know," I breathe, and my cheeks are turning scarlet now.

"What did he say to you?" Evander presses, curiosity burning in his eyes.

I think back through my memories searching for some truth— *any* truth—that could make sense in this situation.

Finally, it occurs to me. "Haldric went to him when Nasgardo tried to rape me. If what you say is true—what if he drew the same conclusions you did?"

Evander ponders that for a moment.

"He most certainly could have. But that was months ago... if he really believed you still had your magic, don't you think he would have done something about it by now?"

Like kidnap me and bind me to killing the King.

It feels so obvious now that they all know. I want to tell Evander everything—to hear what he thinks about it—but I force myself to keep those questions stuffed down until I have a chance to confront the Dissenters.

I owe them at least a conversation before I tell Evander about them.

Well... some of them. Mila, Warren, and Credo.

"I won't let anything happen to you," he promises, his eyes piercing and intense. "If Credo or anyone knows and tries anything —they're dead."

I flinch.

"Because you want me to kill the King?" My voice is shaking.

"Yes." He brushes a lock of hair behind my ear. "But that's not the only reason and you damn well know it."

I drop my eyes. "Because you want to sleep with me."

Never mind the fact that I want that, too.

There's a brief pause. He lifts my chin up, so I'm forced to meet his eyes.

"Is that all you think I care about?" His eyes are serious.

I swallow drily. "Yes." I try to look away, but he's still holding my chin.

He's silent for a long moment. So long that I grow unsure if he will ever respond.

Finally, he does.

"I'll admit I love teasing you," he smiles slightly, his eyes alight with humor. "And I can't promise I won't keep doing that. But if sex is off the table, I'm still here, Fiana. It doesn't change how I feel about you, nor how I will protect you."

My breath catches. "And how do you feel about me?"

He smirks. "A part of me wants to make an absolutely filthy joke right now. But considering my former statement..." He chuckles. "Let's put it this way—you're the only female I've ever brought here. And tomorrow I'm taking you somewhere that I never thought I would share with anyone. That I never *wanted* to share with anyone. So as far as friends go, know that you're the best I've ever had."

"But am I the kind of friend you wouldn't turn in for still having magic?" I question.

He leans in, his lips mere inches from mine. "I'd sooner turn myself in than let anyone harm a single hair on your pretty little head." His breath is hot against my lips. "And that's a goddamn vow."

My heart pounds against my ribs.

He's so close to me.

He lifts his chin slightly and his lips land on my forehead.

I shut my eyes. Wishing with every fiber of my being that he would kiss me for real. And yet knowing that if he did—I wouldn't be able to do this anymore.

I'd have to tell him everything—about the Dissenters, and the dagger, and all of it.

And I will, I vow to myself. *I will speak to Warren and Credo when I get back. I will give them a chance to explain themselves.*

And then I'm telling Evander everything.

I open my eyes.

"We should get to bed. Separately, of course. Big day tomorrow," he says, giving me a half smile.

My heart aches. "Okay," is all I manage to say.

I start to walk back toward the cottage, but my legs turn to jelly underneath me. Evander catches me under the arms before I fall.

"Fuck—too much jad," I say.

"Really? You don't seem drunk..." His tone is light.

I snort. "My legs give out about three drinks before my mind does," I confess. "I think I'm okay though." I push out of his arms and take another few steps, my knees buckling underneath me again.

He's had enough of that, and swoops me up into his arms.

"Hey!" I complain. "Put me down!"

He snorts. "In a moment."

He races at immortal speed inside the cottage and into a room I assume is mine. He puts me down on the bed, then starts taking off my shoes for me.

"I can do that," I say impatiently, trying to yank my ankle out of his grasp. But he's already done.

"I'll get you some pajamas," he says quietly.

"No—" But he's already tossing me a lacy nightgown from the dresser.

"Do you need help getting your dress off?" he asks, a brow raised. Except something in his tone indicates the offer isn't sexual.

I sigh. "No thank you. Goodnight," I say pointedly.

He winks at me and then leaves me briefly, though he doesn't close the door. I hear the faucet in the kitchen running so I wait patiently until I hear his own door open.

But moments later he's back with a glass of water.

"There's a little Curic magic in it that will prevent a hangover. Drink at least half tonight, half in the morning." He sets the glass down on the bedside table closest to me.

"Thanks," I say, truly grateful.

"Goodnight." He hesitates a brief moment at the entryway, and then leaves, closing the door behind himself.

I undress myself without getting out of bed, sliding the nightgown over my head. I chug half of the water, feeling the cooling sensation of his magic sliding down my throat and radiating throughout my body. It takes some of the edge off the alcohol, enough to where I feel well enough to get up and at least wash my face and brush my teeth.

When I'm done in the bathroom, I climb gratefully into bed, my thoughts swirling with the implications of what Evander has revealed.

I think you still have your magic. And I need your help to overthrow the King.

The brand on the back of my head burns again, reminding me I've already pledged my life to this very task.

I just never thought I'd be the one actually holding the golden dagger.

I was right about Evander, though, I realize as I pull the covers tighter around myself. He *is* sympathetic to the Dissenters' cause. I just need to find a way to connect the two without losing the trust of either one.

As I drift into unconsciousness, a troubling thought occurs to me.

Koa can sift through memories. He can even identify if a memory *isn't* there.

Which means there's no way he didn't know that my father never took my magic.

28

I take my time getting ready the next morning. I savor the alone time, letting the shower go longer than necessary. Letting the warm water relax my nerves.

I towel dry my hair and leave it undone in dark brown waves midway down my back. I do my makeup then sift through the closet for something to wear. I settle on a white floral sleeveless sundress that hangs long toward my ankles. I haven't worn a sundress in over a year. It feels like home.

I slip on a pair of golden sandals and then chug the rest of the magicked water. I have the faintest headache, but within moments of his magic filling me, it fades away.

I hesitate for a beat, bracing myself, then finally open my bedroom door.

"Good morning. Did you have a nice rest?" Evander calls from the kitchen.

I walk the few steps down the hall to join him. He's sitting at the tiny kitchen table with a book in hand, a mug of coffee nearly empty in front of him.

My breath snags.

Evander on vacation is a sight.

He's wearing light colors again—a pale pink linen shirt that clings to his chest muscles and a pair of white linen pants.

His beard and hair look messier than usual—perhaps a product of not having to report to the Guard this weekend—with a few pieces of his hair falling into his face. And his eyes—bright blue and dancing with joy at first, and then fire as he takes in the sight of me.

"I hope you never wear black again," he says simply, his gaze running greedily up and down my dress. "Was the bed comfortable for you?" he wonders with a suggestive smile.

"It was. Only... I was a bit *cold,*" I taunt, keeping my expression innocent.

Wickedness flickers in his eyes and I know he'll take the bait.

"They say body heat is an effective remedy for that," he says arching a brow.

"Do they?" I play along. "Perhaps we should try that. I really was freezing..."

"Fiana, it would be my utmost pleasure to warm your sheets tonight," he says with a wide grin.

"I'm sure it would..." I sigh dramatically. "But unfortunately sex is off the table. So I guess—even though I want you to—we can't."

"Mm," he murmurs, his eyes never leaving my body. "I knew you were stubborn, but I never took you for cruel."

I fight a smile as my lower belly tightens under his heated gaze. I move to the chair opposite him and sit down. He conjures a coffee for me instantly.

"No more cruel than you riling me up on the couch and then disappearing before our clothes came off," I say innocently, sipping my coffee.

"I *did* invite you to join me in my bed. You chose to pleasure yourself instead," he counters.

"Maybe I prefer my own company." I sip my coffee again.

"That's only because you've never properly had mine."

I practically choke as I swallow.

"And now sex is off the table, so I guess I'll never know." I shrug, setting my mug back on the table.

His grin makes me squeeze my thighs together. "I'm keeping it in my pants for your sake, but when you change your mind, feel free to seduce me."

"I don't see that happening anytime soon," I say flippantly.

He knows it's a lie. I do, too.

"You're like a ticking time bomb, Fiana. You can play coy all you want, but we both know how this little game of ours ends," he teases.

"Someone seems overly confident."

"Huge cocks do that to a male, from what I hear," he shoots back.

I lift my chin a centimeter. "That's funny. What's your excuse then?"

He bursts out laughing. "Beautiful and funny. You kill me every damn day."

"Good thing you're immortal," I quip, sipping my coffee again.

He laughs harder. "Jokes aside, you up for more secrets that could get us both killed?"

My heart rate spikes. "What's one more?"

He smirks. "You know when I first met you, your blatant disregard for your own safety pissed me off. But now I kind of love it."

I roll my eyes. "So where are you taking me anyway?"

He brightens. "You'll see. Are you hungry or are you ready to go?"

I take one more large gulp of coffee, then wipe my mouth with one of the napkins on the table. "Let's go."

He transports us instantly to some place that is far enough away from Evander's cottage that I have no idea where we are.

We're standing in a dry, grassy field with a towering, craggy mountain in the distance—though only the peak is covered in snow.

There's a sound of rushing water, and I turn to see a river stretching thirty feet across, with a thick forest of oak and other broadleaf trees I don't have the name for on the other side of the water.

More forest surrounds the clearing on each side, about a hundred yards away from where we stand. At one end near the riverbank, there's what looks like a dirt trail leading deeper into the trees.

"Are we still in—"

"No. We're in Lucia."

I turn back to Evander in surprise. His face is unreadable.

"Is this the part where you take me somewhere deep in the forest and murder me? Because I thought we were friends..." I tease, though part of me feels nervous.

He smirks. "Funny—but no. I have some people I want you to meet."

"Oh?" Now I'm actually getting nervous. "Who exactly?"

He starts walking toward the dirt path, grabbing my hand and dragging me with him.

"You'll see."

I quickly wish I hadn't worn a dress. Or white.

We walk—no, we *hike* through the forest, coming upon countless forking paths and intersecting trails, and somehow Evander always knows exactly which way to turn. I don't see him check a map or even a compass, and there's no hesitation in his decision making.

Some insect keeps humming in the trees—not crickets, something more rhythmic.

"What's that sound?" I eventually ask, staring at his back. He has released my hand and is now a few paces ahead of me.

"Cicadas. They're native to Lucia," he replies over his shoulder.

"And that louder squawk—there. What's that?"

"Ah." He slows and glances back at me. "That's a vorger."

"What's a vorger?" Something about the name sends a chill down my spine.

"They're—a kind of bird. Don't worry about them." His tone sounds too casual.

"Are they dangerous to us?" I hurry my pace to stay closer to him.

"Not if I'm here with you. Just don't get lost." He glances over his shoulder again. "We're almost there," he promises.

"Good," I breathe.

We hike another five minutes or so when we happen upon what appears to be a dead end. The trees are so densely packed together with other low lying bushes that there appears to be no way you can keep walking without hacking through it with a machete.

Evander stops a few inches from the first tree, reaching a hand toward it with eyes closed. I watch him, admiring the way his lips part as he uses his magic, his beard twitching as if he were saying his intentions out loud.

I don't notice at first what's happening, but a *crack* in the trees makes me glance up.

My breath catches as I watch the trees split and collapse, transforming into a wooden walkway winding deeper into the forest toward a large clearing—one that only now becomes visible as the bushes sweep out of the path's way, lining the sides of it as if it were a landscaped garden path.

Evander's eyes open and he pauses, giving me a once over. I feel the cool breeze of his magic wash over my skin, over my dress. The thin sheen of sweat on my forehead seems to evaporate. I glance down to see the small scratches from stray branches on my arms healed, and the dirt stains that had accumulated on my white dress gone.

As if I had never hiked at all.

Curiosity sparks within me as we walk across the wooden path, making our way to the clearing up ahead. It's about a hundred feet away. Whoever we are meeting, he wants me to look presentable for them. To impress them, even.

I catch my first glimpse into the clearing and stifle a gasp. There is a massive—what would you call it? It isn't a home.

More like an *estate*.

The sheer size of it suggests that it would take a dozen or so hired helpers to maintain. The front gardens alone are more expansive than any I have ever seen, even in the wealthiest parts of Abyssia. The main building is made of a white stone and towers high above the gardens—I count at least five windows to the top.

Behind the main building, the jagged mountain is much closer than it was before. I gasp as a giant winged creature appears over the top, then lands with an echoing *thunk* on one of the snow-dusted ledges near the peak.

"That's Mount Zora. We're close to dragon country here," Evander says casually.

"You don't say," I murmur as the creature blows out a thick stream of fire toward the sky. It lets out an earth-shattering growl that echoes into the valley, then launches skyward before returning to the unseen side of the mountain.

"They don't bother us, don't worry," Evander encourages.

I lower my eyes to meet his, then resume taking in the estate.

Toward the far right of the main building there's a pair of massive stables, so big they can probably hold twenty or so horses each. A couple of greenhouses lay to the far left, full to the brim with plants of all kinds.

Chickens wander the gardens aimlessly, as do a pair of gargantuan brown dogs, each likely weighing as much as me. One of them sniffs the air and then locks his eyes on me, snarls, then gallops full tilt toward us.

I freeze. Dogs *never* react this harshly to me.

"She's a friend, Dagger," Evander calls out. The dog immediately slows to a gentle trot, releasing some of the tension his body previously held.

Evander pets the giant dog's head as he slowly approaches me. I hold my breath.

"He just needs to sniff you to make sure he agrees with me. Give him a moment..." Evander explains.

My heart pounds as Dagger sniffs the front of my dress, and then circles around me smelling my hand, my back, and my other hand. He finishes his circle, pausing, considering his findings. I glance at Evander, who looks utterly bored. Finally, Dagger head-butts my hand, forcing me to pet him. I gently rub his head as my heart rate begins to slow.

"He's a big sweetheart once he knows you're not a threat. Although usually it takes him longer to warm up to newcomers. I'm surprised he's letting you pet him," Evander reveals, chuckling.

I shrug. It would be weirder to me if he didn't.

Dagger slumps to the ground and lays down, exposing his belly to me. I bend down to rub it.

Evander lets out a low whistle. "Now *that*, I've never seen. And I raised this one from when he was a pup. I'm offended, Dagger!"

The dog just sighs in contentment, his tongue lolling out lazily to the side, completely ignoring Evander. I smirk up at him.

"Dagger likes me more than you," I tease.

"It appears so..." he agrees.

Something in his expression irks me. "What?"

He shrugs. "It's just another sign that you're Natric, that's all." His tone seems artfully casual.

I scowl, straightening back up.

"I don't have magic, Evander."

Dagger whimpers, and then rolls over to stand up. I resume petting him.

"You do, you just don't realize it yet. I'm hoping today we can figure out why," he explains.

"Evander!" A female's voice calls from near the main building. I look to see the source.

Damn. The female looks like a freaking High Guard warrior herself.

She is close to six feet tall, dressed in a simple white sleeveless shirt and black utility pants. Her hair is cropped short with chocolate brown waves grazing her collarbone. Her arms are tan, and as muscular and toned as a female's arms likely can be.

And her face reminds me of Evander's—prominent brow, full lips, and piercing cobalt eyes. Hers don't have the two tone like his, but there is no mistaking the resemblance.

"Fiana, meet my cousin, Rosie," Evander says, gesturing to the tall female. "Although I like to call her Thorny, because she's usually a pain in the ass," he adds under his breath as she approaches. I stifle a laugh.

"I heard that!" Rosie complains. Evander snorts.

"Your cousin? Like first cousin?" I wonder.

"Yup. I'm immortal, too. It's not as fun as it is for the boys, though. I don't get to have male sex slaves at my beck and call... I just get to live forever and run fast. Of course Evander's too old world to have *that* kind of fun, aren't you?" Rosie teases.

My heart jumps at that admission. *Has he really never—?*

"Rose, meet Fiana," Evander says. "A female I'd rather *not* scare off within the first five minutes of meeting my family." His tone is edged with annoyance.

His family. As in—

"I see she broke Dagger. I doubt our family will be much scarier than him," Rosie muses. Dagger is indeed still cuddling against my leg.

"You brought me to meet your family?" I clarify, glancing in Evander's direction. My stomach is suddenly in knots.

"I brought you here to show you our school. It just so happens that my family runs it," he says, shrugging. "If I could have arranged for them to all leave, I would have, trust me," he adds with a grin as he pinches Rosie's arm.

"I fucking dare you," she growls, staring down her nose at him. Evander laughs.

Rosie stares at her cousin for another beat before turning to me. "Let's not cause a scene before poor Fiana even makes it inside. Come, Fiana. I shall show you our school!" she announces in a fake royal accent. I snort.

Rosie leads the way to the main building and I hurry to keep pace with her impossibly long strides, practically skipping with curiosity as Evander trails behind.

"Who do you teach at this school?" I ask, glancing over my shoulder to meet Evander's eyes. I'm surprised to see Dagger following me closely, too.

"You'll see," he says, lips fighting a smile.

"Who else of your family lives here?" We are nearly at the front door.

"My other cousin, Ryder—Rosie's older brother. Their father, my uncle Draven—who's my mother's brother. And my mother," he mentions casually.

I whirl around to glare at him.

"You didn't think to warn me that I was meeting your mother?" I whisper between clenched teeth.

His smile is taunting. "Relax, Fiana. We're friends, aren't we?"

I bite my lip, trying to ignore the panic that is now steadily rising within me at the thought of meeting Evander's mother.

His apparently immortal mother.

"You coming?" Rosie calls, holding the door open for us. I exhale, not realizing I've been holding my breath for so long. I shoot a warning look toward Evander before I follow Rosie inside. Dagger comes with us, and I'm a little surprised he's allowed in.

The inside of the—home?—school?—whatever it is, it's palatial. Marble floors, a pair of big sweeping staircases, gold leaf crown moldings, and vases of fresh flowers greet us in the entrance hall. There's a sitting room on either side of the hall, with archways leading to still more rooms on the far side and toward the back of the building.

Rosie leads us up one of the stairs and down a hall to the left, Dagger staying a few steps behind me the whole way. Evander hangs back further, taking up the rear.

The hallway has the same flooring as the entrance and every inch of the wall is covered in art. Some of it looks priceless; I think I even spot a few Hendrik van der Zee originals, which I have only ever seen in museums in Abyssia.

I honestly didn't think it was possible to be rich enough to own one, especially since he was killed in the Third War of Crimson Eyes. The bold colors and prominent brushstrokes are so distinctly his style but... *it can't be.*

There are other kinds of canvases in between the masterpieces —ones that look like they could have been painted by the students. Some are quite impressive, while others look like the work of a much younger artist.

The juxtaposition of the fine art with the children's art makes my heart swell for some reason; like this school sees its students as just as impressive as the greatest artists of all time. It's beautiful.

"Let's pop into Anita's class, Rose," Evander suggests as we near the end of the hall.

"Ugh—why?" Rosie complains.

"I think Fiana can learn something. She's going over bloodlines today, right?"

I roll my eyes, though no one can see. "I'm not uneducated."

"Even so, I'd like to pop in. I might learn something, too," he says casually. I find that hard to believe considering his three hundred and eighty years of learning things, but I choose not to press the point.

"Your school has lessons on Saturdays?" I ask instead. "Seems kind of cruel."

Rosie snorts. "You'd be surprised. The students here *love* their lessons. It's freaking weird." She pauses outside of a door on the right side of the hallway. "Are you sure you want to do this?" she asks, looking pointedly at Evander.

"Yes," Evander says coolly.

"Fine. In here," Rosie grumbles, pulling on the door. She gives a little wave to the teacher—to Anita—as we quietly shuffle inside. Dagger comes with us and sits down right in front of me.

The class has their backs to us, with Anita standing at the front. She's rather petite with platinum blonde hair that is so light it appears almost silver. It hangs in two long, rope-like braids around her oval-shaped face, and though her features look youthful, there's something about the way her eyes shine that suggests she has many decades already behind her, with hard-earned wisdom to boot.

A white board hangs on the wall behind her with various words written in different colors, but I hardly notice that.

Because I am utterly transfixed by the students.

Sitting in four even rows of five, every chair is full of elven children of all ages. Some look as young as six while others have the longer, leaner body of a twelve-year-old. There are even a few who look as old as fourteen, sitting in the back so as not to block the youngsters' view.

The age discrepancy isn't the strangest part, though. Every single seat is filled with a young female. This is an all-girls class—perhaps an all-girls school.

"As I was saying, each bloodline contains a thread that links all the way back to the preternatural energy of the Maker himself. Some threads are universal to all elves—this would be things like household magic. Others can only be found in certain bloodlines. The higher the concentration of a specific bloodline, the stronger the thread to the Maker's energy. That's why it is sometimes said that more blended bloodlines are less powerful. While it's not necessarily true that they have less power versus a more pure bloodline, their thread to the Maker's energy for all of their various branches of magic is thinner. So it takes more work to tap into the full extent of their magic."

A blonde child in the second row raises her hand.

"Yes, Charlotte?" Anita prompts, smiling at the child.

"If there was someone who had a mix of all of the bloodlines, and they got really good at finding their threads, does that mean they could become the most powerful elf of all time?" she asks, her voice eager.

Anita tilts her head to the right. "Sort of—if a completely blended elf trained really hard for many years, they could learn how to wield *all* of the magic that exists. But that doesn't necessarily mean that they would be the most powerful—they would have extremely diverse skills but there could still be an elf more powerful than them, just based on an individual's genetic power makeup."

Anita jerks her chin toward the back of the room. "Take Mr. Evander for example—"

I bite my lip to suppress a giggle at the formal way she addresses him.

"—you all know he's got a very strong concentration of Havoc in him, a smaller concentration of Premonic, with just a hint of the healing power of the Curic bloodline and the Hermetic protection magic. But you also know that Mr. Evander is very powerful in his own right, regardless of his blend of magic. I would bet you five notes that even if a fully blended elf had trained for decades in all branches of magic, they would *still* be less powerful than our Mr. Evander. Because power isn't just about what exactly you can do with it, it's also about how much you can channel through your cells, which is based on the size and efficiency of your mitochondria—"

"And I happen to have massively huge mitochondria," Evander quips. I snort at that, thinking of a similar joke he made before about a *different* large body part.

The entire class turns to look at me. I cover my mouth as blush creeps into my cheeks.

Anita smiles tightly, and then gestures toward me. "And Miss—"

"Fiana," Evander chimes in. I uncover my face to glare at him.

Anita continues. "Miss Fiana here also has rather large mitochondria. So it's possible that if Miss Fiana faced off with Mr. Evander, depending on Miss Fiana's bloodline, we could see anything happen from a perfectly even match-up to a completely one-sided fight... it just depends on each individual's specific combination of magical branches, their genetic power makeup, and their handle of their gifts."

The blonde child—Charlotte—raises her hand again.

"Yes?" Anita says warmly, meeting her gaze.

"So what you're saying is... I want big mitochondria?" Charlotte asks in a puzzled tone.

Evander is the one who snorts this time. Anita shoots him a glare of her own.

"What I'm saying is... we just can't let any aspect of our genetics determine what's possible for us. Not our bloodline blend. And not the size of our mitochondria, either. Because as you all know, for some branches of magic, not much cell power is required to have a big impact. Take Natrics, for example. They're able to alter weather patterns and even influence animals to suit their needs using only twenty percent of the cell power that Mr. Evander would need to channel his Havoc magic."

"It's *so* unfair," Evander laments, and half the class erupts into girlish giggles.

"It can feel that way. But then again, proper training can help you become more efficient. So even if you have average or smaller than average mitochondria, with enough training you can improve your mitochondrial efficiency and enhance your cells' ability to channel magic," Anita counters.

It's interesting, for sure, yet I find myself wondering why they are even teaching these girls this stuff. The technical aspects of magic are usually taught only to boys, since they are the only ones who would need to know how it all works. None of these girls will ever get the opportunity to *apply* any of this knowledge. It honestly seems... cruel.

Unless you kill the King, a small voice in the back of my mind says.

"Anita, are you able to sense Fiana's bloodline by chance?" Evander asks. I shoot him a horrified look.

"Well—no, actually. I was going to ask you about that after class," she admits, her tone sounding frustrated.

"Is that something you can normally do?" I ask Anita.

She nods, and then addresses the class. "Who can tell Miss Fiana why I can sense people's bloodlines?"

Four different hands shoot up. She calls on a redhead in the front row. "Yes, Maybelle?"

Wha—?

The redheaded child turns to look at me, her sweet face covered in freckles. "Miss Anita is all Relic blood—and though she doesn't still have magic, she has trained herself to understand the signals of her body to help her figure out elven bloodlines. She can also sense the genetic power makeup of elves and can also do a few other things but—" the child giggles, and then turns back to look at Anita, "I forgot the rest."

Anita smiles warmly at the child. "Thank you, Maybelle. That's exactly right."

I pinch Evander's arm. "Maybelle? As in *the* Maybelle?" I murmur almost silently in his direction.

"The very same," he whispers, his eyes bright with pride.

And mine—

Mine well with tears. Dagger whimpers and moves toward me, pressing his body against my leg. Evander glances down at him then catches my eye again, giving me a frustratingly knowing look.

"Thank you, Miss Anita, for letting us pop in. We'll let you get back to it." He glances at the teacher briefly before returning his eyes to me. He gestures toward the door and leads us out of the classroom, with Dagger and Rosie following closely behind.

The door clicks shut.

"That's her? That's really Maybelle? You brought her here?" I choke out. The tears are already falling rapidly.

Evander nods. "Yes. I did." He's smiling.

"I'm going to leave you guys... to talk..." Rosie says casually. "I'll meet up with you in the dining hall."

"Thanks, Rose," Evander says, meeting her eyes and giving her a single nod. He gestures for me to follow and leads me to another room two doors down. It's a small room with a desk, chair, and a couch. Someone's office, I guess.

We sit down, Dagger curling up at our feet, resting his head on his giant front paws.

"What is this place? Where did the other girls come from?" I ask, unsuccessfully trying to wipe away the tears that keep on falling.

"We call it the School for Forgotten Females," Evander says with a half-smile. "I told you that whenever a child is brought to the palace for execution, I secretly intervene and save them. This..." he gestures toward the classroom down the hall, "... this is where I bring them."

My heart squeezes at that. I don't know what to say.

"I started it about two hundred and fifty years ago—the first time the High Guard was assigned a girl to—" He shudders, and he doesn't have to say the word for me to understand. "Once it became law to steal magic from females, when a female was found with magic in the first hundred years, the King simply punished the parents. But when it kept happening—when girls kept reaching their sixth or seventh birthday with their magic still intact, he resorted to more—extreme measures." His throat bobs, his eyes tightening.

"When I understood he had reached a new level of horror, I knew I had to find a way to save these kids. When the next one was assigned to the High Guard only two weeks later, I begged my mother to take the girl. She agreed, and I took the assignment. Anita was the first girl I saved."

My gasp is audible. Over two hundred and fifty years old— though as a pureblood Relic she could still be mortal and live that long and longer. Calimo is a prime example of that. Relic blood was the original elven bloodline, created by the Maker himself over ten thousand years ago.

My tears have slowed, and I wipe away the final few. "How do you get away with it?" I ask. I can't imagine it.

"Well, if the child still has magic, it gets taken by the King directly—as you witnessed in Ador. So that part is always done with an audience. But the King doesn't like to be involved with the second part. So he assigns someone in the High Guard to kill the child. The first time it happened, I was too horrified that he was actually ordering it that I didn't volunteer—not to complete the deed nor to save the child."

He shudders, clearing his throat before he continues.

"But the second time, when it was Anita, I did volunteer. And I convinced the King that their 'poisonous blood' shouldn't be spilt in front of royalty. That I should take them out to the forest and kill them like beasts, like the 'traitors' they are. Of course, he ate that right up."

I nod as I recall him saying something similar on top of the bell tower.

"So I took her to the forest at the base of Ador, but then I dissolved here—to Lucia—to hide her with my mother. Once she was safe, I immediately went back to the forests of Ador and killed a small doe. I burned that body as I was expected to—instead of Anita's. Then I collected the ashes and used Hermetic magic to disguise them as elven remains."

"And that's how all the others got here? You saved them the same way?"

Evander nods.

"But—none of the girls still have their magic?" I clarify.

"No," he says simply.

"Then why teach them about the technical aspects?" I press. It still doesn't make sense to me.

"Because when Anita came here two hundred and fifty years ago she showed us that for many branches of magic, it doesn't *matter* if your magic is gone. Since her bloodline is completely pure, she had such a strong thread to the Maker that her body still knew what to do. She just had to learn how to interpret it."

"For many branches—but not all?"

Evander sighs. "No, not all. What we've learned through our students is that we can teach them to do anything that doesn't change the physical—things like Premonic magic which simply tells you information. Similarly, large aspects of Relic magic are like that. Harmonics still have the ability to be great mediators in relationships, though their skills are less pronounced."

"So no Curics?"

"They can't magically heal but they do have the ability to learn how to identify the exact diagnosis and treatment. One of our students helped us save Dragon—our other guard dog—after he ate a poisonous flower. She knew exactly what he'd eaten and was able to find us the antidote within minutes."

"That's—" I take a breath, struggling for my words. "I can't believe that's possible."

"No Natrics either—that branch seems too physical to be used without magic." He eyes me meaningfully.

I ignore that. "You did all of this—you've *been doing* this—for two hundred and fifty years? All while staying in the High Guard? While being the King's right hand warrior?"

My eyes burn as I understand the depth of his sacrifice—that he would stay in such a precarious position for *centuries*. If he was ever discovered, immortal or not, he would be executed.

Evander remains quiet for a long moment, watching me process it all.

Finally, he speaks. "Yes. I have."

"I'm such an asshole," I cry, covering my face with my hands.

Evander takes a sharp intake of breath. "Why do you say that?"

I part my fingers just enough so I can look through them to meet his curious gaze.

"You *know* why. I treated you *horribly* that night in the forest. Hell, I even tried to *stab* you!" My voice sounds muffled behind my hands.

Evander fights a smile, reaching for my wrists to uncover my face.

"I understand why you did," he soothes. "I don't blame you."

My face feels far too exposed.

"How can you even sit here with me? How can you still—*like* me—after how awful I was to you?" A pit begins forming in my stomach.

"You didn't know the real me. And I wasn't ready to show you, either. So... I don't blame you."

I shake my head in disbelief. "How are you not mad at me for this?"

"Because I don't like being mad at you. I'd much rather feel—*other* things—with you." The look in his eyes turns seductive. He pauses. "*Friendly* things only, of course," he adds, his expression abruptly innocent.

I stare at him. "I don't deserve a friend like you," I admit, feeling the guilt of my own secrets squeezing my chest like a vice. Tears well in my eyes again as the truth of the words sink in. He's saving kids, and at one point I signed up to betray him.

Not anymore, though, a small voice reminds me. It doesn't make me feel much better.

"Fiana!" he exclaims, his eyes admonishing. "It's not like I'm some saint who's never done anything wrong. Take me off the pedestal, love. Because it's *me* who doesn't deserve *you*."

"You've done something that actually benefits these girls' lives —at massive personal risk. Meanwhile, I took all your money, rejected you even when you were kind to me, and oh yeah—tried to *stab* you!" My heart feels like it's been singed.

And I spied on you, I add mentally, unable to say it out loud. *But I didn't tell the Dissenters anything of consequence,* I remind myself. I protected him as much as I could.

Evander snorts. "You didn't take my money, I gave it to you willingly. And it's nowhere close to *all of it,* so take me off the pedestal for that one. And as far as the rejections..." he raises a brow, smirking. "They haven't exactly turned me *off* you. Quite the opposite, in fact."

I glare at him. He laughs.

"And we happen to share a love for violence, Fiana. With me being Havoc born and all..." His eyes rake over me hungrily, as if they can see the flesh beneath my dress.

So much for sex being off the table. I press my lips together to fight a smile. He notices. And correctly guesses where my mind has gone.

"And now that sex *is* off the table, I must insist that you become as docile as Dagger..." His eyes are full of humor. "Though if you bare yourself at *my* feet for a belly rub, don't blame me if my hands start to... *drift...*"

He bites his lip seductively.

I don't want to—I still want to feel horrible about myself. But I can't help it.

I laugh.

"There she is—there's that laugh I love."

My heart skips. *Love.* A far too intimate word for a friend, yet he's said it a few times now. I need a subject change—anything to get him to stop looking at me like that.

"So your mother's here?" I blurt out as I remember.

Evander narrows his eyes at me. "Yes. Is that a problem?"

I sigh. "Why will she think I'm here?"

He shrugs. "She knows I've been saving your ass these past few months. I'm sure she has her own theories."

My cheeks burn scarlet. "You told your mother about me?"

"I did." He shrugs again, though he's fighting a grin.

"When?" Is it me or does the air suddenly feel thinner?

"I'm not going to answer that," he says, his eyes challenging me. "And before you try to seduce me to get the answers you want... I think it's time we join everyone for lunch."

"I'm not going to seduce you," I mutter under my breath.

He hears me anyway, and his tone is chiding. "Fiana, your mere existence is a seduction I can barely withstand. But sex is off the table now, so do try to keep it to yourself."

29

The dining hall is impressive. Like everything else in this place.

Two long tables are full of students—all of them female. Anita's entire class is there along with another three or four dozen students. I gape at the sheer size of the student body. Evander has saved over fifty kids. And many, many more over the centuries.

The third and fourth tables are occupied by adults. There are nearly as many adults as children. Most of them are female too—all of them except two males who sit next to each other, across from where Rosie is sitting. They look strikingly similar to each other and to Rosie, though one appears to have a hint of grey in his chocolate brown hair. They have to be Draven and Ryder.

Next to Rosie is a statuesque female with long brown hair, also tinged with threads of grey. She has her back to us, but I suspect she's Evander's mother.

Evander leads us past the tables of students toward the one where Rosie and the others sit. A few students stare at me. I try not to feel embarrassed by that; newcomers have to be rare, I imagine. It would be too dangerous to bring an outsider in.

My heart skips as I realize exactly how much Evander had to trust me to bring me here. Then my stomach twists, knowing I haven't given him the whole truth.

I will tonight, when we're alone again, I decide.

Fuck the Dissenters.

Mila will just have to forgive me for this one.

Dagger still follows closely behind us and when we approach the table, he finds a spot behind the benches to lay down.

Evander leans down to kiss his mother's cheek.

She turns to look up at him. "You *are* here then? I was beginning to think you wouldn't even say hi to your own mother," she scolds.

Evander rolls his eyes. "Please, Mother."

"And? Did Fiana put up a fight again last night or what?"

Evander turns—I can't believe my eyes. Calm, cool, collected Evander turns beet red. I stifle a snort.

"I see Rosie didn't tell you the news," he says shortly, shooting me a furtive glance.

"The world does not revolve around you, *Evander*," Rosie sneers. "Eloise and I had much more important matters to discuss."

"And what's the news?" Eloise asks. She still hasn't turned around.

Evander clears his throat, his cheeks still pink with embarrassment. "Fiana is *here*. As in *directly behind you*, Mother."

Eloise turns.

It's instantly clear where Evander gets his looks from. Her skin is a bit tanner than his—likely a product of living in sunny Lucia instead of Ador. She has the same two-toned blue eyes under a thick array of brown lashes. Her lips are dark red and full, while her cheekbones are high and slightly sharp under her skin. That— and the threads of grey in her hair—are the only signs of her age. Otherwise, she looks as youthful and vibrant as Evander.

"Well then I'll ask her directly—did you put up a fight again last night, Fiana? Or did you play nice this time?" She meets my eyes and cocks a brow.

Uhh. I take a breath and straighten up taller.

"If Evander considers my behavior last night *a fight*, then I'm not sure how he made it three and a half centuries in the High Guard."

There's a pregnant pause where Eloise, Rosie, Draven, and Ryder stare at me blankly.

They all burst out laughing.

"Well that was unexpected," the younger male—Ryder—says cheerfully.

Eloise shoots her son an amused look. "Is she telling the truth?"

Evander glares at her. "Like you don't know?"

She must be Premonic, too. And must have learned how to use her gifts even without magic.

Eloise laughs. "I do, I'm just surprised." She shifts her eyes to me. "From what he's told me, you're usually quick to draw that dagger of yours."

I fight a smile. "Only when he really deserves it."

Eloise appraises me. "She *is* feisty! I can see why you had so much trouble with her."

"Mother..." Evander complains.

Eloise laughs again. "Oh please, that's a trait I admire in her! Someone has to keep you in line, and I gave up on that job a long time ago."

"I'm never out of line," Evander complains, giving me a wink.

Eloise shoots her son a warning look and then gestures to the free spaces on the benches. "Come—sit. Eat. I have a lot of questions for you."

"I'm sure you do," Evander mumbles sarcastically.

I laugh.

We sit down—me next to Eloise and Evander next to me. Evander starts filling our plates with food from the center of the table, where platters are piled high with brisket, potatoes, green beans, and macaroni.

"She does have lovely green eyes, doesn't she?" Eloise gushes. It's my turn to blush.

"Thank you," I choke out.

"You know who often has green eyes, son?" Eloise adds, glancing past me to Evander. Her expression looks pleased.

"Yup," Evander says through a mouthful of potatoes.

"Interesting," she says, smirking. The same way her son smirks.

"I'm missing something..." I say, turning my head back and forth between Evander and Eloise.

Rosie snorts. "They're trying to guess your bloodline, since Anita couldn't detect it. Natrics often have green eyes."

I shoot a dumbfounded look at Evander, who is still busy stuffing his face. I've never seen him so hungry.

He catches my eye and understands immediately. "Yes, they know what we discussed last night."

I shake my head, reeling at the thought of me being the topic of conversation here before I even knew any of these people existed.

I take a breath, hyper aware of the many pairs of eyes on me. And my reputation among them as a female with a short fuse.

I force my voice to sound casual. "But I thought you researched my bloodline?"

"Only your father's. Your mother's is quite unknown," Evander explains.

Right. "Why do you think Anita can't detect it?"

He swallows. "Same reason as I told you last night. The protection magic."

"And that makes the rest of your bloodline all the more intriguing. Because it could be something we haven't seen in a long time," Draven adds with a wry smile.

"I've tried to tell Evander—I *don't* have magic," I complain, stabbing a macaroni with my fork. Something in my body feels *wrong* as I say that. Because it really *is* so fucked up that I don't.

Evander snorts. "Anita was practically losing her mind when she saw you. Trust me, you do."

I nearly choke on my macaroni. "I *don't*, Evander." The words sound harsh.

"Perhaps we should take this conversation to a more private location," Draven suggests calmly.

"And call upon Anita," Eloise adds.

"Ideally before our new friend stabs Evander with a fork," Ryder teases.

Rosie cackles with laughter.

I shoot them both a glare.

"Careful, cousins. Push her too far and you might become her next victim," Evander quips.

I sneer at him. "On the contrary, Evander. I prefer to take out all of my rage on you."

Ryder snorts. "I like you, Willowbark."

"Me too," Rosie chimes in.

I beam at them.

"Three against one, I see. What else is new?" Evander bemoans.

Draven and Eloise stand from the table then, with Ryder and Rosie following suit. I stand up as well, while Evander looks up with another mouth full of food, annoyed.

Rosie stares down her nose at Evander. "I see your appetite's back, cousin. Wonder what changed..."

Evander looks murderous as he swallows. "I'm going to suggest you run along to the teacher's lounge before I decide to throttle you."

Rosie snickers then holds out her elbow for me. "Shall we?"

I link her arm and send a devilish look in Evander's direction. "We shall. I'd love to know more about this missing appetite."

Ryder, Rosie and I trail behind Draven and Eloise. A quick glance over my shoulder shows Evander still at the table chowing down.

Rosie follows my gaze. "This is the most I've seen him eat in months. He claims he eats in Ador, but I've noticed he's a touch weaker in the training ring."

"I wonder why..." I murmur, cognizant that even Eloise and Draven could probably hear us several paces ahead. We leave the dining hall and start wandering down a long hallway toward the back of the building.

Rosie tugs on my arm. "It's you, of course. He denies it, but I think he was worried being so far away from you."

"How much does he talk about me?" I question.

Rosie snorts. "Too much."

"Easy, Rose," Ryder chides. "Evander's wound pretty tight these days. Unless—?" He gives me a questioning look.

"Unless what?" I raise a brow.

"He's trying to figure out if you've slept together yet," Rosie whispers.

My cheeks heat. "We have *not*," I insist.

"*I* know that. Evander would be all over you if you had," Rosie says, as if it's obvious.

The topic—however embarrassing—*does* jog my memory of something Rosie said earlier.

"You mentioned something before—about Evander being too old world to—" I can't finish the thought.

Rosie eyes me. "Convert every female who bats her eyelashes at him to an immortal? Yeah, him and my brother are boring that way. Although my brother certainly would like one..."

"Tread carefully, sister," Ryder warns through gritted teeth.

My stomach lurches. "Evander hasn't made any immortal females? Like ever? At all?"

She snorts. "Nope. Much to the frustration of half the female population of Ador, I'm sure."

"And Meddia, and Lucia, and Abyssia..." Ryder adds.

"Why not?" The question slips out before I can stop it.

Rosie shrugs. "Beats me. If I could have dozens of males

fawning after me, trust me there'd be a lot more testosterone in this school."

Ryder snorts. "You say that now, but knowing you, you'd kill half of them within a week."

Rosie sighs. "You're probably right about that. You and I share this one thing in common, Fiana: I have a wee bit of a temper."

I smile. "Only when they deserve it though, of course."

She tugs on my arm again. "Of course."

We reach a set of double doors. Anita, Eloise, and Draven are already inside. We unlink arms and enter one by one.

The lounge is luxurious. There is no other word for it. The couches and armchairs are made of supple leather that looks like— *damn*, that looks like dragon skin.

There are not one but *three* fireplaces along the walls, though none are lit since it is already so warm here. It's only the middle of March and Lucia already appears to be well into spring. It's kind of trippy after nearly two years of endless winter.

The lounge is empty other than Evander's family and Anita. They are all seated toward the back of the room, and on the coffee table in front of them, a tea service has been prepared. A bottle of rather expensive jad is also present, which Rosie and Ryder pour for themselves immediately upon entering.

Dagger has followed us in, I notice, and he sits by my side.

Evander enters seconds after we do, and I find myself blushing at the thought of him hearing my conversation with Rosie.

He gives me a look that betrays nothing.

He sits in a chair flanking Eloise's and nods toward the empty one next to his with his eyes fixed on me. I pour myself a tea and sit with him, as Rosie, Anita, and Ryder settle across the table from us.

"Where would you like to start, Evander?" Draven asks once everyone has settled in.

Evander considers that. "The Fated Twins, I suppose. I don't think Fiana's heard the prophecy."

I glance around the room. Everyone is staring at me.

"I haven't, no," I admit.

Draven nods. "It's a story from my and Eloise's time—we were born in the late 100s. Not many have heard it, especially those born after the Third War."

"Especially since Vilero took to altering history books," Eloise adds.

"Exactly." Draven takes a sip of his tea. He conjures a book then, and quickly turns to the page he wants. "This is *The Elven Chronicles: From Old World To New* from 170 A.V. Any edition made after the Third War has this prophecy omitted. Luckily, we Deschamps have a tendency to hold on to things throughout the centuries."

Deschamps—the name seems familiar somehow but I can't quite place it.

Before I can ask, Draven starts reading.

"In the beginning, magic was a sacred union between masculine and feminine, fire and ice, land and ocean, water and wind, day and night. It was tempered and balanced and graceful. It became more potent with trust and flowered with love. It obeyed the dance between the opposites, finding the perfect alignment to create beauty and harmony in the Light Realms. If conflict existed, we knew not of it. For the magic did the work to find the perfect solution for all. Peace and harmony were natural, and it existed that way for thousands of years.

"The Elven territories worked together to grow and expand their health, peace, and prosperity for all. Poverty did not exist. Disease was rare and easy to heal. Joy radiated throughout the realms, with only petty dramas or family squabbles dimming the light.

"One of those squabbles involved a male who desired a female. That female did not return his feelings and she used her magic to set him up with her twin sister, who had confessed to her that she loved the male. Since they were completely identical, the magic allowed the first twin to give her sister the traits that so appealed to the male. In the laws of magic, it was the highest solution for all for the male was happy being

with the female he had fallen for, the second twin was happy to be with the male she desired, and the first twin was happy to be free of his advances."

Something stirs within me, and my thoughts drift to Calimo for some unknown reason. I shiver.

I notice too, that Evander is watching my every move.

Draven continues.

"After a time, the second twin grew tired of pretending to be her sister. She decided to confess to her now husband how her sister had magicked her to appear like the first twin. She blindly hoped that because they had spent so many wonderful years in bliss, that her husband would simply accept her for who she was and love her all the same. After all, she had stayed dutifully by his side and bore him three children.

"But the male became furious with the hidden rejection from the first twin and disgusted by the trick of the second that he had been laying with for nearly a decade. In a blind rage, he stole the second twin's magical abilities and slaughtered her with her own power. He then set out to find the first twin to do the same to her. Along the way, he also stole magic from every female he encountered, including his own two young daughters. He allowed his son to keep his magic, deciding he would be the heir to this new terrifying regime that was just beginning to unfold."

I gasp. "Is this how King Vilero rose to power?"

Draven nods. "Yes, exactly."

"So this whole thing started because two females played a trick on him?" I shake my head in disbelief.

"Indeed," Eloise says.

I feel sick to my stomach as Draven keeps reading.

.   .   .

"The first twin meanwhile could feel through her twin connection what had happened to her sister. She guessed correctly that the male had finally been told the truth, and sought out an elder crone to help her.

"This crone was extremely gifted in the magical arts and could even see the future possible realities that lay before the first twin. The crone tried to see through a million different realities. In every single one, the first twin ended up powerless and dead."

I shudder. Something about this story deeply disturbs me. I have this eerie feeling of impending doom.

Draven turns the page.

"The crone said: 'You cannot hide. You cannot fight. You cannot magic him away. You cannot fix what you have done. And he will come for you, and for all females. The peace in the Elven territories is over.'

"'Please, there must be a way,' the first twin begged. 'I'll do anything.'

"The crone was silent for a moment. 'There is one thing. But the land demands a grave sacrifice from you.'

"The first twin repeated: 'Please, tell me, I'll do anything.'

"The crone looked at her gravely and said: 'You must spill your own blood.'

"The first twin's voice faltered when she spoke next: 'You mean kill myself?' she said."

Tea suddenly doesn't feel strong enough. I stand up and reach for the bottle of jad, pouring myself a shot. Draven pauses to watch me. The whole room is watching me.

I take the shot, making a face as the alcohol burns on the way down.

Draven waits for me to set down my glass before he begins reading again.

"The crone said: 'If you don't, he will. And he will take your power before he does it, ensuring no female can ever have her magical birthright ever again.'

"The first twin said: 'But if I do it—if I spill my blood—what befalls the rest of feminine kind?'

"The crone's eyes were grave. 'There will be many, many years of suffering. I see centuries of this male ruling, indoctrinating fathers to steal the magic from their daughters and wives. As the magic stays with the males and they get drunk off access to more power, they see this male as their god, and he eventually becomes their king.'"

I pour myself another shot. Draven keeps reading, but Evander watches me closely.

"The first twin said: 'King of the Elven territories? But there's never been such a thing.'

"The crone's brow furrowed. 'There will be.'"

I take my shot.

"The first twin felt hopeless. She said: 'But—centuries of suffering—what of the solution? If we're doomed anyway, why should I spill my own blood?'

"The crone replied: 'Because if you choose to sacrifice yourself for feminine kind with your magic still intact, the land will use your blood to nourish strength in future females. The process will be very slow. It will

take many generations of females eating from the land, absorbing the tiny remnants of your magic into their bodies, before any female will be strong enough to overthrow the future King.'

"The twin pressed: 'But there will be some? Eventually?'

"The crone shook her head. 'One. There will be one,' she said.

"The first twin went on: 'And how will she overthrow this all powerful King, if she will have her magic stolen from her just as all the others?'

"The crone replied: 'Because there will be a male who protects her. Who prevents her magic from being stolen.'"

I involuntarily cough, and Draven glances up from the book.

"You don't think?" I look with anxious eyes at Evander.

He smiles gently. "We don't know for sure, but we do suspect."

"That I'm this one?" I laugh without humor. "But that all assumes that I actually *have* magic. Which I told you—I *don't*."

Evander shoots a look toward Anita. "Anything?"

I look at the Relic teacher for the first time since I've sat down. She's staring at me intently, a thin sheen of sweat coating her forehead.

"No," she laments. Annoyed.

Evander sighs. "Draven—please continue."

I can feel my own annoyance building. I don't want to hear anymore. Next to me, Dagger starts growling low in his throat.

Anita looks down at him and her eyes brighten with interest, but Draven clears his throat and begins again.

"The first twin balked. The gravity of her choice to deceive the male fully weighed on her. Centuries of females left powerless, all because of her self-ishness. As terrified as she was about carving her own flesh, she knew she owed it to the females to give them a way—at least one way—to get their magic back.

"She took a deep breath. 'And I have your word, your binding magical word, that what you tell me is true?'

"The crone gave her a wry smile. 'Not that my binding will matter much soon, but yes, child. You have my word.'

"The twin felt the seal of the magical promise caress her skin like a feather-light breeze. The crone meant it.

"She asked the crone: 'Can you procure me an—instrument?' The crone generated a glowing golden blade out of thin air. She instructed the twin: 'Go to the top of the mountain where all streams originate from. Slice each wrist and let your blood drip into the water. Make sure the cuts are deep enough that you die before he comes.'

"The first twin swallowed hard, a lump forming in her throat, but took the blade in her shaking hand. 'How much time do I have?' she asked the crone.

"'Less than a day,' the crone advised.

"The first twin gave the crone a curt nod. 'Thank you for your help. I'm sorry for what I have done.'

"The crone's eyes were grave. 'Thank you for your sacrifice,' she said.

"The first twin dissolved into thin air, becoming the wind itself as she catapulted to the top of Mount Zora, the place where all streams began. The first twin landed lightly on her toes as she became her elven form again, a few feet from the mouth of the streams.

"She waded inside, tears streaming down her face, feeling so terribly alone. 'I don't want to die alone,' she whispered, holding the golden blade against the edge of her wrist.

"She used her magic to summon all the creatures of the mountain. The fish rapidly accumulated around her, weaving in and out of her legs. The birds flew lower than normal to stay close to her. The deer and elk and bears all forgot they were enemies and surrounded the mouth of the stream, watching her. And finally, a swarm of bumblebees landed lightly on her skin, her hair, even her eyelashes.

"She did not fear their stingers. She welcomed their company. And with one last look at her tear-stained face in the clear reflection of the stream, she slit each wrist."

. . .

I flinch as a sharp phantom pain lances across each of my own wrists.

The whole room is quiet for a moment. I can feel everyone's eyes on me, practically branding my skin. The silence feels heavier somehow with each moment that passes. Anxiety has my heart beating faster than a hummingbird's wings.

I shake my head. "Why are you all so *convinced* that I have magic? That I'm the one the prophecy tells of?"

Evander is the one who speaks first. "We can't say for sure— your father's Hermetic magic cannot be unraveled. If Anita can't get a read on you, I'm not sure anyone can. But even so, I've seen you do things that you shouldn't be able to do. Like win Dagger over the moment he meets you."

I furrow my brow. "That's not proof of anything! So your dog likes me—all dogs like me. All *animals* like me."

Evander shakes his head. "Dagger isn't just a dog. He's been embedded with Havoc magic. He's absolutely lethal, and it usually takes at least a month for him to relax around a newcomer. We bred him this way so he could be the best guard dog that ever existed, but it can get inconvenient because new students have to be chaperoned by a teacher anytime they go outside. And that phase usually lasts for weeks—not seconds."

I shake my head. "That doesn't prove anything." As if on cue, Dagger lays his head on my foot. I sigh. "Besides, can't you *feel* your magic buzzing in your cells?" I ask, looking at Draven and then Ryder. "I don't feel anything. And I never have."

Anita shakes her head. "The Hermetic seal—it's double wrapped. Meaning you cannot sense what secret it's protecting any more than an outsider can," she explains.

"Just because you cannot feel it—doesn't mean it's not there," Eloise encourages.

"But I—" I stop myself, looking down at my lap as memories

flash in my mind. Times where I pretended I had magic—and set intentions exactly as males do—and—

And got the tavern job.

And was saved from Nasgardo by Credo—and Haldric.

And was saved by the carriage driver from the butcher.

I had written those times off as luck, but—

"I will be hunted down for this. You all must know that I will. I'm a danger to you—to all the great work you've done here, just by being here." I scan their faces, saving his for last.

Evander reaches for my hand, and I'm too slow to pull it away. "I will make sure that doesn't happen."

"He's not the only one," Rosie chimes in. I shoot her a wary look.

"You all can't seriously be discussing this. *If* what you say is true —and I'm not convinced that it is—you'll all be executed, too. Just for knowing about it and not reporting it. Just for helping me. I won't let you do this," I insist. I don't know these people, Evander's family, but I know I don't want them condemned to such a fate.

Ryder snorts. "What do you think we've been doing for the last two hundred and fifty years with this school? You really think we don't understand the consequences of going against the King?"

"But—"

"No, really think about this for a second. I know you barely know us, but I also know you're not stupid. We've been doing this for *centuries* right under the King's nose with Evander still at the *top* of the High Guard. He is as trusted as he's ever been, since day one, over three hundred and fifty years ago. No one—outside of you and everyone you've seen here today—even knows this school exists. Every student we've ever brought here is required to stay here *for life*. Because we understand the risk of defying the King all too well. If even *one* student left—if even *one* outsider knew this place existed, we'd all be ruined."

I stare at Ryder, utterly speechless.

"But still, we do this. Every fucking day. And some days it's the worst. Some days, Evander brings home a girl so traumatized that it takes us *months* to help her reach some semblance of normalcy again. Even with healing magic. We do this not because it's *fun* or because we're a bunch of bored billionaires. We do this because if we don't, no one else will. And we're tired of things being this way. We will keep running this school for as long as there's a need to, but you better believe if we have a way to change this kingdom so that our school doesn't *need* to exist—we'll do it in heartbeat."

I take a breath, and the fresh oxygen does little to calm my nerves. I pour myself another shot of jad, my eyes catching on the fine print of the label as my mind catches up with a small detail Ryder let slip.

"You're the Deschamps—like *this* Deschamps?" I point to the bottle, where *Deschamps Fine Wine & Spirits* is clearly printed.

Rosie snorts, looking at Evander. "You didn't tell her, cousin?"

Evander shrugs. "She knows I never let her pay for anything."

I yank my hand out of Evander's grasp. "You're liquor billionaires? Turned forgotten female philanthropists?" The level of inadequacy I am now feeling has me wanting to shrink in my chair, but I force myself to sit taller.

Eloise is the one who answers. "We're comfortable. And yes, we want to use our money for good. Our students are a worthy cause. As are *you*," she insists.

Draven clears his throat. "What my sister means to say is that if you are the one the prophecy speaks of—if you still have your magic—we will do everything in our power to protect you."

"And not just because of what *we* want," Eloise adds, her tone softening. "But because you—you are what Evander wants."

"And there's nothing we protect more fiercely than our family," Draven adds.

Our family.

I look at Evander, my heart racing. His cheeks are lifted in a half smile. He doesn't seem uncomfortable by what his mother and uncle have said.

Not even a little.

My eyes are questioning him. I don't have enough space in my body for all the different emotions swimming through me.

Shock—at the prospect of being this alleged female warrior meant to overthrow the King.

More shock, and *fear*—at the prospect of still having magic.

Nervousness—at being the newcomer to this insanely powerful family. Even if Evander and I are just friends.

But we aren't that, are we?

My chest aches as I stare into Evander's easy, open eyes. As I remember that—according to Rosie—he hasn't turned any females immortal.

Not even once.

You are what Evander wants, his own mother said.

And the revelation that he wasn't eating during his visits here for months.

He was worried about being so far away from you, Rosie said.

And then there were Evander's own admissions...

Fiana, your mere existence is a seduction I can barely withstand.

But if sex is off the table, I'm still here. It doesn't change how I feel about you, or how I will protect you.

There she is—there's that laugh I love.

Love.

I am dangerously close to falling into that inescapable, all-consuming, life-altering state.

Thunder crashes outside, interrupting my thoughts. Everyone's eyes shoot to the window. Everyone's except Anita's, which are still fixed on me.

"You're Natric, alright," she breathes, her eyes wide.

"You can read her?" Evander asks, shocked.

Anita shakes her head, glancing briefly in his direction. "No, but that storm was conjured. And there's no signature on it. It's like no one conjured it." She turns her gaze back to me. "But someone did."

"Interesting," Draven replies.

"I- I didn't do that. I swear," I disagree. My voice is breathless as my heart feels tender and exposed.

"Maybe not consciously. But Natrics track very closely with celestials—with gods. Elven lore tells us that the Natric bloodline started when the Goddess of Creation fell in love with an elven male. So Natric magic can act like celestial magic," Anita explains.

"Translation, please?" Rosie grumbles.

Anita turns to face her. "Meaning it can be driven by emotions —not just intentions."

Another clap of thunder rattles outside. Dagger whimpers. Anita's eyes dart to the dog.

"And that confirms it," she breathes.

"How?" Eloise wonders, true curiosity reverberating in her tone.

Anita gives her a tight smile. "Natrics are masters of nature. Especially those with high concentrations of Natric blood. Especially those with a genetic power makeup like Fiana's. Nature isn't just about the weather, though. It's everything natural. The beasts, the birds, the bees—"

"Like Haldric," Evander says to me. "I *told* you."

"What's Haldric?" Anita questions.

"Fiana has a pet owl back in Ador who is unnaturally responsive to her," Evander explains. "He follows her around, brings her things she needs. Even saved her from assault one time and came and got me during the flood."

I shudder.

"But why can't she feel it?" Rosie asks. "The magic? Why would her father make it so she doesn't even know she has it?"

It's like I'm not even in the room anymore.

"I've thought about that—it's brilliant, actually. If she were ever suspected or questioned, she could truthfully say she doesn't have magic. And no Premonic on the planet would know she's lying," Evander says.

"But how would that serve her beyond protection? To have

magic but not be able to feel it—not even to know how to wield it properly?" Ryder says, looking toward Anita.

"There's an expiration date. I just can't figure out why it hasn't let up yet," she says as a furrow forms between her brows.

"What's the date?" I ask. It's not that I'm believing all of this, but—

"Your twenty-fifth birthday," Anita says.

"But you're long past twenty-five. You would have to be to work at the tavern," Evander says, confused.

"I'm actually—not. I lied about my age to get the job," I admit. Evander's eyes widen. "I *will be* twenty-five in a few days though, on March 20th. I hope you're not upset I lied—"

"No, not at all," he reassures. "But—you know what this means, don't you?"

I don't speak. I'm not sure if I can say it.

It's Eloise who answers him.

"You still have your magic. And you're not even done developing yet. Magic gets stronger every day, every hour, even every moment leading up to age twenty-five. Which means—"

"You're going to be more powerful than Evander," Anita finishes. "More powerful than anyone we've seen in centuries."

30

E vander's family is looking at me like I'm an answer to their prayers.

"She *has* to be the one from the prophecy—everything fits!" Rosie exclaims. "The first twin was a Natric, and Fiana is clearly a Natric. She still has her magic. She was protected by someone—her father. And now, Evander. And she's *powerful*." She tucks her feet underneath herself and sits up taller, her eyes alight with excitement.

"It does seem like a perfect fit. The most perfect we have ever found," Draven admits, glancing toward his daughter. "The fact that she still has her magic at this age is an accomplishment in and of itself. To have it *and* be Natric *and* an extremely powerful one at that..."

"Everything fits!" Rosie gushes again, bouncing on her knees in the armchair.

"There is one way to know for sure," Evander suggests. I look at him, panic steadily rising within me. "Ryder could track down the old crone."

Anita's eyes widen. "She's still alive, then?"

Evander nods. "As far as I last checked. She's good at evading capture."

"I could leave tonight," Ryder agrees.

"Wait—stop!" I stand up, too anxious to sit still anymore. I take several steps away from Evander and his overly eager family. "I don't even know if I can *do* this," I admit. "I don't know if I can kill the King."

The brand on the back of my head burns searing hot, reminding me I've pledged my very life to this cause.

I watch each of their faces falter. All except Evander's, which remains confident and steady.

"I mean I *can* do this, but I need time. This is all happening so fast," I say quickly. The tattoo calms down, and with it, so does my heart rate.

"You don't have to if you don't want to," Evander encourages. "We'll still protect you no matter what."

"Yes she *does* have to. Are you fucking kidding me right now, Evander?" Ryder jumps in.

"Ryder—" Evander starts.

"No he's right," I cut in. "I *do* have to do this. I just need some *time*."

"We can train you. Give me a month in the ring and you'll be ready," Rosie says confidently.

"And I can teach you how to use your magic," adds Ryder.

Evander stands up and approaches me, his eyes gentle. "But it's your choice, Fiana. We won't force you into anything."

"Speak for yourself, cousin," Rosie growls.

His jaw ticks. "*I* won't force you into anything," he says to me directly. "And I can take Rosie any day."

"We'll see about that," she huffs.

Evander ignores her. "It's up to you."

I can feel my face flushing. "I have work. Back in Ador."

It's a poor excuse, but I just need to get the hell out of here so I can explain myself to Evander before things go any further.

Ryder snorts. "Stick with us and you'll never have to work again."

Eloise shoots him a disapproving look, but adds, "We do have spare rooms. There's plenty of space here for you."

"I—" I lose my words as Evander takes another step toward me, catching and holding my gaze.

"Perhaps we should let Fiana think about this. It is a large ask of us to make," he says without turning toward the others in the room.

"But, Evander—"

"Enough, Rose. Evander is right. We should let Fiana decide this on her own timing," Draven interjects. "The King isn't going anywhere."

Rosie grumbles. "That's the point, though."

"Rose, give it a rest," Ryder says quietly.

My eyes are still locked with Evander's. "Yes. I just need some time," I finally say.

Evander gives me a wink, then turns back toward his family.

"I think we're going to take off then," he announces.

Eloise's face falls. "You're not staying the whole weekend?"

Evander shakes his head. "I think Fiana might need some time alone to process all of this."

"But you'll come back soon, won't you Fiana?" Eloise demands.

I give her a tentative smile. "As long as I'm welcome."

She raises a brow, smirking. "Just refrain from trying to stab my son again and you're welcome anytime."

I fight a smile. "Sounds fair."

"And on that note—let's go," Evander urges.

"How are you feeling about all of this?" Evander asks me.

I shrug, though he can't see me. We're hiking our way back to the original clearing by the river, the School of Forgotten Females tucked back into the forest's protective embrace, with both Dagger and Dragon defending it again.

"I don't know what to feel," I say honestly.

"That makes a lot of sense."

We grow silent for a while, though the cicadas are humming loudly again.

"Tell me something," I start. I need to get out of the chaos in my own mind.

"What do you want to know?" Evander encourages.

But the question gets stuck in my throat as blush heats my cheeks. I'm losing my damn nerve.

He sneaks a glance over his shoulder at me, his eyes curious. At the sight of my face, he stops short.

I sigh. "Rosie said that you weren't eating before. Why was that?" It isn't the question I actually want answered, but it feels safer to ask.

He closes his eyes, shaking his head once. "My cousin and her big fat mouth."

He opens his eyes, which look wicked now. "You're too reckless for your own good... it made me nervous being away from you."

My heart thuds. "She said you didn't eat for months, Evander."

He raises a brow. "So?"

"So we weren't even friends until recently," I point out.

He shrugs. "Yes, and you were the *most* reckless during that time. Sneaking into The Cave... stealing horses..."

I gasp. "That was right after we met."

"Your point?" He turns and starts leading us through the forest again, at a faster clip.

I race after him. "You were nervous about me getting into trouble before you even knew me? Enough to not want to eat?"

"You say that like it's a bad thing," he says, pausing to pull a branch aside that obscures our path.

My heart is pounding. I move past him then whirl on him so

we're eye to eye, finally feeling brave enough to ask what I really want to know.

"She also said you didn't make any immortal females."

Evander jerks his head back "Did you think that I had?"

"Yes. I thought you'd made *dozens*," I breathe. "You've been alive for how long?" I raise a brow.

He scowls. "You thought that little of me?" His eyes darken.

I don't know how to respond to that.

He starts off on the trail again.

"Yes," I finally admit.

His back muscles tighten. "And why did you think that?"

I scoff. "Well what was I *supposed* to think, Evander? You were parading around a different one each night and they all seemed *obsessed* with you."

I know it's unfair. I know many of them (maybe all of them) were Dissenter plants, but I can't stop the accusations from coming out of my mouth.

He whirls on me. "They are. Most females are—except *you* in some cruel twist of fate. That doesn't mean they *belong* to me. They just smell the wealth and status on me. They know if they're with me, I'll buy their drinks and their carriage rides home. Some probably hope I'll fall in love with them and immortalize them. And I don't blame them. Not one bit. Because they're just trying to survive. Just like me."

"*Survive*? How are *you* fighting for survival?" I demand, my anger rising. "You have magic, you're a *billionaire*, and you're at the top of the High Guard. What hardship is threatening *your* survival, Evander?"

"YOU!" He shouts, his eyes shadowed. I take a step back, my heart racing, but he advances a step of his own. "You heard Rosie— I don't eat because I worry about *you*! First you're stealing horses and sneaking into The Cave. Then you're with Calimo. Then Nasgardo tries to assault you. And all the while you're pissed at me because you think I'm this horrible child murdering monster! And I practically have to *bribe* you to bring your guard down long enough for you to even see the real me. And just when I think we've turned a corner, I find out that all this time you thought I immortalized half of Ador like a fucking pig."

He shakes his head, his magic glowing red with his anger. His voice is pained. "It's *you* I have to survive Fiana. If anything will be the death of me, it's you."

My eyes are wet. "I didn't know!"

"You didn't ask!" he shoots back. He starts off on the trail again, his entire body tense.

I race after him. "Evander, I'm sorry. I- I care about you. Please, slow down and let's talk about this," I beg.

"We have to keep moving," he says gruffly.

"Why?"

Evander abruptly stops walking and I almost ram right into him but he whirls around in a flash and holds out a stiff arm to catch me. There's a look of utter horror on his face.

"What is it?" I whisper, barely loud enough for even my own ears.

He looks over my shoulder. "Vorgers. Six of them," he rasps, and then his eyes slide back to meet mine. "Fiana, don't look. *Run.*"

I can't help myself. I look.

The beasts are nearly eight feet tall with two long, spindly legs coated in a thick black hair. The body is as thick as a horse's, covered in black and dark red feathers that don't look soft at all; they stick out in every direction and look stiff. *Sharp*, even. As if their entire body is covered in a spiky armor.

The neck is longer than average, but it juts forward instead of skyward like a swan's. And the head. Blood red eyes and a waxy black beak full of *teeth*. Razor sharp rows—a jigsaw of teeth—line the inside of the sharp beak.

Because apparently they need more weapons to kill us with.

"Get back!" Evander shoves in front of me, blocking me from view, pulling out a short sword I didn't know he was carrying.

"Give me a weapon!" I hiss.

He tosses me a dagger still in its sheath without turning. I catch it and unsheathe it, my heart a jagged beat in my chest.

The vorger in the front opens his colossal wingspan of spiky feathers and flaps once, letting out an ear-piercing shriek that makes my stomach drop toward my ankles. My legs feel leaden as Evander urges me to *run* again.

But I can't leave him.

Evander glances over his shoulder at me for a split second and then launches himself toward the first vorger. His blade makes a clean cut across the beast's neck and a bloody disembodied head lands with a *thud* at his feet.

Uhh. I fight against an intense wave of nausea at the sight and creep a few steps closer behind Evander, my knife outstretched.

There's a *slash* and several more screeches as Evander works his way through the flock. Two more heads come tumbling to the ground. I avoid looking at them, keeping my eyes on Evander instead. Watching the way his muscles contract and expand as he fights. Seeing the steadiness—the beauty, even—in how he moves.

And yet I can't figure out why he isn't just dissolving us to safety. Or using his Havoc magic to incapacitate them, instead of risking going near them in hand to hand combat. Or shielding us, our scent and our sounds so we can sneak away. These are all things I know he can do.

A fourth head falls with a *thunk*. I keep my eyes lifted. And my knife. I take another cautious step toward him and the vorgers that remain standing.

The two that are left are better at avoiding his quick move-ments. I watch in horror, realizing that they move at a similar speed to immortals. Lightning fast, and utterly lethal.

"Argh!" Evander grunts as a vorger strikes his shoulder. I watch in horror as he is lifted off the ground by the vorgers' beak—no, by his *teeth*—as streaks of blood dribble down the front of his light pink shirt. The other strikes toward him with his razor-sharp teeth like a snake.

Evander swipes out with his free arm, which still holds the short sword, but the vorger in front of him is too quick.

"Use your magic!" I wail, feeling useless even with the dagger in hand. *What is he trying to prove?*

"I can't," he growls through gritted teeth as he swings back to swipe the vorger holding him in the chest.

The beast yelps, finally dropping Evander, who in a flash pulls out the short sword and decapitates the other vorger before he can strike again. Without even pausing to catch his breath, he spins around and finishes off the last one. The head thuds against a tree before tumbling to the ground, Evander's blood still dripping from his hideous teeth.

Evander takes a labored breath, sheathing his short sword (which seems to disappear the moment he does) and turns to meet my eyes. My wide, terrified, eyes.

"Are you okay?" he breathes, taking a few cautious steps toward me.

"Me? You're the one who's bleeding!" I gasp as fresh trickles of blood spurt out of his shoulder.

"I'm okay," he insists, shutting his eyes for the shortest of seconds to heal himself. The bleeding rapidly stops and the wound closes over. The blood stains on his shirt disappear, and when he opens his eyes, I swear he looks *amused*.

"What are you smirking at?" I snap. Though admittedly, I'm glad he isn't still mad at me.

He chuckles. "I shouldn't be laughing because you didn't know, but it's just when you said *use your magic* as if I hadn't thought of that..." His smile widens.

I scowl. "Why couldn't you?"

"Because vorgers have magic, too. One of the ways they incapacitate their prey is by shutting down access to the Maker. So I *literally* didn't have access to magic. At least while they were still alive."

I cross my arms, the dagger jutting out of my fist. "Just *a kind of bird*, huh? Don't *worry* about them?" My glare is meant to punish.

Evander shrugs, eyes dancing with laughter. "I just killed six of 'em single handedly without magic. I don't think you *had* anything to worry about." And then his face falls. "I'm sorry I got mad at you."

My chest aches. I relax my stance, sheathing the dagger and handing it back to him.

"I'm sorry I believed you were a rake."

He fights a smile. He takes another step toward me, the space between us rapidly shrinking. "So *that's* why you wanted sex off the table..."

I take a sharp intake of breath as his hand reaches for my chin. He tilts my head up to look at him, his eyes burning with craving.

"I wonder. If I kissed you right now, would you stop me?" He runs his thumb over the seam of my lips, which part under his touch.

"Friends don't kiss," I say weakly, my heart hammering against my ribs.

"Are you sure about that, Fiana?" He inches his face closer to mine, his eyes challenging me.

"No," I breathe. "I mean, yes," I correct, blush filling my cheeks.

"I think they do sometimes. Like after one saves the other's life..." His mouth is centimeters from mine. His hot breath tickles my lips.

"Yes," I whisper. "I mean, no." He smells like spearmint. I lick my lips.

"You want me to kiss you. Don't you, Fiana?"

My breathing shallows. I can't think straight. "Yes," I admit. I close my eyes.

He chuckles. "That's what I thought," he says against my lips, and then he pulls back instantly. "Too bad sex is off the table..."

My eyes snap open as my jaw drops. "Are you *fucking* kidding me?"

He laughs full out now. "No, I'm not. That's payback for your *no touching* games. Now come on, let's get back to the clearing before another pack of vorgers finds us." He starts off at a brisk pace.

"You already *got* payback. With that stupid *breathing* game of yours! And that stupid *couch* incident!" I hiss as I chase after him.

His laughter grows louder. "You rather enjoyed those times if I recall... I do remember hearing some satisfied screams."

"You did *not!*" I growl.

"It's okay, Fiana. I touched myself those nights too," he encourages, his tone oozing humor. He steps over a fallen tree, then turns, a wide grin on his face. He holds his hand out for me to help me climb over.

I ignore it. "You must have heard the wind."

"Could be, considering you're a Natric. I imagine a shattering orgasm *could* impact weather patterns for someone like you," he teases.

I groan. "That is *not* what I meant."

"Sure it wasn't." He moves to the lead again.

"It wasn't, Evander." I grit my teeth.

We reach the clearing. He turns to me with a barely hidden grin.

"Fiana, please, just relax. It's just a little teasing amongst friends. That's all." He winks.

"Oh is that all?" I ask innocently, a new strategy forming in my mind.

He narrows his eyes at me. "I don't like your tone. Come here and let's dissolve back to Meddia."

I shrug. "Fine."

He wraps his arms around me from behind and with a *crack*, we leave Lucia, landing on the hill where his cottage is.

Before he can unhand me, I grind my ass intentionally against his pelvis.

"Oh, fuck," he breathes against my hair. I smile at his shock and grind a little harder, noticing the exact moment when he starts to get hard.

It barely takes a second.

"What are you trying to do to me?" he curses.

"I don't know what you're talking about," I say innocently, leaning my head back against his chest. His arms tighten around me.

"Is sex still off the table?" he asks, his voice strained.

I don't answer at first. Instead I press harder against his erection.

He groans. "Fucking answer me, Fiana," he pleads.

I turn to face him, wrapping my arms around his neck, watching with satisfaction as his eyes practically pop out of his head. I press my hips into his, feeling his erection along the inner edge of my hipbone.

I kiss his neck, and he scoops his hands underneath my ass, lifting me up into his arms, forcing my lips higher toward his. I wrap my legs around his waist, relishing the feel of him pressed tight against my center.

Our lips haven't yet touched, though we are breathing the same air. His eyes search mine and I can tell he still thinks it's a joke.

And maybe it started out that way.

But now I can't think, can't breathe, can't *see* anything other than his two-toned eyes.

I can't *feel* anything other than raging heat erupting between us —the tension coiling where our centers are connected. The need building between my legs.

I gasp, knowing I am ready to give in. Knowing I am ready to give it all to him. Mind, body, and energy.

"Holy shit," I breathe, realizing what I'm feeling. Realizing this thing with Evander is so much bigger than I thought.

"What is it?" he asks, just as breathless as I am. Our lips still haven't touched.

"Holy shit," I say again as his breath mingles with mine. As everything in me begs me to give in to the divine union pull I am just now recognizing.

"What is it, Fiana?" he pleads, his breath tickling my bottom lip.

"Why haven't you?" I ask finally, my voice barely above a whisper.

He tightens his grip on my ass. "Why haven't I what?"

"Immortalized anyone. How is it even possible that—?"

"That I've gone three hundred and eighty years without turning a female?" He lets out a breathy chuckle. "I guess you don't know how it works."

"I *know* how it works," I snap.

He laughs. "I don't mean *sex*, Fiana." He presses me harder against his erection in emphasis, his eyebrows dancing. "I mean immortalization."

"They're different?" I breathe, as my legs tighten around him of their own accord.

He smirks. "Mmhmm. I have to use magic to immortalize someone. Sex can just be sex."

He raises a brow.

I hear the unspoken invitation.

My body aches in response.

Sex can just be sex.

I can have him, without being devoted to him.

And yet every cell in my body wants to give it *all* to him.

My next breath feels unsteady. I can't think about that now. I need to soothe this ache, taste his lips, feel him on me, feel him *everywhere*.

I need sex to just be sex, and the rest—I'll figure out later.

"I need you," I murmur, weaving my fingers through his hair. I plant a light kiss against his lips then pull back to look into his eyes.

They're heated and soft and wicked all at the same time.

"Don't you tease me," he says. "If you kiss me again, I am going to fuck you tonight," he says, his voice edged with his own salacious need.

"Promise?" I say coyly before leaning in to press my lips against his.

He responds instantly, pulling me tighter against his body and kissing me back.

One of his hands fists in my hair as he takes the kiss deeper, and I shudder with pleasure as he claims me with his hands, his mouth, his breath.

He tastes like spearmint and sin.

I need to get closer to him.

Heat pulses in my core, and I start rocking my hips against him as he carries me toward the cottage. He groans with pleasure, and the sound is *so fucking hot*.

Because he needs me just as badly as I need him.

His lips move to my neck and I shudder as his tongue traces a hungry line up the length of my throat. I yank his chin back up to me, claiming his mouth with mine.

He's mine. He's mine. He's mine.

The door opens somehow, and I hear it slam shut. He gently guides my feet back to the floor, tangling his fingers in my hair as his lips come up to my ear.

"I hope you're ready for a long night, Fiana," he growls.

I moan as he circles around me, his hands fondling my breasts then sliding down the length of my abdomen. I jolt with pleasure as one hand presses against my aching center while the other pulls my hip back so I'm pressed tight against him. He's so *hard*.

He sweeps my hair forward over my shoulder and kisses the tender, exposed skin at the back of my neck.

I grind my ass against him. He twines his fingers through my hair again and the light pull feels good. His lips kiss up the side of my throat and then his grip on my hair tightens and he yanks his lips away from my skin.

He spins me around and I wrap my arms around his neck reaching my lips up for his, but he abruptly pushes me back. My eyes flutter open and I gasp.

"What the hell is on the back of your head?" he growls, and it's fury, not desire that lives in his eyes now.

My heart stops as guilt and shame snake through me.

"I was going to tell you tonight," I explain frantically, still catching my breath.

"Tell me what?" he urges, backing away a step. Anger tinges his power red. My stomach tenses.

"It's not what you think—I never betrayed your trust," I insist.

His eyes darken. "I know what that mark means, Fiana."

"Then you know I only pledged myself to taking down the King! Which is exactly what you and your family want me to do!"

His lip curls in disgust. "I can't believe I took you there," he shakes his head in disbelief. "I can't believe I trusted you!"

"You *can* trust me, Evander. I never told a soul about Maybelle or anything!" I plead.

He grabs my forearm in a tight grip. "But you're working with Koa and Warren, aren't you?" he snaps.

"Yes," I admit. "But I never told them *anything* about you!"

"But you're only here with me because *they* told you to spy on me," he counters.

"No! That's not it at all, I swear! And I'm not working with them anymore!" Hot tears pool in my eyes as my throat feels too tight.

He dissolves us somewhere while my chest caves in. He pushes me back hard and I collapse onto a couch—we're back in his cliff-side home.

"Evander—"

But he dissolves away before I can even get the word out. Tears fall down my cheeks as my heart crumples, breaks, and shatters.

The snow whips around like tornado outside, and it mimics the turmoil now churning in my gut.

Because he's gone. He's left me.

And I can't fucking breathe.

31

The grief is somehow worse than it was when I lost my father for good. Because at least then, I had Evander's soothing arms wrapped around me.

My divine masculine's arms.

My heart burns and aches and *throbs* as I think those words.

It makes no sense—that shouldn't exist anymore—and yet I know to my very core that it's true.

He's supposed to be *mine*.

And I'm supposed to be *his*.

My cries turn hysterical as I realize what I've done.

What I've broken, what I've shattered, what I've mutilated and destroyed.

He was so good to me for *months* on end.

All I had to do was trust him fully—like he trusted me.

And I didn't.

I didn't.

And he's gone.

He's gone.

My sobs turn messy and violent, and my chest feels like it's caving in.

Does he know? Does he feel the pull too?

I want to believe that he does with every fiber of my being. I try to talk myself into it, reminding myself how he's flirted with me from the very beginning.

But then fresh sobs shudder through me as I realize the full extent of what I've lost.

He could have been mine.

He *wanted* to be mine.

I can see that clear as day now.

But I ruined it.

I ruined it.

I fucking ruined it.

And he's gone.

He's gone.

He's gone.

At some point in the early hours of the morning, I crawl up the stairs and into his bed. It still smells like him, and that brings me the tiniest sliver of comfort.

Enough to fall into a depressive, dreamless sleep.

And I secretly hope at some point he will come home and crawl into bed with me.

But when I wake in the morning, I'm still cold and alone.

I stay in bed as fresh tears coat my cheeks. Haldric is perched on the ledge above the fireplace, watching me with warm, sympathetic eyes. He sensed my need the moment I came back and crashed into the window until I let him inside.

It was a kind gesture, but it wasn't enough.

I wipe my face and force myself to get out of bed, hoping I'll find Evander in one of the spare bedrooms. Maybe he came back, but still needed his space.

I grow more disappointed with each door I open.

A pounding at the front door startles me, and I race down the stairs as fast as I can.

It makes no sense, he wouldn't knock on his own door, but I still hope it's Evander somehow.

I swing the door open and shiver as the biting wind whips across my bare arms. I'm still wearing the sundress from Meddia.

It's Warren, looking furious.

I quickly slam the door shut, but he holds it open, forcing his way inside.

"Leave me alone!" I shout as fresh tears drip down my face.

"Woah—what's going on?" he says gently, glancing between my attire and my face.

"I'm done with the Dissenters. I'm out—now get the hell out," I growl, backing toward the kitchen. I yank a chef's knife out of the block.

But he's too quick, and he grabs my wrist in a blindingly fast movement then pries the knife out of my shaking hand.

"Get dressed properly and let's go," he says shortly.

"No." A sob jolts through me, and I shudder.

"I'm not asking, Fiana. Get dressed or I'll make you," he argues.

I glare at him with disbelief. "You are exactly like Koa," I accuse. "You claim to be for freedom, yet all you do is order everyone around."

"No—I'm not. But you made a promise. We need to meet and discuss where you've been. We need you to honor your commitment," he argues.

"Like I said, I'm *out*."

"Fiana, don't make me use magic on you. You have three seconds to go get some warmer clothes on," he retorts.

I glare at him for two seconds. He raises his brows, and I hold my hands up in surrender.

"Fine. Give me ten minutes. I'll meet you outside. Clean up your stench before you leave." I move toward the stairs.

"Will do," he says emotionlessly, and I can feel his eyes burning a hole in my back.

I get dressed in an oversized sweater and pants in two minutes flat, then I race down to the lowest level and grab a few daggers. I shove one in each boot and one in each of my pockets; my sweater is long and heavy enough to completely obscure them from view.

I race back up to Evander's office and find a pen and paper.

I wore blue, if you remember. And I meant it. I'm sorry.

I can't think of anything else to say without revealing too much, and I'm running out of time. So I kiss the note and then leave it on the kitchen counter, hoping it will be enough.

Hoping he will come back and read it, and be here waiting for me to explain when I return.

Koa's fury is written all over his face to the point where he looks centuries older than he actually is. He's at the head of the table waiting for me to explain myself.

Warren sits to my right, looking like he's been raked over the coals. He's looking away from me, and is still as a statue.

Credo sits across from me, concern crinkling his brow. His eyes dart between my face and Warren's, with the occasional tense look in Koa's direction.

Mila sits to my left. She's playing with the end of her long blonde braid, staring at the table, her legs bouncing up and down.

Collette, the raven haired beauty, is tapping her manicured fingernails against the table while she stares at me with a smirk.

Paul keeps looking between me and Warren, his expression wary.

Blaze and his wife Hawley—the blonde with a pixie cut—look as if this is the last place they want to be.

Everyone else looks like they're holding their breath.

"Well?" Koa says finally. He sets his hands on the table at the far end and leans against them, lowering his gaze to my height.

I resist the urge to shift awkwardly in my chair. Instead, I sit up straighter and level a punishing gaze at him.

"I have nothing to say to you." My tone is flat and impolite. The whole room collectively flinches.

"You went somewhere with Evander. Where did you go? What did you see?" Koa presses.

I keep my mouth sealed shut.

Credo sighs, scratching his bearded cheek. "You need to tell us what you know, Fiana. That's the whole point of you being a part of this resistance."

"I don't want to be a Dissenter anymore," I say calmly.

Collette snorts, then rapidly collects herself when Koa levels a look at her.

"Fiana," Warren chides, and his tone rings with warning.

"I joined you guys because I thought we were fighting for freedom. But you are the most controlling male I've ever met," I snap at Koa.

"It's called leadership," Koa seethes.

"It's called abuse of power," I argue.

"Fiana—" Mila starts to say, but Koa snaps, "Tell us or I'll go into your mind and find out for myself!"

I kick back my chair and whip out two of my six daggers. "You do that and you're dead."

Koa laughs. "I know you've learned a few tricks with Warren, but how quickly you forget that I can force you to turn those knives on yourself. Without even breaking a sweat, I might add."

"Koa!" Warren booms, and it's the loudest I've ever heard him speak. He's standing now, towering over me but looking at Koa.

"She has intel we need," Koa counters, glaring.

"We don't use magic on our own," Credo argues, pushing to his feet as well.

"We do when they're disloyal!" Koa insists.

"Disloyal?" I snort. "Yeah, let's *talk* about disloyalty. Tell me Koa, does anyone else know why you *really* picked me to join? Because we both know it has nothing to do with Evander."

Warren's gaze drops to me. "What are you saying?"

I keep my eyes on Koa, my daggers at the ready. "Ask your stupid leader."

"I don't know what you're talking about," Koa says, and my stomach immediately tightens.

"That's a lie," both Warren and I say at the same time.

Koa fumes. "Lower your shield, Warren. We need to know what she knows."

"No," Warren says flatly. "Tell us why you chose her."

"I will take you out with her if you don't lower your damn shield," Koa growls.

Credo grabs Koa's arm with one of his giant hands. "Why are you lying to us?" he bellows.

"Unhand me!" Koa tries to yank his arm free.

"Tell us the truth, Koa," Paul snaps.

"LOWER YOUR SHIELDS!"

There's a hideous cracking sound and Koa goes white in the face as Credo's hand tightens around his forearm, crushing the bones inside.

"Get her out of here," Paul says quickly to Warren. "Blaze—take the others. We'll handle him."

"Do not use those blades," Warren warns as he grips my upper arms and dissolves us away.

We land a hundred feet away from Evander's cliffside home.

"Want to tell me what the hell is going on?" Warren asks the second he unhands me.

"I don't know how much Koa knows, so I'm not telling you a damn thing," I growl, setting off through the deep powder toward the house.

"What about what Evander knows? Does he know you're working with us?" Warren asks, quickly keeping pace with me.

"Considering you keep showing up at his house, I can't imagine it's slipped his notice," I retort.

"I cover my tracks and you know it. Does he know about us, Fiana?" Warren urges, his tone a little softer.

I whirl on him with angry tears in my eyes. "You branded my fucking scalp! Did you really expect him to be too stupid to see it?"

Warren stops short, his expression horrified. "Did he hurt you?"

I narrow my eyes at him. "No! Evander would *never* hurt me."

"How can you be so sure?" he asks.

"Because!" I spit the word out as if it answers his question, then spin on my heel and start jogging back to Evander's home.

The front lights aren't on, and my chest tightens as I realize it might still be empty.

"Did you fall for him, Fiana?" Warren asks from behind me, his tone abruptly gentle.

My heart throbs, and I slow my pace as I near the door.

"So what if I did?" I whisper, knowing he will hear.

"So you would really jeopardize the whole mission—and everything good that can come from it—just for love?" He's caught up to me now and forces his way between me and the door, compelling me to look at him.

"You don't get it." I shake my head, staring at his muscular chest. "It's not that simple."

Warren snorts. "Of course it's not. You really think I've never been in love?" Ancient sadness resonates in his tone, and it sparks something in my memory.

"Actually, you might get it," I breathe, wiping away a stray tear. "Better than anyone else."

"So talk to me," he encourages.

My heart burns as the words come to me again, and I try to choke them out. But fresh cries steal my breath before I can say it.

"Fuck," Warren says. "You're really torn up about this, aren't you?"

I nod. "He found the mark on my scalp and he left—" I gasp as another sob jerks through me.

Warren wraps his arms around me and while they're warm, they do nothing to comfort.

Because they're not *his*.

"He's supposed to be *mine*, Warren," I sob, and Warren tenses at the inflection.

"You don't mean—"

"I do. *That's* why I'm *out*. I can't do it. I can't betray him. And he's *good*, Warren. He's nothing like you think he is. The Dissenters have *no reason* to go after him."

Warren rubs reassuring circles along my upper back. "I understand," he says quietly, and I know in my soul he does.

He gets it better than anyone.

"How long have you known?" he asks gently.

"Just since yesterday. And now he's *gone*." My voice breaks on the last word, my body shaking in his arms. "And he doesn't even know how I feel."

"Aw, shit, Fiana. I'm so sorry." He holds me like he means it. Like he feels my pain—like he knows it intimately.

It's the pain I saw behind his eyes the first time I met him.

"He will come back. Just give him time," he reassures, but I can tell that he doesn't fully believe that.

"You can't tell anyone," I murmur against his tear-soaked shirt. "Don't tell anyone."

His arms tighten around me. "I won't. I promise."

My breathing slows slightly and relief washes through me.

"Thank you," I whisper.

He holds me for another infinite moment. Eventually I shiver, and he unwraps his arms from me to pull back and look at me.

"Will you be safe here?" he asks softly.

I nod my head. "I want to stay in case he comes back."

"He won't hurt you?"

He already has, I want to say.

"No. He won't."

32

Warren nods once, concern evident in his eyes. He moves to leave when an echoing bell sounds from down the mountain.

"Ugh. That's a royal summons. You need to go," he says, annoyed.

"I can't right now," I plead.

He holds out his hand. "Come on. I'll stay with you."

Too weak to fight him further, I take it and we dissolve in a *crack*.

The crowd is already assembling, and Warren leads us to the back. I quickly release his hand and start wiping my eyes, eager to destroy the evidence of how deeply I've fallen, in case Koa happens to be here.

As a resident of Parley, he shouldn't be, but with him you never know.

The King stands on the balcony atop the bell tower, his robes a sea of greens and golds today.

My heart jolts as I spot Evander to his left, slightly behind him.

A horrifying thought occurs to me. Has he already turned us in? Is this *my* hearing? My pulse skyrockets as panic spikes within me.

Evander is casually scanning the crowd, his body language tense. His eyes land on me a split second later, lingering on my face. And then he abruptly looks away, his face utterly composed.

I can't fucking breathe.

The King stomps three times, and I unwillingly turn my gaze to him. I raise the hood of my cloak, resting my hands on the hilts of the daggers in my front pockets.

"My dear people, I have gathered you all here today for a most wonderful occasion! Do you know what today is?" He scans the crowd. "You, sir! What occasion might we be celebrating today?"

My pulse pounds in anticipation.

The villager coughs. "I—uh—don't know, Your Majesty, sir."

The King scoffs. "You *don't know*?" He stares down his nose at the male. "How can you *not know*?"

I wrack my brain trying to come up with a holiday or *something* other than my own impending demise as a reason for this gathering.

By the way Warren tenses next to me, I'm not too optimistic.

The villager lets out a nervous laugh. "Forgive me, Your Majesty. I don't even know what day of the week it is. I've had a bit of jad today, you see."

The King laughs humorlessly. "He's had a bit of jad he says! You've been spending time at the tavern, have you?"

I shudder.

The villager shrugs. "It's a nice place."

"Tell me, good sir—what is your name?" the King asks, his hand sweeping out in a dramatic flourish. I notice Evander shifting his weight uncomfortably.

"Archie Evergreen, Your Majesty." The villager bows.

"Archie Evergreen. Son of Penelope and Arnold Evergreen, is that right?" the King says, clasping his hands together.

"Yes, Your Majesty."

"I knew your mother once, Archie. A fine female. Very submissive, never caused trouble. That is, until she raised a son like you."

My stomach twists.

"I beg your pardon?" The villager's face turns red.

The King ignores him. "Who in the crowd knows what today is? What wondrous holiday we get to celebrate together?"

A timid female near the front raises her hand. My throat feels tight.

The King's eyes widen. "Why yes—and you are?"

The female tightens her cloak around herself. "Ariella Hawthorn, Your Majesty."

"And what event are we celebrating today, Ariella Hawthorn?"

She clears her throat. "Your ascension to the throne," she says, and I exhale in whole body relief. *Of course.* "Six hundred years ago today," she adds, her tone borderline sarcastic.

It makes me stiffen right back up.

The King smiles widely. "Very good! However, Ariella, I must admit you don't sound pleased. Aren't you *proud* to call me your King?"

I feel sick. *What a loaded question.*

"Of course," she says. Her tone is far from convincing.

"Well please, don't be modest on *my* account! Do tell the rest of the village—why are you proud to have me as your King?"

It's a trap. Everyone in the crowd can feel it.

Evander's jaw looks unbearably tense. He shoots a furtive look in my direction. My heart jolts when his eyes meet mine, then aches when they dart away again.

"I'm proud to have you as my King because—" she hesitates, and the King leans forward expectantly. "Because you keep the Shadow Realms at bay, and we haven't had a war in over three hundred years."

The King considers her words carefully for several moments, his forehead creased. Finally, he beams, and the whole crowd collectively exhales.

"That's *right*, Ariella! You are *safer* under my rule! I am so delighted you recognize that," he gushes, but his eyes don't match. "Who else would like to share why they are *proud* to have me as King?"

Evander shoots me another look, and I stare back with apologetic eyes. If this is the only moment I get to see him, I'll make sure he knows I'm sorry.

He looks away.

"You—in the brown cloak. What is your name, good sir?" Vilero asks cheerfully.

"Calder Hollingsworth," he says, his tone bright and obedient. "I'm proud to have you as King because it means we get to have more fun with the females," he chuckles.

A female near the front groans. I tense at the sound.

At the same time, the King's face falters. "You there, what is your name fine lady?"

"Priscilla," she says quickly. "Priscilla Pinegrove, Your Majesty."

"Priscilla, could you please enlighten the crowd as to why you made a dissatisfied sound when Mr. Hollingsworth shared his testimony for why he is proud to call me King?"

Priscilla clears her throat, and her voice is weaker when she speaks. "I didn't mean to, Your Majesty. That was very rude of me." She bows her head in deference.

"It was quite rude—right you are. Do you have anything you wish to say to Mr. Hollingsworth?" the King presses, smoothing a strand of copper hair away from his face.

"I- I'm sorry, Mr. Hollingsworth. And I'm sorry, Your Majesty," she says graciously, bowing her head lower.

"Yes. Good. We can forgive the occasional mistake, Ms. Pinegrove. But do not let it happen again," the King chides, staring down his nose at her. She shudders under his intense gaze, nodding her head in understanding.

The King straightens back up, his expression beaming again.

"My good people, I have not just gathered you here today to share in the glory of my ascension to the throne. I have also called you here to formally invite you to my party tonight! You are *all* invited to this momentous celebration! And in fact, you all are required to attend!"

The crowd fidgets and murmurs.

"Required, Your Majesty? Does this mean I must close the tavern?" Credo bellows, and I jump at the sound.

The King's smile falters slightly. "Yes, Credo. But worry not, there will be plenty of liquor for all to enjoy!"

"Here, here!" says a villager. One who frequently leaves the tavern wasted. A few other males cheer along with him.

"Yes, yes! A fine evening it will be, indeed!" The King smiles, clapping his hands in merriment. "And to make it even more fun, I've decided to make it a masquerade ball! Ladies are expected to wear formal gowns, and fellows should wear suits and ties. And all must wear a mask!"

"But Your Majesty, I cannot afford a formal gown," says a middle aged female on the far left side of the crowd. "And where will I get a mask by tonight?"

"Ah, my dear lady, this is not a problem for the King! I'm certain our local dressmaker can fashion something for everyone—can you not Viktor?"

I shudder as I remember my last encounter with *Viktor*.

"Yes, Your Majesty. Magic will make quick work of it," he grins. "As far as pricing, well, I must charge for the increased demand on such short notice."

The King nods approvingly. "That is quite fair."

"Fair? There's nothing *fair* about this! Half the town will go broke just trying to dress for your affair!" says the female.

Evander moves in a flash, jumping down from the balcony and rushing her in one quick motion, grabbing her by the throat. "Apologize to the King or you're dead," he demands.

My heart gallops at the sight of him overpowering her. She put him in an impossible position—I know that—and yet I cannot stand seeing him like this.

"Apologize to the King," he says again, louder this time.

She flinches. "I'm—" she takes a gasping breath, then seems to soften. "I'm sorry, Your Majesty. I was out of line."

The King watches the exchange with an amused expression. "Apology accepted. However, I do not wish to see your face again on such an important day. Ludo—take her to The Cave. A month in the darkness should teach you proper manners."

The crowd gasps. Another High Guard approaches the female. Evander stares her down a moment longer then unhands her as Ludo cuffs her wrists. They dissolve away a second later. Evander searches the crowd for me again, his forehead tense.

When his eyes find mine, all I see is anger.

It wounds me right to my core.

Warren takes me back to Evander's the moment the King dismisses us. The tears have dried up now that I've seen him, but my pulse is still running in a panicked, unsteady beat.

"I'll give you some time alone. So you can get ready for tonight," he says gently as he releases my arm. We're back on Evander's doorstep, Haldric perched on a nearby aspen watching our exchange.

I nod once, fumbling in my cloak pocket for the set of keys Evander gave me when I first moved in.

My hand shakes as I slide it into the lock. Warren notices, and steadies my hand with his own.

"He'll come around, Fiana," he says in low voice.

"You didn't see his eyes." I turn the key and step inside.

"No, but I know what it feels like to be in his position."

"And what position is that?" I face him, holding my arm out for

Haldric who quickly flies the short distance and lands on my forearm.

Warren jumps. "The hell was that?"

"You've met Haldric," I say with a shrug. "He's my pet."

Warren raises a dark brow, looking as if he wants to say something else, then quickly shakes his head. "Just give him time, Fiana. I'll see you tonight."

I spend the rest of the day meticulously bathing, primping, and coiffing every bit of my body.

The beauty of the King's detestable affair is that Evander is required to attend. Meaning we'll be stuck in the same room together for hours.

And I intend to look impossible to ignore.

Every half hour or so, I poke my head out of my bedroom, listening for the sound of his own shower running.

It stays bone dry all day.

But I don't let that discourage me, and his well-equipped home has every tool I need for tonight.

In my closet, there's already at least ten formal ball gowns to choose from. I settle on an emerald green one-shoulder, chiffon-draped gown with floral detailing at the waist and along the shoulder. A thin velvet cord cinches my waist, a long slit climbs up the skirt to mid-thigh, and there's a small triangle cutout between my breasts.

It's sex in a dress.

My hair is curled and pinned up into an elegant knot, and my lips are painted like red wine. I finish the look with a pair of sparkly gemstone earrings that look suspiciously like two caret diamonds.

They remind me of my thieving days back in Abyssia with Grandmother.

As I catch a final look in the long mirror within the closet, I know I've done all I can to regain the upper hand. The only thing I'm still missing is a mask.

I come down the stairs hoping there might be a wartime one that isn't completely hideous stashed away in the weapons vault, when a glimmer of gold and green catches my eye on the kitchen counter.

It's feminine and feathered, and matches my dress better than any that I could have dreamt up.

My heart swells at the sight of it.

And for the first time since he brought me back to Ador, I feel a sliver of hope.

33

I planned to call a carriage, but the sound of one just outside has me opening the door before I get the chance. I wave to the driver then quickly grab the nicest cloak from my closet—one made of lush mink and supple leather.

The ride to the castle is quicker than I would have expected, yet it makes sense given the cliffside home's impressive altitude.

The driver helps me step out, and when I hand him a fat stack of bills, he bows his head low in appreciation.

I walk carefully up the stone path to the castle's giant double doors, falling in line behind several other lords and ladies on their way in.

They aren't really lords and ladies, though. The King doesn't keep a court, hence why he had to invite the villagers to fill his banquet hall.

Most look like they are wearing hand me down gowns from a hundred years ago. Several appear to be wearing their own wedding dress with colored belts or sashes as accents; it's likely the only formal gowns many of them own.

My cheeks heat as I realize had I not met Evander, I would

have had to rush something from the dressmaker's myself. A gown like the one I'm wearing tonight would have cost me two night's tips.

It's absolutely ridiculous asking us all to participate in this forced pomp and circumstance.

"Name, please?" says a Main Guard at the front.

"Fiana Willowbark," I say calmly.

The Guard searches his scroll for my name. When he finds it, he raises a curious brow. "You've been invited to sit at the royal table."

"I have?" My stomach swirls with butterflies. "Who requested that?"

"Doesn't say. Look for your name at table five," he gestures impatiently for me to move inside. "Follow the other guests down the hall, up the stairs and to the left. Cloaks can be checked at the foot of the stairs."

"Okay," I say timidly as I follow the other guests inside. I check my cloak as instructed then climb the stairs slowly, clutching my skirt to avoid tripping over it.

At the top of the stairs, the small crowd veers left and lines up next to the Master of Ceremonies, who announces each guest's arrival to the ballroom beyond.

My cheeks begin to burn. The whole point of a masquerade is to be *anonymous*. It seems counter-productive to announce each guest's arrival.

My embarrassment heightens as I realize the MC is asking for everyone's birthplace. Nearly everyone was born in one of the villages of Syra—most in Ador, some in Linden or Parley, a few in Veliathon and Petralis.

I'm going to stick out like a sore thumb.

Impossible to ignore, I remind myself. *Perhaps this is a good thing.*

"Please welcome Miss Fiana Willowbark of Heron, Abyssia," the MC shouts.

As expected, every head turns in my direction—including the

King's. I push down my nerves then force myself to smile as I descend the short stairwell leading into the ballroom.

The ballroom is huge. It could easily fit the entire population of Ador and then some; it looks like there are at least a thousand guests milling about.

I scan the crowd searching for the beard, the messy dark hair, the piercing blue eyes. But there's so many people, and nearly every male is dressed in black. The King is the one exception, dressed in a deep burgundy tuxedo. He sits on a throne on an elevated platform, looking down on the crowd with a sneer.

Dozens of round tables circle the perimeter of the space with settings prepared for dinner, though no food is visible. Intricate flower arrangements are centered on each table, with larger ones staggered at various points around the room. Servants are weaving in and out of the crowd, passing around hors d'oeuvres and glasses of champagne.

A large open space lives in the center for dancing, and toward the front of the dance floor is a ten piece band playing an upbeat tune.

"Fiana—you look *stunning!*" says a familiar female voice the moment I make it down the stairs.

I turn to find the source and smile tightly at the sight of the blonde beauty dressed in a simple black silk gown. Her silver mask makes her hazel eyes appear greener.

"Hello, Mila," I say cautiously, swallowing back a lump in my throat. I tilt my head in grateful bow. "Thank you."

"Oh come now, Fiana," she says, linking her arm with mine. "We work together. We're old friends. Don't look so nervous to see me." There's a crisp warning evident in her tone. She leans in to whisper, "I'm with you and Warren. Fuck Koa."

I sigh in relief. "It's good to see you," I say in acknowledgement. She squeezes my arm.

"Seems your landlord delivered on the gown," she teases, moving around to my front again to take in the sight of me.

My heart throbs, but I manage a smile for her benefit.

"That's funny, I wasn't aware I should be collecting rent," says a smooth male voice. One that effectively stops my heart.

I clear my throat as I turn to face him.

He looks so fucking good.

He's wearing black from head to toe as usual, but the materials and cuts are much more formal than his High Guard attire. Even his hair looks more refined in light of the occasion, and his beard is cleanly shaped. His mask is a simple black one that does nothing to dim the vividness of his two-toned eyes.

He looks like he was born to be dressed in finery like this; and given his family's legacy, he absolutely is.

"I wasn't aware you needed the funds," I finally say once I compose myself. "But I'm happy to supply."

Evander's eyes turn disapproving. "You know your money is no good with me."

Mila lets out a nervous laugh. "Well with the tips you give her, it's essentially *your* money she'd be paying back to you."

Neither Evander nor I join in her laughter.

"Will you dance with me?" he asks, holding out his hand as an offering.

"Of course," I breathe, my heart fluttering too fast.

"Catch you later, then I guess," Mila says, disappointed.

I shoot her an apologetic look over my shoulder as he pulls me away. She watches us with wary, curious eyes.

As if on cue, the band shifts their upbeat tune to a slower ballad the moment we arrive on the dance floor.

Evander twirls me once then pulls me into waltz position, leading me into a slow, flowing dance.

"Your breasts are a masterpiece in that dress," he says in a low voice, all pretense of formality gone. His eyes are still serious, but his lips twitch at the corners.

My heart skips, and I want to laugh and cry all at the same time.

Because *this* feels like the Evander I know. It's a small thing, but it makes me believe he's open to forgiving me.

"That is a wildly inappropriate thing to say to a lady at a ball," I chide playfully. "But considering my transgressions, I'll allow it," I add, apologetic.

Evander's jaw tightens. "Let's not discuss your transgressions tonight."

My stomach tightens. "Okay."

We stare at each other for a few seconds as the dance continues, and I can see a hint of pain lingering in the depths of his eyes.

I try changing the subject. "You didn't have to seat me at the royal table, by the way. I would rather sit with strangers than the King—no offense."

His eyes darken underneath his mask. "I didn't seat you at the royal table. *I'm* not even sitting at the royal table."

"You didn't?" My stomach lurches. "Well then who did?"

Evander curses under his breath. "Three guesses who."

My jaw drops a centimeter. "*Calimo*? Why the hell would he do that?"

Evander ponders that briefly, his jaw ticking. More profanities— far more creative ones—start streaming out of him in an endless loop.

"What is it?" I whisper.

"Do you have a dagger hidden somewhere underneath that bodice?" he says, his tone urgent.

"*Where* would I hide a dagger under this?" I hiss.

He rolls his eyes. "I don't know—maybe sheathed to your thigh or something?"

I shake my head. "I'm sure there's a steak knife on the table if I really need a weapon. But why are you so convinced that I will? What do you think he's going to do?"

Evander's jaw ticks. "He has you seated with the King. Can you think of nothing?"

I think for a moment. "Damn," I whisper. "You don't think he's going to offer me up like some prize just to repair his relationship with his father, do you?"

Evander nods once.

It's my turn for an endless stream of profanities.

Evander tightens his grip on my waist. "Take a breath. It's going to be okay."

"*How* is it going to be okay, Evander?" I argue.

"Easy—just breathe. I have a plan," he says calmly.

I glare at him. "Care to inform me of it?"

"I'm still thinking—give me a moment."

He twirls me away from him once, then spins me back in. He dips me back low, then lifts me back upright. All the while his eyes look a million miles away.

"Got it," he says finally, once our eyes are level again. "Calimo's expecting you to fight him on this—he'll want you to make a big scene to piss off the King, and then he'll swoop in at the last minute with what he knows to save the day. He's creating a problem so he can deliver the solution."

"How does that help me?" I say anxiously.

"Don't be a problem. Be an utter delight—to Calimo. To the King. Even try to enamor the King to you. Then Calimo won't say a word, because if he did, then he'd be ruining the King's fun, which would only strain their relationship further."

I let out an exhale of relief. "That's brilliant."

Evander's lips hint at a smile, but his eyes are still hard. "I know."

Just then the song ends and the MC beats his staff, silencing the room.

"If everyone could please make their way to their assigned tables now, we'd like to begin dinner service."

Evander walks me to the edge of the dance floor then leans in close to whisper, "Don't be shy with your steak knife if the need arises."

The royal table is just below the King's raised platform.

The King sits in the chair centered directly in front of his throne, with two masked females on either side of him, one blonde and one brunette. My stomach churns as I realize he has probably immortalized them against their will.

Two males, other than the King, sit at the table as well. One I quickly recognize as Calimo with his warmer skin tone and dark hair. The other looks like a spitting image of the King—pale with red hair. His back is to me, but I imagine he likely also has black eyes.

Intuition hits as I remember the prophecy. The King kept one son alive from his relationship with the second twin. I wonder if that son really made it six hundred years.

Calimo turns as I approach and stands up, a calculating look on the lower half of his face.

I take a deep breath, say a little prayer to the Maker, then fix a fake smile to my face.

"Oh Calimo! I've *missed* you!" I gush, leaning in to kiss his cheek. A big red lip mark stains his skin, and he looks appropriately stunned, even underneath his mask.

"You have?" he says skeptically, pulling out my chair for me and scooting me in as I sit down.

"Who's this, Cal?" asks the King with interest. His eyes scan my mask then drift lower, to my lips.

"I mean of course you have!" Calimo recovers quickly. "Father, this is Fiana Willowbark. We've been courting for a few months." He drapes an arm possessively around my shoulders.

I dig my fingernails into my palm.

"It's an honor to meet you, Your Majesty," I say with a bow of my head.

"Pleasure," the King says with an amused smile. His mask is made of gold and looks rather heavy. "Where did you find this one, Cal?"

"Uh—the Ador Tavern," he says absently.

I breathe a sigh of relief. He certainly seems thrown off.

"Ah a beer maid, eh?" says the redheaded male to my right.

I smile politely at him. "Indeed. And we haven't met. Fiana Willowbark," I say, extending my hand.

"Charles Vilero, Prince of the Elven Kingdom, first son of our King. Pleased to make your acquaintance." He kisses my hand.

Calimo tenses next to me. I quickly snatch my hand away, giving Charles an apologetic smile before turning squarely forward.

Now I'm facing the King.

"Didn't I see you dancing with Evander?" the King asks, his tone utterly amused.

I shrug. "I meet a lot of males working in the tavern. Many of them grow fond of me." I turn toward Calimo. "But I'm rather fond of your son, here," I say with a smile.

The King laughs boisterously. "Now that's a first."

I shoot him a look, fighting to keep my face composed. "Why do you say that?" I wonder, trying to keep my tone light.

Charles laughs this time. "Calimo is what you might call a lady repellant."

"Brother," Calimo warns darkly.

"What? You know it's true, Cal," the King chimes in.

Fuck. I side eye Calimo.

He looks so weak.

My stomach twists. I can't believe it. I'm actually starting to feel a little sorry for Calimo.

The ladies flanking the King have been silent up until now, so when one speaks I jump at the sound.

"What did you say your name was?" says the brunette to the left of the King. She's wearing a pale pink gown with an ornate white bird mask obscuring everything except her lips and chin.

"Fiana," I say, smiling. Her voice strikes me as oddly familiar. Like maybe I've seen her in the tavern at some point.

That thought has my stomach roiling all over again as I realize maybe she was one of the females Evander was with. I force myself to turn away from her curious eyes so as not to throw her a dirty look.

The food appears in front of us then—an impressive pile of meats and potatoes, vegetables and rolls revealing themselves on each plate. I force myself to eat like a lady, even though I really want to dig in like a pig.

All of this posturing is making me hungry.

The table is relatively silent as everyone eats. I notice that both the King and his bird-masked brunette keep staring at me. But maybe that's just because I'm sitting directly across from them.

"Do you plan to wed Calimo, then?" Charles says suddenly as I take a big sip of wine. I nearly choke.

"We haven't discussed it," I hedge, sneaking a glance at Calimo. He looks annoyed. "Enough, brother."

"Well it's a valid question... considering we're royal, the potential for new heirs is always a legitimate curiosity," Charles counters.

I cough. "We are a long ways off from heirs."

The King snorts. "Seems your future bride doesn't care for your bedroom techniques, son."

I squirm in my seat, feeling stuck on how to smooth things over. Before I can think of anything, the King speaks again, drawing my eyes to him.

"Luckily his father doesn't have that same problem," he says with an easy grin.

I taste bile. I force myself to take a deep breath then offer the King a polite smile.

"I'm certain as a male of your stature, you endeavor to keep your ladies entertained." It's an effort not to say it through gritted teeth. Instead, I dig my fingernails into my leg.

The King tosses his head back in raucous laughter. "I would be delighted to show you just how *entertaining* I can be. Would you care to join me in my chambers tonight?"

Calimo chokes on his wine. I place a hand on his leg in reassurance.

"You are much too flattering, Your Majesty. But surely it would be improper given how taken I am with your son."

The King flashes me a smile that's all teeth. "As you wish, Miss Willowbark. However, I must insist you keep me informed of your evolving fancies. Should anything change with Cal—I implore you to allow me to be your first male caller."

"It would be a great honor to be called on by Your Majesty." I bow my head slightly as my stomach tightens in treacherous knots.

"Father, surely we've tortured the lady long enough?" Charles says in a bored tone.

The brunette in the bird mask shoots him a reproachful look. "Yes, perhaps instead of planning her next courtship, we should celebrate your accomplishments this century, my King?"

The King beams. "There are so very many, indeed."

The brunette nods encouragingly. "Of course there are. Our Kingdom has produced triple the wealth of the previous century under your leadership," she enthuses, stroking his arm.

"That's true," the King agrees, his lips curving into a proud smile.

"And the High Guard has incarcerated or eliminated—what is it Charles? Fifty thousand criminals?" she says, looking to the King's son.

"That's right," Charles says with an eager nod. I take a sip of my wine. "And Cal has only ruined three buildings this century," he snorts. "Oh wait—Glacier Pass makes it four."

I cough violently, my eyes watering.

Calimo reaches for my hand under the table, giving me a gentle squeeze. I want to grab my steak knife and stab him in the throat, but I force myself to catch my breath and smile again.

"I beg everyone's pardon, I must have swallowed wrong," I say quickly once I can speak again.

The brunette throws me a dirty look before returning her eyes to the King. "And Charles has shown great initiative in his royal duties."

The King smirks. "Yes, my son has done well this century," he lifts his glass toward Charles, who clinks it across the table.

"And there haven't been any conflicts with the Shadow Realms this century," Calimo says quickly, clearly trying to be seen in a better light.

The King's hand shakes, and he spills wine on the table. He sets the glass down quickly, wiping his hand with his cloth napkin. I study his face and when he lifts his eyes, I see the last thing I ever expect to see.

A subtle hint of fear.

"Yes, well. All in a century's work," he says quickly. He gives me a smile, but it's lost all the luster from before.

Interesting.

"How *do* you keep the peace, Your Majesty? It's an impressive run indeed," I say politely.

The brunette stares at me with venomous eyes, and I quickly center my gaze back on the King, who's wiping the back of his neck with his napkin now. He clears his throat, and I notice the exact moment his composure returns.

"Centuries of diplomacy, of course! I do enjoy negotiating with the demon king." He grins.

The brunette seems to relax slightly, taking a sip of her wine.

Whatever it is, she's in on it.

The band starts up again, and a moment later our plates magically clear.

"Enough diplomacy talk. Miss Willowbark, I must insist your next dance is with me," the King says, rising to his feet.

I glance at Calimo, who looks utterly defeated. "It would be my honor, Your Majesty."

I carefully rise to my feet while avoiding stepping on the hem of my dress. By the time I push my chair in, the King is right behind me, a hand outstretched.

I take his hand as a sickening feeling fills my gut. I force another polite smile. His hand is oddly cold, even in the warmth of the crowded room.

Like the life has been drained right out of him.

He leads us to the dance floor and I catch Evander's eye on the opposite end. He stands on the edges, speaking with someone taller than him. Warren, I realize with a start. He looks so different in formal attire. Evander's eyes are hard, and his beard looks stiff, as if he's clenching his jaw.

Panic courses through me all over again as I imagine what they could possibly be discussing.

The King whirls me into a waltz position obscuring my view, an amused smile stretching across his pale face.

"You are quite the enigma, Miss Willowbark. I don't know what it is, but there's something about you," he murmurs.

I manage a tight smile even as my insides are reeling. "I'm just a simple female, Your Majesty," I attempt to deflect. The *last thing* anyone in this room needs is the King unearthing my secret.

He laughs deeply. "Oh, I doubt that. And as far as your affections for Calimo—how stable are they?"

I swallow thickly. "Quite secure, Your Majesty. And besides, you appear to have two ladies who already have your affections. Surely you don't need a third."

The King's eyes tighten beneath his mask. "As King, I can never have too many ladies," he retorts.

"Of course, Your Majesty. My sincerest apologies," I say quickly, my heart hammering against my ribs.

He appraises me with his coal black eyes. "Why did you come to Ador?"

My stomach jolts. It's only the worst possible question he could ask me. "My grandmother died," I say quickly, without offering any other explanation.

It seems to satisfy him well enough, as he nods in understanding. I let out a silent exhale in relief.

"Do I scare you, Miss Willowbark?" he asks, amused.

My jaw tightens. "Only the appropriate amount, Your Majesty."

He chuckles. "And what amount is that?"

"Enough to respect your rule as my King. Enough to know if I step out of line while in your presence, there is a great lot for me to fear," I say truthfully.

"You have nothing to fear from me tonight, Miss Willowbark. I endeavor to spend my evening celebrating, not punishing."

His admission does not provide me any relief, but I still say, "I appreciate that deeply, Your Majesty."

"Enough to join me in my chambers tonight? Sleeping with my bastard son is one thing. He's not even a Prince. But spending the night with your King? Surely you know it comes with a great many benefits."

I can feel Evander's eyes burning a hole in my back and I know he's somehow hearing every word.

"My heart is already spoken for. But thank you again for your flattery, Your Majesty."

The song ends then and I curtsy deeply the moment the King unhands me.

"Thank you for the dance, but I must retreat to the ladies room," I say, meeting his eyes again.

"Of course," the King says with a slight bow of his head.

I sigh in relief and start walking briskly to the stairs that lead to the hallway. Evander watches me and gives me a subtle nod as I pass him.

I want to throw my arms around him and bury my face in his neck, but I force myself to keep walking, cognizant of the many pairs of eyes on me.

Especially the royal ones.

Calimo catches up to me at the bottom of the stairs and pulls me into an unexpected hug. I freeze in his arms, my insides in turmoil, wishing too late that I'd taken a knife from the table.

"Thank you for refusing him," he murmurs against my hair. "And I didn't start that flood," he adds, in a warmer tone. He pulls back to look at me. "I don't even know what happened. I blacked out that night. I have no memory of even leaving my townhome," he admits, his eyes sincere.

My gut feels calm and open. "You're not using Hypnotic magic right now?" I say, my jaw tight.

He shakes his head. "No. And I'm sorry I did before."

"So if you didn't try to kill me—who did?" I ask in a strangled voice.

He shrugs, his eyes full of concern. "I honestly don't know."

34

I hide myself in the ladies room for a solid fifteen minutes. The first five are spent hyperventilating, and the next ten are spent wracking my brain for other potential suspects who could have caused the flood.

I keep coming back to one person.

Koa.

He has the golden dagger and even admitted to wiping Calimo's memories. No one else makes sense.

It makes me sick to my stomach that he would go to such lengths just to get the dagger back, and at the same time I don't understand why he would want the dagger without me.

He has to know I'm the one the prophecy speaks of. He has to know I'm meant to kill the King.

But why would he value the weapon so highly, and completely disregard the one who's destined to wield it? To the point where he didn't care if I drowned in my sleep?

It doesn't make any sense to me.

But I've wasted too much time pondering it.

I straighten my mask and smooth my dress before forcing myself to rejoin the party.

As I return to the ballroom, I stay far away from the royal table and the King's throne, which he's now returned to. I grab a glass of champagne off a server's tray and take a large pull, scanning the room.

Warren catches my eye and quickly moves through the crowd to join me, grabbing a glass of jad off a table that must have been his.

"You good?" he asks in a low voice. "You've been popular tonight."

I take another sip of my drink and nod once, my mind swimming with thoughts of Koa and the flood. I'm staring at the dance floor when I speak next.

"You've been a good friend for me, Warren. But I'm never trusting Koa again," I say harshly. "So if you're planning on waiting for that day, we should just end things now."

"I know," he murmurs. "Mila, Credo and I have discussed it. We're cutting him off. We're going to try and get others to, as well."

I dart my eyes to his face, which is blank and emotionless.

"You would do that?" I say.

He sighs dramatically then rakes his fingers through his hair. "There's more he's done that we haven't told you. He convinced us it was necessary, but Credo and Mila agree he went too far."

My heart hammers in my chest. If *all* of them knew the truth about the flood and did *nothing* to stop it—

"Like what?" My tone is razor sharp.

"Like compelling Vito Stargrove to murder your father."

"*What?*" I snap, certain I didn't hear that correctly.

Warren sighs. "I know. We should have stopped him then. I'm so sorry." He places a large hand on my shoulder.

I jerk it off. "Let me guess, it was all so I would join you?" I hiss, tearing him down with my eyes.

He doesn't flinch. "Yes. It was."

I scoff. "So help me understand. When he presented this plan, the whole group agreed it was for the best?"

Warren shakes his head once. "No plan. He did it, and told us after the fact. After we already marked you."

It's better, but not by much.

"And you still trusted him for *months* after that," I say, my tone bitter. I toss back the rest of my champagne in a quick gulp and level a punishing glare at him. "Warren, I mean this with my whole heart. *Fuck. You.*"

I slam my empty glass onto the nearest table and head for the stairs.

I make it to the bottom of the main stairwell where the cloak check is when a firm hand grips my arm. Assuming it's Warren, I try yanking my arm away, but it tightens into a vise-like grip.

"Leaving so soon?" says a voice that makes my hair stand on end.

I curse under my breath. "What do you want, Nasgardo?"

He pulls me close, so his mouth is at my ear. I cringe as his breath heats my skin. "I just want to make sure our King didn't hear something about me that he shouldn't have," he sneers.

"I haven't said a word. Now unhand me," I snap.

"You're still mortal I see," he says in a cruel whisper. "I thought for sure Evander would have claimed you by now."

I narrow my eyes at him. "He has," I lie.

Nasgardo laughs darkly. "Not from where I'm standing, he hasn't."

Evander is here now—a few paces behind Nasgardo—holding a finger to his lips. His presence brings instant relief.

I smile at Nasgardo. "Better not let him hear that. Evander can get very jealous," I say threateningly.

"We'll see how jealous he is when it's *my* name on your lips when you come."

Evander's power tinges red. He shakes his head once then grabs Nasgardo by the throat.

"Unhand her. *Now*."

Nasgardo sounds like he's choking. He reluctantly releases my arm.

Evander throws him against the stone wall of the hallway, causing the whole building to shudder. He keeps him pinned to the wall with one hand across his throat.

"Looks like you'll have to share this one with the King," Nasgardo taunts, though his eyes are wide with fear.

Evander ignores him, looking over his shoulder at me. "Fiana darling—do me a favor and get your cloak. We're going to leave in a few minutes."

My heart swells at the prospect of leaving together—of finally having a chance to have him back, all to myself. I hand my slip to the coat check servant, who looks as if he's seen a ghost. He quickly snaps to attention and hands me the cloak. I slip it on.

"Nas, you touch her again, and you're dead. I swear it," he growls, baring his teeth.

Nasgardo laughs nervously. "That's what you said the last five times, and I'm still standing."

"Yes, but the last five times were before Fiana caught the attention of the King. It will be much easier to kill you without repercussions if he knows you harmed his future plaything." Evander's hand tightens on Nasgardo's throat.

My jaw drops in disbelief.

"I am *not* his future plaything!" I argue.

Evander ignores me. "Do we have an understanding, Nas?"

"Well if that's really how you feel, we should just deliver her to the King now, don't you think?" Nasgardo taunts.

"Rot in hell," Evander growls, and then he rips out Nasgardo's throat.

Nasgardo's eyes go glassy as blood gushes from his neck in an endless stream of sickening red. He gasps for breath as he collapses to the ground.

Evander wipes his palm with a wet rag then tosses that on the floor next to him.

"Let's get to the entrance, Fiana," he says coolly.

"Are you *insane*?" I gasp as he pulls me by the arm toward the front.

Evander snorts, anger still radiating from his body. "He's immortal. He'll heal himself or someone will find him and heal him. We do this practically every week."

"You do?!"

Evander sighs. "Yes, and it drives the King nuts so let's get the hell out of here before he finds out."

We're silent the rest of the way out of the castle. When we reach the entrance, Evander pulls me into his arms and dissolves us into his living room. It feels too similar to how he left me before, and as we land my heart aches the moment he unhands me.

"You left," I accuse. And I know deep down I should be the one apologizing, but my heart is still tender after learning how my father died, and I can't think properly.

"I know. I'm sorry," he says, removing his mask and tossing it onto the coffee table. He approaches me slowly then reaches his hands around me to untie the ribbons at the back of my head. As he removes my mask, the look he gives me stops my heart.

"I needed time to think," he says softly.

"I never betrayed you," I breathe.

"I know." He tosses my mask to the side.

"And I never would." I hold his gaze, my heart cleaving open with every second that passes.

"I know." His eyes lower to my lips.

I take a step toward him, but he takes a reactive step back.

"Just—let's talk this through first," he explains. "I need to talk this through first."

It's not a rejection, but it feels like one.

"What do you want to know?" I choke out.

"I saw you speaking to Warren tonight. What did he say to you?" His tone is cautious.

I close my eyes, willing the tears not to fall. "That Koa compelled Vito Stargrove to murder my father so I would join them."

I'm wrapped in a hug so fast it knocks the breath out of me. I bury my face into his neck, inhaling the woodsy scent of his skin. Letting myself pretend that this means he's really mine.

His arms are holding me too tight against his chest, yet for the first time in days I feel like I can breathe.

"I'm so sorry, Fiana," he murmurs against the top of my hair.

"*I'm* sorry," I say, pulling back to look at him. "I'm sorry I didn't tell you sooner. And while I was absolutely trying to get closer to you to learn all of your secrets, it was never for their knowledge or benefit."

His jaw tenses as he considers my words. "Then what was it for?"

I reach my hand for his cheek, my thumb brushing against the bare skin of his cheekbone just above his beard.

He leans into my hand, his eyelids drifting closed.

My breath catches. I know what I want to say, but I can't quite say it.

His eyes flutter open halfway, piercing mine. Making my heart race.

"When you told me my father died," I start, and his eyes widen slightly as he takes in my words. "I hated you," I admit. "And I hated you because I thought you had killed Maybelle. Even though you told me you hadn't."

He watches me with curious eyes as I take a deep breath and continue. "I hated you so much, and yet when you put your arms around me..."

He pulls my hand to his lips and kisses my palm. "Yes?"

"I knew I was safe. And—I felt like I was home," I breathe.

His eyes soften. "I wanted you to feel safe," he murmurs.

I smile slightly. "I did." I wipe a tear from the corner of my eye. "I do."

"I won't hurt you," he promises, and sincerity rings in every word.

"I know you won't."

My heart skips as he looks deep into my eyes. As he removes all my masks and sees me right down to my core.

"The next morning, I knew I wanted to get closer to you. But not for the Dissenters—for me," I explain. "I agreed to join them because otherwise Koa would have wiped my memories. But I kept what you told me about Maybelle a secret. I wanted to understand what the Dissenters were doing, and I definitely was in favor of taking down the King. But from the moment I joined them, I knew deep down where my true loyalties were."

He kisses my wrist now. "And where were they?"

"With you."

His eyes are smoldering. "Tell me why."

I reach for his cheek again and he releases my hand, draping his arms around my waist instead. It feels so natural, being wrapped up in his arms.

"Because no matter who I thought you were, from that first moment outside The Cave, you kept my secrets. You protected me even before you really knew me. And though I didn't understand why, it made me trust you." I drag my thumb across his cheek again. "And I wasn't going to betray that trust."

"I'll always keep your secrets, Fiana," he murmurs, pulling my body tighter against his.

"Tell me why," I breathe as our lips inch closer.

"You know why," he says threading his fingers through my hair and tilting my head back, hovering his lips a half inch over mine. "You feel it too, don't you?" he whispers, true questioning in his eyes.

My breaths are shallow. "Yes."

He crushes his lips against mine. I kiss him back hungrily, wrapping my arms around his neck.

His lower hand presses against the small of my back, fusing our hips together, but it's still not close enough. He deepens the kiss, arching me back slightly as I press my body tighter against his.

"How long—have you wanted this?" he murmurs against my lips between kisses.

An evil thought occurs to me.

"Only for oh, five minutes or so..." I tease.

He pulls me back by the hair to look at me with amused, yet frustrated eyes.

"Well if you're indifferent we can stop right here," he challenges. His hand sneaks underneath the slit of my gown and rubs between my thighs in teasing, sinful strokes.

I flinch, fighting to keep a straight face as my body aches underneath his hand.

"Fine by me," I choke out, eyes fixed squarely on his.

He shakes his head, chuckling. "You are such a fucking liar."

I am, and I'm glad he calls me on it as he pulls my face back up to his. He kisses me again while the hand down below plays with the edges of my lace.

"You can't pretend you don't want me anymore. Your body craves my touch."

I tremble as he rubs me over the lace, desperate to feel him touch the sensitive skin underneath.

"Yes," I moan into his mouth as my hips grind against his hand. "Months," I admit. "I've wanted this for months."

I feel him smile against my lips. "I knew it."

"And you?" I gasp, as heat rapidly builds underneath his teasing touches.

He sucks on my lower lip. "You've ruled my life from the moment I met you."

I choke on my exhale. "Really?"

He dips his nose to my neck, inhaling deeply. "Mmhmm." He plants a tender kiss underneath my ear. His next words are a deadly whisper. "I nearly took you right there in the forest."

I pull his face up to catch his eye. "You're going to tell me the whole story one day."

A smile plays at the corners of his lips. "But not tonight?"

I shake my head, staring him down, my tone intensely serious.

"No. Tonight you're going to touch me. Everywhere. Until I tell you to stop."

His lips part, and a split second later a wicked glint forms in his eyes.

"Wrong, Fiana. Tonight I'm going to touch you, everywhere, until you *beg me* to stop."

A flash of heat has me squeezing my thighs around his hand. He grins as he feels that, then starts rubbing me over the lace again.

"And why would I ever beg?" I choke out.

His eyes turn possessive, but he freezes his hand.

"Because I'll have you trembling in my arms and screaming my name until you're limp, hoarse, and spent."

My lips part. "You think rather highly of yourself," I argue, even as my hips grind against his hand again.

He smirks, pulling his hand back and it feels like a punishment.

"Perhaps, Fiana. But by the end of tonight, *you* will too."

He pulls on the front of my dress now, and it dissolves away with a *crack,* leaving me bare to my lace in the middle of his kitchen.

His eyes are hooded as he takes in my form, and two rough hands drag down my abdomen and naked hips, causing goosebumps to pucker on my exposed skin.

He takes his hands lower, down the lengths of my thighs as he drops to his knees before me. He grabs one of my heels and carefully slides it off, kissing the inner edge of my knee as he tosses it aside. He repeats the same thing on the other side and I shudder as his lips drift higher up my inner thigh.

He climbs back up to his feet, towering over me with hungry eyes. I back up a step, my breath coming in shallow pants as heat builds intensely in my core.

He rips off his own shirt in one quick motion, the buttons flinging against the walls.

Fuck. He is so fucking *hot*.

A wicked smile stretches across my face. He notices, and mirrors my expression. He prowls toward me like a wolf, and I back my way toward the stairs like his prey.

"Look at you running away from me. Does someone want to be chased?" he teases.

Need aches between my thighs, and he isn't even touching me. I bite my lip, eager to prolong this moment. Knowing that so much has already changed between us, and yet nothing will compare to what comes next.

"Someone thinks they can catch me," I challenge, racing at top speed up the stairs and down the hall to his bedroom. He's there on the bed before I even make it inside, a devilish smirk on his beautiful face.

"Fiana my love, you didn't *really* think you could outrun me, did you?"

He races across the room in a flash, spinning me around in his arms and pinning me to the bed.

"Or do you just like to get caught?" he murmurs, his lips dangerously close to mine.

My awareness narrows to the feel of his bare abs against my bare stomach. I arch my back to press tighter up against him. I pull his hand away from my shoulder and guide it up my thigh. His fingers pause just an inch from the top.

"Why don't you find out for yourself?" I taunt, pressing his fingers toward the lace again.

His eyes turn warm and approving. "My pleasure."

He bends down to kiss me at the same time he pulls on the lace.

It dissolves away somewhere and suddenly his hands are everywhere.

And I'm hot, wet, and willing.

His fingers feel like heaven as they tease between my thighs. My hips jolt as little moans escape my throat.

"That's it. Moan for me."

As if I could keep quiet with his fingers right—*there*.

I curse as his fingers start to expertly swirl. "It's not fair," I complain. "You're too good at this."

His lips are inching toward my breast, which is as exposed as my lower half now.

"Mmm," he hums along the top curve of it. "Seems someone has rapidly changed her tune."

Another moan slips through my lips as his fingers pick up the pace and pressure, somehow knowing exactly how I want it.

Tension builds as he sucks on my nipple, and I dig my fingernails into his back, as the hand down below keeps edging me towards a delicious peak.

"Fuck," I curse again, my hips arching up into his hand.

Evander lets out a low chuckle. "Such a filthy mouth." He flicks his tongue teasingly across my nipple. "I love your filthy mouth," he adds, sucking on me again.

A shudder of pleasure rocks through me. My body melts underneath his touch as every cell of my being opens up to be *his*.

And I *am* his. I feel it to my core. This is bigger than love, or lust, or sex.

He's my divine masculine. My other perfect half. My heart thuds chaotically as I wonder if he can feel it, too.

His fingers swirl faster and my thoughts abruptly scatter, as everything dissolves into breathtaking pleasure. I scream his name as my climax rocks through me, as he lets me lose myself in his arms.

He nibbles at my neck as I release, and I feel him moan appreciatively at my throat.

"That's it," he murmurs, stilling his hand. My hips writhe against him, my body aching with pleasure.

"More?" he teases. "Oh, I'll give you more."

His hand starts up again and I grip his waist, my fingernails denting his soft skin. I've barely come down from my first climax—I can hardly breathe—and yet he starts eliciting another one from me.

My body responds so willingly. So quickly, so obediently as he repositions slightly to slide a finger inside me. I quiver at the feel of him claiming me with his hands, my hips rocking as he slides in. And out. And in again.

"Fuck," I gasp as he finds a rhythm that has my core tensing and tightening, all the while his lips leave trails of kisses down my neck.

"Will you come for me again?" he murmurs against my throat.

"Yes," I gasp as the tension builds, and my whole being *aches* to do exactly that.

His lips meet mine in a heated kiss as his hand pushes me over the edge, and I scream into his mouth. He bites my lower lip and I come harder, pleasure thundering through me like a storm.

I'm sensitized, so I try to push his hand away, but he locks it in place and keeps going as another intense release ripples through me, only seconds after the previous.

"*Evander!*" I scream, wanting him to stop and yet wanting him to keep going, as he pushes me to a higher peak.

One I didn't know existed.

Pleasure steals my breath, steals my heart, steals my very sanity as I melt into a mindless heap in his arms. It keeps going, and a part of me wants to fight it. Wants to say that enough is enough.

But Evander isn't stopping.

And I don't ever want him to.

35

Lightning buzzes under my skin, the charge building up so intensely that I have to shake my limbs out to release some of the tension. There is just so much *power*.

And I'm furious.

Because Koa tried to drown me and had my father killed.

I have the inexplicable urge to destroy something, so I settle for the mountain. I start shaking the ground to force an avalanche. Never mind the fact that all that snow will bury me too—that doesn't bother me. It just feels so good to watch the mountain fall apart.

To be the one to end it all.

Warm hands grip my arms and shake me, *hard*. I growl, ready to end whoever is attached to those hands when I hear my name in the sweetest voice I've ever known.

My eyes slide open warily, convinced this isn't real.

Two cobalt-and-ice-blue eyes stare back at me.

"Are you okay?" he says frantically, worry lines creasing his forehead.

"I—" I take a shaky breath. I'm still trembling with whatever the hell is *under my skin.*

"It's your magic. You're feeling your magic, Fiana," Evander breathes. He squeezes my arms a little tighter. "It's your birthday—March 20th. You're feeling your magic."

I sit up and glance out the window, which reveals nothing but night outside, only to became horrified to see giant cracks in the wall of glass.

"Did I do that?" I gasp.

"Yes—you triggered a small earthquake. Don't worry—I'll fix it." Evander closes his eyes and the glass carefully restores itself.

I glance around at the rest of the bedroom noticing dresser drawers are open, the bedside table is overturned, and the art has tumbled down off the walls.

"An earthquake, huh?" I breathe, feeling embarrassment heat my cheeks.

"That's what woke me up. I knew you'd be powerful," he says, his tone approving as the rest of the bedroom magically returns to order.

A shudder rocks through me as more lightning singes under my skin.

My mouth feels dry as sandpaper as I choke out: "Is it always like this?"

"Not for everyone—some feel a low grade faint tickle of their magic all day whether or not they use it. Elves like us—we need to *use* it."

My body is shaking, and I haven't noticed until now. Maybe I've been shaking the whole time.

"Show me how," I beg through chattering teeth.

One of his hands moves to my heart, while the other grips my arm again.

"First, close your eyes," he says calmly. Though I don't want to, something about the feel of his hand on my heart steadies me.

"Good. Now take a deep breath, and try to breathe all the way down into your belly."

I do as he asks and at first I can only get the breath down to my ribcage. It takes me a few tries, but finally I'm able to get the breath lower.

"Good—stay with that for a few breaths and just notice what happens to the feel of your magic."

I focus on the flow of oxygen, marveling at how the lightning begins to feel less dominating. Less chaotic. There is still *so much* there... but it feels less like it's taking over me and more like I have control over it.

"You're doing great. Now, when you're ready, all I want you to do is still the wind."

I open my eyes seeing the wind tossing snow around like a blizzard.

"How?" I lift a brow.

"It's instinctive—the less you think about how, the more naturally it will come to you. Just give it a try," he encourages.

I close my eyes again and take another belly-breath, trying to relax my mind. Just like I had all those months ago on that bench in Ador.

It isn't really an intention, it's more a split second *feeling* of stillness, and before I even register the change, the room goes unnaturally silent.

I open my eyes. The wind is virtually gone, snow floating down gently and peacefully, completely undisturbed by the wind.

"You did it," Evander says, planting a soft kiss on my lips. "How do you feel?"

I let out a sharp exhale. The lightning under my skin still feels *intense* but—perhaps less debilitating. I'm no longer shaking.

"Better," I say, my voice thick.

"Now let's try something a bit harder," he says with a curious smile. He reaches on his bedside table for a dagger and slices quickly and cleanly through his forearm.

"What the—?" I gasp.

"Just heal it. You did it with animals before—remember?"

"That was with tinctures! And luck!" I argue, watching blood drip down his arm.

He grins easily at me. "Just try."

I shake my head, but I take his injured arm in my hands and take another belly-breath. For some reason I don't feel the need to actually think of or imagine or intend the repair process. Instead, my mind just finds the image of his smooth, unblemished forearm.

I watch in amazement as his flesh knits back together. He conjures a wet rag and wipes away the fresh blood, then dissolves it away somewhere.

"See? Knew you could do it," he says with a wink.

"What if I wasn't a Curic?" I shoot back.

He snorts. "I researched your father's bloodline—remember? How do you feel now?"

I narrow my eyes, but consider his words. "Much better. How often do I need to use it to prevent it from building up again?"

"You'll get better at holding it in time—the breathing and focusing really help with that. But I think until you feel totally comfortable with that, it'd be wise to use your magic every hour, and to do something bigger before you go to sleep."

"Every *hour*?" I gasp.

He grins. "You're special, Fiana." He kisses me on the cheek. "Happy birthday, by the way."

I snort. "Twenty-five. It never seemed like a big deal growing up as a female but now... it does."

"Now that you know your age actually *does* coincide with a surge in your magical capacity?" Evander asks.

"Exactly," I say, a faint smile stretching across my lips.

He smiles back, his eyes soft. "I can't sense it on you by the way. I only guessed what you were feeling from the date."

"The protection is still intact?" I say.

He nods. "It is. It's quite impressive."

"Wow." It makes me miss my father. I close my eyes to prevent them from tearing up.

"Do you want to rest some more, or stay up?" Evander says softly as he kisses each of my eyelids, one of his hands dragging gently down the length of my waist.

I'm suddenly hyper aware of how naked we both are.

"I want to touch you," I murmur crawling closer to him on my knees. I straddle him, tugging on the boxers he never even took off last night. "Enough of these," I complain. "I want you to fuck me properly. And I want *you* to come."

A low chuckle rumbles deep in his throat as his rough hands rub up and down my bare back.

"I certainly can fuck you, Fiana—but there's not going to be anything *proper* about it." His teeth tease my bottom lip. "Still want it?"

I grind my hips against him in response. He quickly hardens underneath me.

"Don't make me ask twice, Evander," I growl into his ear.

"Fuck," he groans. "My name on your lips is the best damn thing I've ever heard." He lowers me on my back now, sliding off his boxers. My eyes practically pop out of my head as I see *all* of him.

"What, did you think I was lying?" He raises a brow.

I burst out laughing. "You are so fucking cocky."

He fights a grin. "Comes with the *package*."

My laughter explodes at that, and now I'm shaking the whole bed.

One of his hands finds its way between my legs and I abruptly stop laughing as he languidly slides a finger inside of me.

I moan as his thumb strokes the top.

"Mmm. You're soaking wet for me." He leans down to kiss me. "When did you first get wet for me?"

Breathing is already a challenge with his hand stroking me like *that.* I reach for him, desperate to give *him* some pleasure for once, but he instantly swats my hand away.

"Answer me," he orders, and my stomach clenches at his dominant tone.

"When you laid in my bed," I gasp as his thumb makes tight little circles on my sensitive flesh. "After catching me with the dagger." A ragged breath moves through me.

"Mmm, when I told you I would only fuck you once you *needed* me?"

"Yes," I gasp as he nibbles my neck, the hand down below pushing me closer to the edge.

"So tell me, Fiana. Do you need me?" he taunts.

"Yes," I admit, reaching for him again. He swats me away.

"Say it," he orders. "Tell me what you need, Fiana."

I quiver underneath his thumb.

I'm already close, but I want *him.*

"I need you to fuck me," I say obediently, secretly relishing how he's making me work for it.

"Mmm. Say it again," he says, pulling his hand away and positioning himself over me. I gasp as his eyes bore into mine, as every inch of his naked body hovers centimeters above me. His cock grazes the inner edge of my hip. I reach for it, but he grabs my wrist and pins it down by my face. I try with the other hand, and he does the same thing.

"I need you," I say breathlessly, arching my back up to rub my hips against his length. "I need you to fuck me, Evander."

Pleasure flickers in his eyes as he positions himself at my center. The sliver of contact feels so good that I'm already writhing underneath him.

"Again," he growls, sliding in half an inch. A moan escapes my lips and I'm already desperate for more.

"Fuck me, Evander," I moan.

He crushes his lips against mine in possessive, claiming kisses.

He slides in another half inch as my body stretches to accommodate him. The fit is so tight, so good, so *hot*.

"More. Please. Fuck me, Evander," I beg.

He groans appreciatively against my cheek. He slides in deeper, finally releasing my wrists. I wrap my arms around his neck and try pulling myself up to meet him, but a firm hand pushes my hips back down.

"Don't rush me," he warns, but he slides in another half inch. "You've tortured me for months. It's my turn to torture you."

"If this is how you plan to torture me, I want it every night," I gasp.

"You want it, or you need it?" he prompts.

"Need it," I breathe. "I need *you*." I grip his hips in emphasis.

"Damn right you do," he says, giving me a deliciously deep thrust. I gasp.

"More," I beg as he pulls languidly out.

"Like that?" His gaze is both heated and amused.

"More," I order, looking him dead in the eyes.

"You are so naughty." But he obeys, thrusting deeper. He pulls out slow, pausing at the tip and my core aches and aches for another deep thrust.

"I need more," I complain, knowing that *need* is his magic word.

"Don't worry, I know exactly what you need," he growls, *finally* starting up in a steady, pleasurable rhythm.

"Fuck. Yes."

I soften and surrender, letting him drive into me again and again and again. My body relaxes deeper with every thrust and every part of me feels whole as he claims me as his.

I'm yours I'm yours I'm yours.

"Fuck. Say that again," he groans, and I don't realize that I've said it out loud.

"I'm yours," I gasp as he drives into me harder. He grunts, sliding an arm underneath my back. He kisses me roughly between deep thrusts, and my whole body opens wider to receive each one.

I'm yours. I'm yours.

"You're mine." His tone is possessive, and I whimper at the sweet sound of him claiming me. At the feel of him taking me, again and again.

I tighten my arms around his neck and wrap my legs around his hips. I cling to him like he's oxygen, and I'm all out of air.

"I need you," I breathe into the crook of his neck, breathing in his sultry, woodsy scent. He groans with pure male pleasure, picking up the pace to a delicious, punishing rhythm.

I gasp as our bodies come together again and again, as I feel his need satisfy my own. My core tightens and tenses as our connection deepens.

"Fiana," he growls against my neck, giving me love bites that send shivers down my spine. His next words come out like a command. "Be a good girl and *come for me.*"

My body responds instantly, obediently. It *wants* to do as he says. I tremble and tighten around him as he drives impossibly deeper.

"Fuck," he growls, driving me harder, and I whimper with delight as my release intensifies. "Good girl," he gasps. "*Just* like that."

I grip him harder as pleasure overtakes me, as my whole body responds to his every word.

"You're so fucking good," he praises, and it somehow sends me higher. He roars, burying himself deeper inside of me, finding his own release.

I gasp as he collapses on top of me. His weight is heavy, but unbearably pleasant, and the ache around his cock feels so damn sweet.

He kisses me deeply, our bodies still connected. Then he gently flips us over so I'm on top of him.

We breathe together for several moments, still connected, skin on skin. His hands trace soothing lines up and down my bare back.

He chuckles. "You're purring like a kitten."

"It feels so good," I moan. "All of it. Every bit of it."

He squeezes my ass. "You mean every bit of *me*."

"Yes," I sigh, burying my head into his neck. He kisses my shoulder.

"Can I tell you something?" he says gently, an edge of vulnerability in his tone.

I kiss his neck. "Anything."

His arms tighten around me. He presses his lips against my forehead, then inhales deeply.

"You smell so good," he murmurs.

I giggle. "That's what you wanted to tell me?"

He snorts. "No." There's a long silence. He rubs his hands up and down my back, and I can feel him thinking.

I prop myself up slightly so I can see his face.

He holds my gaze.

A moment later, he sighs. "It's something intimate. Are you ready for that? Because if this is just sex for you—I can keep it to myself."

I brush his hair back from his face. "It's not just sex for me."

He considers my words for a beat, studying my eyes.

"I wasn't kidding when I said you've ruled my life from the moment I met you," he starts, his eyes cautious. He pauses to trace a gentle line up my back. "And I meant it when I said the past several months without you have been torture."

"I'm here now," I reassure, planting a delicate kiss on his lips. "I'm with you," I add, kissing him again.

He softens at that, wrapping his arms around me.

"I'm keeping you," he says against my lips. "And if anyone hurts you, I'll fucking kill them." He somehow makes the harsh words sound sweet.

"I know," I breathe, kissing each one of his cheeks.

"In the flood, when I thought you were dead—" he says, his voice breaking on the last word. "I can't ever lose you."

"You won't," I reassure.

"And you can't ever run away on me."

I pull back to look at him, stroking his beard. Staring into his piercing blue eyes, which are full of emotion.

"I'm yours. And I'm not going anywhere."

He hums with pleasure then pulls me tighter against his chest. He gives me a tender kiss.

"Good, because I'm never letting you go."

36

Evander cooks us an impressive breakfast as the sun starts coming up. There's eggs and bacon and fresh tropical fruit imported from Abyssia that make my mouth water. We eat side by side at the counter, and he steals little kisses from me every few minutes.

My heart is full and swollen, and every moment feels too good to be true.

I want to tell him I love him, that he's meant to be *mine*, that every part of me wants to be *his*.

I want to tell him that I want him to immortalize me. That I want to be with him forever, that I want to share my heart, my mind, my body, my energy, every cell of my being with him.

But that feels way too heavy after our first real night together and right now everything feels too perfect to ruin.

So I keep it to myself.

"He's a good one," says a voice that sounds oddly familiar somewhere in my head. I jump looking for the source, and my eyes land on Haldric's bright yellow eyes. He's expectant, like he's waiting for a response.

"Yes, it's me. Can you finally hear me?" the voice asks. Haldric blinks.

"Holy shit!" I gasp.

"Language," teases the voice. He carries the tone of a grumpy old grandpa.

"What?" Evander startles, looking at me.

"I just heard Haldric. *In my head,*" I exclaim.

"I'll have you know I'm only a fifth of your age," Haldric complains.

"And he can hear my thoughts," I add, walking over to him to stroke his chest.

"Ask him if he knows more about your magic," Evander says, his tone excited.

"How would he know?" I snort.

"I'm not an imbecile," Haldric complains.

"Animals often pick up on things that elves can miss with magic," Evander says, shrugging.

"Exactly. Like I said, he's a good one," Haldric says, clicking his beak once.

"Haldric likes you," I giggle.

"Of course he does. Most males wouldn't let you invite an owl to live inside their homes," Evander quips. "But see what he knows, if he's willing to share."

"I know many things, but this conversation is boring me. Ask me a question, and I may deign to answer," Haldric huffs.

"He's kind of snobby," I giggle. "But I still love you," I add rubbing his plumage. He glares at me.

"Can I speak to all animals or do I need a relationship with them?" I ask mentally.

"You can speak to all, but not all will listen or choose to engage with you. So in a way, yes, you need a relationship with us," Haldric explains.

"He says I can speak to all animals but only some will listen or speak back," I relay to Evander.

"That's impressive. Ask him if you have the ability to control animals," he suggests.

"*Control isn't the right word. Will most be loyal to you? Yes. Will many do as you ask provided it's a reasonable request? Absolutely. But you can only control us if we make you our Queen,*" Haldric says, flapping his wings once.

I relay what Haldric said to Evander. "Not really sure what that means," I add, shrugging.

"I think it means they decide they want to serve you for life. Some will, others won't," Evander suggests.

"*Indeed, he is right again,*" Haldric clicks.

"I'm getting the sense that Haldric likes you more than me, and that's very bad for my self-esteem," I say morosely.

"*Calm yourself. It's his mind I like,*" Haldric argues.

"I'm sure that's not true," Evander answers me with a chuckle.

"He says you're smarter than me," I complain, glaring at Evander, who snorts.

"It's not me saying that so I don't know why you're mad at me," he laughs. "Besides, he probably means wisdom, not intellect. Since I have a couple centuries on you, it would be really embarrassing if you were wiser than me."

"*As I said, he is a good one,*" Haldric praises.

"Fine," I say to both of them, blushing.

Evander laughs and then abruptly freezes, his eyes a million miles away. He dissolves somewhere and is gone and back in less than a second, with two short swords and a half a dozen daggers strapped to his legs.

"What is it?" I ask frantically, still stunned from his abrupt departure and return.

"Warren's here with Credo and Mila. And a few others," he says tightly as he approaches the front door.

"*They know,*" Haldric says cryptically.

I ignore him. "Are they armed?"

"Warren is."

"Let me talk to them," I say quickly, attempting to wedge myself between Evander's swords and the door.

He levels a look at me. "If you think I'm going to let you put yourself in danger less than twelve hours after finally being with you—"

"You are, because you trust me. Right?" I say pointedly, raising a brow.

"It's not you I'm worried about," he argues.

"Give me a weapon then. I can handle myself." I hold out my hand. "Warren trained me."

He startles slightly at that. "For how long?"

"Three months. I'll take a dagger and a short sword, please."

He fights a smile. "You're either overconfident in your training or overconfident in the fact that they mean you no harm."

"This coming from the male who somehow works the size of his dick into every conversation," I snap.

He chuckles. "You certainly didn't seem disappointed this morning. So I don't think it was false advertising, do you?"

"*Maker save me,*" Haldric complains. "*I'll be in the weapons vault.*" He flies downstairs.

I glare at Evander. "I never said it was, and neither is my confidence that I'll be just fine." I reach for the weapons again. He hands me a short sword and unwraps one of the dagger sheaths around his own leg before bending low and wrapping it around mine.

My breath shallows as his fingers linger along the inner edge of my thigh after he buckles it in place. When he stands, he leaves me no room to escape his closeness as I back up against the door.

"If anything happens to you I'm going to kill your friends. And then I'm going to put you through an intensive training regime with Rosie." He kisses me once. "Deal?"

"What if I'm dead? How will Rosie train me?" I tease.

"If you're dead, then I'm going to kill you," he shoots back with a smirk.

"And if everything goes fine, you're going to lick me tonight. Deal?"

He fights a grin. "I was planning to do that anyway, so fine. We have a deal."

He backs away at exactly the moment someone pounds heavily on the door. I jump at the sound.

He raises a brow at my response and I narrow my eyes at him before turning to open the door, sword first.

"Easy, Fiana. We just want to talk," Warren says holding up both of his hands.

"Evander says you're armed. Can you leave your weapons outside, please?"

Warren's throat bobs. "Will you disarm yourselves?"

"No," I say simply.

He studies my face for an infinite beat. "Fine." He starts pulling out various blades hidden in his pockets and presumably in The Ether and tosses them onto the ground.

"The long sword, too," Evander says lazily when he appears to be done.

Warren sighs in annoyance but pulls the final weapon from his hiding place along his back and lays it gently on the ground.

"You do know we still have magic as a weapon, right?" Paul argues.

"That's what shields are for," Evander retorts.

I shoot him an amused look over my shoulder and then fix a serious expression to my face again before turning back to the rest of the Dissenters.

"You're going to come inside and sit at the table. If any one of you give either me or Evander any indication of an attack, we will kill you on the spot," I say darkly.

"Come on, Fiana, we have never put you in danger!" Mila complains.

"Considering Koa compelled a prisoner to kill my father so I would join you in the first place, our entire relationship isn't exactly built on solid trust," I snap.

Everyone shifts uncomfortably.

"She has a point," Credo booms. "Everyone good with her terms? No one attacks and no one dies."

There's mumbles of approval from the whole group.

I smile sweetly and open the door wider, my short sword at the ready as they file inside.

Warren, Credo, and Paul sit side by side on one end with Mila, Blaze, Hawley, and Collette on the other.

Evander and I stand side by side at the head.

No one speaks.

Collette crosses her legs.

Warren clears his throat. "First, we'd like to apologize for Koa's actions against your father."

"And for lying about it," I interrupt.

He sighs. "Yes, and for lying about it. And we would also like to apologize for his actions during our meetings. This group," he gestures to the table. "Is willing to continue planning our ultimate goal—bringing down the King—without him. Assuming you let us into your plans."

I stare at Warren. "Why should I believe he's no longer involved? You've been loyal to him for decades, some of you. And he has the network."

"We have ways of using the network without him if needed. And some of us will be playing both sides," Paul says.

"Nope. Deal breaker," I say sharply. "You're either with us or you're with him."

Warren lowers his chin a centimeter. "Fiana, we want to work with *you*. We understand Koa hasn't told us the whole truth about you, and that Evander obviously is not who we think he is, either. But we can't jump all in without knowing the truth."

"Too bad, because we're not sharing a damn thing unless you're all in." I raise a brow. "Isn't that the same deal Koa gave me?"

"It is, and that's fair. But some of our group still doesn't trust you after what you did with the golden dagger," Warren explains.

"After what *I* did?" I balk. "You have got to be fucking kidding me."

"You had a job to do and you didn't fulfill it. That makes it hard for us to trust you," Warren doubles down.

"All I wanted to know was what it was used for before I handed it over! Was it really so hard to tell me that it's used to kill the King?" I counter.

"But why did you hold on to it in the first place?" Warren presses. "Actions like that make a few in the group wary."

"Then those few in the group should be made aware that Koa nearly murdered me to get it back," I snarl.

"Excuse me?" Evander says, grabbing my arm. "When?" His tone is deadly.

"The flood," I say, meeting his eyes. "Calimo told me last night that he blacked out that night and doesn't remember anything."

Collette snorts. "And you believe Calimo?"

"Can Koa's Hypnotic magic force people to do magic against their will and not remember it?" I shoot back.

Warren looks incredibly uncomfortable. "Yes. It can," he admits.

"Koa wouldn't do that!" Collette argues.

"And yet *he's* the one who found the dagger before the High Guard even narrowed down the signature," I retort.

"Are you serious?" Evander says.

I meet his eyes. "Yes. He came up with some story that he was so 'worried' about me that he looked through everyone's heads to see who did it, then found Calimo and stole back the dagger."

Credo rubs his face. "Bloody hell."

Collette glares at him. "Don't tell me you believe her?"

Credo looks down at her. "Yeah. I do."

"I do too," Warren chimes in. "Damn."

"So here's what's going to happen next. You all are going to leave, and I'm going to go murder Koa. Anyone who wants to join me is welcome to," Evander declares.

"Wait," Paul says, holding up a dark hand. "That's not necessary. We have more to share with you. And we would like to form an alliance if you're willing."

"Unless it's Koa's head on a goddamn platter, I'm not interested," Evander growls.

"We have the golden dagger," Paul says quickly. "And we are willing to give it to Fiana as a measure of good faith. So no murder necessary."

Evander snorts. "I don't give a shit about the weapon. He almost killed her."

"And I understand why you want to retaliate," Warren concedes. "Believe me, I do. But right now we don't understand what Koa's motives are. What his bigger plan is. If we kill him now, we might somehow alert the wrong people that something is amiss."

Evander curses under his breath. "But if we keep him alive, he gets to continue to carry out those plans."

"Which is why," Warren puts his hands up as Evander looks like he might attack him, "some of us want to play both sides. Those of us who can adequately shield against him, that is."

The room is tense and silent for a beat as Evander considers his words.

"How can we trust you? The dagger is all well and good, but it's not enough if you're going to be playing both sides," Evander says tersely.

"Why not?" Credo asks. His tone is not defensive, but genuinely curious.

"Because I have too much to lose if you fuck us over," Evander says evenly. "Much more than you do."

Collette snorts. "I seriously doubt that!"

"He's telling the truth," I growl.

"Let me guess—he's afraid of losing *you*?" She raises a brow.

"Of course I am," he snaps, and my heart flutters in response. "But that's not what I'm referring to. And if you don't check your tone when you speak to Fiana, then this meeting is over."

She looks like she wants to object, but Credo reaches across the table and puts a giant hand on top of hers in warning.

"Despite our lingering mistrust for you, there is another piece of the puzzle that I can offer as proof that we are on your side," Warren says, his gaze lingering on Collette, who's fuming silently.

"Go on," Evander urges.

"We are now aware of Fiana's *individual* significance," he says carefully, his eyes meeting mine. "And considering she is the only one who can return magic back to the females, we have no intentions or motivations to screw that up, and frankly I'm appalled that Koa even tried."

"Seriously," Mila seconds, giving me a look of deep concern.

"How did you become aware?" I ask, as my breathing becomes shallow.

"The earthquake this morning... spoke to me," Credo reveals.

I exchange a loaded glance with Evander.

"Who else knows?" he asks.

"We assume Koa already knew. But other than him, just this group," Warren explains.

"Do you think the King realized what happened?" I ask breathlessly.

Evander's face is unreadable. "I'm not sure."

"I doubt it," Credo says. "The magic is so old, it doesn't read the same way as Natrics today."

"Old?" I crumple my brow.

"Yes, very. You'd have to have a long memory or be a pure-blooded Relic to recognize it," he says confidently.

"How does it read if you don't have a long memory?" Evander questions.

"Well first off, there's no signature which throws off pretty much everyone trying to get a read on it—and most will give up there.

And secondly it's reading as pure celestial magic. It doesn't register as elven to me," he explains. "I don't know about the rest of your bloodline—but the Natric magic seems pretty undetectable."

"Then how did you connect it to me?" I press.

"You look strikingly similar to someone I used to know with this kind of magic. I wrote it off as a coincidence when I first met you, but this morning I immediately thought of you. Must be an ancestor of yours," he says, smiling.

"What would someone think if they pick up on the celestial magic?" Evander asks.

"That the veil has thinned and a god or goddess has come to visit. It happens every few centuries, so it's not out of the realm of possibility." Credo shrugs.

"Would that mobilize anything in the Guard?" I ask Evander.

He shakes his head. "Not unless they start causing damage. We should work on helping you control your magic, though."

"And since you have an important job," Warren says pointedly to Evander. "Perhaps it would be helpful for me to assist in that endeavor."

"I have others that can help," Evander says, and then he softens slightly. "But I am provisionally convinced that you will not harm or betray us," he admits.

"And what exactly is that provisionality based on?" Warren raises a black brow.

"On your deliverance of the dagger and... on a few conversations I need to have first," Evander explains. "And your words last night did give you a leg up, I'll admit," he adds. My curiosity sparks and I look between Evander and Warren.

Warren's lips twitch like he might actually smile. "Thank you. We should leave you to it then—unless you have any other questions."

"None for right now," Evander dismisses.

"Good," Paul says with a curt nod. "We can deliver the dagger this evening. Will you be home?" Everyone starts to stand up.

"Yes," Evander says herding the group toward the front door.

"Thank you again for your trust," Warren says, shaking Evander's lone free hand.

"Provisional trust," Evander corrects, but there's a hint of a smile in his eyes.

37

The next week passes quickly with both Evander and I busy at work. I mostly work with Mila, who is awkward around me after learning of Koa's role in the flood. And Evander's obsession with hurting anyone who might try to harm me.

Or maybe it's my magic that she's more afraid of.

Evander comes to the tavern after work each night and sits at the bar. Mila gets extra jumpy under his watchful gaze.

I try to reassure her that as long as everything we discussed was true, she has nothing to worry about.

"I know, I know. I just feel horrible that we lied to you about your father, too," she explains for the third time. "I'm supposed to be your friend. I should have told you sooner. But Koa convinced us it was for the best, and I thought if I told you, you'd want nothing to do with us."

I sigh. "I've forgiven you for that," I promise.

It took me a few days, but for better or worse, Koa did save her life. I don't fault her for remaining loyal to him or being influenced by him.

"You shouldn't," she insists. "I knew it was wrong, and I agreed to it anyway."

I drop it after that. She continues to squirm.

Credo is remarkably relaxed. But then again, I've never really seen Credo phased by much of anything.

Warren continues to train me in the mornings, which Evander has no problem with. Warren seems to be the one Dissenter that Evander actually trusts.

I try asking Warren about it, but his responses are vague.

When I ask Evander, he gives me a look that cracks my heart open all over again.

"We have an understanding," is all he says.

Each day, I practice talking to animals and healing my own bruises from training. I'm too nervous to use too much of my magic so close to the King, and Evander agrees we should wait until we get back to the school before affecting the weather again.

I also practice breathing exercises with Warren during our sessions, which helps tamp down the intensity of the magic enough to where I feel less panicky.

When I close up the tavern each night, Evander is always with me, dissolving us home and pulling me into bed.

Even though my body is tired from training and work, when he strips me bare and runs his hands all over me, I rapidly forget my need for sleep.

On Friday night, he takes us to Meddia instead of back to his cliffside home. Credo has given me another weekend off at Evander's request.

It hits me that this is where everything fell apart before, and my chest tightens up when we land.

Evander is none the wiser, and he starts pulling out food that his offsite chefs prepared—which I've now learned work for the school in Lucia. He's pulling a bottle of wine out of the cellar when he sees my face.

"What's wrong, beautiful?" he says as he cuts the foil.

"Nothing—I just," I take a deep breath. "I'm sorry."

He unscrews the cork, his forehead creased. "You have nothing to be sorry about."

"I can't lose you either," I admit as a lump forms in my throat. "I'm keeping you, too."

His smile makes my heart clench. He pours us each a glass of burgundy-colored wine, then hands me a glass while raising his own.

"To keeping each other," he says, clinking my glass.

"In a totally, non-desperate, emotionally stable way," I add with a smirk.

We drink then he lowers his glass, fighting a smile. "You may want to return me then, because I'm desperate and emotionally unstable for you."

I almost spit out my wine. "You are not."

"Don't tell me what I feel, Fiana," he chides, brushing a strand of hair behind my ear.

My breath shallows as his fingers linger on my neck. He takes our glasses and sets them down on the counter before backing me against it, trapping me with his arms.

Trapping me with his eyes.

My heart jumps. "What do you feel?"

He leans his body into me, gripping my neck as he presses his lips against mine. There's a roughness to his kiss. A hint of urgency. It has me breathless in a matter of seconds.

"Like if I ever stop kissing you, you'll somehow disappear," he says against my lips. "And I'll never get you back."

"I'm not—going anywhere." I gasp as he picks me up and seats me on the counter, his lips moving to my neck now.

"Like I wish it could be me who kills the King," he groans. "Just so I can keep you out of harm's way." His kisses turn to nibbles and I jolt at the pleasant change, threading my fingers through his hair and wrapping my legs around him.

"I won't get hurt," I promise, sighing as his tongue soothes the spots where his teeth have marked me.

"I won't let you." He kisses his way along my jaw until his lips find mine again. He fists his hand in my hair and tilts my head back, claiming me with a deeper kiss. I start pulling open the buttons of his shirt, desperate for the feel of his silky skin.

"Tell me more," I beg as my fingers brush against the scalding heat of his abs. He slides his rough hands under my shirt and I raise my arms up so he can pull it over my head. He slips a finger under the lace of my bra, unhooking it and tossing it away. He lays me back on the counter and I shiver at the coldness, but he quickly sends a pulse of magical heat into the granite beneath me.

He stares at me with hooded eyes as he starts to remove my pants. He does it the slow way, the non-magical way; like he's unwrapping a present and wants to take his time.

He bows low as his mouth moves to my abdomen. I shudder as his tongue traces a slow, scorching line up the length of me. He pauses to kiss the tender spot between my breasts.

"Like I live and breathe by your heartbeats," he murmurs and my back arches as he takes my nipple in his mouth.

"And your moans," he adds, sucking harder as his hand slips between my thighs. He pulls on the lace around my hipbones and it quickly dissolves away. A desperate moan escapes my throat as his fingers graze over my sensitive center.

He groans in approval, stroking me again, quickly eliciting more moans from me.

"Desperate for you," he repeats, pulling my hips back to the very edge of the counter. He drops to his knees in front of me and lowers his head between my thighs. I gasp as his tongue makes contact with my naked flesh.

I writhe on the counter as he takes his time devouring me. His hands move to my hips, holding me steady as he licks and sucks.

"Keep doing that—" I choke out. "And I'll be the one who's desperate."

"Mmm," he grunts in approval, without ever pulling his mouth away.

His next lick has my hips rocking in pleasure as little whimpers make their way out of my lips.

"You taste so fucking good," he groans before stealing another taste. He slides a finger into me as his tongue keeps teasing me.

I gasp as it all intensifies, threading my fingers through his hair. He groans with pleasure as he feels my release, sucking harder on me. When he lifts his lips away from me, I see the desperation in his eyes.

The hunger for more.

I sit up gingerly, still catching my breath. Yanking open the buttons of his pants. He kicks them off, and the boxers too.

I stroke the hard length of him, and his eyes drift lazily shut. I slide my hips closer to him and position him at my center. He pushes in slow and the breath whooshes out of me as he fills me all the way up.

"That look right there," he says softly, and I notice his eyes are open a sliver. He slides himself back out before pushing in again. "That look makes me emotionally unstable."

"It's just a look," I dismiss, wrapping my legs around his hips and my arms around his neck. I gasp as he pulls back the very tip before diving back into the depths of me.

"It kills me," he says, except the words are anything but violent. He grips my hips and picks up the pace, keeping my gaze locked with his.

"You kill me," he murmurs, lowering his lips back to meet mine. His hands rake up my naked back as he deepens his thrusts, fusing our bodies together again and again.

I pull him closer as he pulls me tighter, and it's still not close enough.

All the while, his eyes are open. Watching me.

It feels like worship.

And I get how he feels.

Because having him look at me like that?

It makes me emotionally unstable, too.

The next morning we're back in Lucia. "Hop on my back—it will be faster," he instructs as we approach the hiking trail to the school.

I giggle but do as I'm told. The close contact brings my mind back to last night. I kiss his neck once I'm in position and he hums with satisfaction.

"Hang on tight," he says, and then he launches like a gazelle into the trees. It's like riding Sterling at full tilt, only faster, and far more elegant. I marvel at how even and steady Evander's breathing is, despite the supernatural speed. The trees race by like green and brown blurs, the wind whipping my hair back away from my face. The hike that originally took us about an hour is over in about a minute.

He helps me down after skidding to a graceful stop, then moves toward the thickest section to ask the entrance to open.

"It only opens for me, Draven, and Ryder," he explains as we watch the path form. "Rosie and my mother don't leave the grounds. And you can't dissolve directly onto the grounds. So no one can enter or exit except this way. And we never dissolve directly to the entrance. We always dissolve to the clearing then hike in, that way there's no trace magic right at the entrance."

"What about the magic used to open it?" I wonder as we start walking across the path.

"Cloaked, with Hermetic magic. Only me, Draven, and Ryder can trace it. Not even Anita can trace it—so we know our cloaking works. And the large population of vorgers in the area also discourages people from even coming into these woods. Not to mention the dragons up on the mountain."

I shiver. I can more than understand that.

When we make to the edge of the path I glance up at the mountain and nearly do a double take. Three giant dragons are perched near the peak, seemingly looking down right at us. A navy blue one flaps her wings once, as if about to take flight, but the biggest of the three smacks her with his dark red tail. She lets out a stream of blue flames skyward.

Evander follows my gaze. "That's odd. I don't normally see more than one," he says absently.

Dagger barks once in greeting and I tear my eyes away from the dragons. He gallops up to meet us, with Dragon tagging along a few feet behind. I scratch each of them behind the ear.

"They'll be in the teacher's lounge," Evander announces as we approach the castle. "Stay here, Dragon," Evander orders as we make it to the door.

The dog whimpers, but does as he's told.

"We need at least *one* of our guard dogs actually guarding this place while you're here," he chuckles.

"Isn't Dagger more vicious? Should I tell him to stay instead?" I wonder.

Evander eyes me, amused. "No. Dagger might be imbedded with Havoc magic, but Dragon's name isn't a misnomer."

My jaw drops. "You're telling me that sweet baby breathes fire?"

Evander snorts. "The fact that you think either dog is *sweet* is baffling to me. Must be a Natric thing." He winks.

The hallways are full of kids laughing and chattering, and some of them greet Evander and Dagger before running away giggling. A few give me a shy wave, while others just stare at me wide-eyed. I smile in what I hope is a non-confrontational way.

"No lessons today?" I wonder.

Evander shakes his head. "It's the spring holidays. You're seeing the tail end of it, when they're extra energetic."

We make it to the teacher's lounge. As Evander predicted, his family is all there, along with Anita. A few other teachers are milling about, but as soon as Eloise catches her son's eye, she kindly dismisses them.

"We have a few things to discuss," Evander says.

Rosie claps her hands together. "She's agreed to kill the King—excellent!" She launches over to me at immortal speed and pulls me into suffocating hug. "I knew you had it in you. We can start training today. Right now even. We can—"

"Way to steal my thunder, Rose," Evander complains. "But there's more, cousin."

Rosie inhales deeply and then finally releases me from the hug. "Oh! I see." She giggles.

"What do you see, Rose?" Eloise asks.

"Don't say another word," Evander warns. Rosie giggles again, but covers her mouth.

"What is it? I don't understand..." Eloise complains.

I blush crimson.

Evander clears his throat. "It's nothing, Mother, Rosie is just being inappropriate. Actually what I have to say isn't quite so amusing, Rose."

"Perhaps we should all sit down," Draven suggests.

The whole room looks at Draven then does exactly that.

Evander reaches for my hand. I let him take it.

Rosie and Eloise's eyes laser in on the casual touch.

"Oh," Eloise remarks with a hint of blush creeping into her cheeks.

I'm pretty close to wishing I was hidden somewhere in The Ether when Evander clears his throat and says, "Others now know that Fiana is prophesied to kill the King."

The room is silent in shock for a beat.

Draven speaks first. "What others?"

Evander takes a deep breath. "The Dissenters, as led by Koa."

"*What?*" Ryder gasps.

"As in killed our *mother* Koa?" Rosie growls.

My mouth drops open. I try to catch Evander's eye but he's looking reassuringly at Rosie.

"It's gotten a bit complicated, so please try to keep an open mind as we explain," he says, his tone compassionate.

"That's going to be pretty fucking difficult, Evander," Rosie says, gripping the leather cushion beneath her.

"Rose—take a breath," Ryder says softly, but his eyes look pained.

"Fiana's magic has come in," Evander says quickly as Rosie looks like she wants to speak again. "And she triggered an earthquake in Ador that Credo—the owner of the tavern and known Dissenter—was able to ascertain linked back to her."

"That's impressive," Anita says with wide golden eyes.

"How so?" Ryder asks, pulling gently on her silvery blonde braid.

"The way Credo explained it, her magic reads like celestial magic," Evander supplies.

Anita nods, unsurprised. "That's how I get it, too."

"How do you know they know?" Eloise asks, concern evident in her tone.

Evander sighs. "As I said, please keep an open mind." He locks eyes with Ryder and Rosie before continuing. "Before Fiana came to the school, she had already pledged herself to kill the King."

Eloise looks confused. "To whom?"

"No," Ryder says nervously.

"To the Dissenters. But she *only* pledged to kill the King and has no other loyalties to them," Evander explains.

"You're serious," Rosie says, her cobalt eyes brimming with tears.

"I never intended to put Evander or this school or any of you in danger," I say quickly, sensing the rising tension.

Ryder's jaw tenses. "Who knows?"

"No one knows about the school or the family," Evander says firmly. "They only know that Fiana has her magic and is meant to kill the King."

"What about you?" Draven wonders. "Do they know you have been compromised?"

Evander squeezes my hand. "They know I want to protect Fiana at all costs, but they know nothing about me being compromised before meeting her."

"Why do they think you would go to such lengths to protect her?" Ryder asks.

"They have a theory, one I've encouraged, because it protects the school," Evander says vaguely.

"Theory? What theory?" Eloise questions.

"They think she holds the divine union pull for me," Evander says, his tone matter of fact. My heart pounds in my chest as I watch him out of the corner of my eye.

"That is a good cover," Draven admits.

Cover?

As in—I don't?

I feel like my heart has been shredded. I force myself to take a deep breath. I slide my hand out of Evander's grasp and wrap my arms around my chest.

He glances at me briefly, his eyes unreadable, before turning back to his family.

"There's more," he says, his tone apologetic. "The Dissenters would like to join forces with Fiana and myself—and presumably anyone else we might be working with—to take down the King."

"Absolutely not!" Rosie barks, crossing her arms and slumping back in her chair. "No way in hell am I working with Koa Zell."

Evander lifts a hand to calm her. "Koa is not part of the group that wants to join with us."

"How is that?" Draven asks, curious.

"Koa has shown his true colors in recent months to the larger group. He had Fiana's father murdered, for one. And he compelled Calimo to start the flood that nearly killed her," Evander explains. "He's lost favor with his own group. They want to split off and work with Fiana instead. And us, if we're willing."

"You can't expect us to believe that Zell will let them go," Ryder counters. "Not after—"

"Don't," Rosie says, tears pooling in her eyes.

"The ones who can shield are planning to play double agent. The ones who can't don't have enough power to be missed," Evander explains.

Draven tenses, gripping the arms of his chair. "Double agent? That is a tremendous risk, Evander."

"I know," Evander nods. "But Warren Volkov is part of the group and—"

"The one who's divine feminine you watched the King burn alive, heal, rinse and repeat—for eighty-six hours straight?" Ryder urges, dumbfounded. His eyes throw daggers at Evander. "You really think after all of that, Volkov will submit to *you*?"

I shudder at the mental image. No wonder Warren looks dead inside.

"I think," Evander says, his voice steady and controlled, "that Warren and the others care more about helping Fiana *win* than making sure I *lose*."

"Which means we have a common goal," Eloise remarks.

"By a stretch of the imagination, sure, Fiana will be safe from their harm," Ryder starts. "But that doesn't mean the rest of us—or the school—will be on their 'don't kill' list."

"If they want Fiana to succeed, they won't want to harm our students," Anita says quietly.

Ryder sighs, but meets her eyes. "It's still a huge risk."

"One we won't be taking if they're playing double agent with Koa Zell," Rosie snaps.

"Can't we just kill Zell instead?" Ryder asks. "The fucker more than deserves it."

Evander sighs dramatically. "I did suggest that—and believe me, I want to. But they want to keep him in the dark and spy on him instead. They say they're worried that killing him might 'alert the wrong people.'" He shrugs, annoyed.

"I am not fully comfortable with the idea of double agents," Draven admits.

"I'm not fully comfortable with *any* of this!" Rosie complains.

Draven glances at his daughter, then sighs. "It *would* be nice to have more boots on the ground for when we take on the King."

"Oh! I nearly forgot..." Evander says. "Fiana, reach into your back pocket."

"What?" I stare at him blankly.

"Just do it—grab what you feel and pull it out," he encourages.

I narrow my eyes at him but do as he asks. My hand touches nothing but air for the first half second, but then a cold metal hilt seems to form out of nowhere in my palm. I pull it out.

"Holy shit," Rosie gasps.

Anita's eyes go wide. "How did you get it out of the palace?"

It's the golden dagger.

I turn to Evander. "How did you get it into my back pocket?"

"Fiana stole it when she was still working on behalf of the Dissenters. I was able to catch her immediately," he says, grinning mischievously at me, "and told her not to give it up without talking to me first. I didn't know she stole it for Koa at the time, and she didn't know she could trust me, but she did. That's why Koa flooded her apartment—so he could steal it from her when she didn't hand it over."

"How did you get it back from Zell?" Ryder wonders.

"We didn't," Evander explains. "Warren and the other Dissenters stole it from Koa and gave it to us as a measure of good faith." He turns to face me directly. "And I had Paul hide it in your 'back pocket' in The Ether, since I can't touch it without alerting the King."

I raise a brow. "How did you know I would wear the right pants today?"

Ryder snorts, and I shoot him a glare.

Evander's fighting a smile. "It doesn't quite work like that—it's not attached to any clothing. It's attached to your energy body in The Ether."

"What will Koa think now that the golden dagger is gone?" Draven wonders.

Evander shrugs. "Paul said they gave him an identical weapon. Apparently the Dissenters have a particular specialty with forgeries."

"They do," I chime in. "They've been funneling weapons that cannot cut through magically derived shields into the Guard's rotation, and they're identical to the ones that can. That's how the King didn't realize the original one was stolen—I replaced it with an identical one."

Ryder whistles. "That's a pretty sophisticated operation."

Eloise looks puzzled. "But then how did you know she stole it, son?"

"Her scent, Mother," he says dismissively.

Eloise blushes slightly. "Ah."

Rosie rolls her eyes. "Please tell me we're not actually considering this," she complains.

Draven appraises her. "I think it may be worth considering, Rosie."

She groans.

"If nothing else, it is more help against the Guard," Ryder agrees. "I don't like the double agent thing, but we have enough Premonics in this family to catch them in a lie should they try to cross us."

"More than enough," Eloise agrees, nodding.

"I do think the children will be safe if they truly want the King dead," Anita adds.

"As do I," Draven agrees.

"Seems you're outnumbered, Rose," Evander says gently.

"As usual," she growls.

Draven looks toward Evander. "What happens next?"

Evander gives his uncle a tight smile. "I think next we have to bring them here for training and planning."

"They're all trained by Warren," I interject.

"Volkov has nothing on Rose—they'll need to train with us," Ryder says, squeezing his sister's shoulder. She jerks away from his touch, looking annoyed.

"As will you," Evander says, fighting a smile.

I meet Rosie's cobalt eyes as nervous flutters fill my stomach.

"I would be honored," I say tentatively.

She snorts. "We'll see how long that sentiment lasts."

"Well there's no time like the present—in the meantime I can return to Ador and gather our new allies," Evander encourages, pushing me to my feet.

"Uh—"

Rosie stands as well, an evil grin spreading across her face. "Yes! Let's strike while the iron is hot."

I manage a polite smile.

But the feeling of honor is already long gone.

Thirty minutes later, I'm horrified to find out that it won't just be me training with Rosie. A handful of students follow the two of us out past the greenhouses and into the training ring.

"What happened to spring holidays?" I ask nervously.

"They're still on holiday, some of them just love to fight," she says, shrugging.

"How did that happen?" I wonder as I see a six-year-old start sparring with a girl a whole head taller than her.

"Not now Jessa—wait for instructions please," Rosie calls. Jessa drops her fists, looking deflated.

Rosie answers me. "Since they don't have magic right now, we want them able to defend themselves should our security measures ever fail.

They train five times a week for three hours each, and weekends and holidays are optional for girls that want more practice," she explains as she lays out various dull practice weapons. "But some of them just like the physicality of it. It's easy to feel trapped here. The activity helps."

Rosie instructs the small group to get into equal rows of six. She pulls me to her side when I start to file in line. "No, you'll be with me," she murmurs. I repress a groan.

Once the girls are lined up, she instructs them to start a series of warm up movements that remind me vaguely of something Tarletan used to do for exercise—burpees, squats, jogging in place —followed by a complex series of punches, kicks, and jabs through the air.

Despite my sessions with Warren, it's kicking my ass.

I've already felt pretty inadequate a few times at the school. First, when I learned that it even existed, and that Evander and his family risked their lives to protect these girls. Second, when I realized Evander came from a family of billionaires.

But this becomes a new low for my self-esteem as I watch *six-year-olds* effortlessly flow through the same warm up that has me out of breath within five minutes.

"Stamina needs work. And your muscle tone could be better— that's why you're tiring so quickly," Rosie says shortly.

Seems her frustration is still alive and well.

"What did Warren teach you, exactly?" she prods.

"Sparring mostly," I say between labored breaths.

"Got it. We'll see how you do with that."

I repress an eye roll, knowing that on some level her shortness with me must come from her grief for her mother, and at Koa's hand no less.

I'll have to get the rest of the story from Evander later.

I should be reasonably confident in my mat skills after training with Warren for months, but as I watch two fifteen-year-olds sparring, I quickly realize these kids are on a different level.

"Nora has a hint of Havoc in her," Rosie explains, pointing to the striking teen with golden skin and black hair. "And Layla is just vicious," she laughs, gesturing to her redheaded sparring partner.

As if on cue, Layla tackles Nora to the ground and pins her down between her knees, a dull knife pressed against her throat.

"Yield!" she demands, and Nora lifts her hand in acquiescence.

"Ah," I mumble, feeling more anxious by the minute.

After a few rounds of watching the students, Rosie asks everyone to "observe" and I almost have a panic attack as she pulls me into the ring.

"Take a breath, Fiana," she says quietly.

All I can feel are their eyes on me.

I'm supposed to be their champion. Never mind if they know that or not. *I* know it. And after watching the girls all afternoon, I can't shake the feeling that anyone one of *them* would be a better choice than *me*.

"Ready?" Rosie prompts, brow raised.

I take a deep breath and tighten my grip on my dull training sword.

I nod once.

And we begin.

38

"You weren't that bad!" Rosie promises as I practically limp back to the castle. We stopped training only for a brief lunch right there in the ring. At that point, all the students left and it was just me and Rosie.

For another five hours.

My body aches with every step I take.

"Even Jessa thought I was bad," I complain, thinking of the six-year-old who giggled after Rosie pinned me to the ground in less than a second.

"Jessa's really good—she has Havoc in her. And she's been training for almost a year. Don't compare yourself to her," she encourages.

I sigh. "I guess I thought Warren prepared me better."

"He did a decent job, I'll admit. I wasn't expecting you to be so aggressive when you can get a jab in. It's just technique and stamina for you at this point, which we can keep working on together. Just use your magic to heal all those muscle tears so you're not sore tomorrow," she adds.

My heart brightens at that. "Good idea." I close my eyes and let the magic do its thing. My next inhale hurts measurably less as the ache in my ribs is dulled.

"I'm sorry I was a pain in the ass earlier," she sighs.

I look at her, surprised that she's admitting fault. She usually seems so... cocky.

A bit like her cousin.

We're near the greenhouses. I lean against one for a moment to adjust my shoes. Rosie gave me another training wardrobe this morning, one fit for spring and summer. Though Draven had to shrink it to my size since she's six inches taller than me.

"I didn't know Koa killed your mother," I admit in a low voice.

She leans against the greenhouse with me, combing her fingers through her shoulder-length brown hair.

She exhales. "I know. It's not your fault. And it seems we have that in common since he had your father killed."

"I don't want to pry—but I'm really sorry if my involvement with him hurt you," I say gently.

"Why *did* you get involved with him?" she asks, turning her body sideways to stare at me, her shoulder pressed against the greenhouse glass.

My tone is bitter. "He didn't exactly give me much of a choice. They kidnapped me once it was clear Evander liked me. Told me I had to join them to spy on him and steal things on their behalf. All in service of killing the King, somehow."

"What did they think you would find out about him?" she wonders.

I lift a shoulder, and then lower it. "They wanted to find his weakness and kill him, so he couldn't interfere with their plans to end the King."

She snorts. "Guess they found it after all."

I turn to face her, crumpling my forehead. "What do you mean?"

"The flood?" she says, arching a brow, her blue eyes looking convinced. "If Koa really just wanted the golden dagger, he would have gotten it without all the dramatics."

"I don't follow..."

She kicks her boot against mine. "You, silly. *You* are his weakness."

"Oh," I breathe, my heart rate unsteady.

"Don't tell me you're surprised," she snorts. "I smelled him all over you this morning." She gives me a knowing look.

"Oh," I giggle. "Yes, we've gotten—closer."

She sighs dramatically. "I *really* miss that."

I shift my weight awkwardly. "Evander says you never leave..."

"Not for two hundred and forty-eight years," she complains.

"Fuck," I blurt out.

She snorts. "I *wish*."

I laugh at that.

"My blood relatives are the only males we've had here since then. I envy Anita, except for the fact that it's my *brother* she's sleeping with. And I envy you, except for the fact that it's my idiot cousin who's warming your bed."

"Does your father have anyone?" I ask awkwardly.

"No, not since our mother." She looks depressed. "Back where we started, aren't we?"

"You don't have to tell me anything you don't want to," I say quickly.

"My family used to think my mother was the prophesied one," she reveals.

My heart stops.

"My father wouldn't take her magic, and with our family's wealth, she was very well protected. But she didn't have a drop of Natric blood."

She's silent for a long moment, wiping the corners of her eyes.

"What happened?" I ask when she lifts her gaze again.

"Koa's nearly a pureblooded Hypnotic. As lethal as Evander is physically, Koa is mentally. At first my parents and aunt and uncle worked with him thinking he could be a powerful weapon to help them take down the King."

She clears her throat, pressing her back against the glass, staring toward the trees on the other side of the gardens.

I watch her patiently, the hum of the cicadas the only sound between us.

"Something changed the week they decided to act. I was only ten at the time, but I remember it like it was yesterday." Her throat bobs as she swallows. "Uncle Koa, as we used to call him, started acting weird. My father says he chalked it up to nerves, and didn't think anything of it. Then my mother goes on to convince my father that she wants to go alone to kill the King, with only Koa by her side."

Dread carves out a pit in my stomach. "What was her reasoning?"

"She wanted us—me and Ryder—to have someone to raise us in case anything happened to her, so she begged him to stay home." Her voice breaks. "It could have worked with just my mother and Koa. He really is that powerful. He could have easily incapacitated the King and the whole Guard, giving her an easy opportunity to stab him with the dagger."

She digs her heel into the dirt with enough force to dent the earth.

"But instead, something went wrong. And she ended up dead. Koa claims someone in the High Guard killed her as they approached the palace, but he should have been able to prevent that." She shakes her head bitterly.

"Did your father detect a lie?" I wonder.

Rosie shakes her head. "No. Which is why he didn't kill Koa. But we've always had the sneaking suspicion that Koa compelled her to go with him alone."

"Why would he do that though, if even now he still wants to kill the King?" I puzzle.

"That is the magic question. One we haven't been able to

answer in hundreds of years," Rosie admits. "When he started the Dissenters, he tried to get us involved again. But at that point we were secretly starting the school, so my father basically told him to go fuck himself."

"I don't like this." My stomach churns. "He's got too many secrets and zero clear motives."

Rosie looks at me with wide eyes for a beat and then pulls me into an unexpected hug.

"No—I'm sweaty," I complain.

"Shut up, we're having a moment," she argues.

I soften in her arms, ignoring the fact that I'm eye level with her breasts.

She pulls away and then laughs at my expression.

"You look like you've just been violated," she quips.

"Sorry—you just caught me off guard," I say biting a lip.

"I'm just glad you're not holding a secret candle for Koa, that's all. I was trying to suss you out, but it turns out you're alright, Fiana," she reveals.

I swallow over a lump in my throat. "Thanks."

"Stop—I'm the one that should be thanking you. You're doing us all such a big service. I don't think you realize how much it means to us—to our students. And to me," she says kindly.

"I'm happy to do it," I say honestly. "Vilero's a dick." I pause, fighting a smile. "And—it's high time we get you some," I add, pinching her waist.

She cackles with laughter. "I can see why Evander's obsessed with you. You share our sick sense of humor," she says, wiping lingering tears from her eyes. "You must think our family is nuts."

I shake my head. "Not at all."

She starts walking back to the castle, and I follow close behind.

"Stick around a century or two, and we'll see if you change your tune," she laughs.

I'm glad she can't see my face, because it instantly falls.

I don't *have* a century or two, at least not yet.

And I have no idea if Evander even wants me around for that long.

~

Shortly after dinner, Dagger and Dragon are going nuts. It's to the point where my Natric instincts kick in and I rush outside.

"What's with Fiana?" Ryder asks.

"What's with the dogs?" Rosie counters.

"Evander has returned," Draven says simply. "With the Dissenters."

It's all the same people that were at Evander's cliffside home: Mila, Warren, Credo, Paul, Blaze, Hawley, and Collette.

They're all severely overdressed, and most of the males have already peeled off their cloaks and sweaters. Warren is completely shirtless, which draws Rosie's eye instantly.

It sort of draws mine too, but not in an *I want him* kind of way. More just like his eight pack abs are staring at me and there's nowhere else to look.

"Already delivering on the D, I see," Rosie murmurs as we watch the dogs sniff each newcomer.

I snort. "That's Warren. Sadly, I don't think he has eyes for *any* female," I admit.

"Like he's gay?" she says. "Just my luck."

"No—he's the one who watched his divine feminine be tortured to death," I whisper awkwardly, hoping that Warren can't hear us across the field. "Don't think he's recovered in the fifty years since."

"I'm willing to do us both a favor and find out," she murmurs, a predatory look in her eyes. "I'll share details, don't you worry," she adds, licking her lips.

"Please don't," I giggle.

"The tall one—who's that?" Eloise asks in a casual tone.

"Credo. He owns the tavern where I work, and Mila—the little blonde girl with the thick eyebrows? She's a bartender, too."

"If muscles isn't up for it, tell me about the buff black one."
Rosie's practically drooling.

"Paul?" I bite a lip to keep from laughing. "He's quite—strict."

Rosie shoots me an amused look. "Like dominant?"

I blush crimson, putting my face in my hands. "Oh my fucking
Maker."

"Two hundred and forty-eight *years*, Fiana," Rosie complains.

"I don't think he's seeing anyone, no," I say quickly, repressing a
giggle. "The pale blonde ones are together—Blaze and Hawley."

"Not into blondes, so we're good there," Rosie confirms.

"And the other female? What's her name?" Eloise asks.

I groan, because that female is currently smiling flirtatiously at
Evander.

"Collette," I say curtly.

Rosie shoots me a look. "Guess we don't like Collette."

I sigh. "No, she's fine she's just—"

"Batting her eyelashes at *your* male? I don't think so," Rosie
growls, stalking off in her direction.

Eloise cuts in front of her with a quick immortal dash. "Be nice
to our guests, Rose."

I repress a satisfied grin. Rosie is *a lot*, but I'm starting to quite
like her.

Especially when she calls Evander *mine*.

Mila is watching the two of us, a wistful look in her eyes. I try to offer
her a warm smile, but she quickly looks away, guilt evident on her face.

Guess she still hasn't forgiven herself.

Warren looks upward just then and lifts his brows. I follow his
gaze and see the giant burgundy dragon perched on the mountain,
seemingly watching us again.

"Hey, Rose—how often do you usually see the dragons?" I ask
as the Dissenters start approaching the castle.

"Huh? Oh. Like once a year," she shrugs. "The school is warded
to deter them. It's not foolproof considering they're not elves, so our

magic doesn't work the same way on them. But we've never had an issue."

"Gotcha," I say, lowering my gaze. I shake off a sudden chill and catch Warren's eye. He has the smallest hint of a smile on his face. Like he's glad he decided to trust us.

Like he went to bat for us with all the others, and we proved him right.

The group assembles in the teacher's lounge several minutes later, and the room feels slightly crowded with over a dozen of us inside.

There's an armchair for everyone, though, and all the Dissenters seem to have lost the look of fear they initially had upon arrival. It's been replaced with hopeful curiosity.

Even Collette looks less defiant.

"Thank you all for making the long journey," Draven says, standing at the head of the room where everyone can see him. "As you can see, we have a lot to protect and a lot to lose if Fiana is not successful. We are delighted that you all have agreed to help her, and in turn, help us."

He pauses, meeting each Dissenter's gaze with a warm smile.

"My nephew as well as Fiana have informed me of some of the functions of your vast network, but we are hoping you can give us a more detailed overview of how your work can help us overtake the King."

Paul glances at Warren, who is now clothed in a tight-fitting tank top Ryder lent him. Warren nods and Paul stands to speak.

"We have Dissenters in every territory, but especially Syra due to its proximity to the King, and Abyssia, since it's a major port of entry. Outside of this group, we haven't yet attempted to recruit other Dissenters to break away from Koa's influence, so we can only count on them when we are acting in alignment with his wishes. Koa's strategy has always been to weaken supply networks, compromise imported weapons, and breed mistrust and confusion within the Guard. He does the last part on his own, and the rest he relies on us for."

Warren clears his throat and adds, "We also have thoroughly trained our network for battle. Everyone you see here is well versed in High Guard fighting techniques, and we've even invented amulets to shield everyone—but especially the females—from magic. Havoc especially. Basically anything that leads to physical harm."

"Are you wearing them now?" Ryder asks with a smirk.

"Naturally," Warren says with emotionless eyes.

Ryder suddenly looks like he's concentrating, but Warren just stares at him completely unaffected. A few seconds later Ryder's expression changes.

"Impressive," he admits. "Where is it?"

Warren reaches his fingertips near his collarbone and a second later a corded necklace with a black tourmaline crystal pendant appears out of thin air.

"Why the hell didn't I get one of those when I stole the dagger?" I complain.

Warren sighs. "Now that you mention it, I have reason to believe that Koa implanted a false memory of me giving you one during one of our training sessions."

"I'm struggling to understand why that male is still alive," Eloise says shortly.

Credo's eyes lock with hers. "He's on our hit list next to the King, milady."

A hint of a smile plays on Eloise's face.

"Exactly," Warren says. "Which is yet another reason why we want to continue to meet with Koa as if nothing is wrong. We're hoping we can lure both the King and Koa to the same place at the same time, then kill them both."

"You think they're working together?" Evander wonders.

Warren glances meaningfully at Credo, who fiddles with his long grey beard before answering.

"We believe the King has something that Koa wants," Credo starts, glancing between Evander and Draven. "Which is unchecked power. For centuries Koa has claimed he wants to kill the King for the good of the females and our society." He shifts his gaze to me. "But as our lovely Fiana has pointed out, he does not act like a freedom fighter with those of us that are closest to him."

"He *acts* like a power hungry asshole," Mila clarifies, tossing a lock of blonde hair over her shoulder.

Rosie gives her an amused look.

"That would make more sense given what our family knows of him," Draven says curtly.

All of the Dissenters turn their heads to face him.

He notices, and clears his throat. "He worked with us prior to starting your network. My wife was going to attempt to kill the King, but Koa ended up getting her killed when he was supposed to protect her."

"If his real goal is unchecked power, perhaps Koa realized at the last minute he needed more infrastructure to successfully challenge the throne," Evander muses.

"The son is still alive right?" Eloise wonders, arching a brow.

"Yes, Charles lives," I say, recalling the masquerade. "He has a lot of favor with the King, but I don't get the sense that he would be a very strong leader in the event of the King's death."

"You know him well?" Draven wonders.

"I was invited to sit at the royal table at the King's six-hundred-year celebration. By his other son, Calimo," I say, blush heating my cheeks. It feels awkward bringing up a past lover in front of Evander's mother.

"And you made quite the impression," Warren adds.

I shoot him a look.

"The King requested a dance," Evander explains, looking at his mother.

"He's a pig," I mutter.

"The King is aware of Fiana?" Draven asks, his shoulders tensing.

"Only in the sense of a male is aware of a female, Uncle," Evander dismisses.

"He is under the impression that Calimo and I still see each other and requested I notify him the moment our 'courtship' ends so he can have me next," I add with a look of disgust.

Ryder snorts. "Well that's convenient."

"Excuse me?" I glare at him.

"Not him recruiting lovers from Cal. But the King fancying you? I'd say that's really convenient *for us*," Ryder clarifies.

Evander huffs. "I didn't even think of it that way."

Warren nods in agreement. "It certainly gives us a leg up."

"So what? Fiana's going to seduce the King and then stab him instead?" Rosie quips.

Evander meets Ryder's eyes, then Warren's, then finally, mine.

"It's not the worst idea I've ever heard," he says directly to me.

I feel like I'm the one who's been stabbed.

"No," I say quietly.

"It doesn't have to be a real seduction, Fiana, nor anything long term," Warren assures.

"You can keep your clothes on and everything," Ryder encourages with a teasing grin.

"It *is* endless winter up in Ador, after all," Evander adds, winking.

I exhale hotly. "Fine, we can keep that open as an option. What else you got?" I say, looking to Warren and Paul.

"Well, our other plan where you are concerned is to sneak you in and have you kill him in his sleep. With backup throughout the castle, of course," Warren explains.

"Not a good plan because once you're in, it's easy for us to keep you in," Evander counters, and it's weird to hear him speak from the perspective of the High Guard.

Lately I'd forgotten he even works for the King...

"We're prepared to fight our way out if necessary," Warren says with a shrug.

"What if we just stay prepared and the next time he does a public trial or announcement, we get him then?" I suggest. "Maybe we could even cause one by reporting one of our group as committing a small crime, one that wouldn't get them killed on the spot but would warrant a public trial. Then on his way down from the castle, we get him then?"

Evander smirks. "Beauty and brains," he says with admiring eyes. "That idea has potential. The forces surrounding him would be diminished compared to inside the castle, and it wouldn't be that difficult to catch him by surprise."

"But if something goes wrong, then one of us gets thrown in The Cave. Or worse," Collette complains.

Warren shrugs. "I'd be willing to take that chance, if it's our best plan."

Rosie is practically drooling as she looks at Warren.

"The next question is—when is the best time to act?" Draven asks.

Rosie clears her throat, snapping out of her day dream. "Fiana needs another three months to train at a minimum."

"I've been training her since January," Warren argues, and Rosie fights to keep a smile off her face. She's relishing his attention on her.

"Her stamina sucks and she reacts way too slowly," she taunts.

"Which are things that could easily be improved upon when—" Ryder starts.

"Shut it, cousin," Evander barks.

I glance between the two of them. Evander is seething. Ryder looks annoyed.

"It's an option, that's all," he snaps back.

"I think the point is, there's no rush," Evander says, his eyes hard with warning. "And we want Fiana to be well prepared."

"Which brings us to our next request," Warren says, looking at Credo and Paul.

Paul nods once. "We need to create a distraction for Koa. Something to keep him busy while we prepare on our end to keep him from looking too closely at the rest of our group."

"What are you proposing?" Evander asks.

"For the females who have no way of keeping Koa out—Mila, Collette, and Hawley—we want Koa to think that Fiana convinced the three of them to leave the Dissenters, and more importantly, to leave town. We would like for them to stay here, if you are willing to house them, and for them to receive additional training alongside Fiana," Paul explains.

Anita perks up. "I can teach you ladies how to access your gifts even before your magic comes in," she says with a smile.

Mila's eyes widen. "What?"

"You're half Chamelic, which isn't very useful right now, but your Premonic and Curic gifts can easily be tapped into," Anita explains.

"You're Chamelic?" I say, grinning at Mila.

She blushes. "My mother was a pureblood, but obviously had no magic. But what do you mean I can tap into the other gifts?"

Eloise jumps in to explain. "It's what we teach our students at this school. That and how to defend themselves."

Collette and Hawley exchange curious glances.

"Great, so you'll be plenty occupied," Warren says, attempting to keep the room focused. "The rest of us can play double agent, keeping Koa fixated on locating the females. We can give him false trails and keep him occupied to keep his eyes off of the bigger prize —Fiana."

Collette snorts at the last part. He throws her an annoyed look.

"That is, if you're open to housing us," Mila says gently.

"Of course we can house you," Eloise insists. "We have plenty of space."

"Great. More estrogen under this roof," Rosie huffs, crossing her arms. Paul glances at her briefly, and I swear I see a flicker of a smile cross his features.

I stifle a giggle, and Mila notices. She drops her eyes, looking forlorn.

"How often will the rest of you check in with us?" Draven asks.

"Considering I'm losing two of my barkeeps, I'll hold down the fort in Ador," Credo booms.

Eloise suddenly becomes transfixed with removing a piece of lint from her dress.

"Blaze, Paul, and I will take turns coming in on weekends. The fewer of us gone at once, the less likely we are to tip Koa off," Warren explains.

Draven nods once. "I think it is a solid plan for now."

Moments later, the group starts filtering out.

I grab Mila's arm and pull her into an empty classroom.

She flinches at the touch but doesn't fight me, and when the door clicks shut she lets out a colossal sigh.

"Enough punishing yourself," I say sternly. "I'm not mad at you for my father. You didn't tell Koa to organize the hit, and didn't even know about it until after the fact. I've forgiven you already. It's time for you to forgive yourself."

She exhales hotly. "I can't! I should have told you, and I didn't."

"Yes you can. In case you didn't notice, I kept secrets from you too," I say, gesturing to the room surrounding us.

She shakes her head. "Your secrets were to protect innocent children. My secret was to keep you on our side to do our bidding."

I sigh. "Would you ever do it again?"

She studies me, wary. "No. I wouldn't."

"Then please. Let's move forward. I see you looking all sad when I'm laughing with Rosie. Which is stupid, because you should be laughing with Rosie and me, too," I tease. "Especially since you're going to be living here."

She fights a smile. "She does seem pretty great."

"She is," I assure. "So what do you think? Friends again?"

She rolls her eyes. "Fine. I'll stop being such a bitch to myself." She sighs. "And yeah, friends again," she adds with a grin.

39

The next day, I develop a deeper appreciation for breathing. And muscles. And stamina.

Warren, Paul, Blaze, and Credo all left late last night while Mila, Collette, and Hawley were shown to sleeping quarters on the fifth floor. This morning, they've paired up with Rosie and Ryder to have their fighting skills assessed, while I work on learning how to use my magic.

Evander drags me out of bed at six.

"I want to know your limits, so when we need to *push* the limit in a life or death situation, we'll know where that lands for you. Plus, it will give us a chance to see what all you can do, and teach you about the finer points of different branches of magic," he explains.

When we make it out to the gardens where we'll be practicing, Draven, Anita, and a young student are waiting.

"This is Lily," Anita says with a warm smile.

She's two heads shorter than me, and looks probably about eight years old. Her long brown hair is twisted into an intricate braid, and she wears the same uniform all the students wear for training with Rosie. But what stands out to me most are her giant, doe-like, bright green eyes.

"Are you Natric, too?" I ask her with a smile.

Lily yawns hugely. "That's what Miss Anita says."

"She had about two years of using her magic before Evander brought her here. Magic is pretty weak in those early stages and she might not remember much, but I figured she might be able to help," Anita explains.

"High five," Evander says, holding up his hand to Lily.

She grins and slaps his hand. Evander clasps his hand and groans like he's been mortally wounded, falling to his knees and then collapsing to the ground.

Lily giggles uncontrollably.

I fall a little deeper for him as I watch.

"Alright, time to focus," Anita prods, though she's smiling too. "Lily, can you share what it felt like when you used your magic before? Just tell us anything you remember."

"Well, I made it rain one time when I was sad, but I also made it rain when I was angry," she says, shrugging. "And then one time I made it rain when I was really, really hungry," she says, giggling.

Anita nods as if she understands the implications of all of that. "So it's not the type of emotion that changes the weather, but maybe the strength of the emotion?" Anita asks.

Lily considers that, and then nods. "The weather does its own thing unless you *really* want to change it."

"And if you *really* want to change it, do you remember thinking of what you wanted to happen or did it just happen?" Anita prompts.

Lily thinks for a moment. "I didn't *think* about what I wanted so much as I kind of just *knew* somehow. Does that make sense?"

Anita nods. "Like it was more instinctive, or kind of in the back of your mind?"

Lily smiles. "Yeah, exactly."

Anita looks at me with an expectant smile. "Ready to try it out?"

I look to Evander, who just nods.

"So tap into a strong emotion, and have in the back of your mind what you want to happen," Anita instructs. She really is a natural born teacher.

I take a deep breath and close my eyes.

The only thing that comes to mind that draws any kind of emotional response is my father's death. Sadness hits me pretty quickly, but then it quickly morphs into a rage so intense that if he were here, I could claw Koa's eyes out for organizing the hit.

The earth starts to shake.

"Woah!" Lily squeals, which immediately snaps me out of it, causing everything to still.

"Impressive," Draven says, a hint of shock in his eyes.

"What was your experience?" Anita asks, like a scientist interviewing a test subject.

"I tapped into grief, and then anger swallowed me whole seconds later," I explain.

"Was it anger that caused the earthquake in Ador?" Evander wonders.

I think back to that. "Yes."

"Earthquakes are pretty dramatic—probably the hardest phenomena to conjure don't you think?" Draven asks Anita.

"I would agree with that based on what I've read. Perhaps anger is your strongest emotion," Anita muses.

Evander snorts. "I would agree with *that*."

I glare at him.

Anita's face lights up. "Good—stay with that annoyance and see if you can do anything else," she instructs.

I want to glare at her next. The wind subtly starts to swirl faster.

"Good—stay with that—and see if you can feel anything more subtle. Like a sense of control over the wind," Anita encourages.

My annoyance grows a bit more now that we're turning my every emotion into a magic lesson, but that subtle rise gives me a window into exactly what she's asking me to do.

It's like there are two towers I can funnel my emotional energy into. One leads to nowhere but increasingly heightened emotional distress. The other leads to channels where I can extend out and touch different aspects of the elements.

"Woah," I say as I explore the second tower—the one that lets me feel the fabric of the wind and taste the texture of rain.

I lean into that.

Lily squeals as rain starts to fall in steady, warm droplets.

I lean in a little deeper and increase the speed, as euphoria becomes my dominant emotion.

"I see what she means, it's not the type that matters," I say, tilting my face up to the rain.

It reminds me of Abyssia.

"I can move in and out of different emotions, as long as I channel them where I want them to go."

"Can you make it stop?" Anita asks.

I pull back my emotional energy slightly and the rain instantly begins to slow. I pull it all back inside of my body and seconds before it fully returns, the rain slows to a stop.

"That was awesome!" Lily cheers, and I open my eyes to see her jumping up and down in a puddle.

I giggle.

Evander plants a wet kiss on my rain-soaked cheek. "That really *was* awesome," he agrees.

"*Rain, rain, pretty pretty rain,*" Lily sings.

I startle. "You can speak it!"

"What language is that?" Draven asks, curiosity in his tone.

"Natric, I guess. The animals speak it—all of them do, even different species," I explain. "I just can't figure out how Lily can speak it if she doesn't have magic."

"I've been practicing," she says with a shrug. "They took my magic a year ago and when Mr. Evander brought me here and I learned we could still use some of it, I wrote down all the words I could remember, and what they mean."

Anita looks as if she might cry with pride. "Very good, Lily."

"I wish I could still hear animals speak it back, though," she laments. "That went away when..." she bows her head then, tears forming in her eyes. She wipes them away with the top part of her shirt.

I bend down to get on her level. "Was it very painful?" My heart cracks at the sight of her tears.

"It hurt a little," she admits. "But the worst part is losing my abilities. All animals used to love me, but when I got here Dagger didn't like me at first. Mr. Evander said it was because I didn't have my magic anymore."

I rest my hand gently on her shoulder. "If it makes you feel any better, I *do* still have magic and Dagger still thought I was an intruder at first. At least until Mr. Evander told him I was a friend."

Her eyes water with more tears. "But it took him a month to like me. And I even tried to speak to him. *Friend. No harm. Not enemy.* Nothing worked."

A lump forms in my throat. "I'm sorry that happened," I say roughly.

"Lily, if it makes you feel any better, Dagger also likes Miss Fiana more because it's *my* magic imbedded in him," Evander explains. "And you know how much I care about Miss Fiana, right?"

My heart practically bursts in my chest.

Lily wipes her eyes again. "Sure, I get that. But it won't be like this anymore soon—right? That's why Miss Fiana is here?"

"Yes. That's exactly right," Evander says firmly.

My stomach knots. I squeeze Lily's shoulder, giving her a warm smile then straighten back up.

"Perhaps we should get back to it," I say nervously.

Evander meets my eyes briefly, then looks to Anita. "I think we can give Lily the rest of the day off, don't you think? We can work on some other branches of magic?"

Anita nods. "Of course. Lily, would you like to go join Miss Rosie's training or take the rest of the day off?"

Lily looks like she's been punched in the gut.

"Can't I stay here?" she asks, her doe eyes growing impossibly wider.

"Well, I think they're going to work on other kinds of magic, which means we won't need your input. You're welcome to stay and observe if you'd like, but only if Mr. Evander and Miss Fiana say it's okay," Anita explains.

Lily tugs on her braid. Evander meets my gaze.

"Of course she can stay," I say quickly.

"Yay!" Lily cheers. "But if I stay, can Mr. Evander dry me off?"

Everyone cracks up laughing.

"Yes, of course," he says, and seconds later we're all dry.

Next, we work briefly on Premonic magic. Since Evander already taught me how to use it months ago, my connection to that branch of magic feels very solid as we practice it.

Evander starts by telling me a subtle lie—*You look pretty today*—and my stomach erupts into flames.

I quickly gain a new appreciation for Evander's description of 'alarm bells' because there is nothing subtle about the lie detection now.

When I ask him how it could have been a lie, he says "Beautiful. I really meant beautiful."

We move on quickly after that.

"You have a tiny hint of Hypnotic on your father's side from what I could gather," Evander suggests.

I play with it a little bit, but it feels far away. I try compelling Anita to close her eyes.

"They feel heavy, but I can resist with effort," she explains.

"Try me!" Lily asks.

I focus the heavy, sleepy energy on her.

She lets out a colossal yawn, but her eyes remain squarely open.

"I can resist too," she says a few moments later.

"Most struggle to tap into it," Evander admits. "With a lot of practice you *can*, but you usually need at least twenty-five percent in your bloodline to be proficient at it."

Hermetic magic feels a little easier. I'm able to form an invisible glass wall much like Evander so frequently likes to use. It's satisfying to watch him try to break through it, like I had back in The Alcove all those months ago.

Lily tries launching all of her weight against it, and then falls back on her bum clutching her shoulder with pain in her eyes.

"Oh this is good—try taking her pain away!" Anita says quickly as Lily's eyes water.

I bite my lip but kneel next to her, placing my hands gently on the shoulder she's gripping. She jerks, and her face twists in agony, and I yank my hands away instantly.

"Sorry!" I gasp.

"No—no—I'm okay, it just felt really intense," she breathes.

"Is the pain gone?" Evander asks, concern in his tone.

"Yeah, it just felt kind of like she was pushing it down to remove it," she says, twisting her features.

"I'm so sorry!" I say, covering my face with my hands.

"That is not uncommon," Draven explains gently. "We need to teach you how to anesthetize before repairing broken capillaries, that is all."

Lily shrugs. "Yeah don't worry. I've had way worse in Miss Rosie's class."

Beyond the glass wall, I don't immediately grasp the finer points of protection or shielding; I can't shield my mind, my scent, sight or sounds.

"We'll work on that more later. If you need any shielding when you attack the King, we'll add it for you before you leave," Evander advises.

Dissolution comes next. It's a subtle aspect of household magic that some elves never master, though not due to a lack of skill.

Some elves just have a phobia of The Ether.

After dissolving with Evander and Warren for several weeks—and even with Calimo prior to that—I've developed a decent tolerance to existing temporarily in the in-between space.

It takes about an hour, but eventually I dissolve twenty feet away. Evander declares that a victory.

"Is there any more?" Anita wonders. "Natric, Premonic, Hypnotic, Hermetic, household... am I missing any?"

Evander looks awkward for a split second before shaking his head. "That's all for now. Should we take a break or go back to Natric?" he asks Draven.

Draven glances up at the sky.

"Take the remainder of the night to rest. Fiana, practice shielding some more on your own if you would like—otherwise let us give your body a chance to integrate all that you have learned."

"Sounds good," I say with a tired smile. It's nearly sunset.

As we walk back, a dragon perched on the mountain catches my eye. It's the navy blue one I saw before. She lets out a stream of dark blue flames.

It feels a bit like she's mocking me.

I do notice I feel much more grounded than normal, having used magic all day. The jittery feel of the energy has dulled.

Despite that, there's a different nervous energy buzzing in my cells now. One that appears to pick up the winds as I follow everyone else back to the castle.

Lily and the other students know that I'm here to overthrow the King, and return magic back to the females.

They know that's what I'm training for, and they understand the outcome if I succeed.

Which makes me all the more anxious as I think about what will happen to them if I fail.

~

At dinner, Mila, Collette, and Hawley sit with us. I shoot Mila a look, which she returns with a friendly smile. The air feels much clearer between us, and I'm grateful for that.

Still, everyone has an air of exhaustion; even Ryder and Rosie look like they've seen better days.

"That Collette is a complainer," Rosie murmurs in my ear as I slide in next to her at the long table. "But a vicious fighter," she adds, approvingly. "Still, I don't like how she looks at my cousin."

I bite my lip to hide my frown.

With all the activity of the weekend, I feel like Evander and I haven't had a chance to talk.

Was it really only a week ago when we first slept together?

We've continued to be intimate each night and are sharing a bed, but it feels like we're somehow farther apart than ever before.

"Blondie is a delight," Rosie adds, loud enough for Mila to hear.

Mila snorts. "And by delight she means I'm easy to beat in the ring."

Rosie shakes her head. "I wouldn't say easy."

Mila rolls her eyes. "Please, you had me grounded within seconds."

"That's because *I* wasn't going easy on you! You were getting the real immortal Rosie, and you more than held your own as a mere mortal." Rosie holds her wine up to clink glasses with Mila, who gives her a skeptical smile.

"So what you're getting at is that you dumbed it down for me yesterday?" I raise a brow.

Rosie grimaces. "Only because Evander would kill me if I hurt you. I can go full out once you're—"

"Rose," Evander says suddenly.

I shoot him a look, but his face his unreadable.

Rosie sighs, then looks squarely at me. "I promise, you're doing well. Better than I expected, to be honest."

"Better than me, I'm sure," Hawley mumbles, drooping her chin.

Ryder, who's sitting to her left, taps her arm with his fist. "What did we talk about today?"

Hawley groans. "The power of positive thinking."

Mila snickers.

"Shut up!" Hawley snaps.

"What's this?" I say, unable to keep the amusement off my face.

Ryder wraps an arm around Anita's shoulders, who is on his other side. "My lovely partner here believes strongly in the power of the subconscious mind. And after watching her help our most traumatized students, I've embraced her teachings myself."

"And imposed them on me," Hawley groans.

I fight a grin, meeting Anita's eyes.

"It's science, really," Anita says defensively. "Our brains are a lot like our muscles. If you do a bicep curl over and over again for weeks, you get stronger and your body moves in a more functional way when you lift. If instead, you avoid lifting anything heavy and let your muscles atrophy, you get weaker. The next time you lift something, you might strain a muscle."

"I'm straining a muscle just trying to keep up," Rosie quips.

Anita throws her an amused look. "For the brain, if you keep focusing on negative thoughts—for example 'I suck at fighting'— then your brain forms a habit of believing you suck at fighting, which means when you want to be *good* at fighting, you likely won't be able to, because your brain has no concept of that reality. Just like if you try to lift something heavy *without* training, you might not be able to, at least without hurting yourself."

"That makes a lot of sense," I admit.

"And if you let her keep talking, she'll inform you about how our brainwaves create our reality," Ryder teases, planting a kiss on her temple. Anita remains unfazed.

"This *is* a vibrational universe, you know." She shrugs as if it's common knowledge. "Brainwaves carry vibrations, which magnetize the experiences that match those vibrations."

"So how did Vilero stay on the throne for six hundred years then?" Mila asks. "There have to have been about a million females who wished him dead over the centuries—wouldn't their vibrations affect him?"

Anita smiles wistfully. "It does, but you misinterpret what it is these females are actually feeling. Most feel like victims. Like they're oppressed. Like the King, the males, even the world is out to get them. They've lost faith in the Maker, and they've lost faith in themselves. So they keep attracting the experience of being oppressed."

Collette snorts. "Are you saying the females are *asking* for this oppression?"

Anita shakes her head. "No—not in the slightest. They're simply not aware of what it is they're attracting."

"But they *are* oppressed," Collette counters. "They're not imagining it."

Anita offers a stiff smile. "I never said they were *imagining* their oppression. But that doesn't change the fact that they're keeping it alive."

"And you're not?" Collette crosses her arms.

"No. If I was, I wouldn't have discovered how we can tap into our gifts even without magic," Anita counters delicately. "Victims don't look for options or solutions, they look for problems and people to blame. They keep their liberation at arms' length when really they have the power to change everything if they change their mind."

Collette is fuming now. "Except we *don't* have the power to change *everything* if we change our mind. In case you didn't notice, no matter what tricks you can do, *you still don't have magic.*"

Anita—to her credit—keeps her composure. "And we always have the choice to dwell on what we don't have. Instead I choose—and teach our students to choose—to work with what we've got and to find our power despite having it taken away."

A wave of emotion comes over me. "That's beautiful, Anita," I admit. Evander reaches down to squeeze my hand.

"It's not beautiful, it's deceptive," Collette hisses. "These girls may never get access to their magic, meanwhile you've sold them a pipe dream."

I flinch, knowing exactly what would cause them not to get their magic back even if Collette doesn't spell it out.

"They miss their magic, but that lack doesn't define them," Anita says smoothly. "They've found a way to create empowerment and purpose without it—which means they never needed it to feel whole to begin with. *When* they get it back," she meets my eyes with a look of confidence. "They won't ever feel like they have to rely on it to feel strong. They'll know they're strong with it or without it."

"But that magic is their birthright. They shouldn't *have* to feel strong without it," Collette argues.

"I agree with you, but the truth is we can continue to argue about right and wrong until we're blue in the face, but at the end of the day all that really matters is *what is*. We can't change *what is*, or at least we couldn't until Fiana came along, so we found a way to help our students feel strong based on their current circumstances."

"It really is beautiful, Anita," Mila says softly.

Collette scoffs. "It's a lie is what it is."

Ryder levels a look at her. "If you want all females to feel weak and helpless, by all means. But that's not what my partner teaches and it's not what we believe in at this school. We believe that strength isn't dependent on external factors. If it was, no one would ever be truly strong."

Collette's face turns beet red, but she doesn't retort.

"Considering our dear Anita has yet to lose an argument on this topic, perhaps we should change the subject," Evander suggests smoothly. Anita smirks at him, but doesn't open her mouth.

Collette takes a pull of her wine, then slams her glass down. It's a miracle it doesn't shatter.

"I'm going to bed. See you in the morning," she huffs, stalking off.

40

"**D**o you think that positive thinking stuff works when it comes to killing the King?" I ask Evander in our room later as he undresses me for the shower.

He starts the water, letting it heat slightly before removing the rest of my clothes and his own.

"It worked for you," he murmurs, pulling me gently underneath the stream of hot water. It feels like heaven after our long day of training. I tilt my head back and let it soak my hair.

"What do you mean by that?" I ask as he starts rubbing soap up and down my body.

"I held the belief that I would find the prophesied female before Vilero had a chance to find you or kill you," he says, rubbing the soap on his own chest now.

"Oh." I rinse the soap off.

Feeling like a fool.

He notices my mood shift. "What's wrong, love?"

My heart jumps. "Nothing." I turn my back to him and look for shampoo on the small shelf.

Before I can reach for it, he wraps his warm, wet body around me, pulling me tight against him. One arm drapes possessively across my hips while the other strokes my breasts. My breathing shallows as my nipples peak underneath his teasing touches.

"It worked for this, too," he says, his voice low and sensual. "That's what you thought I would say, isn't it?"

His bottom hand drifts a few inches lower as his lips graze my neck.

"Mmm," I purr as his fingers slide between my thighs. My eyes roll into the back of my head and then slide shut as he keeps touching me.

"Don't you know how I feel about you?" he murmurs, teasing my center to a swollen peak.

My legs feel weak as the pleasure intensifies, so I lean back against his chest with more of my weight. He takes it easily, backing himself against the shower wall and pulling me tight to him as I go limp in his arms.

He hardens underneath me and grinds against my ass. "Don't you know how much I need you?"

I'm moaning now as his fingers begin to swirl. The pressure is exquisitely firm.

"No," I breathe. "Show me."

"I will," he promises, his voice full of craving. "But just relax for me and enjoy this first."

Ahh. His fingers pick up the pace. The arm across my breasts slides underneath them, and he hugs me back by my ribs so tight that I'm not supporting an ounce of my own weight.

His hips tilt out slightly, propping mine up. I can see every bit of his hand worshipping me.

He's hot and wet and hard underneath me as he guides me closer and closer to the peak. I'm trembling now, my toes grazing the tile floor as little whimpers escape my throat.

"I love those little sounds," he groans in my ear. "I love the way your body responds to me."

"I love *this*," I gasp.

And I love hearing you say love.

"I love touching you," he says, and for a brief moment I think I said the second part out loud. His lips graze my neck as his fingers take me to the edge. "And I especially love making you *come*."

Pleasure overtakes me the moment he says the filthy word and I writhe in his arms while he grips me tight.

It feels so possessive as he holds me up, like I'm his toy to pleasure and play with. I'm weightless in his arms and he doesn't let me escape as his hand coaxes another blinding release out of me.

I shouldn't like how touches me like he owns me. It shouldn't turn me on so much to know how helpless I am to escape his iron grip.

I should hate the way he nudges a third release out of me before I even have a chance to catch my breath. And the way he presses harder against my swollen flesh at the peak, forcing my moans to turn into screams.

Ones that echo off the walls.

Ones that make him grunt in approval.

I should hate the way he dominates my body, teasing and taunting me any way he pleases. I should want more control over what he does to me, but I don't.

I don't.

I don't.

Because he somehow knows exactly what I want.

Exactly what I need.

Exactly what I didn't know I absolutely crave.

I'm panting as he gently lowers my feet to the floor, my core still rippling with aftershocks of pleasure. He spins me around to face him, then spins again so I'm against the shower wall.

His cobalt-and-ice-blue eyes are hooded and hungry and totally fixated on mine. He grips my hips tight, then lifts me just high enough so he can sheath himself inside of me.

The first thrust nearly makes me come again.

"Fuck," he groans, tilting his forehead against mine as he rocks his hips gently. "You ruin me."

I tighten my arms around his dripping wet neck, and my legs around his back. He pumps in and out on a gentle rhythm while his lips bend to reach mine in a heated kiss.

It's too damn gentle. Much too slow.

"Show me how badly you need me," I whisper against his mouth.

"Fuck," he growls. "Can you take it?" There's uncertainty in his tone.

"I said show me," I command, digging my fingernails into his upper back.

He groans with pleasure, then obeys.

He slams into me harder and faster as my body splits apart and takes it all. His teeth scrape against my lower lip and I moan as pleasure and pain collide. His hands tighten around my hips, locking me into place. I widen my legs, encouraging him deeper, knowing he's still holding back on me.

After all that he gave me, I want him to take every damn thing he pleases.

His eyes heat as if he understands, and he pulls one of my legs up to rest on his shoulder. The other makes its way up there too, and soon he's so deep I can hardly breathe. I soften and relax as he drives into me harder, like my body already knows it's meant to be his.

And it is.

It is.

It is.

He could fuck me so hard it hurts, and I'd enjoy every second of it.

Just then he slows it down to a languid pace and I shudder at the pleasant change.

His voice sends chills up my overheated flesh.

"I *love* fucking you, but I love making love to you *more*."

His penetrating eyes hold mine hostage as his thrusts turn slow and deep.

"Love," I breathe, and his eyes are like a challenge.

Like they want me to ask the question.

Or say the words first.

I stare right back at him as he goes deeper still. He rocks his hips in a gentle swirl and the fullness feels like bliss.

Neither one of us says it, but I can see it in his eyes.

I can feel it in the tender way he moves his hips with mine. I know it in the excruciating slowness of his deep, exquisite thrusts.

And in the way he holds my gaze and kisses me softly right as we both come.

The next morning I wake with him still wrapped around me. There's a pleasant ache between my legs that already has me craving more.

As if in response, his hand reaches for my center.

"You're already wet for me," he groans against my hair. He pulls me tighter to his chest then nudges himself between my legs.

I gasp as the length of him slides in, my heart rate climbing as his fingers soothe my need for friction with firm, delicious strokes.

"How are you—so good—" I breathe as my core tenses and coils with pleasure. My mind flits to the dozens of lovers he must have had in the past three centuries. "Actually—don't answer that."

He chuckles into my hair. "I do have a little Hedonic blood from my mother's side."

I gasp again as his fingers swirl in tight circles. "Hedonic?" I manage through a quivering breath.

"Masters of pleasure... food, wine... *flesh*," he growls as he thrusts into me harder.

"You're telling me—" his finger presses hard before resuming tight circles. "That you have *sex magic*?"

He chuckles again and slides out of me, pushing me onto my back and reentering me from above. His eyes bore into mine.

"Are you complaining?" he teases. A hand of his starts stroking me again as he pumps himself in and out. He leans down to suck my nipple and my body shudders with aching pleasure.

"No," I groan, intensity building in my core.

"Good. Because I want you to *come*."

Fahhh—

And I *feel* it now. The teasing of his magic penetrating every cell of my being, racketing up the pleasure to a place where I have no choice but to do as he asks. To release, to surrender, to *melt* underneath him as he slides deeper into me. As he finds his release too.

He collapses on top of me, his pleasant weight sinking me deeper into the mattress.

I choke on a sudden fit of giggles.

"What?" he demands, pressing up off me to catch my eye.

The laughter shakes through me so hard that he's jiggling on top of me. He smirks, slides himself out and moves to the side of me. He props himself up on an arm.

"Why are you laughing at me?" He lifts a brow.

I catch my breath. "Because—" I choke down another giggle. "You're immortal, you're a billionaire, you're at the top of the High Guard, you've created a school where you save girls who otherwise would have been executed. You have literally every unfair advantage under the sun and as if that weren't enough—you have *sex magic*."

He snorts. "Unfair advantage for what?"

I bite my lip as the giggles finally die down. "For making me fall for you."

His eyes brighten subtly. He pushes a lock of hair behind my ear, a hint of a smile playing on his lips.

"You know three of those things used to be reasons why you hated me," he says.

"True," I admit. "But it would be nice if I had even *one* of those things going for me. Just to level the playing field a bit."

He rolls his eyes. "It's not a competition."

"But if it were, you would be winning," I complain, fighting a grin.

His eyes turn admonishing. "You have unfair advantages of your own, Fiana."

"Like what?" I poke his impossibly ripped abs.

He smirks. "Like the fact that you're doing the most selfless thing in the world by risking your life to return magic back to the females."

I shake my head. "That's a selfish thing. I want the King to lose power."

"But you don't *need* him to. You already have your magic. You could hide out here with me for the rest of our days and reject the prophecy. Instead, you choose to fight," he says, his tone admiring.

"You wouldn't hide out here with me," I argue. "You'd stay in the High Guard and keep saving girls."

He studies me intently. "I don't know if I would. Not if you asked me to stay."

I slap his chest.

He looks amused. "What?"

I shake my head. "I would *never* let you do that."

He fights a smile. "Exactly. Because you're selfless."

"Fine. I'm not a horrible person. Still, you have way more advantages," I counter.

He leans in and kisses me. "Wrong again, my love. It doesn't matter if you think I'm winning now, because truthfully, you've already won."

My heart swells in my chest. "Don't say things you don't mean," I warn him.

He kisses me again and then climbs out of bed, grabbing my hand and pulling me up with him.

"Fiana, I needed every unfair advantage I could get," he says, sliding on his work clothes and tossing me a training uniform.

I slide on my pants and shirt as I wait for him to continue. When he doesn't, I gather my hair up into knot and say, "Why's that?"

He sighs. "Because I fell for you before you even stopped hating me. And I've been fighting like hell to get you to feel the same way ever since."

He kisses me before I can react, then adds, "I have to go. Stay on the grounds. I'll be back as soon as I can."

"But Evander—" There are a million other things I want to ask him, but he shoots me a quick grin before dissolving away.

I run to the window and see him waving from the garden.

You're such a goddamn tease saying something like that and then just running away, I groan internally as I wave back.

I swear I can practically hear what he would say to that.

But Fiana, you love it when I tease you. And I'm not running, I have work.

A hard knock at the door jolts me awake from the fake conversation I'm having with myself.

"I saw my cousin leave. Assume you're ready to train?" It's Ryder.

"Where's Rosie?" I say nervously.

"Eloise needed her help with something or another. It's you and me today—meet you downstairs in five?" he presses.

Another five minutes alone sounds like a terrible idea. The last thing I need is more time analyzing everything Evander just said.

"No—I'm ready now."

I open the door and smile at Ryder as my stomach twists and tumbles. I take a deep breath and set off down the hall at a brisk pace. Leaving my unanswered questions in the bedroom behind.

Evander's fake voice pops back into my head like a playful taunt.

Look who's running now.

It's mental, but I respond in kind.

Shut up, shut up, shut up.

There aren't any students at the training ring this early in the morning, nor are Mila, Hawley, or Collette around.

"Anita's got them in lessons in the mornings. They'll join us after lunch," he explains when I ask.

"Got it. She's pretty interesting, Ryder," I say with a smirk as he leads us through a short warm up.

"Anita? She was like that as a kid, too. Always won her arguments and always made you think in new ways. I don't think we would have discovered the girls can still use their gifts if she was more normal," Ryder admits with a smile.

"When did you—"

"She was forty when she seduced me. I wouldn't touch any of the girls even as they aged out of respect, but as I mentioned, Anita always wins her arguments," he explains, chuckling.

"You seem well matched," I say with a smile. "Are any of the girls here your kids?"

Ryder narrows his eyes at me. "Why are you asking that?"

"Oh—sorry. I just assumed with how long you've been together."

"Enough warm up—let's spar," Ryder says brusquely.

I sigh. "Okay."

"Use your magic to shield when you can," he encourages as he picks up a pair of dull swords and tosses me one.

It doesn't take long for me to realize that Rosie was kind when training me—as was Warren. Neither one had used their full speed or strength. Both clearly dumbed down their reflexes to give me a chance to practice.

Ryder did no such thing.

I felt like I was fighting against a god. One that had me pinned to the ground fifty times within the first ten minutes. By the end of the first hour, it honestly was starting to feel kind of personal.

"You *could* give me a chance you know," I growl as he helps me up from his latest tackle.

He snorts, giving me a smug grin. "You need to be prepared, Willowbark. The King is immortal, his entire High Guard is immortal. Therefore, you need to be ready to fight against an immortal."

I curse under my breath. "You think I don't know that?"

He eyes me skeptically. "Then why haven't you let Evander immortalize you yet? I promise—you will be much better at this once you do."

"What?" My heart starts racing way too fast. "Evander wants to immortalize me?"

Ryder lifts a brow. "You guys haven't talked about it?"

"No." My cheeks flush red.

He ignores me throwing a jab at my ribs that I successfully block with a quick shield. His sword reverberates off the glass and he curses as he shakes out his arm.

"Nice one," he says before repositioning himself for the next round.

"I don't think Evander wants to," I say as my heart aches. "He's never so much as mentioned it."

"Bullshit," he accuses.

I tighten my grip on my dull training sword. "Nope—not bullshit." I swing for his neck.

The trees blur into the sky as my back hits the ground.

Hard.

"Argh!"

"Sorry! That one sounded bad. Stay down, I'll check if anything's broken." Ryder kneels next to me, running his hands over my legs and arms. He hesitates over my rib cage. "Shit—sorry, Willowbark. It's dislocated," he says, and I feel the cooling sensation of his magic underneath my skin. There's a nauseating *crack* as my rib snaps back into place.

I let out a colossal stream of profanities.

"Just lay there a minute and let things settle," he says uncomfortably.

"If Evander wants to immortalize me, believe me, I'm willing," I reveal as I catch my breath.

"Dang. I guess I'm projecting my own shit onto you," he says sheepishly.

"What do you mean?" I raise a brow.

He sighs. "Anita won't agree to immortalization as long as the King is alive." He scratches the stubble at his cheek. "And when you asked about kids—that's another thing she won't agree to until he's gone."

I sit up, groaning a little as I do. "Why not?"

He grimaces. "She loves me—*I* think we're meant to be a divine union. But as much as she loves me, she hates the King more. She doesn't want to live forever or have any kids if he's still on the throne. She'd rather enjoy the time we do have, and eventually pass on. My one saving grace is her bloodline keeps her alive much longer than most."

I stare at him. "That's got to be really hard."

He shrugs. "It is what it is."

"Did Evander say something about immortalizing me?" I press.

Ryder looks like he wishes he hadn't said anything. "Not directly, no. I just thought both of you wouldn't want to risk your death, especially with the prophecy. It pays to have that second and third chance."

"Oh," I say, feeling crestfallen. So he *doesn't* feel the divine union pull.

Give him time, a voice says in my mind. It kind of reminds me of Haldric's voice, which causes me to search the grounds expectantly. Dagger is wagging his tail at me when my eyes land on him.

"Was that you?" I ask with a grin. He lopes over to me excitedly.

"What?" Ryder asks, confused.

I glance at him. "Oh. Sometimes the animals speak to me. I

think Dagger did this time." I scratch behind his ears as his tongue lolls out of his mouth. "Evander said something about Dagger being embedded with his magic. How does that work exactly?"

Ryder snorts. "That's my father's project. He likes experimenting with magic and animals. Basically we gave Dagger transfusions of Evander's blood every week his first year of life."

"Seriously?" I raise a brow.

"Yup. And Dragon got dragon blood infusions—but we were only able to sustain those for about a month," he explains, glancing at Mount Zora.

I follow his gaze. "How did you get the dragon blood?"

He clears his throat. "Five years ago a dragon fell ill near the school grounds. My father and I attempted healing him, but for days he wouldn't let us get close enough to touch him. At some point he fell into a kind of coma, and we were able to do some healing magic on him.

"We collected his blood to run tests and see if there was an infection or something we weren't detecting with magic. But his blood was clean. None of our Curic students could figure out what was wrong, either. There was seemingly no cause for his symptoms, yet about a month later he died. My father had preserved his blood samples, and once he passed on he decided to experiment with our new puppy just to see if anything would take."

"What could have happened to that dragon?" I wonder. They usually live for thousands of years.

"No idea. We think if anything it was old age. Maybe he was ten thousand years old or something." Ryder shrugs. "But enough chit chat—let's go again." He grabs my hand and hoists me to a standing position. "I'll go slower this time—mortal speed. Let's see what you've got, Willowbark."

I take a deep breath then lift my dull training sword. He lifts his own.

Our swords come together in a hard clash, echoing in the open space.

"Not bad," he compliments.

I yank the sword back and strike again. Lower this time, but he deflects it again.

"Try faking me out. Go left, and then jerk your sword to the right at the last moment," he suggests.

I try that, except of course his sword blocks the fake out.

He grins at me. "Almost."

I strike high this time, and he catches the dull wooden blade with his hand.

"You're dead," I say matter of factly.

He shakes his head. "If anything my fingers are gone, but I'm still kicking. Finish me off."

I strike low. He blocks it with his sword. I try high again, but this time he ducks and swipes his sword at my shins.

"Shit!"

"You're dead," he says with a chuckle.

I glare at him. "No—if anything, my ankles are gone. But I'm still kicking."

He snorts. "No, without ankles you most certainly aren't still *kicking*."

I roll my eyes. "I'm still *alive* then."

"Okay, then. Get on your knees and finish me off," he jokes. Then he grimaces. "Don't tell Evander I said that."

I smirk as I lower to my knees, throwing three quick strikes at Ryder's thighs, groin, and stomach. He blocks all three easily and lifts his blade to my neck. I block him with a glass wall shield and his sword ricochets back. I drop the shield a split second later and jam my sword at his stomach.

"Oof," he groans, stumbling back a step. "That was good thinking with that shield," he chokes out, rubbing his abdomen.

"Thanks," I say, getting to my feet and dusting off my knees.

After lunch in the dining hall, Mila, Collette, and Hawley join us in the training ring. Rosie is back as our lead trainer, along with the students.

We start the typical warm up and I notice with satisfaction that I'm not the only former Dissenter who struggles through it.

After that, Rosie has the students begin their sparring matches while we initially observe from the sidelines.

"We've sent Ryder to locate the crone," Rosie explains as I ask where he's gone. "Hit back faster, Willa!" she shouts.

"Crone?" Mila asks, tightening her shoelaces.

"She channeled the prophecy initially," Rosie says in a lower voice again. "Evander met her centuries ago during one of the portal crises—when elves were getting trapped in The Ether. She had a vision when he saved her of him working with a female to overthrow the King."

"Wait, really?" I ask. "She saw me coming? And Evander knew?"

Rosie nods. "Nice dodge, Aurora!" she calls to a lanky teenager, before continuing in a lower voice. "She never said what you looked like or anything, so we've always been blind to who it might be. Just that he would be there with you. For ages, he thought one of our students would be the one. And honestly... we all did."

"So this crone can give us an edge then?" Mila wonders.

Rosie shrugs. "That's the hope. She's quite skilled with magic and to our knowledge, has kept hers throughout the centuries. Not in the eye, Poppy!" she shouts suddenly at a brunette teen with biceps that rival Rosie's. "You know better than that! Take a lap and cool off. Aurora—go see Draven for healing."

Rosie shakes her head as the offending student slinks away from her victim, a look of innocence on her face.

She drops her voice again. "The crone helped Evander become an expert at Hermetic magic, which helped him keep his position in the Guard while keeping the school safe."

"And she's still alive?" I raise a brow.

"Yup," Rosie says. "And my mother was half Possessic, so Ryder should find her pretty easily."

"What do you think she will know?" I question, stretching out my quadriceps.

"Not sure, but every bit of information helps, right?" she adds, shrugging. "Alright, students take a break while the grownups give it a shot. Hawley with Mila, and Fiana with Collette."

My stomach turns but I keep the emotion off my face as I enter the training ring and face my opponent.

Collette is sneering at me as I fist a dull dagger in each hand.

Rosie calls out for us to begin.

Collette and I circle each other for a few seconds.

"Afraid to wound first?" she taunts, shrinking our circle on her next go round.

"No," I mutter, my muscles tensed and ready to react.

She drives at me, grabbing my arm and flipping me onto my back. I grunt as the wind knocks out of me. She straddles me, bringing her blade to my throat.

"Yield," she demands.

I drive both blades toward her kidneys. "You yield," I hiss.

"Draw," Rosie calls.

Collette rolls her eyes then slides off me. "That was *not* a draw."

Rosie ignores that. "Go again."

We go again.

And again.

And I land on my back again.

And again.

I try to remind myself that she's coming at me fresh while I'm a little slower because of my earlier session with Ryder. But it's honestly embarrassing how many times she pins me to the ground.

Because she isn't even immortal.

The students leave around four, but Rosie has us stay for the adult session in the evening too.

I get a short break from Collette while fighting some of the other teachers, but Rosie has us round robin so everyone spars with everyone.

And eventually I make it back to Collette.

She drives at me with a vicious look in her eyes. I dodge her first attempt, but she kicks her foot behind my knees then tackles me to the ground, ramming her forearm against my throat so hard that I start coughing uncontrollably.

"That's a yield, Collette. Back off," Rosie chides.

"Fine," she mutters, climbing off me.

"What's your problem anyway?" I choke out as I force myself back to my feet.

She ignores me, driving again before I even have a chance to stand all the way up. I tip backwards landing on my back for the hundredth time with agonizing force, but I jam my blades between her ribs before she has a chance to get my throat again.

"FUCK!" She groans, jumping back, my dull blades protruding from her armor.

Because I *actually* stabbed her.

"Shit—sorry," I say quickly. "Let me heal you."

"Don't you fucking touch me!" she growls, stalking off the field toward the castle. "I'll go see Draven."

"Fiana..." Rosie chastises, but there's a hint of approval in her eyes.

"I know, I know. I'm sorry. I lost my temper," I say with a forceful exhale.

"She *did* nearly collapse your trachea," Evander counters, and I jump at the sound.

"You're back!" I squeal, spotting him behind Rosie and launching myself into his arms.

He lets out a laugh into my hair. "I've been here for two rounds."

He presses his fingertips lightly against the back of my throat, and the pain starts to recede from all corners of my body.

"And there's someone else who's just arrived," he adds, and I pull back to look at him. "Reina."

The crone.

41

Evander leads us to the teacher's lounge at a quick pace, his back muscles tense. He's nervous, I realize.

That makes *me* nervous.

We don't speak while we walk. The hallways are emptier than normal with most of the students and teachers at dinner. It gives the school the eerie feel of the ostentatious mansion it was once built to be.

The home it was for Evander, over three hundred years ago.

We make it to the teacher's lounge, and he guides me inside, keeping a hand low on my back.

The crone sits with her back to us at the farthest end of the room. She's wearing a tattered grey cloak, her wiry white hair braided in a long rope at her back. Something about her presence feels... off.

I sneak a glance at Evander. His mouth is pressed into a thin line.

Ryder glances up at us and then returns his gaze to the crone.

"Evander is here now. And—the one I've told you about," he says carefully. The crone turns in her seat to face us. She sees

Evander first, looking somewhat bored by the sight of him. And then her eyes fixate on me.

Her ice blue eyes pop out of her head. A split second later, she appears inches away from me.

"Diana!" she exclaims, grabbing my upper arms in a firm grip.

"Easy, Reina," Evander orders and her hands fall at her sides. "Her name is Fiana."

She shoots him an angry glare. "No, her name is *Diana*."

My vision blurs as a series of images flash in my mind. I'm looking through the crone's eyes at myself. For a split second I think she's showing me her current perspective, but the setting doesn't make sense.

She's looking at me not in the teacher's lounge, but in a small one-room hut. There's no icebox, not even a stove. Just a roaring fireplace with a tea kettle hung above. The furnishings are simple, just wood and nails, with no attempt at craftsmanship evident in their designs.

My face looks haggard—my green eyes red with tears, my mahogany hair braided in a coronet atop my head. And my clothing; I'm wearing something I've never worn before. A long tunic and leggings—a fashion from the old world. The whole scene looks *ancient*.

"That's—" I gasp as I realize what she's showing me. "That's not me," I decide. "I'm Fiana."

"You may be Fiana now, but you were Diana then. You are the first twin of the Fated Twins. This isn't good—the King will want her," she says, and my vision finally returns to the present.

I shoot a look at Evander. His jaw is tense, his hands curling into fists at his sides.

"I'm *not* Diana," I insist. "I see what you mean—we do look alike—but I was only born twenty-five years ago. And I don't have a twin. I'm *not* her, I'm Fiana."

The crone looks unconvinced. "What you're planning—it's a death wish." She turns her gaze back to Evander. "She's the King's divine feminine. You can't bring her in front of the King. He will either slaughter her, or enslave her."

I scoff. "That's impossible." Evander gives me a side eye. "I *loathe* the King. I'm not his divine anything," I add.

I can't be. I'm not.

I'm Evander's.

Aren't I?

The crone snorts. She looks at me like I'm stupid, her lip curving into a pitying smile. "You don't get to choose these things. They choose you. You are the King's divine feminine, and he is your divine masculine."

No fucking way.

My stomach tightens. I take a step back, wanting more space between me and the crone. My back collides with the door, and I palm it, staying pressed back against it.

Evander turns to face me, his eyes tight.

Does he *believe* her?

This can't be right.

Confusion, anger, fear—I'm not sure *which* emotion it is but it starts shaking the ground.

Pictures come tumbling off the walls as books crash down off the bookcase. The tea service on the coffee table spills, then shatters on the ground.

Ryder's eyes are wide, staring at me like I'm the devil's spawn, and he clutches the arms of his vibrating chair as the *walls* start to groan.

Reina watches me with interest, seemingly unfazed by the earthquake I'm generating, propping herself up against the back of a leather armchair that shakes her petite form violently.

It's Evander who I'm afraid to look at, but his hands are already on my shoulders, all warm and soothing. He's standing in front of me trying to catch my eye, reminding me to breathe.

"No," I insist, and I finally get a grip on my magic. The earth begins to still. Ryder lets out a measured breath, relief loosening his tense stance. Evander rubs my shoulders then moves to my side, draping an arm around me.

The crone notices the gesture and something shifts in her expression. She lifts a brow, crossing her arms.

And then she *laughs*.

I glare at her.

"Don't tell me *you two* are together?" she accuses.

I ignore her question. "Diana was the King's divine feminine?"

The crone smirks. "Of course. And the King is her divine masculine. That's why he went ballistic when he found out it was Delilah, and not Diana who he ended up with."

Delilah. The name stirs something in me, but I ignore the feeling.

"Why would Delilah even want him?" I press. "Why trick him in the first place?"

She uncrosses her arms, resting her hands against the armchair. "Twins are a tricky thing, especially identical twins. It's possible the divine union pull passed to both sisters in the womb."

"So Delilah was also the King's divine feminine?" Evander asks.

Also? He can't really be buying this, can he?

The crone frowns. "Why else would she have agreed to lie about her identity for nearly a decade?"

Why indeed?

My chest hollows out.

"Could the Maker really have made such a mistake? Two divine feminines for one male?" I ask.

"The Maker works in mysterious ways." The crone shrugs. "What you call a mistake could have been quite intentional. Still, as I said, the King will want you."

I dig my nails into my palms. "Well I'm not *his* to have. And I'm *not* Diana."

Evander's grip tightens on my shoulders. I can't tell if it's possessive or if he's worried I'll start another earthquake.

"Perhaps you are Fiana now, but you were also Diana. You're her soul reborn," the crone insists.

"Reborn?" I rasp, as a tingly sensation reverberates under my skin.

The crone smirks, shifting her eyes to Evander. "I never told you the whole truth about the vision. Part of me didn't really believe it. But now," she looks back at me, "everything is much clearer."

"What did you leave out?" Evander asks. His voice sounds rough.

Like he's finding out I'm the catalyst for six hundred years of collective suffering.

Panic builds in my chest. I need him to know that I'm *not*.

The crone answers him. "That Diana herself would be reborn and would fight alongside you to overthrow the King. I suppose I didn't *want* to believe it," she admits, and I detect a hint of bitterness in her tone. "Few are given a second chance at life."

"I'm *not* Diana," I insist through gritted teeth. "I was born a quarter century ago."

"You were *reborn* a quarter century ago," the crone corrects. "But never mind that—we have much more important matters to discuss. Like how you will slay the King."

Her eyes go glassy then and I glance between her and Evander as a low humming sound emits from somewhere deep in her throat.

"She's seeing," Evander says quietly. His face is unreadable.

I swallow back a lump in my throat.

She appears like she's in another world for at least a minute. It's so long that Ryder walks over to join us watching her, then clears his throat a few times when she still doesn't come back to the now.

"The King will be furious to discover this," she says finally, her hand gesturing loosely toward Evander and me, though her eyes are still far away. "Don't reveal your relationship. Don't act like lovers, act like you hardly know each other."

I glance sidelong at Evander, whose throat bobs as he swallows. My heart feels like it's being torn in two. He's *believing* this madness.

She starts humming again and her eyes roll upward slightly then flit side to side rapidly.

"It will benefit you if you use your original name. He will recognize you as Diana immediately. Going along with it will cause his emotions to cloud his judgment. He won't be as guarded if you keep him talking about the way you once were. About why you tricked him."

"But I *didn't!*" I insist, tears pooling in my eyes. Why doesn't she get it? I had *nothing* to do with Vilero's six hundred years of terror.

Evander pulls me in tighter to his side, but his eyes, still fixed on the crone, look haunted.

He's believing every word.

The humming continues as her eyes speed up in every direction. She coughs loudly, and then finally her eyes come back to now. She takes a labored breath and then moves to the nearest chair.

She collapses with a huff.

"How many chances, Reina?" Evander asks gently.

She coughs again. "Out of infinite possible realities? Six chances."

A chill snakes down my spine. "What does that mean?"

She leans back further in her chair turning lazily to look at me. "It means you have six chances out of infinity to succeed in this mission."

"And how many do we make it out—alive?" Ryder asks. Evander shoots him a hard look.

She chuckles, and the sound of her laugh makes me sick. "So eager to know your fate, eh?"

"Well?" Ryder pushes. "Are you going to answer the question?"

"If you insist. Four," she replies with a chilling grin.

I shudder. Four chances to succeed and stay alive.

Out of *infinity*.

"And why are you so convinced that this is Diana?" Evander says, unwrapping himself from me and gesturing toward me. "Do they look similar?"

The spot where his arm was wrapped around me throbs in its absence.

"She doesn't just look *like* her. She *is* her. I'll prove it to you all in a moment, but we need to discuss what will happen *after* you overthrow the King. Assuming you somehow manage to land yourselves in one of the six successful chances," the crone clucks.

"Go on," encourages Ryder, his face utterly calm despite the knowledge that we're most likely going to fail, and most definitely going to *die*.

"In all of the six, Diana will save her magic until the last moment. If she uses it any sooner, you will fail. You'll know it's the last moment when it looks as if you will all die," she starts, her voice utterly detached.

"How reassuring," Ryder quips.

Reina ignores him. "When you kill him, you'll have to burn his body lest his Guard try to revive him. Once he's dead, you'll have the ability to set a communication spell to all of the females in the realms. You'll want to do this immediately after he dies because they will start to feel their magic within seconds of his death. You'll communicate this through *his* magic, so when they receive *theirs* back, they'll have an understanding of what is happening.

"Tell them that they have their magic back and they have two choices. They can choose to come to a secure location and be trained to fight—perhaps here at the school—or they can keep their magic hidden."

"Fight?" I choke out. I advance a step toward her. "Why would they need to *fight*?"

The crone snorts. "The Guard will immediately declare war on you, and all those who helped you. And since killing the King also returns magic that other males stole from females, you will need all the help you can get. Some males won't like reverting to just their own stores of magic. But I do see that you will have tremendous support. Some females will be too frightened, but many will rise to the occasion."

"And how many chances to win the war?" Evander asks calmly.

"If you succeed in killing the King and all survive—one of those four chances I mentioned before—there's one reality where you win the war."

"*One*?" I cry.

"Yes. Just one," Reina says, turning her icy gaze upon me. A pit forms in my stomach as something about her words strike me.

They *remind me* of something, though I can't quite place what.

"Yes—that's it. It's coming back, isn't it?" She cocks a brow.

"What?" I look at her blankly.

"Oh for magic's sake," she growls, and again my vision blurs as she sweeps me away—six hundred years away—to a different place, time, and life.

Diana's life.

Except this time I'm not looking through the crone's eyes.

I'm looking through my own.

DIANA

I'm crying, the tears coming faster than my magic can wipe them away. A deep emptiness fills my gut.

I did this.

I'm alone, on top of Mount Zora, the golden blade shaking in my quivering hand.

Delilah is dead because of you, my darkest self accuses.

Females will suffer for centuries because of you.

Because you didn't return his love.

Because you naively believed that there would be another.

One who would activate your own divine pull.

One who would wait centuries for you, just as you'd wait centuries for him.

One who would stand by you no matter what.

One that you *would get to choose.*

The sky darkens as my emotions spiral out of control.

Damn Natric magic. Thunder crashes as a sob shudders through me.

You'll never get to choose.

You'll never have that love.

You failed. And not just yourself—but every female in these realms and millions that haven't even been born yet.

"I failed," I sob, and my whole body convulses as the ache in my heart cuts deeper. "I thought—I felt—"

The sobs overtake me again and I can't finish.

I thought he was coming soon. That he'd be here soon.

I thought Delilah was happy—that Anthony was happy.

I thought the magic would only allow this if it was for the highest good of all.

I gasp as another cry shakes me to my core. "How was *this* for the highest good?" I demand, and my magic overtakes the skies as sheets of powerful rain come tumbling down.

Why was I given so much power if this *is how the Maker ends it?*

I clear the sky in a flash and sunshine warms the crown of my damp head and my tear-stained cheeks.

Why do you let me do this—no one can *do this—and then just let it all go to waste?*

Even Delilah's magic is weaker than mine. It was always a point of contention with us.

Though she's a Natric too, her ability to wield it always somehow fell short of mine. We had to come up with a story for why she no longer changed the weather with her emotions when she agreed to marry Vilero in my place.

We said she'd learned to control herself.

I laugh darkly. Delilah—though I love her—could *never* control herself. Which is exactly why she likely chose to come clean with him, eventually. She couldn't control that nagging feeling of living a lie.

No matter how much she claimed to love him—and how devoted to him she became after he immortalized her—she couldn't control the urge to be honest.

I don't blame her for that. I'm not sure I could have, either.

Though she's dead—I send my thoughts to her anyway.

I forgive you Delilah. This wasn't your fault. This is mine.

My fault.

It's my fault that Anthony is on a murderous, magic-stealing rampage.

It's my fault that millions of females will grow up without magic.

It's my fault that Anthony will crown himself King of the elves.

This is all my fault. It is now—and it will be for centuries.

No one will ever forgive me. I will be forever remembered as the female who betrayed all of feminine kind.

The female who ruined Elven society.

The female who created the Dark Ages of the Light Realms, as Reina said they will come to be called.

And for what?

For love?

A love that doesn't even exist.

And now—never will.

I take a deep breath. There's no more putting this off. I walk over to the stream. It's time to die.

Alone.

I don't want to die alone, I whimper. Pathetically.

But my magic reaches out anyway, despite how weak I feel.

The small mammals come first—jack rabbits and marmots and foxes. Neither care who's predator or prey as they walk with me toward the stream. I wade inside. The water is unseasonably warm, I notice. It comforts me.

The fish come next, feeling my magic calling them through the water. Dozens, and then hundreds of carp and trout weave in and out of my legs, some of their scales grazing the tops of my bare feet. I watch the weaving patterns as my tears fall into the stream.

There's a whoosh of wind as the birds sweep lower as my magic beckons them. Sparrows, cardinals, and falcons alike fly in concentric circles over my head. I look up at the beauty and impossibility of such a sight, my chest aching knowing that I may never see such a thing again.

Then the large mammals arrive with heavy footsteps, as bears, elk, deer, and bison run onto the scene. They nearly collide with the smaller mammals already crowded around the edge.

A lone cougar prowls through the group, laying her majestic form down along the riverbank. Her tail reaches across the small distance between us and rests heavily on my shoulder.

My chest caves at the warm contact and fresh sobs rock through me.

Finally, the smallest creatures of all make their way to meet me. Lightflies—which have graciously awakened during their daytime slumber to show me their mystical beauty one last time.

I watch their vibrant light show of purples, pinks, greens, and blues. They seem to know exactly what patterns will comfort me, and my heart feels a little lighter as I watch.

Thick, fluffy bumblebees arrive last, landing on every inch of my skin, my hair, even my eyelashes. Thousands of stingers at the ready, yet all I feel is comfort.

I won't die alone after all.

I take a shaky breath—one of my last.

I lift the blade to my wrist, letting the sharpness barely pierce the skin.

If I can have a second chance, give it to me. If I can fix this, let me. If I can be reborn, let me. If I can meet my one true love, make it happen for me. Please.

I close my eyes as I use the knife.

Lightheadedness finds me quicker than I expect.

I drop the blade and use magic for the second wound, and within seconds me, the cougar's tail, and the bees all fall heavily into the water.

I try to make the bees leave—they need not die with me. But they don't.

They stay with me.

And I'm fading.

Going.

Gone.

42

Hot acid bubbles in my stomach as tears fill my eyes in the *now*. It was me—*I* am responsible for this. For *all* of this.

I meet Evander's gaze, and it only makes me feel worse.

I immediately dissolve outside. Out by the horse stables, and I hardly notice the fact that I beat my best distance because I have to *get away*.

The warmth of Lucia coalesces around me as I bolt for the trees and I curse under my breath—wishing for once for the biting cold of Ador. Wishing for the harshness of the wind and ice. Wishing the realm would punish me for all the suffering I've caused.

Because it was me. I did this.

Clouds gather overhead, obscuring the light of the moon. The temperature nosedives as I run through the trees, in the opposite direction of the main entrance, needing to put as much space between me and Evander as possible.

I did this. I'm at fault for this.

The truth eats my insides as I run.

How can he love me after *that*? How can *Evander*—who loathes the King, who tricked him into killing seven of his best friends—how can he *ever* look at me the same way again?

You're the reason for his suffering. You're the reason for everyone's *suffering. You're the problem.*

The tears run down my face before I can stop them.

I run faster, my stomach twisting.

I have to get *away*.

The sky opens up into a cold rain. As if the realm itself is punishing me for the centuries of suffering I've caused.

The King is your divine masculine. The King will want you.

"STOP!" I shout—at the voice in my head.

Because there's no fucking way I'm ending up eternally tied to the King.

I'm Evander's. I *want* to be Evander's.

Doesn't matter what you want. No way he'll want you anymore.

I trip over a bulky tree root and collapse to the ground. Sobs jerk through me as the cold rain turns even colder. Ice pellets smack my head and shoulders.

I don't get up.

I curl myself around my legs, hiding my face between my knees, letting every bit of dignity leave me. I give myself to the hail—to the punishment. I deserve it. And so much more.

My stomach churns. I feel sick, but not nauseous.

Guilt.

I feel guilty.

You are *guilty. This is all your fault.*

"We'd like to have a word with you," says a deep and resonant voice somewhere deep in my mind. I startle to an upright position, shielding my face from the hail.

"Who's there?" I ask, scanning my surroundings.

"My name is Zyrran. I'm going to pick you up," the voice replies.

"Pick me... up?" I breathe, pushing to my feet. The hail has slowed to a gentle rain. I don't see any animals anywhere in the forest.

I turn, trying to glimpse through the darkness formed by the clouds, but the shadows seem to darken further. I take a breath, trying to force the emotions down so the clouds will expose the moon and I can see properly again.

The rain slows and then stops, but it's still too dark under the cloud cover. There's an odd whooshing sound coming from somewhere up above, and the wind blows my hair back. I look up.

"Holy—"

The rest of the words get lost in a blood-curdling scream, as a massive claw wraps around my torso and I get *yanked* toward the sky.

I'm face down, parallel to the ground now, which is rapidly shrinking away as this giant scaled beast gains altitude at an astonishing rate.

The school is swallowed up by a thick grove of trees and disappears from view entirely—as if it doesn't exist. We make it past the wards in a matter of seconds.

I want to fight out of the claw's grip, but the second I do, I'll go tumbling down to a quick and painful death.

I'm going to be sick.

"*Relax Natric one, we mean you no harm,*" says the same resonant voice.

"Where are you taking me?" I manage to choke out as the giant winged creature propels us higher. I can hardly hear my own voice over the rush of wind but the creature responds instantly.

"*Your kind calls it Mount Zora. We call it home.*"

"You're a dragon," I realize. Fear grips my chest so tightly I struggle to breathe.

"*Indeed.*"

He arcs high and the peak of Mount Zora appears in my field of vision for a split second before he launches into a terrifying nose-dive on the other side.

My breath rushes out of me as I count the dozens of powerful winged beasts gathered in a large circle just below the peak. Most have their wings tucked in tight, their powerful claws digging into the sheer rock face.

As if it's soft and pliable.

"When you say *we*..."

"*I mean the Havordians*," Zyrran says, leveling out as we near the landing spot.

"*Watch your head*," he adds, and my stomach drops as he tosses me into a section that mercifully is still covered in thick, fluffy snow from last winter.

I cover my face as I hit the ground. It's a painful landing even with the soft snow, and I'm shivering as my bare arms sink into the powder. The wind is knocked out of me, but I force myself to push up out of the snow. There's a dull rumbling all around me as I make it to my feet.

I'm trembling.

My eyes are wide as I take in the Havordians in the bright light of the moon.

The dragons are a rainbow of colors—shades of green, reds, dark blues and yellows. Some have spiky tails that look like the weapons Evander keeps in his cliffside home. Others have smoother tails, but sharp points staggered up the length of their spine like giant lethal porcupines.

The one who took me—Zyrran—is a deep burgundy color with orange eyes and black horns that look needle-sharp, even from down here. He's the tallest. Thirty feet at least.

The rest seem to adjust their positions to make room for him. Like he's their leader.

I start to count. Five, ten, twenty—there are more dragons clustered further down the slope of the mountain, wedged between evergreen trees that may as well be blades of grass for these colossal, fearsome beasts.

"*For your sake, I would advise you think of a different term for us. Some of the young ones take deep offense to your word choice*," Zyrran snips.

My jaw drops. "You can hear me?"

"Certainly. We've been able to hear you for several days now, though many of us prefer to block you out."

"Several days—like since my birthday?" I take a step forward, somehow no longer feeling my fear despite the fact that I'm now in the center of the deadliest circle I could ever imagine. "Does Natric magic include—"

"Communicating with dragons? No, not typically. We haven't bonded with a Natric since Anadyna walked these realms," he replies, his tone melancholy.

"Anadyna—as in the daughter of Eldris the Great and the Goddess of Creation?"

As in the first Natric elf to ever be created?

"Precisely."

"Wait—what do you mean by *bonded*?" My stomach turns at the word. Elven bindings are breakable in one way only.

Death.

"We've chosen to serve you in your mission to overthrow the King. That is—if you're able to accomplish it in a timely manner," Zyrran says, tilting his head slightly.

A grass-colored dragon to his left adds, *"And if not, we'll take matters into our own claws."* He snarls, his razor sharp teeth peeking out of his enormous jaws. I take an unconscious step back.

Zyrran shoots him a reproachful look.

"You're going to help me kill the King?" I breathe, turning in the circle, meeting each creatures' eyes. "But why?"

The green one smacks his spiky tail against a tree behind him, causing me to jump. *"So many questions!"*

"Silence, Gorvorian. It's only natural for her to be curious. She is the first elf we've spoken to in over five thousand years," Zyrran scolds with a withering look at the green one.

Gorvorian snorts, and I feel the heat of his breath like hot steam over my head.

"Your King isn't just upsetting the balance with the elves. His relent-

less hunger for power has led to consequences for us, as well as every other creature in the Light Realms," Zyrran explains.

"What kinds of consequences?" I ask, staring into Zyrran's orange eyes. There's a rumble all around me, and the vibrations sound like outrage.

"*We cannot trust her, Zy. Be wise with your words,*" says a dark blue female to my right that's almost as big as Zyrran.

"*She's inextricably linked to our fate, Lozana. We owe her an explanation,*" Zyrran counters.

Lozana flaps her wings once, snarling. "*Didn't you hear her mere moments ago? She believes she is Diana Pryndale, the original catalyst of this entire abomination!*"

There are sounds of agreement from a few dragons behind me. My stomach lurches, and I spin around nervously.

Dozens of giant eyes are staring me down.

Zyrran snaps his teeth, his front claws digging deep grooves into the earth, as if he's preparing to launch himself across the circle at the female.

"*Which is exactly* why *we are bonded to her. Did you not realize the importance of her soul returning reborn? The Maker has not allowed such a thing in even* my *lifetime, Loz,*" he presses.

Lozana sends a fiery breath skyward. I gasp, throwing myself onto the ground. I cover my head with my hands as my whole body jerks with fear.

Burning alive—that's one way I *refuse* to go.

Better they snap my neck in their giant jaws.

"*At ease, Natric one. Lozana will not harm you. We are forbidden from harming those we are bonded to,*" Zyrran insists, his tone gentler in my mind.

I look up. "Am I bonded to all of you?" I push myself up onto my knees, wiping my hands against my pants to get the snow off.

"*All of the Havordians, yes. There are thirteen of us. The rest of our species are not able to bond with elves,*" he explains.

"Havordians are the elders, right? The dragon council?" I finally stand back up.

Zyrran bows his giant head. *"Indeed, and bonded elves are also protected from the rest of our species. It is law, though not one we've had to enforce in thousands of years."*

Some of the tension leaves my shoulders, but I can still feel Lozana's fiery glare on my back.

"Why *did* you bond with me?" I ask. "And what happens to you and the rest of the realm if I don't kill the King?"

Zyrran shoots a warning look over my shoulder then bows his head so he's eye level with me. *"The King has disrupted the natural order of the Light Realms in more ways than one. Stealing magic from the females was a disgrace, but even that does not compare to his biggest sin."*

I swallow drily. What could be a bigger sin than that?

"That much power is too much for any elf to hold in their cells," Zyrran explains, and I get the feeling that he's watching my reaction carefully. *"It's not natural, what he's done. And in the early days he nearly died struggling to contain it all."*

He pauses, his eyes narrowing to slits.

The other dragons tense.

"King Vilero has been conspiring with demons in the Shadow Realms for the past six centuries. He channels dark magic. He's mutated his genes with it so he could hold more power. And he lowers the vibration of the entire realm in the process, cursing the land and all who inhabit it."

Fear makes my voice rough. "How does it impact you?"

Zyrran's eyelids droop. *"We're dying. Slowly—so slowly that we didn't notice for six centuries. But we Havordians used to be sixteen five years ago—now we are only thirteen. And we're losing weaker dragons at a faster rate."*

My heart clenches as I remember the dragon Ryder mentioned who died by the school. "Is it a sickness?" I breathe.

Zyrran nods his head once. *"A blight on the realms. And the guardians of the realms."*

470

"How long do you have? Before another one of you gets sick?" I scan their scaly faces. My heart catches as I see a small lavender dragon peak out from behind a larger violet one.

"We are all in some stage of sickness now. Our stamina has dropped. I noticed it first three hundred years ago, but I believed I was simply getting older. But then our young started hatching smaller. And weaker. And now it is difficult for our females to conceive at all. This year, we have seen five eggs never hatch."

Zyrran's voice catches on the last part. He clears his throat in a mighty rumble, then coughs up steam.

"With the three Havordians that have passed, their wings gave out about three months before they died. Then they lost the ability to breathe fire one month later. The final month, they fall into a coma. They die within weeks at that point."

Exactly like the dragon Ryder described.

My eyes are watering, but I'm angry not sad. "And all of this is because Vilero is channeling dark magic? Just so he can keep more power for himself? So much power that he had to defile himself just to be able to hang on to it?"

"You understand our desire to end the King, then. However, we were told simply ending him is not enough. That there's ancient magic attached to his life. Magic that you intended, in your life as Diana."

"Told?"

"Surely you know we have a direct link to the Maker, Natric one," Zyrran says, straightening back up to his full height.

I let out a short exhale. "I've heard the legends. I just never imagined I would have a way to confirm them."

"If you kill the King, the balance of magic is fated to be restored. If we kill him, the magic dies with him."

"A sacrifice we are willing to make, Zyrran," Gorvorian complains, whipping his tail against another tree. It collapses into a splintered heap.

"No you can't!" My heart starts galloping at an unsettling speed. "Let me do it—I can do this," I insist, pacing closer toward Zyrran.

Zyrran throws another death glare in Gorvorian's direction before turning back to face me. *"We will give you a fair chance. We can still end him on our own—and we will if you do not act quickly. Three other Havordians have lost their flight this week. We cannot delay more than a month."*

"A month?"

Panic rises like a tidal wave threatening to pull me under.

"I can try..."

Lozana throws another fiery blaze upward, though on a low diagonal angled suspiciously close to my head. *"A month is too long. Let me take her tonight."*

"No, Lozana," Zyrran warns, hurling a fireball at her. I flinch, but her scales are fireproof and the flames are merely absorbed into her skin.

She growls back. *"I will not lose my flight! We don't even know if it will come back once the King is dead!"*

"Tonight?" I say quietly as more dragons start arguing in my mind—new voices hitting me from every different angle. It's so disorienting that I find myself sinking to my knees again and covering my ears. But the sound doesn't stop.

"Jeptolia, Freva and Plodius cannot fly anymore! It's barbaric asking them to wait a month!" says a male whose tone is more of a rasp.

"Do you really want Sashaya growing up with a mother who cannot fly?" This one's a female, and she's pleading.

"Or worse yet—one who cannot breathe fire to protect her?" It's Lozana again, pure anger in her voice.

The arguments grow louder as I sink deeper into myself trying unsuccessfully to block it all out.

"I am confident the Maker would not have told us of the Natric one if we weren't supposed to work with her. If she needs a month—we should give her a month. We can spare that much time," Zyrran insists.

"She is the cause of this! She doesn't deserve more preparation! Throw her to the wolves and see if she succeeds. And if not, we torch him tonight!" Lozana pushes.

"*Aye!*" Gorvorian agrees.

"*No—we give her more time,*" Zyrran growls, puffing up his chest.

The whole circle starts hissing and growling as fire crackles deep in their throats.

And I'm standing right smack in the middle of it all.

Guilt and grief sicken my stomach as I realize the whole realm is suffering because of *me*.

Not just female elves.

Not just the animals Nasgardo has been killing.

But even the guardians of the realms—the thousand-year-old dragons.

I'm like a plague that's been unleashed, tainting every aspect of life. Children have died, animals have died, dragons have died.

Because of me.

So what if I did it in a previous lifetime? It's still my fault.

And no wonder Evander hasn't felt the divine union pull or wanted to immortalize me. He was never meant to feel it.

So why did I?

Your punishment, a cruel voice says in my mind. And though the dragons are still arguing, I know it's my own. *So you know the pain you dealt Vilero, you feel for Evander what he could never feel for you.*

Maybe he loved who he thought I was, the idea of this female coming to fulfill the prophecy.

Maybe he put me up on a pedestal and saw me as his savior for his students and his double life.

Maybe he believed I was good and selfless, just like he is.

But now?

I'm the source of his students' nightmares, the catalyst for everyone's suffering.

I'm not good or selfless, and I'm definitely not a savior.

I'm the villain in this story.

I'm the villain in *his* story.

I'm the one who—after the initial shock of this realization—he'll grow to hate.

He must feel so betrayed right now. He must wish he never met me. He must wish he never kissed me, never slept with me, and never fell for me.

It was one thing to hide the resistance from him.

But this?

Will he even believe I didn't know this all along?

The dragons are still arguing over how much time to give me to kill the King.

I can't let them kill him without returning the magic back. And I can't ask them to wait for me to better prepare. Not when they're sick and dying because of my stupid trick.

"I'll do it," I say shakily. "I'll do it tonight. Fly me to the base of Ador and I can dissolve the rest of the way myself." I palm the golden dagger, still sheathed in my back pocket in The Ether. The cold metal sends a jolt of electricity down my spine, mingling with the intense waves of panic churning in my gut.

"*Are you sure, Natric one? We don't want you to get yourself killed in the process...*" Zyrran protests.

"I won't. I'll wait until the middle of the night, and then I'll sneak into the castle. I've done it before once already," I explain, moving to his side. "I'll slit his throat in his sleep. He won't even have time to scream."

"*You will need to burn the body too...*" Zyrran says skeptically. "*Wouldn't it better to lure him out of the castle somehow? Then we can back you.*"

"No," I say, and my heart hammers in my chest. "I want this to be a stealth attack. The crone said they would declare war on me and anyone who helps me—including you. I've put you into a horrible position as it is. Let me make this right."

Zyrran side-eyes me. "*What about your... friend? The Havoc-born one. Would you like us to retrieve him for you?*"

I shake my head violently, tears streaming from my eyes. "No. It's better if it's just me. I- I work well alone. I can handle this," I say, and the last part is more for myself than anyone else.

Zyrran groans. He levels a look at every Havordian in the circle. *"I don't want to hear another complaint about her from any of you from this point forward. Are we clear?"*

There are rumblings of approval from everyone.

Lozana, the dark blue one, snorts out a puff of hot air. *"Clear."*

Zyrran faces me head on. *"I will take you. Do you think you can hold on if I let you ride on my back?"* It's as if he's raised a brow, though dragons don't have any.

"I can try." My whole body is charged with anxious energy, and yet I somehow simultaneously feel completely numb.

Zyrran lays down on his belly, sweeping a wing out long to the side like a ramp.

I stare at his burgundy wing, noticing the scales are each rimmed in black. "Will it hurt you? If I—"

"Just climb on, Natric one. We have a King to kill and balance to restore," Zyrran urges.

I take a breath that was intended to be deep, but it barely makes it down my throat.

I crawl up his wing and seat myself just behind his shoulders. I wrap my arms around this neck. It's thicker than a tree trunk. It's awkward, and my mouth goes dry as I feel him backing up to launch himself skyward.

"Hold on tight," he bellows, and the dragon chatter in my mind grows silent, as if they've all left the room.

Seconds later, we're airborne.

43

The forests of Lucia thin out within an hour of flight. There's a long expanse of barren land leading into the southern tip of Syra, and the temperature steadily drops.

It's too late to wish I'd worn a sweater, and soon I'm shivering.

"Open up your senses and I can share heat with you," Zyrran says gently. There's an edge of concern in his tone.

"How do I do that?" I say mind to mind.

"Take your awareness wider out to the sides of your body instead of concentrated just in your mind," he instructs.

I don't exactly know what he means by that but I try it anyway.

I focus on the wind, the feel of his wings flapping and the muscles in his back working, and the steady rhythm of his breath. It instantly relieves some pressure in my head and my thoughts feel further away. Everything comes into sharper focus, like I've entered a meditative state.

"Good. Now tune your awareness into my molten core. It's located just above my diaphragm in my lower abdomen," he encourages. *"Find the fire burning there and let that heat move into your body."*

Again, his instructions don't make sense, but I still attempt to do as he says without thinking too hard about it. I can imagine the feel of the fire he describes, and I send my awareness in the location he specified.

"Woah," I breathe as the heat jolts through me, and my breath comes out hotter than is normal for an elf.

"*Is that magic?*" I ask, as the heat moves into my frozen arms and legs. I shake out my numb fingers as hot blood rushes into them.

"*Any creature can sense these things with their awareness. The problem is most do not test the limits of their divine mind, nor train their focus to stay out of needless thoughts. It is a bit easier for Natrics to tap into, though,*" he explains.

"*Needless thoughts?*" I've never heard thinking described in such a way.

"*Most thoughts are needless. They simply waste energy. And the part of your mind that thinks is spiritually immature. Which is why thinking causes your kind so much suffering.*"

Zyrran dips a touch lower, sneaking below the cloud cover for a moment before climbing higher again, obscuring us from view from down below.

He continues. "*Being is much more efficient, and spiritually wise. Another way the Maker describes it is like being in your body, instead of in your mind.*"

"*Is that how I sense wounded animals?*" I wonder, remembering how viscerally I feel it throughout my body.

He nods his head once. "*Indeed. With your Natric gifts, it seems your awareness is naturally more open to animals than is typical for your kind. Combine that with staying out of your thoughts, and you'll find yourself entering a state aligned with the Maker himself, which bodes well in situations where you desire an advantage.*"

"*Why don't more elves know this?*" I ask dubiously.

"*Too many of your kind have forgotten that your power originally comes from the Maker. You think yourselves gods in and of yourselves, meaning you limit your magic tremendously by relying only on yourself.*

"*It is not that your kind does not know—it is that they do not* want to *know. To merge yourself with the Maker's omnipresence means you must admit you are not the most powerful thing in this universe. It means you must submit to a power greater than you, and trust that that power will not punish or harm you. For most of your kind under this King's rule, that is too great a sacrifice to comprehend. The last thing your kind can stomach is submitting to a bigger power when you have already been forced to submit to one against your will."*

"*Indeed,*" I think, feeling extremely resistant to this concept myself—even if it means I'll have the Maker's help with what comes next.

"*You cling to your independence thinking it gives you more power, freedom, and choice. But we dragons know that the Maker always chooses the highest good for all. The thing you would choose for yourself —that's what the Maker chooses for you. But your kind is too skittish to trust in this. So you cling to your power thinking it's your own, cutting yourself off from the source of all that is, and thereby weakening your own power in the process.*"

I can feel my mind and heart opening a sliver to this at the same time another part of me wants to fight against it.

Instinctively I know our magic comes from the Maker and there's something in Zyrran's words that speaks to an ancient part of me. Like he's awakening wisdom buried deep within my cells.

At the same time, my body rejects the idea of giving my power away to something bigger, however benevolent that thing might be.

"*It is not giving your power away, Natric one. It is letting the Maker channel his power through you supplementing your own, instead of relying only on yourself,*" Zyrran chimes in.

I let those words sink in as Zyrran dips beneath the cloud cover again. It's snowing below, and it coats my bare arms for a fraction of a second before melting to liquid on my unnaturally heated skin.

"*Ador is there,*" he advises, angling his head to the approaching silhouette of a mountain. The lights of the village are illuminated.

"*Drop me at the bottom and I'll dissolve up to the castle,*" I instruct as my heart rate starts to climb.

"*Are you sure you want to do this alone?*" Zyrran asks, an edge of nervousness in his tone.

I take a deep breath and then rub the side of his neck.

"*It's my actions that caused this. It's my mess to clean up.*"

"*May the Maker guide your actions and clear all obstacles in your path,*" Zyrran prays.

A pleasant chill rushes into the crown of my head, as if the Maker himself were responding to the prayer.

"*He is,*" Zyrran answers my thoughts. "*When you let the Maker in as we dragons have done for centuries, you are never forgotten, nor alone.*"

He drifts even lower, galloping on the snow as he touches down. I tighten my grip on his neck as the jerking motion threatens to buck me off. He skids to a stop two hundred feet later, and I let out a shaky breath.

"*I will remain here until you are ready to return,*" Zyrran says.

"*That's not necessary,*" I contradict, feeling guilty about the dragons that have died. "*I won't be entering the castle until after midnight, anyway, and your presence might alert the Guard.*"

"*What if you need help? What if you are in danger?*" he says, an edge of anxiety in his tone.

"*This is my mess,*" I say firmly.

He stares at me for a long moment with his giant orange eyes.

"*I will go hunting in the southern region and return in three hours when you enter the castle. Do not be a hero, Natric one. Call me if you need help,*" he urges.

I give him a weak smile. "*Fine.*"

"*Good luck.*" He backs up about fifty feet, then runs and launches himself skyward.

I take a few deep breaths as cold rushes back into my veins the further he gets away from me. I need proper clothes immediately.

I glance at the entrance to The Cave just ahead, and feel a sharp pang of grief.

How much did my father know?

Did he know I was Diana from the very beginning? Did my mother as well?

Was that why she sold her soul?

To save herself?

Did she name me Fiana as some sick joke, and then bailed on the whole mission the closer I got to actually having my magic come in?

Fresh anger at Koa's hit heats my freezing skin, and the burst of energy has me wanting to push my magic somewhere.

Like into the winds to whip up a tornado.

One that will travel to Koa's home in Parley and kill him in the destruction.

I fantasize about that for a few seconds before a *crack* draws my attention back to The Cave.

I immediately dissolve away myself before I can see who it is. Not a good time to get caught.

I make it a quarter of the way up the mountain in my first go, and pause to take a few deep breaths before dissolving the next quarter.

It occurs to me that attacking tonight after a long day of training isn't my best strategy, but Evander healed me in the training ring, so I don't really feel the fatigue.

And adrenaline is a powerful stimulant.

My next leg leads me to just above the village, making the distance to Evander's cliffside home quite manageable. I dissolve directly into his living room. I'm a little surprised his wards don't keep me out.

But I'm also not.

Haldric isn't around and nor do I 'hear' his voice. He must be out hunting.

I get some food into my system and venture into Evander's closet. All of my armor is back in Lucia, but I think I can figure out how to fit his to my size with magic.

I slip it on and it swallows me whole, and brings hot tears to my eyes as his scent envelopes me. I wipe those quickly away and intend the clothes to shrink.

I gasp as everything tightens to a compressive state, then urge the fabric to give just a touch.

A quick look in the mirror shows I've done a fair job.

I have the golden dagger hidden in The Ether, but I need extra weapons, so I venture down to the vault. I check the clock in the kitchen on my way down. It's almost half past ten.

I strap a few daggers to my thighs, cursing the fact that I haven't learned how to hide them in The Ether yet.

Perhaps if I succeed and survive tonight, Evander will forgive me enough to teach me.

My heart aches at that.

And then it fucking *aches*.

I gasp for breath, recognizing that the wounds are not my own. But they're close.

I sink to my knees, sending my thoughts out.

"I'm on my way," I urge, forcing Curic magic into my own system. It takes the edge off enough to where I can get back to my feet and follow the thread of searing pain out of Evander's front door.

It lures me toward the stables and my heart cleaves open at the thought of Sterling being harmed.

"I'm almost there," I send out, hoping like hell I make it soon enough.

The pain takes me behind the stables instead of inside it, and I gasp as I take in the horrific sight.

It's a massacre.

I run to the first animal—a fallen doe with a giant wound across her chest. Her eyes look glassy—I quickly check her pulse.

Damn. Dead.

The next one—another deer—is actively choking on blood or bile or something. I race to his side and put my hands lightly on his fur coat.

I take a deep breath, moving my hands up and down his throat. I feel it then—a collapsed trachea. I imagine the cartilage separating and opening and weaving itself back into the proper places.

The deer gasps for breath, then takes three shallow breaths. He meets my eyes and I hear him.

"*Thank you.*"

I quickly focus on his next wound: a deep gash across his abdomen. A pool of blood stains the snow red beneath him.

I shut my eyes again, imagining the blood flowing in the opposite direction—back into his body. Back into his veins, his arteries, his heart. Then I envision the flesh and sinew knitting back together, his organs becoming whole again, and his skin and coat smoothing back into perfection.

I open my eyes. The deer stands up and grunts another word in the mystical language.

"*Run.*"

And then he bolts away. I stare after him, in awe of the life I just saved.

Someone starts clapping their hands behind me in a slow, mocking beat. I jump to my feet and turn in one quick motion, pulling a dagger out of one of the sheaths at my thighs. My heart leaps into my throat when I see who it is.

"You know I wondered what would happen if I laid this little trap for you."

The male prowls closer, unsheathing his own weapon from some hidden holster behind his back. A short sword.

"I've kept a trace on Evander's home waiting for you to show yourself. And after he so rudely made me *bleed*..."

He strikes once in a blindingly fast motion. I feel the pain before I understand fully what has happened. I double over for the second time tonight—only this wound isn't a phantom one.

"I thought it was time I returned the favor," Nasgardo finishes with a sneer.

I unconsciously drop the dagger, my hands feeling something warm and wet spilling out of my stomach.

"Evander will kill you," I croak. My voice sounds too weak. I fall to my knees in the bloodied snow, fisting my hand around the dagger again and pulling out another one for good measure.

"Evander's the one who will get killed once I tell the King he's been hiding a fully grown female *with magic* from His Majesty," Nasgardo counters.

Evander will murder him, I promise myself, even though a part of me fears he hates me now.

Even if I don't survive this, he will *get justice.*

It might be a lie, but I try not to think of that.

If it's delusion that gets me through this, I'll drink it down like medicine.

He takes two quick steps toward me then pushes me down so I'm on my back, facing up toward him. I clutch my daggers tighter by my hips.

"How did you hide it all these years?" he demands, kneeling over me and pinning my shoulders to the ground.

My breathing becomes shallower as more blood leaks out of my open wound. I try to tend to my healing without closing my eyes, but it's harder to do with them open.

"Answer me!" Nasgardo demands.

"Hermetic magic. My father did it." It feels like something is happening to my stomach, but I force myself not to look so Nasgardo won't see.

"Why?" he presses. I see the vein in his neck bulge for me. Like an invitation. I know exactly where I want to cut once I get my moment.

I force my expression to look blank. "I don't know. He got arrested eight years ago and never told me. And now he's dead. I've been living in fear of getting found out ever since."

If only I had some Havoc in my bloodline, I think bitterly to myself.

Evander could stop Nasgardo's heartbeat with a single electrical pulse.

"You're lying. Tell the truth—why do you still have your magic?" he growls.

I spit in his face. He jerks his head back to wipe it away.

Before he has time to move his hand, I slice both daggers clean across his throat. He makes a gurgling sound then clutches his wounds, his eyes sliding closed. I wriggle out from under him and scramble to my feet, daggers still in hand.

I freeze.

Should I stab him again?

Should I let him bleed out and then burn the body?

I start shaking as I try to decide what to do. I don't have matches or any kind of fire starter with me, and Ador is always *wet* with the never-ending snow.

And I sent the damn fire breather to hunt for dinner. FUCK!

I groan. *Make a decision!*

He collapses to the ground at my feet. I exhale in relief.

At least he's dead now.

I look down at my armor, grateful that it's black. Because I'm absolutely soaked in blood.

I need to get something to start a fire with, and fast. I take a step away and start to take another when an iron fist grips my ankle and I tumble face first to the ground.

He healed himself before he died!

His heavy body climbs over the top of mine, pinning me down against the frigid snow. I sink a few inches under his weight, my face burning with the intense cold contact on my bare skin.

I scream as he yanks my head back by my hair, arching me up and exposing my jugular to him. He bites my neck hard enough to draw blood. I scream louder.

He won't make this quick like I tried to do.

He wants me to suffer.

"Shut up!" He growls in my ear, tightening his grip on my hair. I start sobbing as his knees press my thighs down harder, bruising them as the cold seeps through the armor and underneath my skin.

He forces the daggers out of my hands now, breaking the fingers in each hand in the process. I sob harder, wanting it to be over. Wanting it all to stop.

At least he'll find my body, I realize, thinking again of Evander. *Just behind the stables.*

An ungodly roar erupts above me and Nasgardo launches off me.

I flip over and back up several feet in the snow as I watch Evander ripping limbs off my attacker. Nasgardo wails as he loses both arms, then both legs in a matter of seconds. The wailing abruptly stops as Evander tears off his head with his bare hands. I cover my mouth as vomit threatens in my throat.

Evander pours liquor all over Nasgardo's disembodied limbs, collecting them into a pile at his feet. He lights a match and drops it, steps back and lights another, tossing it onto Nasgardo's lifeless flesh.

The pile erupts into flames. Evander watches him burn for several endless moments while I'm still catching my breath, tears streaming down my face.

The fire ignites something in me as I watch—and suddenly *I* am the fire burning my attacker's flesh. I climb to my feet, ignoring the pains in my body, seeing nothing but the deplorable male who tormented me for months.

How *dare* he harm these animals!

How *dare* he try to rape me!

How *dare* he try to kill me!

The fire changes colors before my eyes, going from orange to an eerie white as my anger grows. A hotter flame, I instinctively know. One that will burn his flesh and bone so much faster.

I want him to be nothing but ash.

The pile shrinks as the flames burn brighter, fueled entirely by my anger.

Out of the corner of my eye, I see Evander watching me, but I stay focused on punishing the evil one before me.

Is it seconds?

Is it minutes?

It feels too short to be more than that.

But eventually the pile isn't a pile of limbs, or flesh, or blood.

It's nothing. It's gone.

He is gone.

I let out a breath.

The flames fizzle out.

Seconds later, Evander hugs me tight to his chest. I burst into tears as he dissolves us somewhere far away.

Meddia—I realize as a warm breeze chases the cold away.

He runs us inside his cottage at immortal speed, then runs a hot shower as he strips off my bloody armor.

He guides me into the shower as sobs rattle my bones.

The warmth feels good.

And the water feels safe.

He washes my body gently, his healing magic finding all the spots that are bruised and broken.

When he guides me out and dries me off, the tears seem to dry up, too.

He pulls me into bed and cradles me in his arms.

And I sleep.

And sleep.

And sleep.

44

I must be dead. I have to be dead. Because the warm, muscled arms wrapping around me in sleep can't be real. This soft bed can't be real. The pitter patter of rain on the roof—it *isn't* real.

Those muscled arms squeeze me tighter and a nose sniffs my hair, as those arms pull me closer up against a warm male body.

Oh yeah, I'm definitely dead.

I'm not in Meddia.

I'm not in bed with Evander.

"I love you," he whispers against my hair. "I love you," he repeats, so quiet that maybe he doesn't know if I'm awake.

I pinch his arm. "Ow!" he grumbles, though he pulls me tighter against his chest. "What was that for?"

I hitch a breath. "So this—this is real then?" My heart comes in a gallop.

He kisses my hair. "It's real. And you're supposed to pinch your *own* arm, you silly killer."

I flinch. "Is that what I am? A killer?" I twist to face him. His eyes are gentle.

"Nasgardo was already dead by my hands—you just pushed him to the Final Death."

I shudder. Last night it had felt *right* to punish.

This morning—I've developed a conscience.

"He tried to kill you, Fiana."

As if that makes it better. As if that makes it different.

"It does," he says, answering my thoughts. *"You are not a monster. You did what you had to do to survive,"* his voice echoes in my head.

In my head. I gasp. He reassures me with his eyes.

"I can hear you. I *could* hear you—that's how I knew where you were. I'm sorry I didn't get there sooner. I searched the forests tracking your scent, but then all of a sudden it was just *gone.*

"Ryder, Warren, my uncle and I all spread out in different directions hunting for you, trying to pick it back up. Eventually Ryder caught it up on the peak of Mount Zora. We thought maybe the dragons had harmed you and were trying to find them, thinking we'd find you. That's when I heard you, clear as day, as if you were speaking to me in the same room. *'Evander will murder him'* you said, and I nearly destroyed the whole mountain."

Worry lines crease his brow.

"You heard that?" I breathe.

"Yes. Exactly like you're hearing me now," he replies silently.

"But that—that was minutes *before you found me,"* I want to say. *"What took you so long?"*

"I didn't know where you were yet—and to be honest, I thought I was hallucinating. But then you did it again, a short time later. 'If only I had some Havoc in my bloodline' and 'Should I stab him again? Should I let him bleed out and then burn the body?' And at that point I *knew* I wasn't hallucinating because—" he pauses, chuckling. "Because I never have thoughts like that."

He continues silently, and the purr of his voice in my mind sends shivers down my spine.

"I realized you must be in Ador if someone was attacking you. I quickly dissolved to the palace, thinking maybe you were there or nearby

when I heard you again—'He wants me to suffer'—and the wind blew your scent from the south, so I figured you were at my home. I dissolved there when you said 'At least he'll find my body. Just behind the stables' so I dissolved the rest of the way, found you, and pulled him off you."

Tears well in my eyes as I remember him biting my neck. My hand drifts there, only to find smooth, unbroken skin. I exhale with relief.

"He set a trap. And he realized I had magic—he watched me heal a deer. He's been doing demonic rituals with them—siphoning dark magic from the Shadow Realms," I explain. "I caught him months ago. That's why he assaulted me. Why he's had it out for me for so long."

Evander's brow crumples. "He's gone now."

"He said he put a trace on your home," I add. "Do you think anyone else knows?"

Evander studies my face. "No. No one else saw us in the forest. But I'm not going to take any chances. I will not risk losing you again." He kisses me then, his lips urgent and passionate. "I need you," he murmurs. "I love you."

I pull away, studying his two toned eyes. "You don't care that I'm Diana? You don't care about what I've done?"

He shakes his head, looking as if that's the least of his concerns.

"It is," he answers my thoughts, leaning in to kiss me again. *"Being with you is my only concern. What you did in a past life changes nothing. You are not at fault."*

I pull back again. "How can you say that? I'm the reason that every single one of your students has to suffer. I'm the reason why Rosie has been stuck there for over two hundred years. I'm the reason why you've had to risk your life for centuries."

He pulls me into another kiss. *"I don't care."*

I scoot back further from him. "How can you not care, Evander? I'm the reason why Ryder and Rosie no longer have a mother! And why Vilero tricked you into killing your own friends!"

He shakes his head. "No you're *not*, Fiana. Stop taking credit for all of Vilero's sins. And mine."

I jump out of bed. "But I deserve credit! *I'm* the one who tricked him! I'm the one who fucked over every female for the past *six hundred years*! How can you even look at me the same way?"

He joins me on his feet. "Because I love you. Because you're not responsible."

"But I *am* responsible!" I argue, backing away as he keeps following my movements. "I remember doing it myself!" My back slams into the wall but he keeps advancing toward me. He traps me with a hand on either side of my shoulders.

His closeness turns my stomach as shame rushes through me.

"Fiana, listen to me. If anything, you are responsible for *one thing* only. And that's tricking Vilero with Delilah. But you are *not* responsible for everything he's done since," Evander says sharply.

"But he wouldn't have done those things if *I* hadn't tricked him." Hot tears rim my eyes.

"Fiana, the reaction does not fit the crime!" Evander insists. "If anything, he should have punished you, not the whole realm. Put yourself in his shoes, if he did the same thing to you, would you have stolen magic from half of the realm in retaliation?"

"I don't know!" I mutter, wiping the tears at the corners of my eyes. He tilts my chin up so I'm forced to look at him.

"You wouldn't, Fiana," he says softly. "People are rejected and manipulated by lovers all the time. That doesn't mean they then go on to condemn the entire opposite sex to subservience. Vilero alone is responsible for his actions."

"But the crone said I'm his divine feminine!" I counter. "Why would I do something like that to my divine masculine if I'm not an evil, manipulative bitch?"

His eyes shadow. "Don't you ever speak to yourself that way again. And you are not his divine feminine."

"The crone said I am," I counter.

"The crone is wrong," he says with certainty.

"No she's not."

"*Yes she is*," he urges mind to mind.

"*Get out of my head*," I complain.

"*No*."

"*Why not*?"

"*Because you're* mine." He kisses me urgently again. I push him off me and run for the door.

"Stop running away from me!" he complains, frustration evident in his tone.

"No!" I yank open the door and race to the front. He's there before I can make it outside. I dissolve away, but his hand grabs me before I fully disappear. We land outside on one of the neighboring hills as rain pours down on us both.

"Why won't you let me walk away?" I shout over the thunder, trying to wrench my arm out of his iron grip.

"Because you're not fucking getting it!" he yells back.

I stop struggling and glare at him. "*What?* What am I not *getting*, Evander?"

"You're not the King's divine feminine." He stares at me with fervent eyes, willing me to understand. "You're *mine*."

"That's impossible," I argue. "I thought you were too, but I was wrong," I say in a lower voice.

"No you weren't." And then silently he adds, "*Why else would we have* one mind?"

I repeat his words again in my head, struggling to make sense of them.

My heart rate picks up. "What? But you didn't—"

"Immortalize you? No, I didn't," he assures. "*Yet I can hear you, and you can hear me*."

"How can that be?" I demand.

"Seems you accepted the bond without needing the magic." He pulls me into his arms as the rain slows to a gentle drizzle. "But if you're willing, I want to do it right. I want to share my magic with you. It will make you stronger and faster. It will make you a better fighter and—"

"So you want me to be stronger to kill the King?" I say, my heart aching as the whole truth finally comes spilling out.

"Of course," he says, his brow furrowing. "And it will give you immortality, too."

"So if I fail the first time, you can revive me and start me up to try again?" I snap.

"If that's what it takes," he says nodding.

I feel sick. Because he only wants me forever if it means his own misery ends.

"For fuck's sake, Fiana! Wake up and realize that I'm *madly* in love with you! Do I want you to kill the King? Of course. Do I want you to have more chances at life if you need them? Absolutely. But not because it will end my misery, or my family's, or our students'."

"Then why? So I'll be devoted to you and do everything you say?" I accuse.

"I'm in love with you! How many times do I have to say it? The only *misery* I can't live with is the thought of ever losing you!"

His eyes blaze with anger. He drops his arms and backs away from me.

"Fuck the King, fuck my family, fuck the school if that's what it takes for you to realize that the *only* thing that matters to me is whether you live or die, whether you breathe or drown, whether you're mine to keep or mine to mourn for the rest of my damned existence!"

I stare at him.

"You love me?" Hope builds in my chest for the first time since meeting the crone. "After everything I've done?"

"Yes!" he says, and a humorless laugh escapes his throat. "Notwithstanding this *maddening* conversation, *yes*, I do. I love you."

"You felt the pull?" I say, softening my defenses. I take a cautious step toward him.

"You've ruled my life from the moment I met you," he repeats, his eyes hinting at a smile.

"That long?" I ask, my breath hitching. "You've known you're my divine masculine for that long?"

"Yes," he says softly, his blue eyes open. And loving.

And warm.

I wrap my arms around his neck. "And you still feel it, even though I was Diana?"

He wraps his arms around my waist. "It never goes away. And I don't ever want it to."

"Because you love me," I exhale slowly, and I know the words are true. "I feel it, too."

"I know." His eyes soften.

I hug him closer. "I love you, too."

"I know," he murmurs, pressing his lips against mine. "*Now are we done fighting yet?*"

I kiss him back. "*Yes, we're done fighting.*"

"*Can I make you mine?*" he asks, as his arms tighten around my waist. There's an edge of vulnerability in his tone.

"Yes," I sigh against his lips.

He pulls back slightly to look into my eyes. "In every way that I want?"

"Yes," I repeat as nerves and excitement send flutters through my chest.

He pulls away from me suddenly and drops to his knee.

"What are you doing?" I complain, trying to pull him back up.

"I'm asking you to marry me," he says, pulling out a small black box.

"What?" My heart skips.

"I bought this ring the morning after I healed the doe," he murmurs, opening the box. "After I saw your eyes."

My breath catches in my throat.

Nestled in the box, in a crevice between silk pillows lays a white gold ring with a giant, oval-shaped mint garnet gem. It's easily as big as my thumb nail, in the exact same shade as my eyes. The center stone is flanked by two slightly smaller epaulette cut diamonds that are as clear as glass, sparkling in the dim moonlight.

I stare at the ring, speechless.

"Will you marry me?" he says again, a hint of impatience in his tone.

I burst out laughing then kneel with him, wrapping my arms around his neck.

We just got done fighting and are soaking wet from the rain, our knees sinking into mud, but I kiss him like it's the most romantic proposal of anyone's life.

"Yes," I gasp before kissing him again. "My answer is yes."

He smiles against my lips then pulls back just to slide the ring up my fourth finger on my left hand.

"I'm going to marry the fuck out of you," he murmurs before pulling me back into a kiss.

"No, *I'm* going to marry the fuck out of *you*," I argue, giggling at the stupid joke.

He kisses me again. "It's not stupid," he laughs. "Not if it makes you laugh." Another kiss.

"True," I murmur, grinning against his lips. I start ripping his wet shirt off. I rub my hands down his damp muscles, then lower, over the front of his pants. He groans, grinding against my hand, running his fingers underneath the hem of my shirt.

"If you keep touching me like that, I'm going to fuck you right here on this hill," he warns.

"Mmm," I moan as his lips move to my neck. I rub him a little harder.

"And if I fuck you on this muddy hill," he growls, licking the raindrops dusting the top of my collarbone. "You're going to get absolutely filthy. And I don't want to hear a single complaint."

"The only thing I have to complain about right now," I say, gripping his package possessively. "Is the fact that you're taking so long to get us both naked."

He lifts his head from my chest, a wicked glint in his eyes.

"I fucking love you."

He tackles me like an animal, ripping my shirt off before I hit the ground. I gasp for breath as he dissolves away my pants, and then his own. The ground is soft and sticky under my naked back, but I don't care.

Because it doesn't matter what I did, or who I was meant for in the past.

Evander is *mine*.

"*Yes, but let's make it official,*" he says mind to mind. "*Unless—*"

I slap his ass. "*I said yes, Evander.*"

"Just making sure," he whispers before entering me in a deep, delicious thrust. He slides his arm underneath my head, cradling me as he drives into me slow and deep.

Our eyes are locked as the rain continues to fall, dripping from his hair and his beard as our bodies connect.

"I've wanted this for centuries," he confesses as his magic seeps under my skin. Not Hedonic magic—this feels different. *Much* different. My eyes slide shut as I give myself over to the feel of it.

"Centuries?" I gasp as he slides his other arm underneath me. He picks me up mid thrust and backs me up against the trunk of a tree before starting up in a sensual rhythm again.

More magic seeps into me, and I shudder with delight.

I'm buzzing. Phantom sparks heat every cell in my body, the energy building to a peak that has nothing to do with sex, even as Evander keeps driving into me, gripping my hips with exquisite force.

"I've wanted *you* for centuries. Even before you came back to these realms."

His words jog something in my recent memory, and my eyes flutter open.

"I've wanted you for centuries, too," I say and the words feel true as I say them. "When I was shown Diana's death, my final thoughts were coming back for you."

"Don't you lie to me," he says, but his eyes are approving and warm. I moan as he drives deeper, swirling his hips in a way that makes my core ache for more.

And more.

"Never," I gasp, my eyes sliding shut again. "You feel so *good*."

"Mm," he grunts, sucking on my bottom lip, shrinking the space between us again and again.

More magic sinks into my cells and soon I'm trembling with pure pleasure and *power*.

And it feels even more intense than my own.

The smells hit me first—rain and peaches and the exquisite palo santo aroma of him. And then other smells—flowers on other hillsides, birds and animals and even the scent of Evander's cottage become discernible even at a distance.

I open my eyes and gasp at the clarity in my vision—as I see Evander's eyes for the first *real* time. The cobalt is even more vibrant than it seemed only seconds ago, and the icy blue parts appear to slightly glow.

His power ripples off him like a vibrant blue mist, and my breath snags as I follow the waves that now ripple around *my* skin, as if his magic is fusing us together.

Not as if. That's *exactly* what is happening.

My breathing is coming in heavy pants now as Evander continues to connect us—mind, body, and energy—as my core tightens and coils and aches for release.

A new kind of release, I realize as the *feel* of our fusion somehow intensifies, beyond what my mortal mind could have ever comprehended.

He slows his rhythm down now and I yank him tighter to me in protest. Hard. I need it *hard*.

He grunts in shock but obliges.

"*You're strong*," he admits as he leans in to kiss me. Our tongues dance together before I take his in my mouth and suck.

The fucking *taste* of him. Like musk and chocolate and rich red wine—I moan as it hits my heightened senses.

He starts pounding into me on a punishing rhythm, and perhaps as a mortal, it would hurt.

Not now. I notice too that the tree ceases to feel quite so *rough*. It was slightly scratchy at first, but now...

Now my *skin* is somehow stronger.

And the roughness just feels like *sin*.

Underripe peaches tumble off the tree as our bodies collide again and again. My heart thumps harder as new sensations ripple underneath my skin.

Magic, Evander purrs mind to mind. *What's mine is now yours.*

A jolt of energy shoots up my spine, and my eyes slide shut for half a beat. Evander roars as a clap of thunder echoes all around us and the tree shakes as we both reach our peak.

Power ripples around us like a cloud as we gasp for breath, our bodies still joined.

We stare at each other for a long moment. One of his hands leaves my hip, trailing lightly up the length of my waist before grazing over the curve of my breast.

He slides his fingertips up the length of my neck before cupping my face.

I start trembling.

So does he.

"*The power,*" he explains. "*Our bodies are adjusting to it.*"

"*It's intense,*" I think as we work to catch our breath, our eyes locked.

"*We need to use some up—it'll help.*" His tone sounds a little strained.

He keeps his eyes on mine as the rain slows down and then soon after, stops. Moonlight filters through the clouds and the damp leaves of the peach tree, illuminating our naked skin.

I'm still shaking, but he seems more grounded now.

"*I liked the rain,*" I complain, narrowing my eyes at him.

"*So summon it,*" he challenges, eyes taunting me.

I shoot him a glare, but then close my eyes. I take my mind back a few minutes ago when we were still in the thick of it—

"*Fuck*," Evander groans in my mind as I feel him harden again inside of me. "*I love seeing it through your eyes.*"

I open mine. "*You can see it?*"

"*Yes, as I told you.*"

"*Show me your version,*" I demand.

He smirks. "*As you wish.*"

I stop breathing as the images hit me. As I see and *feel* the relentless hunger he has for *me*.

How even one touch of my hand against him sends jolts of pleasure through his whole body.

How seeing me naked and wet in the mud made him so hard, he couldn't help it but take me right there on the ground.

I push that intense craving and need energetically toward what I want. Droplets begin to fall from the sky again, and I open my eyes just a sliver to see him watching me.

"That's it," he says out loud and the sound of his voice sends another shiver through me. His now-hard-again cock grinds into me and a moan escapes my lips.

"*Try Havoc magic now,*" he encourages.

"*First show me the rest,*" I demand, my eyes now open wide in a challenge.

He chuckles, and the movement causes him to slide deeper into me. I groan, my eyes sliding shut as he takes me back to—

My old bedroom, in his cliffside home.

45

EVANDER

"Fiana!" I call, sitting on the edge of her bed. Fuck, that looks like a bad one. Her eyes fly open finally and instantly find mine.

Terror. Nothing but terror in those gorgeous green eyes.

She catches her breath, her gaze still focusing on me. Looking at my body, with an odd look in her eyes.

"Are you alright?" I ask cautiously. Is she still afraid of me? I hope not.

Haven't I done enough to show her that I care for her?

That she has nothing to be afraid of with me?

That I live and breathe by her heartbeats?

She finally looks back up at me.

"I'm okay. I'm okay," she says, though her voice is shaky.

I raise a brow. "Do you want to talk about it?" Maybe she *is* still afraid, despite everything. Maybe she wants me to leave.

"It's the flood." She pauses, her eyes beginning to water. "I can't breathe," she chokes.

My own breathing stops and I gently place my fingertips on her inner arm, channeling healing magic into her to soothe her panic attack before it has a chance to take off. She takes a breath that goes all the way into her belly. And another. And another.

I exhale on her fourth one, squeezing her arm in relief. She jolts, blood pooling in her cheeks.

Fuck. Of course.

"Oh sorry..." I pull my hand away.

She thinks you're disgusting. She hates you. Stop deluding yourself into thinking she could ever want you back.

"No touching..." I give her an apologetic smile.

I didn't mean to break her rules. I *want* to follow them. And make her feel safe.

She sits up in bed suddenly. "Tell me something. Tell me a story or something."

Oh... guess I'm not in trouble. "What kind of story?"

Why is her heart beating so fast?

"I don't know. Something happy, I guess," she explains.

A happy story...

Well you—being here, in one of my beds.

That's a happy fucking story.

But I can't tell her that one.

"Before I joined the Guard," I clear my throat, taking my mind back hundreds of years, "I used to love playing tricks on the grey ones. One time, I set a spell on one that made his pants invisible anytime he talked to a female, except he wouldn't be able to see that they had gone, only the female could. I followed him to the tavern—your tavern—and watched from the windows how many times he struck out."

I start laughing at the memory.

"He starts out strong... all confident as he struts over toward the first one. But the second he opens his mouth to speak, boom—his pants are gone. The female takes one look at him and gives him the biggest scowl I've ever seen. A few threw their drinks at him..."

She giggles with me. *That damn laugh*—it does things to me. I fight to ignore the turn on that starts heating and hardening my cock.

"How old were you?" she asks. Oblivious to the effect she has on me.

I shrug. "Only about ten or so. My parents made me join the Guard a few weeks later."

"Why did they make you?" she wonders.

I shrug again. "They knew I was valuable. The Guard—not my parents. My parents were just glad to be rid of me." My gaze slides back to hers and I keep my face blank and neutral. "I guess they thought I was a trouble maker..."

Her lips twitch at the corners. "Can't imagine why..." She winks.
She fucking winked.

At *me*.

My heart rate spikes.

"Is this...? Can it be?" I tease, widening my eyes with mock incredulity.

She furrows her brow. "What?"

She doesn't get the joke yet. *Well... I'm dragging this one out then.*

I shake my head slowly. Dramatically. "I can't believe it..." Laughter is already threatening to ruin my façade, but I force myself to hold it in.

"What?" she demands, still completely clueless.

"In my nearly four hundred years... I never thought..." I can't hold it in much longer...

Her voice grows louder. "WHAT?"

That sends me over the edge. I burst out laughing.

She tackles me, pushing me back onto the bed, which only makes me laugh harder, tears pooling in the corners of my eyes.

Because how many times have I wished she'd touch me like this?

Sure, this is driven by anger, but I'll take it like the gift it is and enjoy every last second of it.

She climbs on top of me now, pinning me down between her thighs and starts slapping my bare chest.

So angry. So passionate.

She probably wants me to stop laughing but I can't. Not when I'm only getting what I want because she's furious with me. The absurdity of this can only be seen as hilarious, or just plain sad.

And I'm an optimist.

I shake violently with laughter, relishing the feel of her heated thighs pressed up tight against my bare hips.

"TELL ME!" she shouts. *So damn angry.* I don't think she realizes how attractive she is to me right now.

Sensing my good fortune is coming to an end, I let out a few more weak chuckles, wiping the tears from my eyes and then finally look up at her.

"I just can't believe you actually flirted with me just now." Another chuckle ripples through me.

Her jaw drops. "I *wasn't* flirting with you!"

Bull. Fucking. Shit. "Please." I say, my tone indicating I don't believe her for a second.

"I wasn't!" she insists.

"Mmhmm... please." *She knew exactly what she was doing.*

She glares at me, and then a calculating look slides across her face briefly before melting into a coy smile.

I jolt as her hand runs lightly over my chest, her teasing touch setting fire to my skin as blood rushes toward my cock.

Her hand drifts lower as—*shit shit shit shit shit.*

Everything in me aches to rip off that flimsy night gown and fuck her against the wall. I can do it in one quick motion—I can have her trembling in my arms and moaning my name before she even realizes what is happening.

Hedonic magic pulses in my cells, aching to be used to show her just how much pleasure she's giving me with her teasing little fingertips.

Hedonic magic always aches to give pleasure, especially when I'm receiving it. I have to close down the urge, or I'll be breaking one of her rules in the next split second.

She leans in toward me, her eyes boring into mine, nothing but pure confidence and challenge in her gaze. She presses her hands on either side of me and hovers her tight little body a few inches above mine. And then closer.

Does she...?

My breathing picks up as her lips dip toward mine and my heart sprints as I realize I might actually get to taste those sweet, full lips of hers.

Her scent, which already lives permanently in my head, fully envelopes me now in a heady cloud.

Like fresh cut flowers and honey and rain.

I need her lips on mine, but I force myself not to steal a kiss even though she's so damn close to me. I can be patient for one more second.

But she doesn't kiss me. She presses her body against mine, her hot breath tickling my ear as my cock reacts wildly to the feel of her weight on top of me.

Her teeth nibble my earlobe and I can't take it anymore, I pull her hips against mine—relishing the feel of her heated center pressing tight against my cock.

There's too much clothing between us. I need to fix that—

"No touching," she purrs in my ear before my magic has a chance to strip her bare.

FUCK!

I groan, pulling her greedily against me, savoring the feel of what she almost let happen for another moment before I force myself to let go.

She sits up, grinning wickedly. I'm still rock hard beneath her.

"What was the point of that?" I accuse.

Do you want me or not?

"That's me flirting. I just thought you should know the difference..." she shrugs.

Naughty little devil...

Well two can play at that game.

I smirk at her, sneaking another gyration against her ass. "I'd like to see that more often."

She shakes her head. "Nope. Now you know, so there's no point in me showing you again." She bites her lip and slides to the side of me, my cock practically pitching a tent in my sweatpants.

"Now get out," she orders with a taunting little grin.

Nope. No fucking way.

I sit up, but don't leave. Because *no way* am I letting that slide. No way am I going to let her work me up like that and *not* return the favor...

I crawl toward her, my mind made up, as Hedonic magic buzzes in my cells. She backs up against the headboard, her eyes widening like a doe's. I fight a grin as I press my hands against the headboard on either side of her.

There's so many things I want to say to her as I capture her eyes with mine. As she's caught like a little mouse in the space between my arms.

You're the most important thing in the world to me.

You're fated to be mine, though you don't know it yet.

I'm madly, deeply, stupidly in love with you.

I'm your protector.

Your goddamn servant.

Your divine masculine.

The one who would sooner die than let anything happen to you.

I could say all of that and other romantic, devotional things. But she just asked for trouble, so that's what she's going to get.

"I don't have to touch you," I whisper, leaning in close, bringing my lips near her silky neck. Close enough to where she can feel the teasing heat of my breath. "To drive you crazy..."

Hedonic magic slides into her body now, teasing and tantalizing all of her nerve endings.

She doesn't move a muscle as I blow gently against the skin at her neck... then her collarbone... then just above her full breasts.

I fight the urge to get closer—to taste the skin I'm breathing on —as goosebumps erupt wherever my breath moves. Her nipples peek through her gown, and it takes everything I have not to take one into my mouth.

I resist—just barely—and channel all of that craving into the Hedonic magic that I channel into her now. Showing her exactly how much pleasure my touch can bring her... if one day she will finally allow it.

I back my knees up and walk my hands down to the bed on either side of her barely covered hips, carefully avoiding touching her legs.

I dip my head lower, worshiping her breasts with breath as my magic drives her into a frenzy. Her abdomen twitches as I work my way lower.

She hasn't asked me to stop.

I glance up briefly and see nothing but ecstasy on her beautiful face... so I keep working my way toward exactly what I want.

My lips almost caress the inner edge of her bare knee, and I fight the potent need I have to lick up the length of her leg.

Instead, I let my breath tease up the inner edge of her thigh. My mouth starts to water as she opens her legs up wider.

Like a goddamn invitation.

I can smell her arousal, and the delicate rosewater scent acts like a magnet for my tongue. I inch closer to what I want, her back arching as I take my breath higher, and I nearly come as I realize she's naked underneath that gown.

I need a fucking taste.

And I'm getting one, I decide.

But only when she begs me for it.

I blow, and blow... careful not to touch her legs, nor any other part of her, as I concentrate all of my magic on the thousands of nerves of her clit.

Forcing her all the way to the very edge.

A little moan escapes her throat, and I know I've won.

She tangles her fingers in my hair and pulls me against her swollen flesh with urgent, raw need.

She's fucking feral.

I give her one pressurized lick. Not enough to soothe her ache, and I fight the clawing impulse to keep going. To give her everything she wants, and to take everything I want.

Because fuck—her goddamn taste.

I pull myself away even as my mouth waters, before the hungry part of me can fully take over. Before I won't be able to stop my desperate, thirsty tongue.

I back up, hiding the craving I feel. Teasing her with my eyes.

"No touching," I chide. I grin, even though a part of me is in agony that I stopped. "Goodnight..."

I dissolve back to my room before the weaker part of me can kick in. I chuckle despite myself.

She wants me. Hedonic magic or not... that shit only works if she's already attracted to me.

She wants me bad.

And I could have had her tonight. She wouldn't have stopped me.

But I'm not ready for her yet. She isn't ready for me yet.

She needs time to heal. I need to let her heal.

And I will.

She's worth waiting for.

Best damn thing I've ever tasted.

I savor what's left of her on my tongue. My cock is still aching for release, so I let myself picture what would have happened if I was still there. If she let me keep going.

If I got another taste.

I hear a delicious scream of pleasure from her room—too faint for mortal ears but—*fuck*.

She's touching herself too.

I come instantly at that because—*fuck*.

She wants me.

Finally.

FIANA

I'm panting. He's panting.

Rain is coming down in sheets and even the tree can't keep us sheltered anymore. Our connection is still intact, Evander hard as steel inside of me. Our eyes meet.

We don't need words.

We don't even need *thought*.

We just needed to *move*.

He moves, gripping my hips tight as he pumps into me on a desperate rhythm. Little whimpers escape me with each punishing thrust. It's hard and deep and exactly what I *need*.

I grip the muscles of his back tightly, digging my fingernails into his heated flesh. He groans at the pressure, driving into me harder as something warm teases against my clit.

Hedonic magic. He's fucking me with magic.

It takes me over the edge.

I scream, my eyes holding his gaze as I release around him, against the tree, his hair dripping rain onto my swollen lips. I kiss him and he groans, deep in his throat, gripping the tree with one hand as he finds his own release.

He catches his breath for a few seconds, and the next few kisses he gives me are pure decadence.

I shiver, and before I can ask we're back in the cottage, pressed against the shower wall. He turns the hot water on.

"*That was...*" I start, finding myself unable to complete the thought.

"*I know,*" he replies, gently sliding himself out of me. "*Sensational.*"

He starts rubbing soap gently over my body.

"*I don't think I can live without that. Without this,*" I add, running a hand down his abdomen.

"*Good thing we don't have to. It's you and me. Forever.*"

"I love you," I say aloud, my voice hoarse.

He kisses my lips. "And I love you."

I feel the weight of my new ring on my left hand and a sudden fit of giggles comes over me.

"I can't believe you fucked your future wife in the mud," I tease, biting a lip.

His eyes darken, and an image of me bent over his knee floods into my mind. My jaw drops.

"I said no complaints, Fiana," he growls, as his imaginary hand smacks my ass until it's rosy in the mental picture. Pleasure jolts through me at the sight of his raw punishment.

I take a ragged breath.

He smirks, sensing my turn on. "And don't pretend you're innocent. Unless you *really* want to get spanked."

I widen my eyes like a doe's. "I don't know what you're talking about."

His eyes light up with amusement. "I'll deliver your punishment later. For now—we should get cleaned up and get you back to Lucia."

I sigh dramatically, letting disappointment color my tone. "Fine."

He flicks my nipple playfully.

"Don't worry, love. We have centuries for me to give you all the spankings you want."

Once we're clean, we get dressed and Evander dissolves us to the clearing in Lucia right as the sun begins to rise. As we hike our way to the school, Evander breaks out into a run.

"*Try and keep up,*" he goads as he flashes through the trees faster than a prized stallion.

I bolt after him, marveling at how quickly my now immortal legs can move. When I skid to a stop next to Evander at the thickest part of the trees where the hidden entrance is, I'm not even out of breath.

"Not bad," he says as he asks the entrance to open.

Dagger and Dragon quickly greet us, and on their approach I hear the Natric language filter through to me.

"*Friend.*"

"Did you say something?" Evander asks, startled.

I glance at him as I pet Dagger. "No, that was Dagger."

"Damn," he laughs. "I keep forgetting I got your magic, too."

A flash of burgundy draws my eyes up to Mount Zora.

"There's something else I forgot to tell you," I say as the giant takes flight.

"What's that?" Evander is absentmindedly scratching Dragon behind the ear.

"When you found my scent on the mountain, it was because I was taken there," I explain. "By dragons."

Evander's hand freezes on the dog. He stares at me. "What are you saying?"

I meet his eyes briefly then turn my eyes skyward again. "I'm saying there's more at stake than we originally thought when it comes to killing the King."

Evander follows my gaze then lets out a stream of expletives. Zyrran, Gorvorian, and Lozana are all pummeling toward us at a frightening speed.

"Dragons?" he shouts, yanking the dogs back by their collars as their muscles coil for attack.

"Not just dragons," I say letting out a shallow breath. "Havordians."

"As in the elders." Evander shakes his head, his eyes wide as the three dragons land with a resounding *thunk* before us. "We're fucked."

46

"*R*elax, Havoc born. We mean you no harm,*" Zyrran instructs mind to mind.

Evander jolts. "*Did you hear that?*" he asks me silently.

"*Of course she heard that. You only hear me because of her,*" Zyrran snaps.

"It's okay," I say aloud to Evander, before turning back to the Havordians. "*I'm sorry I failed you last night. But I still have every intention of killing the King.*"

"*Great, let's take you back now,*" Lozana says brusquely, whipping her dark blue tail against a stray chicken. It goes flying through the air before crashing into the stables and collapsing in a feathery heap on the ground.

I wince, throwing my healing magic out toward the poor bird. He snaps back up to his feet, shooting me a grateful look. A small part of me realizes with shock that I just cured him at a distance.

Evander is a Curic too, I remember.

Guess we really are stronger together than apart.

"We need to make a plan," Evander says, his body tensed for a fight. "Give us some time."

"*As we told the Natric one, we do not have any time to spare,*" Gorvorian argues.

Zyrran levels a disapproving look at his green companion. "*We can spare them a few weeks,*" he says, turning his orange gaze back on me. "*Nothing more.*"

"*I understand,*" I say quickly.

"I don't," Evander growls.

"Let me explain it in private," I snap at him. I meet Zyrran's eyes. "*You have my word that we will move forward within two weeks.*"

"Fiana!" Evander complains, but the dragon elders are already preparing to take flight.

"*Call my name if you need me. Otherwise we will be tuning you out,*" Zyrran instructs as the three of them launch toward the sky.

"What have you done?" Evander asks, his face twisted in anguish. He's pacing in the teacher's lounge. The Dissenters and the Deschamps family are all present, looking confused and tense. Credo, Warren, Paul, and Blaze are all here together for the first time since our initial meeting.

"They're dying. The one who's blood you infused your dog Dragon with? He's the first of several that are dying from a blight," I explain calmly. Anita's eyes fix squarely on mine.

"Because of the dark magic," she breathes. I nod.

"What?" Ryder looks to her, furrowing his brow.

"It's been happening for years," she explains.

"And you're only sharing this now?" Evander snaps.

Anita smooths a lock of her silvery blonde hair, her golden eyes defensive. "It's not like I can detect the source. We have enough to contend with as it is. If I shared everything I've detected throughout the years, you all would go catatonic."

Eloise looks at her with concern. "Do you mean that?"

Credo places a giant hand on Eloise's. "It's the curse of being a

Relic. You come to know way too much. More than you *want* to know, and definitely more than you can act on."

Eloise looks at his hand on top of hers then meets his golden gaze briefly before looking quickly away.

"But Nasgardo is dead," Evander says, confused. "Shouldn't that end the dark magic problem?"

I shake my head. "He's not the source of the blight. The King has also used dark magic to mutate his cells, so he can hold more power than is natural."

Evander's eyes darken. "How long have you known this?"

"Just since the Havordians picked me up a few days ago."

"So Nasgardo wasn't doing it for himself—he was doing it for Vilero?" Evander asks.

My thoughts flicker back to the night I stole the dagger.

I shake my head again. "No—I think he was using it for something else. I think he wanted to undermine the King somehow. For a female."

"What?" Warren and Evander say simultaneously.

I look to Warren. "I saw him arguing with a female about it the night we stole the dagger."

"What female?" Draven asks, pouring himself a glass of jad.

"Don't know," I admit. "She might have been the same one at the royal table at the King's ball. They both had dark hair and their voices are similar."

Everyone looks at Evander, who shrugs. "I don't meet his females. He's very possessive of them. Doesn't like when they have a wandering eye."

"And let's face it, cousin, females are simply incapable of resisting you," Ryder says in a deadpan voice.

Rosie snickers.

I glare at him. "She wanted 'more freedoms'. Whatever that means."

"How would the demons provide her with more freedom?" Eloise wonders.

"It seemed like she wanted more *control* actually," I clarify. "I wonder if they weren't trying to work with demons behind the King's back so that they could get secret leverage over him."

"Well that is now neutralized, at least for the time being," Evander says, moving to the chair next to me and taking a seat. "But if the King has been using dark magic…"

"That means the Shadow Realms will know it when he's dead," Warren finishes.

"And may declare war," Paul adds, his eyes bleak.

"Are you serious?" Rosie blurts out, all trace of her buoyant mood now gone.

Warren's eyes flicker in her direction. "We knew that could be a possibility regardless. Death of a monarch is the prime time to strike."

"And the coronation of a new Queen after a six century patriarchy certainly may lead to us looking weak," Eloise adds, pouring herself a shot of jad. It's the first time I've seen her drink hard liquor.

"A new Queen?" I say, as I watch her bring the glass to her lips.

Eloise meets my gaze then turns her eyes on Evander before taking a huge pull.

Evander sighs. "Yes, my love. After killing Vilero, you will become the new Queen."

I narrow my eyes at him and say mind to mind. *"You could have told me that sooner."*

He fights a smile. *"Trust me, you have nothing to worry about."*

"I've never ruled a kingdom. I've never so much as held a management position," I argue.

"I'll be by your side the whole time," he assures. *"And you can more than hold your own, especially considering all the times you've done the exact opposite of what I've said and still made it out okay."*

"What is happening?" Mila says, an edge of frustration in her tone. "They look like they—"

Warren snorts. "I fucking knew it."

"Knew what?" Draven asks.

Rosie scoffs. "Guess she's a Havoc now, too."

"What is going on?" Eloise questions.

"Auntie, it seems your son has immortalized Willowbark," Ryder says indelicately.

Both Evander and I shoot him a glare.

"What? It's not like you're trying to hide it," he shrugs.

"Oh," Eloise says, true shock on her face. Her eyes laser in on the ring on my left hand. "*Oh!* And you're engaged?"

"What?" Collette snaps.

I shoot her a dirty look, and she promptly schools her features into a neutral expression.

"Yes," Evander says, beaming. "Fiana has agreed to marry me."

The entire Deschamps family launches to their feet and starts pulling Evander and me into warm hugs.

"So that means you'll be the King," Blaze announces, his tone full of meaning. "That's rather convenient."

Evander glares at him. "Just what are you implying?"

Blaze shrinks an inch, and then shrugs. "Nothing."

"Evander isn't marrying me for a stupid title," I snap.

"*The title I could take or leave. It's that booty I absolutely cannot live without,*" Evander teases silently.

I snort.

Meanwhile, Collette is looking me up and down.

As if I'm delusional.

It sets me off.

"Not that we have to explain ourselves," I say, seeing red as I speak. "But we have a *true* divine union. Meaning we *both* have chosen to be devoted to one another."

"Good for you," Collette says sarcastically, her eyes condescending.

"Tread lightly, Collette. My future bride hasn't yet learned how to control all of her magic," Evander says delicately. "And if you keep up that tone, I won't fault her if she feels inclined to break your arm."

"Try her leg," I growl, feeling the Havoc magic buzzing in my cells. It's so much more potent and *present* than Natric magic. Like a barely leashed dog springing for attack.

"Easy, Willowbark," Warren says, and I feel a shield go up between me and Collette.

"Perhaps you should leave the room," Draven suggests, looking at Collette.

"Me? *She's* the one who can't control herself!" Collette complains.

"With all due respect, you baited her, so it seems you too are struggling with self-control," Draven counters, his tone firm but diplomatic.

"Come, Collette. We can take a walk in the gardens," Hawley suggests swiftly.

"A lovely idea," Eloise agrees with a small smile, though her cobalt-and-ice eyes are punishing.

The room is silent for a beat while Collette assesses her options.

"Go," Warren urges when she doesn't move after a few seconds.

She scoffs at him but then stalks out, hooking her arm through Hawley's elbow as she leaves. Blaze follows quickly behind.

I take a breath.

"If you need to get some out, you can break my arm," Evander encourages.

"Oh yes! *Do* break Evander's arm!" Rosie cheers, clapping her hands. Mila snickers.

I shake my head. "No. I don't need to."

Both Ryder and Warren snort.

"What?" I snap at them.

"You're still glowing red, my love. It might help to let off some steam," Evander soothes, holding out his arm. "Besides, you need the practice," he adds with a crooked grin.

I huff a breath. "Fine."

The room is filled with an earsplitting *crack*.

Evander winces, but gives me an approving grin all the same.

"Holy Maker! You really did it!" Mila laughs.

"Now try to heal him," Draven encourages, but I'm already there with a *snap*.

Evander grunts and then shakes out his arm. "Thanks."

"You healed him without touching him," Anita notices.

"I know! It's gotten stronger," I say, and then I glance at Warren and Ryder with a sheepish grin. "And I do feel a lot better, I'll admit."

"And it appears Evander's magic is not concealed by the Hermetic magic," Draven adds, and Anita nods solemnly.

"We expected that might be the case," she sighs.

The room grows silent for a moment.

Credo clears his throat. "Perhaps now we should discuss what our plan is for the King?"

Ryder glances meaningfully at Evander, who nods.

"Based on the information Reina gave to us before Fiana left, we have good reason to believe the King will be quite keen to meet with her," Ryder explains.

"She was the only female he danced with at the ball," Mila interjects. "I found that quite strange. He didn't even dance with his dates." Everyone stares at Mila, and she blushes. "I was only paying such close attention in case we learned something of interest," she hastily adds.

"Forgive me, I don't mean to be rude. But what is it that is so fascinating about this female?" Paul says, true curiosity ringing in his tone.

Evander sends him a death glare, but Warren clears his throat and says, "What Paul means is, it is a bit odd for one female to capture the attention of the King's bastard son, two High Guards, and His Majesty all in less than a year."

"Sounds like royal pussy energy to me," Rosie murmurs low in my ear. I fight a fit of giggles.

"Calimo only cared about me because he sensed my protection magic and wanted to use me. And because Evander showed interest in me," I clarify. "Nasgardo has had it out for me since he met me and I refused to kiss him, and it got worse when he caught me saving an animal from his demonic ritual."

"And as far as the King," Evander says, glancing at me and then at Ryder. "We believe Fiana looks a lot like the original twin in the prophecy. She must be a direct ancestor."

"*Do not say anything more with the Dissenters here*," Evander adds mind to mind.

Credo drops his glass of jad, and it shatters on the wooden floor. "Ah, sorry everyone," he says quickly. He drops his eyes and cleans up the mess with magic.

Warren registers what Credo isn't saying. "You recognized her, too."

Credo clears his throat, the sound rattling the various glasses on the table in front of him.

"I did say that before, yes," he acknowledges.

"So why is it such a shock now?" Eloise asks, glancing between Credo and Evander.

"It's not a shock," Ryder says quickly. "The point is, the King will recognize Fiana as someone he desperately wants."

"And we can use that to our advantage," Evander adds, nodding once at his cousin.

"Guess we're setting you up on a date with the King after all," Rosie quips, nudging me with her elbow.

"It's not a terrible idea," Warren says. "From what I remember, the King keeps no Guards as he entertains females."

"Fiana's not going to *entertain* him," Eloise complains, shooting me a protective look. "And besides, don't we want to try and take Koa down as well? That wouldn't work if it was a date."

"Perhaps we should focus on one enemy at a time given the shortened timeline," Ryder suggests.

"In that case I think we should revisit Fiana's plan to implicate one of our own so the King calls a public trial," Evander says.

"I do not favor the idea of one of us going to jail," Draven counters.

"I've already volunteered," Warren says, pouring himself a shot from the communal jad. "Besides, would you prefer your future niece seducing the King?"

"Warren," Evander growls.

"I'm not seducing the King," I say quickly before he starts glowing red. I turn to Warren. "And you're not volunteering to go to The Cave. We need to find a different reason to lure him out of the castle, so we can use our reinforcements."

"Meaning what?" Warren snaps.

"The Havordians have already told me that they'd like to help," I explain. "And considering they can burn entire armies in one breath, I think we should take them up on their generous offer."

"How the hell are we going to control dragons on a battlefield?" Warren argues.

Evander snorts. "We can hear them. They're bonded to Fiana."

"Bonded?" Paul asks, and there's a hint of recognition in his eyes.

"What do you know of it?" Evander prompts.

Paul shrugs. "My family is from the lands south of Mount Zora —right on the border of Abyssia near where they lay their eggs. They haven't bonded with elves since—"

"Since Anadyna walked these realms," I finish for him. "They told me."

Anita gasps. "Anadyna? She was half celestial half elven."

"Like your magic," Credo adds, looking me right in the eye.

"So if Fiana is bonded like Anadyna was bonded, we can expect them to be extremely loyal to her," Paul concludes.

Warren looks annoyed. "Fine. Then how do we lure the King out into our little dragon trap?"

The room is silent for a long moment. My heart jolts as the idea comes to me, and Evander whistles as he hears it in my mind.

"That could work," he says, rubbing my hand.

"What could?" Rosie says impatiently.

I glance at Evander, who nods in encouragement. "We send anonymous word to the King that the golden dagger was stolen, and the one in his possession is a forgery."

"Then we tell him Koa has it, and where Koa will be," Evander adds. "Meanwhile, Fiana sends word to Koa that she's stolen the real one back."

"And we have them all meet us in the forest at the bottom of Parley," I say.

"Where we ambush them," Warren finishes, and the first real smile I've ever seen him make stretches wide across his face.

It's half pleased, half vengeful, and yet somehow still suits his harsh features. Rosie practically bats her eyelashes at him, but he doesn't notice.

"I like it, Willowbark," he says finally, leaning back in his chair.

"When should we set up the meet?" Ryder asks, and it appears the whole room has agreed to the plan.

Paul clears his throat. "The Dissenters are planning another weapons swap in ten days. Koa is at his worst on those days. He's always jumpy and distracted. It'd be best if we set the meeting then."

Draven turns to me. "Can you be ready in ten days? That's shorter than the Havordian's timeline."

I let out a sigh. "I have to be. I'm not putting this off longer with everything that's at stake."

"We will be ready to join you," Zyrran adds, and Evander and I exchange an amused look.

"I thought you weren't listening," I chide.

Zyrran huffs. *"Sometimes I slip. We all have our faults."*

"The Havordians are in agreement," Evander relays for the

group. He meets my eyes for a beat before turning back to face the group. "In ten days, we murder the King."

The next ten days are torture, and not even because of the impending mission.

Evander goes away to work every weekday. At first he considered taking leave, but given Nasgardo's sudden 'disappearance', he wants to remain connected to the investigation.

There are currently no leads.

It's a small but welcome relief.

A slightly larger relief is testing out the limits of my new stronger body.

Ryder grows particularly fond of being my sparring partner, and even encourages me to 'go all out' with my new Havoc abilities.

Rosie enjoys going full speed and full strength with me as well, but prohibits any use of magic.

"At least for now! In two weeks once we start prepping for war, we'll *really* go head to head," she gushes.

Only Rosie could make training for war sound like an utter delight.

"Why two weeks?" I ask, lifting a brow.

She looks at me like I've forgotten to wear pants, or something equally appalling.

"We need a few days to celebrate the win, *obviously*. You think liquor billionaires are all work and no play?"

It's a valid point. "Who runs the company anyway?" I ask.

"Draven oversees, but there are all kinds of managers and supervisors who keep things running," she says, shrugging.

Quite efficiently, it seems, since Draven rarely leaves the grounds for meetings.

Mila trains with us each day, sparring with some of the teachers and former students during the adult sessions. I attempt sparring with her once, but accidentally break her rib on my first hit.

I heal her instantly, and she forgives me once the pain recedes, but Rosie puts her foot down and relegates me to only training with immortals.

A handful of the adults are, and are more than willing to help me practice.

Hawley and Collette spar with each other and ignore Rosie's instructions to switch partners. I can tell it grates on her nerves, but she doesn't push it. As the days tick by, I feel her approach is appropriate.

Better to keep them happy so they don't decide to screw up our plan.

Credo remains in Ador, but we hear updates from him as the other males filter in and out.

Paul and Blaze come by once more each, and I swear I see Paul sneaking out of Rosie's bedroom early one morning.

When I see her in the training ring that day, she holds her hands up like a measuring stick. There's practically a foot between them.

"You're exaggerating," I snort.

"No, Fiana. Not even a little bit," she says, her face blissfully relaxed.

Like after a nice good lay.

I giggle.

"And his *tongue*," she groans.

"I'm so glad you had a good night," I tease. *And so glad you're not still pining for a male who can't return your affections*, I add silently. Evander hears it—even in Ador—and sends me a curious thought.

"Rosie's sex life, not important," I hastily tell him.

"Gross. Got it. Bye," he sends back.

"Night... morning... it all runs together," Rosie says with a sigh.

I notice she's a touch less aggressive in the ring that day, but refrain from making those observations out loud.

As far as the male who can't return her affections...

Warren comes back three times a week—more often than in previous weeks. He insists on taking over my training whenever he's here.

I quickly learn why.

If I thought Rosie was taking it easy on me before, Warren was practically massaging my damn ego.

The male is so strong that even Ryder yields in an all-out fight against him. Despite my stronger body and stores of Havoc magic, he fights like a male with nothing to lose. His blows are fast and ferocious, and he somehow snakes his way out of holds that should render him utterly useless.

Evander comes home during one of our sessions and I can feel his anguish in our mental connection as he watches.

He doesn't stop it, though.

Because deep down he knows I need to fight as viciously as Warren.

The difference is, I have way too much to lose.

Two days before the meeting day, Paul sends word to Koa. He doesn't return to Lucia, but Warren does and lets us know that all is going according to plan.

Evander plans to get the message to the King an hour before the meeting.

"The less time he has to investigate the validity of it, the more likely we are to get him and Koa in the same place at once," he explains.

Tonight is our last night.

Evander cuts off my training at four, much to Rosie and Warren's chagrin. He says it's so I can rest.

But when he takes me to our bedroom after dinner, we do anything but.

The love we make has a desperate edge in every kiss and touch.

It feels too much like goodbye for me, and despite my best efforts, tears keep falling down my cheeks.

It doesn't seem to bother him. He kisses them away.

A part of me knows we need to rest, but I can't stop holding him. My lips are raw, but kissing him is all I want to do until the sun comes up.

He hears as much in our mind connection and gives me everything I want.

At some point we must have both drifted off, because I wake up on top of him, naked, still wrapped up in his arms.

47

Shortly after sunrise, we meet the others in the entrance hall. Evander, Ryder, Rosie, Mila, Hawley, Collette, and I are all dressed in winter fighting leathers.

Ryder and Evander spend the first fifteen minutes positioning various weapons in The Ether for each of us and showing us where all of the access points are. Beyond that, we all also have a visible set of daggers and short swords for easy access.

"More weapons than the High Guard has," Evander assures as he finishes hiding the last of mine. The golden dagger is still in the same back pocket in The Ether, but I check it three times just to be sure.

Mila then passes out magic blocking amulets for Rosie, Ryder, Evander, and myself, and we hide those in the space around our necks.

Credo, Warren, Paul, and Blaze are already up in Parley. They're going with Koa to the meeting point, still posing as his loyal fighters.

Zyrran checked in with me around sunrise letting me know that the Havordians are already in Parley. They're hiding in some of the more thickly forested areas at the base of the mountain, awaiting instructions.

Draven, Eloise and Anita are all staying back to care for the students, but they meet the rest of us downstairs, hugging and kissing their loved ones and wishing us all good luck.

Eloise tries to give us pastries to eat for breakfast, but none of us are hungry. Draven offers shots of jad instead, and all three of the Deschamps take him up on that.

When there's no more reason to delay, the seven of us head outside. Dagger quickly lopes over toward me and I give him a kiss on the top of his head.

He whimpers, sensing this isn't a normal morning stroll. My heart cracks as I tell him to *stay*—as Evander, the other five and I leave through the school's only entrance, Ryder pausing to seal it once we are all in the forest.

Mila, Hawley, and Collette ride on each of the Deschamps' backs as we sprint to the clearing in quick succession. We pause in the clearing, meeting each other's eyes in stoic solidarity, and then Ryder and Evander dissolve us all in two small groups.

We make it to the forests of Parley.

The cold cuts deeper than it ever has before, and the wind is like a jagged knife slashing across my cheeks.

Evander is still holding my hand, and the warmth of his hold soothes some of the anxiety. I squeeze it. The wind slows, and then it stills altogether.

I turn to look at him at the same moment he turns to look at me, knowing his magic stilled the wind.

"You can do this. You are strong." Every word rings with sincerity.

"Not as strong as you," I sigh.

"You're the one who's got thirteen dragons bonded to you," he reminds me.

"And we are happy to fry any elf who gets in your way," Zyrran adds.

"And even the ones who don't," Lozana quips.

Except knowing her, it isn't a joke.

I give Evander a weak smile and take a huge breath.

The rest of the group is watching us.

"How long until the King gets the message?" Ryder asks.

Evander checks his watch. "Shouldn't be long now."

"Not long at all, you'll find," a sneering male voice announces. "Considering the King is here now."

"Blaze," Mila says, true betrayal in her tone. "What the hell have you done?"

"Yes, Blaze, what the *hell* have you done?" Hawley seethes, crossing the short distance to where Blaze stands at the edge of the trees. "You're thirty minutes early!"

"Damnit, Hawley you might have *tried* to hide our involvement," Collette complains, sidling up alongside her and drawing her visible weapons.

Ryder, Rosie, and Evander already have theirs out. Mila quickly moves behind us, drawing hers at the same time I draw mine.

"Guess we should have expected this," Ryder says in a low voice while keeping his eyes on the traitors, though it's loud enough for my immortal ears to hear.

Which means Rosie and Evander heard it too.

"I told you I wanted to kick them out," Rosie hisses so quietly I have to strain to hear the words.

"I don't see the King yet—do you?" Evander murmurs.

"A hundred paces back in the trees. Taking his sweet time," Ryder murmurs.

"How long until Paul and the others show up?" Rosie says.

"Thirty minutes," Evander and Ryder say at the same time.

"I really don't like being this outnumbered," she admits.

"The dragons are ready to help whenever we need them," I remind her.

"Are we certain they didn't account for that when they chose to betray us?" Ryder asks.

"*We are loyal only to you, Natric one. And somewhat reluctantly, to your bonded male,*" Zyrran interjects.

"*Keep an eye out for traps,*" Evander sends down the dragon bond.

"*We can sense them before they have even been laid,*" Gorvorian says haughtily.

"The dragons are fine," I relay to the others in low whisper.

"Keep them in position until we need them," Ryder instructs.

The King is within view now, about forty paces away, led by a large entourage of High Guards at the front and Main Guards on the sides and along the back.

"He's brought the whole Syran Guard," Evander says in an anxious tone.

"How many?" Rosie asks.

"Five hundred," he murmurs. My stomach drops.

"Four hundred and ninety nine without you, cousin," Ryder quips.

"*Mere kindling for our fire,*" Lozana sneers, and I can feel her practically chomping at the bit down the bond.

"Should we draw the dragons out sooner, then?" Rosie says, and I sense a little anxiety in the way she tightens her grip on her swords.

"No. Some of them struggle with self-control," I say quickly. "I need my one chance before they take over and destroy it."

"Then we fight like hell as long as we can," Ryder says. "To give you the best chance."

"*I love you,*" Evander says privately down our bond.

I say it back.

Mila, to her credit, doesn't say a word. She's bouncing on the balls of her feet, weapons out and hazel eyes steely.

"Let's let him lead the conversation," Evander suggests. "Perhaps he will waste enough time for Paul and the others to get here."

"Are we convinced they haven't been compromised too?" Ryder wonders.

"Yes," Rosie snaps, a little louder than the rest of our voices.

"What I meant by that was—are we convinced Koa isn't neutralizing them as we speak?" Ryder clarifies.

There's a long pause.

"I could ask Warren magically, but it might backfire," Evander suggests. "Might tip Koa off if he isn't shielded properly."

"We keep them in the dark then," Ryder decides.

The King's Guard is directly behind Blaze, Hawley, and Collette now. They edge out of the way as the Guard filters through, stopping about thirty feet away from us in the small clearing.

"Evander," King Vilero says. "Well this is a surprise." His Guard parts slightly to give him an unobstructed view of the rest of us. He's dressed in dark blue velvet robes with his copper hair slicked back underneath his golden crown. He's clearly not dressed for battle or bloodshed.

"Not as big as a surprise as me," I say loudly, stepping through the small space between Evander and Ryder.

"*Fiana*—" Evander complains mind to mind, but he quickly shuts up as the King takes in my face.

His jaw drops a full inch. A moment passes, with the Guard's eyes flitting between my face and the King's, confusion taking shape on each of their many faces.

"So you finally made it out," he says with a sigh. "Did Evander find you at last? Is that why you chose to betray me after over three hundred and fifty years?" He directs the last part toward Evander.

There's a long silence.

"*Do you know what he's talking about?*" I ask Evander.

"*Not in the slightest.*"

"Well?" Vilero prompts. "How did you get out of the tower?"

I sneak a quick glance back at Evander. "Tower?"

Vilero snorts. "Playing dumb is an interesting tactic, Delilah, but I'm not sure it's a very effective one."

"*Delilah?*" Evander and I think at the same time.

I clear my throat. "I'm not Delilah. I didn't realize she was still alive."

The King rolls his eyes. "Nice try. You've proven your point. You can escape and gain the favor of the High Guard closest to me and swindle him into betraying me. Very impressive, Delilah. Now let's get you back to your tower."

"I don't live in a tower. I never have. And I'm not Delilah," I retort. "Though if she's still alive, I would very much like to see her."

The King stares at me for a long moment. His sneer abruptly transforms into a look of confused horror.

"Ludo," he says in a lower voice. "Go to the north wing tower of the castle on the top floor and ask the handmaiden to get the female that's kept there. Bring them both here immediately, and if no female is there send immediate word."

"Yes, Your Majesty," Ludo says before dissolving away with a *crack.*

"The female in the mask," I say to Evander. *"The female with Nasgardo. You don't think?"*

"That she was Delilah? As in the original second twin from six hundred years ago?" Evander finishes. *"I have no clue,"* he admits.

"While we wait to confirm your claims, perhaps you can explain to me why you've summoned me here," the King says, his tone edged with boredom.

"You never got the message?" Evander asks, positioning himself next to me.

Vilero crinkles his nose. "What message?"

"Do not bring up the dagger," Evander urges silently.

"What did your informants tell you?" I hedge.

"That my most prized High Guard warrior has been stabbing me repeatedly in the back for hundreds of years. And that if I came here, I'd find proof," he says, kicking off the patch of snow caked on the bottoms of his robes.

"Alas, you've caught me," Evander says.

"Indeed. Though I'm still unsure of the exact crime," the King admits.

"Certainly all will become much clearer once Ludo returns," Evander retorts. "Fiana and I are both anxious to see the proof that Delilah lives."

The King's eyes lock with mine. "Fiana Willowbark." He takes several paces toward me, urging his Guard to stay behind as he passes the front line. He's about fifteen feet away now. "*You* are Fiana Willowbark?" he asks pointedly.

"I am," I say with a cold smile. "But perhaps you know me by a different name."

"What is *with* this chick?" Collette complains from the sidelines.

The King whirls on her, strangling her from a distance with magic as she clutches her throat and falls to her knees. Hawley and Blaze watch in horror as she gasps and gargles.

And eventually dies.

Her body falls forward with a *thud* against the snow, sinking into the powder.

I flinch, tearing my eyes away from her and return my gaze to the King's.

He advances another five feet. "If you are lying to me, Delilah, I swear to the Maker you'll regret this," he growls.

There's a *crack* as Ludo returns with two females. One is clearly the handmaiden.

The other has my face. And she's glaring daggers at me.

"She isn't lying," a male's voice says from the lefthand edge of the forest. I snap my head in that direction and feel my pulse quicken as I spot Koa.

He's alone. "Nor is she Delilah. I think Diana is the name you're looking for."

"Look who joined the fucking party," Ryder growls under his breath.

Paul, Warren, and Credo are still nowhere to be found.

"Koa," the King says. "Your presence is not appreciated at this time."

"Oh but I think it will be," Koa counters, advancing toward the King. He stops about fifteen paces away.

The King sighs. "Fine. Enlighten me."

Koa slowly advances closer. "You see, they've brought you here to kill you, my King."

"Can't one of you kill him?" Rosie hisses.

"He's shielded," Evander complains.

"Oh?" Vilero snorts. He turns his gaze on Evander and me. "Best of luck with that."

"With all due respect Your Highness, though they seem outnumbered, they're better equipped than you know," Koa counters.

"Koa, if you know what's good for you, you'll shut the fuck up now," Evander snaps.

"Easy, Evander. We're just talking here, son," Vilero chastises. He gestures to Koa. "Explain."

"I would be most delighted to share all of their secrets, Your Highness. Including one involving a secret school full of children that Evander was supposed to dispose of," Koa taunts.

"No," Rosie breathes, pain evident in her tone.

"I'm listening," Vilero says, his eyes darting between Evander and Koa.

"But first I require a prize of my own," Koa says, turning to look toward the crowd of Guards behind the King. His gaze zeros in on Ludo.

And Delilah.

"Fuck you," she hisses, spitting in his direction.

The King glances back at his mistress. "She's a peach, isn't she? Unfortunately she's bound by our divine union and will never care for another."

"Doesn't matter to me," Koa says with certainty. "In time she will grow to love the one she was always supposed to end up with."

Delilah scowls. "Anthony is who I'm *supposed to* end up with."

Vilero whips his magic across her throat and she gags as her voice leaves her. "Silence, pet. Let the grownups talk here." He turns back to Koa. "She's not for sale."

Koa shrugs. "Then I cannot offer my services."

"Then you are dismissed," the King says with a shrug.

Koa balks. He clearly didn't expect this.

The King returns his gaze to me.

"Diana, my darling, this is a surprise," he says in a softer tone. "I tried to revive you, but you wouldn't wake." Ancient sadness seeps through the cracks in his royal posturing.

"I've been given a second chance at life, it seems. But Koa's right —I am here to kill you," I admit.

"But darling, surely we can discuss whatever it is that has led to you this point like adults," Vilero says gently.

Over the King's shoulder, I witness Delilah's face turning beet red.

I decide to play the game he's invited me to join.

"You've made a mess of our world, Anthony. Some things cannot be fixed with words alone," I say, mimicking his tone.

The King advances closer, only five feet away now. His Guard inches closer behind him, narrowing the distance between our tiny army and his massive one.

"Diana, please. Come to the castle. We can sort it all out with champagne and oysters," he says with grin that turns my stomach. "I have missed your company more than I can explain."

"My company is not yours to have, Anthony." I brush my fingers against the hidden golden dagger. "It never was."

"She has the dagger, Your Majesty!" Koa interjects.

The King's eyes harden and he backs away several steps. He glares at Koa.

"You're only telling me this now?" he barks as his Guard coalesces around him, weapons drawn and eyes fixed on us.

"As I said, Your Majesty, I can be of great service to you now. All you have to do is give me Delilah," he urges, glancing back at my twin.

The King snarls then straightens up taller. "Fine. You may have her when we're done here. Ludo, please return her to her tower." The three of them (including the handmaiden) disappear with a *crack*.

"That's not what I meant!" Koa complains. "Release her to me now and then I will help you!"

The King snorts. "Too late. You can have her when we're done here."

Koa ponders that for a moment, his face turning redder by the second.

"Fine!"

My vision abruptly darkens as the King fades from view.

"*I can't see—can you see?!*" I think frantically.

Evander's reply is strained. "*No.*"

Dread fills my stomach as I brace for an attack. I strain my ears to try and hear their approach and anticipate where it might come from.

"*What's going on?*" Zyrran urges.

"*We're completely blinded.*"

"They can't see a thing. Do what you will," Koa's voice filters through the blackness.

Evander's thoughts are seething with rage.

"*Koa blinded us,*" I relay to Zyrran and the other dragons.

"*Allow me to intervene,*" Zyrran says, and I hear a hint of a thrill in his tone. "*Sixty seconds.*"

"Why don't they look more frightened?" Vilero says skeptically. "I thought you said you blinded them."

Koa speaks through his teeth. "I did. Now kill them or arrest them or do whatever the hell you want to do with them so you can bring me to Delilah."

"And yet they aren't afraid. What haven't you told me, Koa?" Vilero presses. His voice sounds closer now, and I can feel his gaze burning a hole in my cheeks.

"*Kill him now*," I order Zyrran.

"*Thirty seconds.*" Zyrran sounds hungry.

"If you want Diana to stay alive, make your move now," Koa growls. He feels closer now too, like he's advancing on the King. I feel a shield come up.

Evander's? I'm not sure.

"*He will not harm you*," Zyrran promises. I sense the beat of his wings on the wind. He's close.

"Make your move, Vilero," Koa sounds panicked now.

"Holy SHIT!" Someone says—a Guard, maybe.

"GET DOWN!" Another Guard.

"*Do not take one step forward*," Zyrran urges at the same time I feel a hot stream of air in front of me.

The magic wears off a fraction of a second before Koa's bones disintegrate into ash. The horrifying image of his skeleton ablaze burns behind my eyes as I frantically take in our surroundings.

The Guards are all on the ground, some of them shielding themselves and others. The King looks wide-eyed and stunned, staring up at Zyrran who is now circling above. Our small group already has their weapons out and is charging at the Guards. I gasp as I realize Warren, Paul, and Credo have emerged from somewhere behind us while we were blind.

Warren grabs a Guard by the shoulder and skewers him with his sword. Blood spills out in a gushing stream, staining the snow a sickening red.

Ryder rushes at two Guards at once. A jab through the heart and another across the throat, blood splattering his face as the carotid gets sliced.

He dodges as a third Guard charges with two swords, putting up a shield of glass as he charges again. The Guard rebounds off it so hard he knocks himself out.

The Guards are charging back now.

The first one to get to me jabs his blade toward my middle. I block it with my sword as my heart practically beats out of my chest.

His blade strikes again, high this time, and I duck, sending a hit of magic to break his sword arm. I scurry to the side as he yelps in pain, dropping his weapon in the spot where my head just was. I whip my blade across his throat and his head goes flying off.

Bile churns in my throat as I watch his beheaded form collapse in a crumpled heap.

I catch my breath for a split second before the next one charges with two blades. Magic locks up my muscles, immobilizing me, but I slip my shield up quick. His blades hit glass, lancing him backwards onto his bottom. Sweat drips down my back as I fight to keep the shield up while Curic magic slowly heals the paralysis in my body.

"Amulets don't work!" I shout to the others.

The Guard is already on his feet and rushing me again, but my shield holds strong. He expects it, and only stumbles back a step. Feeling finally returns to my limbs and before he rushes again and I drop my shield in time to shove my blade deep into his middle.

Bloody entrails drip from the sword when I yank it out.

My stomach turns. *Disgusting.*

"We can eradicate the rest if you would like," Zyrran offers, and I can sense the rest of the Havordians circling just above the cloud cover.

I scan our surroundings, my chest tight as I catch my breath. There's already so many bodies.

Ryder is working his way through the crowd to my left, dodging jabs and lancing open critical arteries in a blindingly fast flash. Warren is just as lethal, ripping off limbs and sending more heads flying in bloody arcs. Paul and Rosie are surging the center of the King's battalion.

Swords clink.

Blood sprays.

Bodies collapse.

And yet there's still hundreds of Guards lined up to accept the same fate.

"*I don't want unnecessary deaths,*" I admit to Zyrran.

"*Then do your job so we may end this,*" he advises.

Right. Kill the King.

I scan the field.

Evander and Vilero are circling each other, somehow protected from of the field of battle surrounding them while still being right in the middle of it.

"Three hundred and fifty five years of service—and mutiny is how you repay me?" Vilero growls. He's unarmed and yet seems completely unruffled. Evander sends a wave of rippling black smoke toward the King to suffocate him, but he shields in time, sending it out to either side. Evander redirects it and kills two Guards encroaching on Mila.

"I think you missed the fact that I was serving you, Anthony. Not the other way around," Evander says, his lip curling into a sneer. Vilero's face reddens at the use of his first name, and sends a jolt of electricity at Evander, who dodges it in a flash.

"How long have you been planning this?" Vilero asks, disgruntled that his hits haven't landed yet.

Evander smirks. "Since you made me kill my best friends." Evander hurls a wave of bone breaking magic toward the King that he redirects behind himself, shattering the femurs of ten of his own Guards. They collapse to the ground in agony, some healing themselves within seconds and then springing back up.

"Why Diana?" the King asks. "How does she fit in with you?"

"*Get behind him while I distract him,*" Evander orders. "*Zyrran, watch her back,*" he adds down the dragon bond.

"She can do what I can't," he says.

Vilero whips his head around, sensing my approach. I feel a shield go up at the same moment he sends a hit of paralysis in my direction. It rebounds off the shield back toward Vilero, but he redirects it behind him and it hits Evander full force.

"No!" I shout, throwing my own shield up to guard him as Vilero advances the short distance to Evander's frozen form.

I yank the golden dagger out of its sheath, but the King launches another attack that breaks my shield down the middle and hits Evander square in the chest.

It's an electric pulse strong enough to stop an elven heart.

Evander's eyes meet mine in split second horror.

And then they turn to glass.

"NO!" I scream. Vilero ignores me, conjuring accelerant and tossing it on his body. He lights a match and throws it on top, and I watch my love erupt into flames.

I re-sheath the dagger, shoving Vilero out of my way and dropping to my knees in front of the blaze.

"Watch my back," I growl to Zyrran, though the words escape my lips.

"*Kill the King first,*" he urges. "*Others are getting impatient.*"

"Give me five minutes," I beg, tears streaming down my cheeks as I grab piles of snow and toss them on top of the flames.

"*I can give you three,*" he says tensely.

The snow isn't working fast enough. I wrack my brain thinking of other ways to put out the flames.

"*You are a Natric, stupid,*" Lozana taunts from the sky. "*Conjure some rain.*"

It's at least thirty degrees too cold for that.

"*I did not take you for a quitter,*" Lozana snaps back.

My panic and grief morph into anger.

"*Not helping!*" I growl as my whole body feels too hot.

"*All of these people are fighting for you, meanwhile you are fighting for someone who's already dead,*" she hisses.

Throwing salt in the fucking wound.

Rage pulses through me so intensely that I want to shake the damn ground.

"*Not shake, Natric one.*" Zyrran instructs. "*Flood.*"

Of course!

I shove that rage up the Natric channels, driving the temperature higher and higher.

The snow shifts to sleet, and it starts to put out the flames a little quicker but I need a real downpour.

"You are so weak. Anadyna could conjure rain on a whim," Lozana taunts.

I hate Lozana's guts right now, but I use that hatred to speed up the magic.

Sleet turns to rain, and then rain turns to a downpour. The flames snuff out Evander's body and I breathe a sigh of relief.

"He's behind you," Zyrran urges.

I whirl around and get to my feet.

"You really are Diana," the King gasps, backing slowly away from me.

Zyrran lets out a fiery blaze that tickles the King's back.

"What the—?" He jumps forward. "The dragons are here for *you?*"

I pull out the golden dagger.

"No," I hiss. "They're here for you."

And I plunge the dagger into his heart.

48

I am Fiana Willowbark and I have just slain King Vilero making me your new Queen. With his death by my hands, magic is returning to you and all other females in this kingdom.

It is my intention to restore balance to our society—to allow females to keep their magic and to eliminate the toxicity males developed under King Vilero's rule—and with this I need your help. Those who do not wish to see females in their power again will immediately declare war on me for ending the King.

If you agree to help me take back the Elven Kingdom for all of feminine kind, meet me at the clearing at 43.5671° N, 10.9807° E in Lucia in seventy-two hours and wait for further instructions. We will teach you how to use your magic and how to fight, and will offer you a safe place to call home during the upcoming war.

If you do not wish to help us fight, you are advised to keep your magic a secret from all males. You will be in grave danger should anyone find out, and many will want to steal your magic again. If you'd like sanctuary but do not wish to fight, you may also join us at the clearing in Lucia and we will keep you safe. Otherwise I recommend you find other females to lean on in this challenging time.

The message flows out of me, hitching a ride to the waves of stolen magic that are rapidly emanating out of Vilero's body.

I stare at his body for a long moment, as every horrible trauma in my life flashes through my mind.

All because of him.

I grab a fallen sword and pummel it into his chest. Again. And again. Blood spatters onto my face but I don't care.

My father's arrest and death. *Stab.*

Calimo's mind control. *Slice.*

Nasgardo's attempted rape and murder. *Jab.*

Evander's death. *Stab stab STAB!*

My eyes are burning and my arms are shaking, and I'm absolutely drenched in Vilero's blood. Sobs jerk through me and even though I know we'll be able to revive Evander, I'm sick to my stomach with grief.

"*Focus, Natric one. Step aside so I can burn the body,*" Zyrran says gently.

"Not yet," I grit out, wiping a streak of blood off my forehead. I slice my sword across Vilero's throat. Once. Twice. My muscles ache as I force the blade deeper, slicing off the head of the tyrant ruler that caused six centuries of suffering.

Adrenaline keeps the disgust at bay as I lift him by his hair. I toss his head unceremoniously next to Evander's mangled body, knowing both will come with me later.

"*Fry him,*" I say to Zyrran, stepping back at the same moment I clear the rain.

A blaze of red flames licks at the King's bloodied body. Within seconds, he's reduced to splinters, and then rapidly to ash.

I stare at the pile of ash as a sickening smile stretches across my face.

He who was once so powerful, reduced to nothing but dust. And a severed head. I pick it back up and face the battle.

"*Join us below the clouds,*" I send down the dragon bond.

"*With pleasure,*" Gorvorian cheers.

Dragons descend from the cloud cover now, and their ear splitting roars draw every Guard's eyes upward.

"The Havordians are under my command," I shout. "And I have slain your King." I hold up his head. "Drop your weapons and dissolve away or I will unleash the fire breathing guardians of these realms upon you!"

It takes about fifteen seconds for everyone to dissolve away. Some drop their weapons, others take them with them.

I scan the clearing, noting the faces of the few who remain.

Warren has wounds in each arm and slices in each cheek, but his eyes are bright and steady despite his injuries.

Ryder looks unscathed but is healing Mila, who has a deep wound near her groin that is gushing blood.

Credo is clutching a gaping wound at his gut. I send my healing magic his way and he coughs as his skin seals up.

Paul is unscathed and is helping Rosie to her feet. My heart stops, but she appears to only have a broken leg. I heal her next and she curses as her bone snaps back into place.

"Thanks, Fiana," she groans.

I turn to face Evander.

He's lifeless and mutilated on the ground. I run over to him, fresh tears forming in my eyes.

"Warren and Paul—are you strong enough to take him?" I ask as I hover a shaking hand over his blistered chest.

"We've got him," Warren promises.

I meet his eyes. He nods once.

I clutch the head of my enemy and link arms with Ryder and Rosie to take us back to Lucia.

Back to home.

~

I'm pacing. Eloise is pacing. Rosie is pacing.

We are *all* pacing.

Because Evander isn't waking yet.

"Maybe I was too late," I say as I look at his form. He's back to his beautiful wholeness, but his heart isn't beating.

And his eyes won't open.

We spent two hours meticulously healing his flesh wounds. Draven and Ryder led the healing, and I helped when I could. When they tired, one of the students who's grown now—a forty-something-year-old named Harlow—stepped in. She's a pure blooded Curic.

And thanks to me, she has magic now.

But he still isn't waking.

"You weren't too late—sometimes with injuries this severe it takes a little time for the organs to start working again," Harlow advises.

None of us question her knowledge. As each female has realized they have magic, it's like they were also given a deep well of knowledge they never had before.

We suspect it's *Vilero's* knowledge, somehow imprinted on the stolen magic.

An intriguing form of justice.

But my fiancé is still dead.

"There's someone at the entrance—she was stopped by Dragon and Dagger," announces another grown student. Alice, if I'm not mistaken.

"Who? It is too soon to expect the females," says Draven.

"She says her name is Reina," Alice says with a shrug. "She said she wants to speak to—to Diana," she says, puzzled.

Draven and Eloise exchange a loaded glance.

"She must have gotten the names mixed up, but go ahead and send her in," Draven says smoothly.

"What could she possibly want?" I complain. I don't want to leave Evander's side for a second.

"I am not sure," Draven admits. "But I think it is best we do not deny her the conference."

"I want to see Diana," the crone demands, her voice rough.

"Please, come inside," Draven says cordially. "Harlow, Alice—leave us for a few minutes if you please."

"Thank you," Reina says brusquely, pushing past him and Ryder to find me.

"You succeeded," she says flatly. It isn't a question. Her eyes dance over Evander's prone form and then center back on my face.

My stomach feels uneasy. "Yes," I say carefully. "We did."

She nods once. "Good."

A long silence passes while Reina just stares at me.

"Do you want this back?" I say awkwardly, remembering the golden blade was originally hers before the King found it. I cleaned it and re-sheathed it once we arrived back in Lucia.

"No," she grumbles. "But I'd like to have a minute alone with you," she says, glancing at the rest of the group warily.

"Why?" Warren questions.

Reina narrows her eyes at him. "You've changed the fabric of the future. There's a lot to *see*. Some that Diana should know privately, since it concerns her."

"I'm not leaving Evander's side," I say curtly.

She turns her ancient eyes toward me. "Let him stay. Everyone else goes."

"Are you *sure*, Fiana?" Warren asks, his tone reeking of distrust.

"I'm sure," I say flatly.

Draven lets out a measured exhale. "We will be right outside," he says, catching Reina's eye. Him and the rest of the group reluctantly funnel out.

Reina approaches me slowly, coming to sit on the leather armchair next to mine.

"First, I want to congratulate you. Your chances of success were quite slim," Reina acknowledges.

"Thank you," I mutter. I'm too tired to force a smile.

"You are now Queen of the Elves. That's a huge honor. Someone in your position should train with someone extremely skilled in the magical arts," she says thoughtfully. "Someone like me."

"Oh—that's very—generous of you. You helped Evander learn Hermetic magic, right?" I remember.

"Yes. And you are Premonic among other things—I can teach you to see the future, too."

My heart speeds up. "Really?"

She nods. "That would be a great skill for someone who faces a challenging road ahead, don't you think?"

I swallow, my throat suddenly feeling dry. "Yes. It would."

Reina smiles. "So it's settled then. I'll join you back here in a few days' time and we'll get started."

I manage a small smile, though my stomach feels uneasy. "That sounds great—thank you."

Reina beams. "Shall we toast to it then?" She doesn't wait for my answer as she procures a bottle of champagne from nowhere. Two flutes appear on the table between our chairs. She pours generously in each glass then hands me one.

"To Queen Diana—Queen of the Elves," she says cheerfully.

I pick up the glass, clink hers, and drink deeply.

When I raise my eyes, she's gone.

"Reina?" I call. I start coughing uncontrollably. "Draven?"

Draven, Ryder and Warren rush into the room, with the others trailing close behind. "What's wrong? Where's Reina?"

"What's happened, Natric one?" Zyrran says frantically.

"I don't—" *cough* "know—" *cough*. Weakness spreads throughout my body as the champagne flute falls from my grasp. Ryder catches it with immortal speed as more coughs rattle through my chest and my insides begin to feel inflamed.

Ryder's eyes grow concerned as he watches me. He sniffs the glass, and swears.

"What—" *cough* "—is it?" *cough*.

My vision begins to blur and my eyes want to close.

Warren's voice is frantic. "What is it, Ryder?"

"Vampire venom—she's swallowed it. Can she be revived after this?" Ryder asks frantically.

Warren swears.

Draven answers. "She just drank it—right? It has not entered her bloodstream?"

"I don't know," Ryder complains, his voice panicked. "Damnit—Evander is going to murder us all."

"Get Harlow back in here. Her digestion might keep it from entering her bloodstream but—"

My eyelids feel so heavy. I let them slide shut.

"But what?" Warren demands.

"It is vampire venom." Draven's voice is grave.

As the darkness threatens to pull me under, Evander's words come back to me.

Their venom can be fatal—even to us.

Even to immortals.

49

Delilah kneels before me, tears streaming down her face. The face we share as twins.

"If you don't want him—let me have him. *Please*, Diana," she begs.

"You *can* have him. I'm not stopping you. Go be with him," I encourage, though I know exactly what she will say next.

"He doesn't *want* me. He wants *you!*" she wails.

"Well, maybe give it some time," I say flatly. We've had this conversation hundreds of times over the years. It's exhausting; especially because Delilah blames *me* for her misery, instead of her beloved Anthony.

"I *have* given it time! *Years*, Diana! How could he possibly need any *more* time?" she complains.

"Well, then maybe it's time to move on," I sigh.

She stands up. "I CAN'T!"

"Well you can't force someone to love you, Delilah. I don't know what you want me to tell you. If I could trade spots with you I would. To be honest I don't know why he *hasn't* moved on to you yet, since we look exactly alike," I admit.

Delilah falls back a step, a curious look coming over her face.

"What?" I say warily.

"That's it, Diana," she breathes.

"What?" I narrow my eyes at her.

"Trade spots with me—make me seem like you and you seem like me," she explains.

I glare at her. "That's extremely manipulative."

"No... it's... it's..." Her face scrunches with effort as she searches for the word.

"Manipulative," I repeat, and she scowls.

"It's *not* manipulative if everyone is happy in the end!" she disagrees.

"Manipulation is manipulation, period," I counter.

"Well, it's manipulation for *a good reason*. That ultimately makes *everyone* happier as a result. It's positive manipulation," she reasons.

"There's no such thing, sister," I argue.

"But there is! Think about it—all Anthony wants in the world is *you*, but all *you* want in the world is to wait for your own divine masculine. Meanwhile, all *I* want in the world is Anthony, and I happen to look *exactly* like you—who Anthony truly wants. What harm could it really cause if we just fooled him? Anthony would get what he wants—a female exactly like you. I would get what I want. And you would get what you want, too."

My sister, the realm's best salesman. "It still feels wrong," I argue, though I can feel my opinion slowly shifting.

"It's not wrong if everyone is happier as a result. What we're doing now—all three of us miserable—*that* is wrong. *This* is for the highest good of all," she says confidently, putting her hands on her hips.

"How would we even do that?" I ask, despite the part of me that is begging me to end this plan before it even starts.

"Hermetic and Hypnotic magic, of course! Just cloak the parts of me that seem too Delilah-y, and alter the way I'm perceived by others to more closely match Diana," she says excitedly. "It could work—you *know* it could!"

I snort. It *could* work. "But it's not just a matter of it working. It's a matter of if the magic will even let us do that—it's not exactly for the highest good of all like you say…"

"But it *is*, Diana. Don't you see?" she insists.

"It might be temporarily—but what of the consequences? What do you think Anthony will do when he finds out he was lied to?"

"He won't find out," she says, her tone certain. "You'll go away— you'll settle somewhere far away from here. You've always wanted to go to Abyssia, haven't you?"

"Sure," I agree. I *am* tired of the endless cold of Ador.

"And you'll live your life down there. Meanwhile, I'll live your life *up here*," she says with a grin. "I'll *become* you, inside and out. I know you so well—it won't even be hard."

"But can you really lie to Anthony forever?" I press.

"I love him, Diana. He's *my* divine masculine. As much as you long for yours—and Maker knows if *yours* has even been *born* yet— that's how much I long for Anthony. I need him, even if I can only have him as you," she confesses, her eyes pleading.

I shake my head slowly.

This whole thing feels too good to be true.

Like there will be some unknown consequence.

Maybe not now, but years from now.

It feels like this stupid plan could end up being the death of me.

"Alright," I say finally, and Delilah's face lights up like the sun. "I'll do it."

It was the death of me. Not once, but twice.

Because I'm dead right now.

At first, nothing exists in death.

I have no body.

No thought.
No magic.
No voice.
A void.
An empty space.
The universe before creation exists.
Consciousness.
Awareness.
Blackness.
Space.

And then, comes the reflection.

On what I've done.

On where I've gone wrong.

I can guess why the crone poisoned me.

I allowed my sister to talk me into the biggest mistake in Elven history.

A six-hundred-year-long mistake.

All because I enabled her delusions.

I didn't stand up for what was right—I gave in to what made her happy.

When I did it, I thought what I did was fueled by love.

But it wasn't love.

It was the furthest thing from love that can exist.

Love doesn't manipulate or trick.

Love doesn't lie.

Love doesn't pretend.

Love holds the highest vision for the one they love—even when they can't see it for themselves.

Even when they *refuse* to see it for themselves.

Even when they *beg you* to see it how they see it.

. . .

Love chooses that highest vision even when it's hard.

Even when it hurts.

Even when it means you don't get what you want.

Even when it means the one you love will end up hating you.

Temporarily—you hope.

But there is no guarantee.

Love is cruel like that.

But death—death is kind.

It frees you from those hard decisions.

It frees you from living with the consequences of love.

Someone beautiful is standing there, just up ahead. I find myself admiring the waves of his chocolate brown hair. It contrasts beautifully with the whiteness of the snow surrounding him.

And then there's his eyes.

I grew up next to the bluest sea in all of the Elven Kingdom, and yet nothing compares to my divine masculine's eyes.

Evander's eyes.

"I missed you," I murmur as tears fall steadily down my cheeks. "You wouldn't wake."

His eyes tighten in shock as I approach him, and then he pulls me into a bone-crushing hug.

"You're not supposed to be dead. Why are you dead?" he murmurs into my hair.

I don't know what he's talking about, because he feels alive enough to me.

I kiss him on the lips and my heart throbs at the contact. A memory hits the back of my mind, and I pull back to look at him.

"You're supposed to be dead. You wouldn't wake."

He sighs. "I am dead. And so are you, my love."

I consider that for a moment, looking around us for proof that he's lying. That's when I realize the whiteness surrounding us isn't snow.

It's light.

"Is this it then? We're dead?" Hot tears fill my eyes.

"You were supposed to survive. I've lived a long life—but you, Fiana. You've waited too long to really live. You have to go back," he pleads.

I look at him like he's crazy.

"Why would I go back if we're together right here?" I counter.

"Because you have to be Queen. You have to go back," he begs. He's leading me somewhere. To a portal, I realize. A giant doorway of rainbow light that goes somewhere—beyond.

"I'm only going back if you go back with me." I cross my arms.

"I can't go back, Fiana. This is a doorway for one." His voice breaks on the last word, his eyes utterly bleak.

"No. I'm not going back without you." My heart throbs harder.

"You *have* to go back. You *have* to rise again. And be Queen. The Kingdom needs you." He's pushing me toward the portal now.

"Not without you! Not without my King!" My chest feels too tight. I'm suffocating.

"You don't need me. I've played my role. I've done my part," he insists, his eyes pained.

"But this doorway right here—we can *both* go in," I argue. "Don't make me live without you."

"Only one of us can go back, Fiana." He strokes my cheek.

"No! It can't be like this—it can't end this way. What's the point of us becoming one if you're just going to rip us back in two?"

"It's not my choice to make. I'm so sorry, Fiana," he says weakly.

"What if we go together? At the exact same time?" I plead.

"It won't work," he warns.

"But what if it does? If we can both go back at the same time—will you go back with me?" My heart stops as I wait for his reply.

"We might get kicked back here. It might not work how you think," he says warily.

"I don't care. I'm not going back without you. We became one for a reason. I'm not going back split in two."

I grab his neck and hug him tight to my chest. His arms hang limp at his sides.

"Evander, I swear to the Maker, if you don't put your arms around me and hold on tight, I am going to murder you over and over again in the afterlife."

He snorts. "So fucking violent."

But he wraps his arms around me.

And he holds me tight.

And as we jump through the door of rainbow light, neither one of us is willing to let go.

EPILOGUE

My son holds the package gingerly, shooting me a wary glance.

"Do you want to open it?" he asks. "It feels kind of heavy," he says with a chuckle.

"Who is it addressed to?" I push a lock of brown hair behind my ear.

"All it says is: 'to whom it may concern.'" He shrugs.

I sigh impatiently. I really don't have time for this.

Our castle is a wreck. Half of the Guard is dead. And we still haven't found Anthony's body.

It's a long shot to think that we can still revive him at this point; it has been twenty-five hours since Diana showed her loathsome face.

My loathsome face, I have to remind myself.

I fucking hate being her twin.

Still, he was alive for at least another hour after that point—maybe more.

I'd gotten the message from Diana when my magic was

returned to me, but by that point my keeper had already locked me back in my tower.

Which is completely void of clocks.

And windows.

All a part of my centuries-long penance.

You'll only exist when I want you to. Otherwise, you won't exist at all.

Anthony was quite creative with his choice of punishment.

He kept me reasonably well fed, and my chambers were somewhat comfortable.

He let me see my son, as long as Charles wanted to see me.

When he felt needy for Diana, he summoned me to his chambers for a quick fuck.

Sometimes he let me sleep there, other times he sent me back to my tower.

But otherwise I lived in solitude with no way of knowing that time was passing.

Even meals weren't a good judge of time, since this body could go weeks without food.

It was the most exquisite kind of torture for an immortal who doesn't age.

It was brilliant, actually.

I had to respect that kind of malevolence.

So I got Diana's message, but I have no concept of precisely *when* that was. And the Guards who remain alive can't tell me exactly when he died.

They're all useless.

It makes me long for Nasgardo.

He was one of the few Guards who knew I existed.

Until now.

Now the whole kingdom knows Delilah Pryndale is still alive.

And one day soon they'll know that Diana Pryndale is alive, too.

It does irk me that Nasgardo hadn't mentioned seeing *her*. He'd spoken of a *Fiana Willowbark* when he visited my bedroom, but never said a damn thing about her having *my* face.

He was young, though.

He didn't know the prophecy.

And I never told him my story.

Perhaps he was trying to figure it out for himself, so he could have something of value to offer the King. He was always looking for some sort of edge over his commander.

Evander something.

Nasgardo never shared his last name.

And I wasn't allowed to meet the Guards.

Nasgardo was a pure accident.

One that had made the past few months (or years?) a little more bearable.

Which is why it infuriates me that he never mentioned her.

I do get a sick sort of enjoyment at the thought of him assaulting *Fiana Willowbark*, though.

Clearly he wanted more of *me* if he went after *her*.

He'd wanted to immortalize me until he realized I was already immortal.

And devoted to his master, the King.

My heart burns as I remember *my* master is gone.

Unless we can find him in the next five minutes or so...

"Fuck—FUCK!"

"Language, Charles!" I scold.

He's opened the package, then shut it again. He stares at the lid like he can't look away.

I approach him warily.

"Ugh. That's nasty. No, don't look, Ma," he insists.

"Step aside." My tone is ice cold.

I lift the lid off the box.

And nearly puke on the floor.

Nestled on a red velvet pillow, face up, black eyes staring into the Beyond.

My husband's severed head.

I smooth my dress, take a step back, and square a cold look at Charles.

"I hope you're ready to act like a King, because this is a declaration of war. And I intend to fucking win."

ACKNOWLEDGMENTS

Holy Maker! I wrote a book! There's so many people who helped me achieve this lifelong dream, and I have to celebrate them publicly because without them, this book would not have gotten written and definitely would not have been published!

First and foremost—thank you to God and my Lord and Savior, Jesus Christ. You helped me fulfill a lifelong dream in less than a year. One that I was so afraid to chase, and yet one You put me in the exact right circumstances to create. You woke me up at five in the morning to give me the themes, outline, and energetic momentum to tell this incredible story. You gave me the space and financial security to write with my whole heart. You also guided me through all of my insecurities and limiting beliefs along the way, ensuring this book got finished. You led me to the perfect editors and protected me from countless wrong turns. And I know it might be strange to some that I'm thanking Jesus for this spicy romantic fantasy novel, but truly, I couldn't have done it without Him. So thank you.

To Ralph—the love of my life and my biggest supporter in all of my ventures (and there's easily been about 14,234 of them in our ten years together). Thank you for cheering me and this book on from day one. Thank you for acting out fight scenes with me, giving me the best book boyfriend inspiration, making me laugh and feeding me epic one liners (versions of which may or may not have ended up in this book!). You helped me get an amazing editor and pushed me to keep going when I was feeling discouraged. You talked through fixes to plot holes with me and helped me maintain my creative vision while making it even better. You even told everyone you know about my book and convinced everyone from your barber to your colleagues to preorder it. You're the best husband anyone could have asked for, and I am beyond lucky to call you mine.

To Taylor—my biggest book fan, beta reader and best friend! You encouraged me to get back into reading and writing again this year, and if it wasn't for you, I wouldn't have had the idea for this book. Thank you for reading *all* of my drafts, telling me what you loved and what you thought could be better, and being my sounding board when deciding what edits to take and which to pass on. I am so grateful for every word you read and for your sweet text message mini reviews. I live for your feedback and can't wait to share book two with you soon!

To Corin—my emotional support human, best friend, and guide! Thank you for building me up every day of our friendship and reminding me of who the fuck I am. You helped me through the indecision and coached me through trusting my gut vs. "the rules" of writing. You helped me break the ones I needed to break, and helped me make this story powerful, unique, and fully mine. You also gave me one of my favorite pieces of feedback in the early stages... "the smut is smuttin'". I think about that all the time. It makes me giggle and blush and feel proud of myself all at the same time!

To my nail salon crew and facial ladies (you know who you are!). Every month I got to gush about my book, and every month y'all convinced me it was worth publishing. I'll never forget the first time I shared the plot with everyone and one of you at the nail salon asked me "What streaming platform is that on? Where do I watch that?" You ladies (and one man!) gave me the confidence to take this story public—beyond my friends and family and out into the world. Thank you.

To Laura—my amazing editor! You kept me honest and helped me take this story from good to great. You delivered your feedback with kindness and a genuine love for the story, and I can't thank you enough for guiding me through the process of deconstructing and reassembling my first ever novel. This book got a thousand times better with your magical touch. Truly, I couldn't have done it without you and I feel so lucky to have found you on the first try.

To Kerry—you freaking nailed the cover. You are such a talented designer and I'm so grateful to have you in my circle. I can't wait for the whole internet to talk about how amazing the cover is. It's all because of you. Thank you, thank you, thank you.

To Leo and Kingsley, my sweet amazing puppies! You were with me almost every step of the way with this book (I *did* send you guys to doggie daycare a time or two during my rewrites) and your cuddles and kisses really made all the difference. In fact, I'm cuddling with both of you right now as I write this. You bring me and Ralph so much joy every single day, and I'm so grateful I get to be your mama.

To my ARC and beta readers—thank you for your time and energy and devotion to this book! I am beyond grateful to have humans all over the place reading my work, building it up, and spreading the word so that more people can fall in love with the icy village of Ador, the secret School of Forgotten Females, and our favorite bearded male with two-toned eyes.

And to my readers—I don't know who you are yet, but I can't freaking wait to meet you. I poured my heart and soul into this book for you, and this is only the beginning of our journey together. So do me a favor—if you loved this book, please keep in touch. You can join my email list at kristencipriano.com to stay up to date on future releases. You'll also find my social media handles there. I'm an independent author (Iconic Publishing is my company!) which means everything I write, I write only for YOU. There's no publisher agendas. No storylines I "must" include to fulfill any quotas or make my bosses happy. It's just me and you, and the stories that are begging to be told in their absolute purest form. Thank you for supporting me so I can keep telling them.

Get excited for book two...

Love,
Kristen

ABOUT THE AUTHOR

Kristen Cipriano lives in Texas with her husband, Ralph, and their adorable Cavapoo puppies, Leo and Kingsley. The story that inspired *The Queen Rises* came to Kristen one fateful morning at 5 am. She immediately snuck out of bed, leaving Ralph and her fur babies snoozing away, and manically typed out an outline. Within 111 days, her first draft was completed. A few short months later, the final book was ready for publishing. Kristen is convinced that this story "wrote itself" but her husband *probably* begs to differ...

instagram.com/kristen.cipriano
tiktok.com/@kristen.cipriano

Made in the USA
Columbia, SC
07 February 2025

52697053R00343